Pyrates
Shifting Flames
Book 2
By Hollow

Table of Contents

This book is dedicated to Kauffman, who inspires me daily to keep writing and has helped me grow as a writer.

"It may be unfair, but what happens in a few days, sometimes even a single day, can change the course of a whole lifetime." — Khaled Hosseini, *The Kite Runner*

Names & Pronunciations

Ironwood Crew

"Ironwood" Thukuli – captain, small, dark brown hair with blonde streaks, brown eyes with green flecks, ivy/plant genetic

Bek *(beck)* – 1st mate of Ironwoods first crew, treasurer, tall, dark-skinned, blue eyes, shifter genetic, captain of 1st ship in Ironwoods fleet

Feluna – ship's doctor, thickly built woman, previous ward of Brinar

Velu – crew member, red hair, pale skin with dark freckles, skinny

"Flame" Kasai – long black hair, scar over left eye from hairline to neck, tanned olive skin, 7th gen heat genetic

Sibra *(see-bra)* – ships girl, extremely skinny, platinum blonde hair, blue and brown eyes, magnetic genetic

Linota *(li-no-ta)* – ebony skin, black curly hair, True Shapeshifter genetic, *special note:* lives as a permanent colf after being unable to shift human

Geralf *(g-air-all-f)* – new first mate after Bek leaves, black hair

Kelin *(kell-in)* – scout for Ironwood's crew, looks for new crew members or sneaks ahead to find targets on land, speed genetic, dark blonde hair

Jen – member of Ironwood's main crew

Daro *(dah-row)* – newer member of Ironwood's crew

Delta – 1st mate of Bek's crew then Ironwoods, extremely pale eyes, pale with dark freckles, white-blonde hair, file-sharpened teeth

Yizaan *(yee-zah-n)* – member of Bek's crew, speaker for the crew when neither mates nor captain is around

Dina *(dee-na)* – member of Bek's crew, navigator

"Distortion" Nona – pressure genetic, ex-prisoner, 2nd mate of Ironwood's flagship

Waveborn Crew

"Fatal" North Bukazo – captain, skinny man with dark brown hair and blue eyes, navigation genetic, navigator for Ironwood's flagship after a time

Arat *(ah-rah-t)* - ship's cook and second mate, dark olive skin, black hair, pistol user

Sioco *(see-oh-ko)* – first mate, former member of Lightning Crew

Seaborne

Leil – elderly Seaborne Admiral, lives in Cernu, grandmother of Doux and Kasai

Doux *(doh)*—Kasai's brother, iron-skin genetic, black hair, forehead scar, light brown eyes, Seaborne captain

Other Characters

Oxe/Oxeanukatahishi *(ox/ox-ah-nu-ka-ta-hee-shi)* – tall, dark-skinned, black hair, blue-green eyes, True Shapeshifter, Nuveri Warrior, Kasai's mate, known as Tamotsu *(ta-moat-su)* when on Ironwood's crew

Brinar *(brin-are)* – head researcher of Witch Island, salt and pepper brown hair, known as Eaden *(ee-den)* for a while

Amalia – blonde hair, fair skin, from Witch Island, Brinar's partner, mother to Bronwen and River

Bronwen – dark blonde hair, vitiligo brown and fair skin, grey eyes, Brinar's daughter

River – black hair, blue eye and green eye, pale skin, Brinar's son

Cifius *(sigh-fee-us)* – tall, tattoos along his arms and around his neck, thickly muscled, white hair with grey streaks, pale brown eyes with yellowish hue, unknown genetic

Na'vira *(na vee-rah)* – Doux's wife, detection genetic, tall, black hair, light tan

Xicía *(zee-she-ah)* – ice genetic, prior member of Razora's collection, dark tanned skin, white hair, white-blue eyes, known as Akir *(ah-k-ear)* on Ironwood's crew

Yan *(ya-n)* – stout, dark brown hair, a merchant in the Northern Waters

Iono *(ee-oh-no)* – thin, black hair flecked with silver, Yan's wife

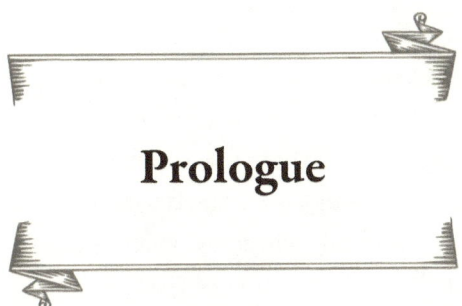

Prologue

SUNLIGHT SHONE BRIGHTLY on the fishing village. At a table set out on the docks, a small man sat observing the people scrambling over the docks. Running a hand through his hair, he gazed towards the village thoughtfully.

A deep voice called out, "Captain, here's today's haul!" as a bag of coins clanked onto the table, drawing his gaze.

The captain's cruel dark brown and green-flecked eyes glared at the bag with disdain. "Is that it?" He opened the bag briefly, then closed it and shoved it to the side. It scraped against the table, falling over. A few kinas spilled out, clattering softly against the wood.

"We also found books, some fine clothes, and a ton of fish by the harbor," the other man said. Tall, dark-skinned, with deep blue eyes, he sneered at a group of rowdy people nearby. "However, the crew might drink all the le if we're not careful."

They watched the group for a few minutes; the people were laughing and singing drunkenly. A barrel sat open in the middle of the crowd, and people kept dipping tankards into it. Several other similar barrels were stacked nearby.

"Captain! We found something!" They turned as another man ran up to them. He skidded to a stop, panting. "You need to see this, sir!" His face was flushed with excitement, his red hair sticking up wildly.

The captain paused, then nodded. "Show me." He stood and followed the newer man. The dark skin man hesitated, looked at the crowd, then walked after the two shorter men.

The red-haired man led them to a small building down the street. A medical center sign hung above the doorway, skewed slightly. The captain eyed the warped windows with interest; that signified intense heat, but the air here was cool thanks to the ocean.

But there was nowhere on this island that produced enough heat to cause that.

The door was cracked just enough to let in some air, and he felt a brush of heat blow through. He sneered, turning to the red-haired man. "Let Feluna know about this place. She's the ship's doctor." He turned away but was stopped when the younger man tapped his arm.

"But you'll never guess who's in here." He was almost buzzing. "You talked about recruiting someone who can help us get other ships, right?" His eyes were bright, a wide grin crossing his face.

The captain shot him a sharp look, but nodded. "Yes, what about it? Some small village isn't likely to have someone with that kind of power, though." The dark-skinned man gave them a curious look, casting a glance at the door with interest.

"Not even him?" The younger man opened the door and pointed at the single cot inside the small room. Despite the breeze from the sea, the room was blistering.

A tall, slender man with black hair lay unconscious, his hair spread out on the pillows. They could see numerous bandages and possibly a splint over an ankle. What they could see of his face was little, but the edges of a scar were visible.

The captain nodded. "Well, you were right. We can use him. Good find, Velu." His lips curled into a strange grin, his eyes gleaming as possibilities unfurled in his mind.

Part I

Spark

Chapter 1

Oxe

DESPITE THE GLARING sunlight, the air felt cold.

"North, can we check here one more time?" The words came out slowly, painfully. His voice cracked softly, his gaze flicking around almost erratically.

A tall blonde-haired man turned toward him; his eyes were dark but not unkind. "We've looked here already, Oxe. I'm not sure they'll be any news." He sounded sympathetic, yet it was evident that he expected a certain response.

A stocky black-haired man shook his head, laying a hand on North's shoulder, and murmured, "North, let him look. This is our last time coming this far south, anyway. He might as well try."

Oxe leaned against the railing, but he felt their gazes like a weight. Since he began looking, he lost weight, and his hair grew long enough to tie back.

He looked out over the town. Erith, once a small fishing village, was now a decent sized port full of larger fishing vessels and a fish market. In the distance, a tower striped in beige, blue, and green could be seen above the trees.

Oxe flinched internally and tried not to think about the last time he was there.

"Oxe, we'll be here two days. But this is the last time we can come this far south." There was a tense pause, then North continued.

"Razora is causing problems, as is that new pirate, Ironwood." He kept his voice even, but Oxe could see they were observing him.

He took a deep breath and nodded. "Alright. Thanks North." He tried to ignore the sadness in his gaze. Arat's eyes were full of pity, but he said nothing as Oxe turned away.

Before he could step off though, North laid a hand on his shoulder. "After this, you need to decide what to do next, alright. But...no rush."

Oxe glanced at him, but said nothing. Stepping off the ship, he moved away from the docks. The sea air was fresh at first, but his nose burned as he walked through the market. Caught fish, spices, too many people. He stopped by several stalls, asked a few questions, but no one had any answers.

"No, we haven't seen anyone like that around here."

"Sorry, still no sign."

"I saw a woman like that, but no scar."

He hated the looks, the pity that some people gave him. They had answered these questions, or similar ones, before.

And it was clear they remembered him doing this two years ago, and a few times since.

Making his way through the town, he noticed the new homes, the medical facility, the horks and carts. A few ulcats prowled around the homes but avoided him as he passed. Little by little, the town was growing.

He noticed the kids dodging around homes and tried not to stare. Being at sea for over four years now, kids were an anomaly to him. He used to love interacting with the kids in his tribe's home, playing with them as a wolf and helping the younger shifters when they appeared, teaching them the tribes crafts, telling stories around the fire with the elders and other adults.

He wished he were there now, maybe even raising a kid of his own. He halted under a thick leaved koris tree, clutching his arm to his side. Oxe took a shuddering breath and tried not to imagine what that would've been like.

Shaking his head, he headed out of town. He barely noticed where he was until he nearly bumped into a new sign that had been placed along a well-worn path. He jerked to a stop, staring at the sign.

Seaborne Base and Medical Facility >
Erith <
Sedgeliss Wharf ^

He sighed and sank against the pole, his head between his legs. "Why do I keep looking?"

The wind sighed through the forest ahead of him. A few leaves drifted down, the slight breeze stirring the thin branches; summer was coming to a close, though he didn't see any changing colors yet.

"It has been two years. No one has found him." Oxe stared at a small insect crawling in front of him. "Brinar thinks he..." He couldn't finish the sentence aloud.

He refused to believe Kasai was dead. Let alone by his own hand.

But Oxe had no idea where to look anymore.

"Maybe I should go home." The words came out hollow. He hadn't wanted to go home at first, but he was even more reluctant now.

The thought of being Alpha no longer appealed to him, not that it did when he was first told. He hadn't wanted the responsibility over the entire tribe. But when Kasai had disappeared after they had captured Blacksmoke...

He didn't want to give up, but he didn't think there was anyplace left to look. The Seaborne were keeping an eye out, and Leil had been keeping in touch with him when she could. Even Brinar was keeping an eye out on anything unusual from Witch Island.

But so far, all they had told him was that aside from a report of a pirate crew setting fires to port villages, there had been no signs of Kasai. And Brinar knew Kasai wouldn't attack innocents.

The fires were also confirmed to have been set by Ironwood. He had been getting bold in the past year, but Oxe didn't want to think about that.

He also didn't want to face Idan. She had asked the elders for him when he was injured, but they had rejected her. While they were not closely related, Oxe had been Promised to Kasai already. She had refused to accept that because Kasai hadn't been one of the tribe at the time, but when the elders marked her for arguing...

She could not accept that Oxe did not want her, and she pressed him. At seventeen springs now, she was beautiful, but she was also incredibly harsh. She grated against his nerves terribly, and at his last call...Oxe had called her a name that was reserved for the worst of their tribe because she had mocked Kasai. He would not have accepted her while he did not know where Kasai was.

But after that, he never would. She had become worse than nothing to him.

He clenched his fangs, feeling his jaw elongate. "Why did you run Kasai?"

A branch fell from a nearby tree, but the fleeing squirrel told him it was just rotten and only animals were near.

He stared at where the squirrel disappeared. "I love you. I always will. But you are gone...and maybe I should accept that."

His eyes blurred as tears threatened to spill out. He could still feel Kasai next to him, the intense heat he radiated almost scorching Oxe's fur. His jaw shifted back into place.

"How can I go on without you?" His voice broke, and he held back a sob.

His mind drifted back to the day Kasai had disappeared.

"He's gone." Oxe's breath exploded out, painful and cold.

Brinar looked at him, then scrambled to his feet. "What do you mean? He's barely been conscious!" While his eyes showed worry, it was his voice that revealed the extent of his concern.

"He..." Oxe's voice failed, his throat tight.

Brinar glanced at him, then entered the thickly scented medical room. Despite the overly potent smell of medicine, Oxe followed him. But the small room held nothing but Kasai's scent and a few bandages that had been ripped off from his escape through the window. Oxe leaped through and followed it for a short distance, but it quickly dissipated.

The lack of scent erased any chance of following Kasai. Oxe leaped back through the window and looked at Brinar. "His scent disappeared into the trees, but I saw no sign of him."

Kasai had been coherent enough to hide his tracks, or didn't go the way they thought. But the stream close to the trees' edge stopped the scent cold. Oxe had crossed the stream, but there was no trail on the other side.

"Why would he run?" Doux had asked no one specifically when they came back out, but North and Arat had exchanged a dark look.

"Do you have an idea?" Brinar asked North, noticing.

North nodded, his face grim. "It's just a guess, but what if Kasai doesn't remember the past couple of weeks?"

Everyone stared at him except Arat, who nodded.

"If you're a pyrate and you wake up in some Seaborne facility with no memory of how you got there, what would you think?" North continued. "He probably doesn't know we brought him here, or that Brinar's been treating him."

Oxe closed his eyes against the pain. "He thought the Seaborne caught him."

North nodded. "Oxe, go follow his scent. Look in the woods. Brinar, can you tell the Captain here what happened? Arat, Doux, let's split up and look around. I'm sure he didn't get far."

Everyone gave a nod and split up. Amalia pulled Oxe to her and hugged him tight briefly. "We'll find him."

Oxe blinked back tears and tore himself away. His paws met the ground and he flew into the trees.

Oxe shook his head. They had spent a week looking for Kasai, but there were no signs aside from another bandage at the edge of the road leading away from the Seaborne tower. His scent gone, no scuff marks in the dirt. If Oxe hadn't known better, Kasai had deliberately walked on exposed rocks, roots, or through water, as if he didn't want to be found by anyone.

And nowhere was there a body, or weapons, or blood. No footprints either, or strands of hair. Nothing Oxe could use to track him.

Oxe had even questioned if Kasai remembered what happened during that fight, but no one would answer him.

He stood, trying not to sink into any dark thoughts. "I need to get back to North. I will ask if he can take me home, or at least to

Witch Island." He wouldn't mind seeing Brinar and his family again. Bronwen and River had been getting big and would be over a year old by now.

He had turned back toward Erith when running footsteps caught his attention.

"Help!" The long, drawn-out cry came echoing through the trees, and a moment later, a young girl came pounding down the path that led to Sedgeliss Wharf.

Oxe stepped back as she skidded to a stop in front of him. "What is wrong?" Fear came rolling off her in waves, acrid and thick.

"Pyrates are attacking Sedgeliss!" She gasped. "Please, I'm heading for the tower, but can you go help? Just get people out!" Her breathing was jagged and rough; she had been running hard.

Without another word, she pounded off towards the Seaborne tower.

Oxe watched her for a moment, then turned towards Sedgeliss Wharf. It was a small port, where the families of the nearby Seaborne lived. It wasn't much to look at. What could pyrates want with it?

He paused, then shifted his ears and immediately heard faint screams. Without another moment, he shifted to his wolf form, his muscles sliding smoothly under his skin and a barely audible *click* as his bones fit into place. It had been years since this had been painful, and he merely felt a pinch as his joints moved, bones stretched and shrank, and his muscles swelled. The fur just itched as it sprouted along his skin.

His waistcloth, a kind of loose skirt-like garment he had fashioned recently that conformed better to his wolf body, fit him snuggly and didn't rub his fur like most clothes did. And when he ran, it didn't hinder him. He was suddenly glad he wore no shirt.

The trees flashed by as his paws flew over the ground; the scents touched his nose briefly telling him about the neixe herds, squirrels, and a litter of ulcats nearby, and his ears caught snatches of birdsong and a stream headed for the sea.

As he got closer, however, the scent of ash and wood-smoke touched his nose. Screams got louder, children crying, and occasionally cruel laughter wove through the other sounds. The creaking and crashing of falling wood, shattering glass, and the occasional triumphant laugh could be heard, but they were fainter.

He growled as he came into sight of Sedgeliss and took in the burning buildings. Charred trees fell around him as he left the forest. He halted as people came rushing out. The smoke hung thick and black above the little village.

He yelped to get their attention and the small group of women and children took one look at him, then after a glance at the burning homes, they turned and ran towards him. He dodged to the side as they ran past, terrified of something worse than a strange creature.

The fear that rolled from them was strong enough to make him whimper and want to cover his nose.

His hackles rose instinctively and he took a few steps towards the town.

"Hey, what's this?" A man's voice came pealing out like a bell through the smoke. The man stepped out and Oxe growled.

Oxe's growl petered out and he stared. He had seen this man on posters before, but *this* was Ironwood Thukuli? He wasn't that impressive just from his looks; a small man, shorter than Oxe by at least a foot, his hair was tied back and brown with sun-bleached blonde streaks. He wore a typical sleeveless coth shirt, black breech shorts, and no shoes, and a bag of what smelled like earth at his waist. But his eyes...

Oxe was reminded of Grimshaw. When he aimed to kill Oxe before Kasai had killed him, his eyes had the same look. Heartless, sadistic, almost inhuman, enjoying the kill. Oxe felt a cold trickle along his spine.

"Now what are you?" The man regarded Oxe curiously, his head cocked. "You aren't a colf." His tone boarded on being bored, and there was a cruel hint to it.

Oxe snarled, his fangs clacking together as he snapped at the pyrate captain. He didn't trust this man. Every nerve in his body screamed to get away. His hackles bristled almost painfully.

"Hm. Well, we could use the meat." Ironwood smirked. "And most of us could do with cold weather gear." He jerked his hand, palm up, twisting it at the wrist upwards.

Oxe leaped back just as a sharp root suddenly burst up from the ground. He stared at it for a heartbeat, then dashed away. Was Ironwood a genetic? Or someone else nearby? He had never heard of plants growing so quickly, or looking like a rase thorn but over three times the size.

He dashed through a narrow opening between two stucca and wood homes, not flinching away from the heat emanating from them. He had felt worse when he had been with Kasai.

On the other side of the houses, though, he stumbled to a stop. The houses were falling, some already in ruins, and fire blistered every surface and the air was thick with smoke. He wanted to cough, to rid his chest of the acrid air.

The wails were louder here. He spotted a young child, a toddler, sitting in the center of the road. Without a moment of hesitation, he sprang forward, his eyes watering, and nudged the boy towards an open space where he could see an untouched house.

He wasn't surprised when the kid flinched and screamed at the sight of him, but he gave a gentle whine and licked the boy's face. It had never failed with his tribe's children, but then again, they were used to wolves.

Thankfully, the boy understood Oxe wasn't a threat and clung to his fur as Oxe led him as quickly as he could toward the unburned home. The child's steps were hesitant and unsteady, but Oxe didn't stop. He had just gotten them clear of the smoke when a gasp drew his attention.

He paused and the boy whimpered, flinching into his fur. He flicked one ear back briefly. His heart thudded almost painfully in his chest. That gasp...was something familiar about it? He mentally shook himself and started walking, forcing the boy to stumble, but quickly nudged him up and didn't stop until they had reached the space behind the house.

He tried to ignore the footsteps and a strange tapping sound behind him. Whoever had gasped was following them, but the kid was crying and Oxe wanted to get him to safety first.

The kid suddenly cried, "Mommy!" He ran toward a woman who was peering out from behind a tree.

"Rik!" she cried and gathered him up. She glanced at Oxe. "Thank you, creature." She froze, then whirled around, the boy in her arms, and raced into the forest. Oxe was alone in less than a heartbeat.

He was shocked at the fear that had suddenly overwhelmed his nose and flicked his ears back. She had seen something, something that had frightened her, but it wasn't him. His ears twitched.

The footsteps and tapping had stopped.

The wind shifted, blowing from the village now, and Oxe turned toward the stranger.

But he stopped dead when he caught sight of the person standing behind the house. The scent filled his nose and he whined, his tail giving an involuntary wag.

Nearly as tall as Oxe in his human form, his beard was twisted into a short braid, and his black hair was tied back and braided in a half familiar way. A cane, the source of the tapping noise, was held in the right hand. He leaned heavily onto his left leg in a strange stance, but then he met Oxe's eyes and Oxe couldn't hold back anymore.

He shifted at once into his human form, so quickly that his muscles protested and hurt for once. He stared into the familiar green eyes, drinking in the scar that stretched down the left side of the face and the almost spicy scent he could detect under the smell of smoke and ash.

He opened his mouth, and a single word escaped in a heartbroken cry. "Kasai?"

Chapter 2

Kasai

KASAI STARED AT THE wolf, barely registering when it shifted into a tall man with black hair, blue-green eyes, and a familiar geometric pattern tattooed on his chest.

"Kasai?" Oxe's voice flowed through his ears, sounding more pained than he had imagined it would be. He sounded heartbroken.

Not that Kasai blamed him. He stared at his mate, his heart suddenly crying out. It had been two years since he had seen him, since he had last heard his voice. He struggled to resist running forward.

Oxe's face looked drawn, his body skinnier than Kasai had ever seen. His curly hair hung loosely around his face. Kasai didn't see any new scars, but his tan was darker than before.

But he was confused. Had Oxe been here this whole time? Why hadn't the Seaborne taken him? Or maybe they released Oxe? Or had Oxe left, but then why did he come back?

"Oxe?" His voice came out in a harsh croak and the Nuveri warrior flinched. "What are you doing here?" His throat spasmed with pain and he said no more. It rarely hurt this much, but the smoke wasn't helping.

Oxe stared at him, his eyes wide, then lurched forward. Before he reached Kasai however, there was a tongue of fire between them. He stopped, almost stumbled, and stared again. "We...I thought...you were dead."

Kasai flinched and closed his eyes. Behind him were footsteps, steady and slow. "Get out of here." He hissed harshly. His left hand twitched and the flames between them simmered along the ground.

Oxe flinched. "No." The word came out as a growl.

The footsteps came closer, their pace unchanging.

"Leave." Kasai opened his eyes, ignoring how close Oxe looked, and glared. "Now." Before Thukuli got here. The captain didn't appreciate when his crew did anything he perceived as slacking off. And he offed people for the fun of it, let alone if they pissed him off.

But Kasai still had a debt to pay and didn't want to screw things up. Even if it meant not leaving that very moment.

Oxe's ears pricked, the tips sharpening. "Why?"

"Get lost." Thukuli's voice growled out behind Kasai. "We don't need some punk causing trouble."

Kasai moved aside as Thukuli took his place on the left, tapping his cane once before stepping. Oxe tilted his head slightly but said nothing.

"Kasai, head back to the ship." Thukuli didn't look at him, only glared at Oxe. "We're done here."

Kasai nodded and took a step back.

"Kasai please, come back." Oxe's voice came out in a rush.

Thukuli suddenly slammed his heel onto the ground and a massive thorn shot through the dirt, the sharp point stopping just before Oxe's nose. "I don't know who you are, but get out now." He shot a glare at Kasai. "Get back to the ship now or your friend here pays the price."

The loaded words lashed out, and Kasai cringed back. He turned away, calling over his shoulder. "I'm going, leave him." His heart ached, but he couldn't risk Oxe's life. He heard slow footsteps retreat behind him, breaking into a run after a few feet, and he knew Oxe had left.

If Thukuli hadn't been there, and Kasai didn't owe him for saving his life, he would've left with Oxe at that moment. But his right arm twitched, a twinge of pain shooting through his shoulder, reminding him of the reason for his payment.

He wanted to go home, but he couldn't. It wasn't safe. The Seaborne had caught him once, he wouldn't let them again.

He tapped his way through the town, turning when he got too close to a wall, or debris appeared in his path. Around him the fires raged, but he felt no heat. None of these fires were hot enough for him to feel anymore. He silently cursed the smoke that was making his eyes sting and obscuring his already faltering vision.

It didn't take long until the last section of houses, now mostly ash and rubble, gave way to the open market space before the docks.

He stumbled as he approached the wharf, hissing under his breath.

"Kasai, need any help?" A man's voice rang out.

Kasai looked up and tried to keep his face calm. "I'm fine Velu, thanks." He swallowed the annoyed sigh that threatened to escape.

The skinny red-headed man frowned. "Seriously, the wharf here is warped. It's easy even for us to trip." His freckles seemed darker than usual; Kasai wondered if he had forgotten his suncare again. He hung from the ratlines with a few others.

Heat flared out, making several people flinch. In front of him, the gangplank was lowered to the wharf's edge, and someone moved out of his way. "I said I'm fine." He tapped the gangplank once with his cane, then made it up with no issues. "You need to stop worrying about me."

Velu swung down and met him at the rail. "Fat chance. Thukuli would have our heads if we didn't help each other." The sails fluttered slightly, closed while they waited for the captain. There wasn't much of a breeze, but enough that they could leave without using the engine thankfully.

Kasai glanced at him and shrugged. "Fine. But seriously, I will hit you with this." He raised the cane and started towards the helm, making it up the stairs with no issue. He knew this ship well enough by now he didn't need his cane, but he kept it in his hand, just in case.

His eyesight hadn't bugged him for a few weeks, but today it was acting up and he hated it. He couldn't wait to be able to walk at least semi normally.

Velu grinned at the empty threat and shook his head, walking just behind Kasai.

A young girl met him at the stern. "Can I get you anything?" She asked, her head down.

Kasai frowned. "I'm fine. Go help in the kitchen for now," he told her.

She ran off, and Velu sighed. "I hate how she worships you..."

Kasai gave a snort in agreement and leaned against the rail. "Can you blame her? She took too long on a chore, just once, and Thukuli hit her hard enough she got knocked out for almost a full day." He lowered his voice, "and I'm the only one who stood up for her."

Velu just shook his head as Thukuli ran up the gangplank. The captain stood in the center of the ship and looked around. "Crew, what's the haul?"

"Not much, sir." A tall man called out from his spot in front of the captain's cabin. It was Bek; the first mate of the crew was also in charge of the ledger when they raided towns. And Kasai hated him. He mocked others and was just as cruel as Thukuli, even if he didn't have genetic abilities.

Thukuli frowned. "Well, did we get *anything*?" His voice took on a barely detectible edge, and the crew held its collective breath. He looked around slowly, leaning back slightly.

There was silence for a few minutes while Bek checked the papers in front of him.

After a few more uncomfortable moments, he looked up. "We have food, but that's about it. There were fine clothes in one house, and some silver in another, but it wasn't much."

Kasai ignored the pang of guilt he felt; by now he should be used to this.

Thukuli's eye twitched. "That's it?"

The ship grew quiet as they all waited for the outburst, the tension thick enough to choke on.

"Fine," he said coolly. "Prepare to leave. We're heading back north and taking a few ships while we're moving." He gave Kasai a significant look. "Kasai, check the engine and make sure it's in working order."

Kasai gave a single nod, not relaxing until Thukuli disappeared into his cabin. He turned to Velu briefly, murmuring. "Send Sibra to me when she's done in the kitchen."

Velu nodded and disappeared up the ratlines as Bek took the helm.

THE ENGINE HUMMED SMOOTHLY under Kasai's fingertips, and he relaxed against the wall. Alone, finally. The engine room was cool, being at the waterline, and it felt nice combined with the heat he usually gave off.

The engine had taken no damage since they had come into port, unsurprisingly, and Kasai had barely to glance at it to know that. After almost two years of working on this engine, he knew it by heart. But took no pride in it.

He closed his eyes and took a deep breath. Oxe...

He remembered clearly the day he woke to Thukuli's face and Feluna's relieved sigh, unaware of what had happened.

Feluna had explained they found Kasai nearly dead in a small medical facility on Veridey's Island, but no one knew how he got there, and the doctor had fled during the raid so he couldn't answer. And Kasai didn't remember how he had escaped the Seaborne. Only before...

He glanced at his right arm and flexed it unconsciously, but his fingers moved with only a second's delay.

"Oxe..." he whispered the name and closed his eyes against the pain. He wished he could've had time to explain to Oxe about everything. The months of pain and recovery. Of nightmares, screaming, and desolation he felt. The sense of loss when his arm...

He snapped his eyes open, heat flaring out; a faint sizzling noise was heard from the bottom of the walls. He wouldn't think of that.

A door opened somewhere nearby, sending down a cool waft of salty air, and rapid footsteps heralded the approach of Sibra. Her hair was tangled and she was out of breath when she approached Kasai. "Sorry, the cook had me scrub out one of the small cauldrons."

"It's fine. Why don't you sit?" Kasai phrased it as a question, but nodded towards a crate nearby. He frowned at her slightly as she sat down. "You didn't go into town, did you?" He reduced the heat for her.

She shook her head. "The captain still won't let me."

He didn't think Thukuli ever would at this point. "I'll talk to him, see if you can't tag along with me next time." He knew why Thukuli didn't let her, but Kasai didn't think he should worry about that anymore.

He internally winced as he remembered the smoking village where Sibra came from, and her mother's dying request for Kasai to protect the girl. He had had no choice but to at least try, as the guilt would've eaten him alive if he hadn't, but he didn't anticipate she would've attached herself to him after that.

But that had been a year ago. Thukuli had ordered she help Kasai to earn her keep, but she was billeted as a ship's girl officially.

He felt uneasy giving her any orders, but she was bright and willing to help at least, and it kept her out of Thukuli's sight.

"Who was that man? The one that turned into a wolf?" Her question caught him off guard, and he glared at her.

"I thought you didn't go into town?" He asked, his voice hard.

She shrugged, clearly unbothered. "Who was he? You looked like you had seen a ghost."

He grit his teeth, his eyes closed, and the temperature rose.

"Kasai?" Her voice was pained, and he relaxed the heat. "Sorry, I won't pry."

He shook his head. "I'm not mad at you for prying. I'm mad that you went on shore without telling someone." Mostly the truth.

She nodded and looked down. "So who was he?"

Kasai sighed. "I don't know if I want to talk about that right now."

She nodded slowly, downcast.

Kasai closed his eyes, then looked at her after several moments. "I'm sorry. It's just...painful," he explained.

"Is he important to you?" Sibra's expression was unreadable, but she seemed genuinely curious. And he knew she wouldn't tell anything to Thukuli.

He shrugged uncomfortably. "You could say that..." Oxe was more than important, but unfortunately there was no way to get to back to him. Not safely, and not before he had repaid his debt to Thukuli.

She was watching him expectantly when there was movement and Thukuli appeared. "Kasai, I think we need to talk about that man. Sibra, get." Kasai hadn't even heard his footsteps.

Sibra nodded meekly and scurried away, racing past Thukuli.

Kasai eyed Thukuli warily. "What about him?"

"I just want to ask you about him, is all." Thukuli said this with a shrug, but Kasai heard the warning in his voice. "Who was he? You knew him."

How much had he heard? "A friend of mine, from before I got injured." Kasai was reluctant to acknowledge that he had a partner. Thukuli had enough resources to find out who Oxe was and hurt him as it was. Admitting who Oxe really was would just make it worse.

"A friend? Seemed like more than a friend. What with the way you looked at him, he looked at you." Thukuli's voice grated harshly, his eyes flashing. Jealous. Again.

Kasai sighed internally. Thukuli had made a few advances in the past year, and Kasai hated it from the start. "Close friend. The last time he saw me, I was just about to fight someone, but then I got hurt and the Seaborne got me."

"I wondered if you had been in a fight, but you never said anything." Thukuli glared at him but shrugged, leaning back against the wall. "Wish you had gone with him?"

Kasai narrowed his eyes. "I still have to pay you back." He said the words carefully, trying to gauge Thukuli's reaction.

Thukuli gave him a strange look. "I was surprised when you flamed your partner."

Kasai flinched. How had he guessed? How *much* had he guessed?

"I'm seriously surprised you didn't run off with him. I could tell you were on the verge of it right then." Thukuli's voice turned to a sneer. "Maybe when you've paid off that arm, you can go."

Kasai resisted the urge to glare. He leaned back against the wall, heat flaring out. "Until that's repaid, I'm not leaving," he said evenly.

"Tone down the heat Kasai. I'm not mad." Thukuli's voice certainly didn't sound like he *wasn't* mad, but he knew he had Kasai trapped. And worse, he knew Kasai knew it.

Kasai tried to ignore the contempt dripping from his words.

The heat dissipated at once, and Kasai opened his eyes. Thukuli's face was barely an inch from his. Kasai tried not to flinch. "I said I would pay back the debt I owe. I won't leave until that's done."

One of the worst things about Thukuli was the fact that he could move silently. It was creepy.

Thukuli backed off after a moment, nodding. "Good. The medicine wasn't cheap, nor was the time we worked on you, so you still owe quite a bit." He paused for a moment, his eyes hard. "Stay here for now. I'll send Sibra down myself later."

Kasai watched him walk off, then turned to the cot hidden in the corner. Laying down, he stared at the ceiling, feeling the ship rock in the waves, and closed his eyes with a sigh.

Chapter 3

Oxe

"HE *what*?!" North's jaw dropped and Arat stared at Oxe. Several people turned, the shock clear on their faces.

"He is alive." Oxe repeated. "But he was hurt badly. And scared." He shuddered as he recalled the wave of fear that had rolled off Kasai when Ironwood showed up. "He seemed to be connected to Ironwood, but I could not understand why."

North's face twisted into a snarl. "But he was hurting people? Those fires, he started them?"

Arat just looked concerned.

Oxe frowned. "No. At least, he was not hurting people on purpose. Ironwood's crew was behind the attack; he may have forced Kasai." He refused to believe that Kasai would hurt people on purpose. It wasn't like him. It had taken months for him to recover from killing Grimshaw, and he was still having nightmares before that last fight.

But to hurt others on purpose...he didn't think anyone could change that much, especially Kasai.

Arat stepped forward. "Oxe, call Brinar. Use the face-crys this time."

Oxe grimaced but nodded. The face-crys, a new piece of technology developed just over two years ago, was still confusing for him. A ground crys mixed with sand, then melted into glass and coated with a special substance, allowed people to talk face-to-face over long distances. The hookup was expensive, but Brinar had given Oxe one when they returned the clipper ship.

He entered his room quickly, ignoring the open porthole and the thick smell of salt permeating the air, and flipped through the stiff book that held the distinct patterns for other crys' in the world. He found Brinar's and tapped the code onto the metal pad below the screen.

The ten-inch square flickered as the en coursed through it, and through the speaker along the side a static sound could be heard. After a few moments, Brinar's face appeared distorted but quickly smoothed out as the connection held.

"Oxe? Is everything okay?" Brinar's voice hadn't changed, aside from being a little tired, since the last time Oxe had called several months ago. He looked fine though, his island's medicine finally taking the full effect.

When they had met, Brinar had appeared in his sixties. His silver hair had been long, braided, and he wore rose-tinted lenses. Now, back on the medicine his island made for its inhabitants, he appeared much closer to forty. He had slimmed down and his hair was a salt-and-pepper brown color, and his strength had only increased since his body reacted to the younger muscles.

Oxe still didn't understand how it worked, even though Brinar had explained it some. They took medicine that slowed the aging process once they turned eighteen, and as a result, they lived much longer than everyone else. After thirty years off the islands version, Brinar had aged slower than other people but faster than he was meant to, but now he could take the medicine monthly and could fit in better with his people. He was still older, but much closer to the people that all appeared in their twenties and thirties.

Oxe shook his head, trying to focus. "Kasai's alive."

Brinar held a hand up. "Hold on. Amalia will want to hear this." His voice was immediately alert, his gaze wary.

He disappeared off the screen. Oxe waited impatiently, his fingers drumming on the bed. The ship creaked, and he could hear people working in the rigging or at the wheel or heading to or from the mess area.

"Bronwen, put that down!" His voice sounded further away and if he weren't still in a state of shock, Oxe would have smiled. "Amalia, come here. Oxe found Kasai."

After a moment, a blonde-haired woman holding a small boy appeared. "Oxe? Is he there? How is he?" Amalia looked more tired than Brinar; having twins probably was a bit much for them. River squirmed in her arms, but she readjusted him easily.

Oxe shook his head. "No. I...I don't know what happened, but he was with Ironwood's crew. They were attacking a town close to Erith."

Brinar appeared to the side. "Ironwood's crew? They were attacking a *town*?"

Oxe nodded. "Kasai was injured. He walked with a cane. I could not talk to him long before Ironwood showed up and attacked me."

He regretting having to run, but had no choice. He knew that trying to make Kasai leave would've gotten someone hurt, and Kasai had seemed reluctant. If it hadn't been for Ironwood, maybe there would've been at least a chance.

Amalia closed her eyes briefly. "Oxe, what did he look like?"

Oxe thought for a moment. "He grew a beard, and his hair was longer and braided. He leaned to the left greatly, and when he walked, he seemed hesitant about his movements. I don't think he could see very well, like when he first got injured from the lightning. He used a cane to get around."

Amalia nodded and looked at Brinar. "The brain damage did more than we thought."

Oxe held back from flinching. When Kasai had exploded the arrow on himself and Brinar, he had been hurt gravely. His skull hadn't fractured like they told him.

It had broken, and a piece had to be removed to let everything heal correctly. The bone had punctured a portion of his brain, resulting in bleeding, but they were unaware of how to treat it then. By the time they knew, Kasai was already out of surgery and waking up.

Kasai's condition seemed to improve after a few months at sea, leading them to believe that the damage was not as bad as initially thought. He was distant, and struggled with his powers for a while, but improved with practice and time.

But then during the fight with Blacksmoke, a kick to the face had caused more damage and possibly made things worse. North and Arat had been there. They had seen him nearly get killed; it had been an act of desperation when North shot him.

But then he disappeared before they knew the full extent of the damage.

"Oxe." Brinar's voice brought him out of his thoughts and Oxe realized he had been staring off for a few minutes. "Did he recognize you?"

"Yes. I think he recognized me as a wolf first, then followed me when I moved a child away from the town." He had, as who else would've not attacked immediately? "But he...he shot flame at me when I tried to approach him." Oxe's voice broke a bit; his hand was shaking.

Amalia and Brinar exchanged a worried look, then Amalia spoke. "We know his powers are affected by his emotions. He probably didn't do that on purpose, Oxe." Her tone was reassuring, but her eyes betrayed the depth of her worry. She had been one of the doctors to treat Kasai after his fight with Brinar. She knew about the deeper injuries he had even before his fight with Blacksmoke.

Brinar nodded. "Did he say anything?" He sounded almost...sad, but Oxe wasn't sure.

Oxe nodded, his throat tight with pain. "Yes. His voice...he sounds like Sonus now. Rough. I do not think he recovered from that fight very well. But he only told me to leave, then Ironwood showed up."

Brinar's eyes narrowed. "He didn't say anything more?" River started fussing and Brinar held him; the boy calmed down and pulled on Brinar's beard. Brinar flinched and made him let go.

Oxe said grimly, "No. He was scared. I think Ironwood has some kind of hold on him."

There were footsteps outside the ship's room, but they disappeared quickly. The ship creaked and rolled, but Oxe gripped the table hard enough his knuckles were white.

Amalia looked grim as she spoke. "He might. We don't know what happened when Kasai disappeared. We don't know how he ended up with Ironwood."

"What should I do?" Oxe asked them. His voice was on the verge of cracking and he had to suppress a shudder.

It was silent for a few moments, then Brinar spoke. "Meet me in Surval. You're still with North's crew, right?" Oxe nodded. "Let them know we'll meet at Nakan's shipyard. Call the Nuveri, let them know. Maybe they have an idea."

Oxe nodded again, and the connection ended.

A sob choked out before he could stop it. This was too much. He curled over, his body shuddering and jerking, sobs escaping in gasps. His hand clenched over the scar on his ribs, the lightning strike marks almost burning against his hand.

It was several minutes before he slowly uncurled, his hand still clutching his side. Kasai was alive, but none of that made sense. Why would he be so attached to someone he clearly feared? He was still Oxe's mate.

Right?

He hadn't looked angry, looked upset, like Oxe might have expected, but the pained look of love in his eyes wasn't that different from what Oxe had seen before. He had *wanted* to leave, but somehow he couldn't. That was the only explanation.

Oxe finally stood up. It would take three months to get to Surval if they used the engine. He looked at his bracelet and the two wolves that hung from it.

Kasai's bracelet had been gone, but that was only because it was sitting in Oxe's bag. His bag held an assortment of items of Kasai's, or things that needed to be given to him. His bangles, a logbook that had belonged to Sonus, and a photoglass of Sonus, Kira, and the newborn Kasai and young Doux.

Oxe didn't know if Kasai could handle what had happened, or how much he remembered, but he knew they had to get him back. He stared at the face-crys and growled, his fangs showing.

"Brinar, I hope your family is okay with you leaving for a while. I think we are going to need your help." Oxe spoke the words aloud, then left the room.

Chapter 4

Kasai

"KASAI, CAN YOU SEND them our welcome?" Thukuli's voice oozed out, and Kasai barely concealed his grimace. The ship was moving along quickly, keeping pace with another ship just ahead. The breeze was strong enough to make a few stray strands of hair blow across his face.

He raised the bow and quickly formed an arrow, the tip a swirling point of red and orange. He shot it high, aiming towards the fleeing ship. Without flinching, he watched as the mainmast went up in flames and the ship jerked to a stop. Grappling hooks pulled it closer.

If he flinched, Thukuli would start asking questions, and Kasai was in no mood for that. Two months of nightmares, each one showing Oxe getting hurt. Sometimes he remembered Blacksmoke, sometimes it was Thukuli, and once...Kasai himself. He was exhausted, mainly emotionally, and wasn't sure how much more he could take.

He shook his head, firing another arrow. It ripped through a hanging from the crows nest, sending a man crashing to the deck. Kasai ignored the faint snapping sound, the wrong angle of his head, and leaped over with everyone else.

He wasn't a fan of the bow in his hands; it was simple, made of wood, and was maybe the sixth or seventh he'd had in the last few months. He could already feel the wood in this one cracking. There were spares below, but he missed the custom-

No, he wouldn't think of that now.

The merchants fought hard, much harder than when Kasai had fought at someone else's side. However, he was kinder back then. He didn't try to hurt people then; here, he didn't have a choice.

His footsteps faltered only slightly, more because of the rocking of the ships than sight right now. Luckily, that wasn't bothering him today.

"Get back!" Thukuli leaped over and joined Kasai, knocking away a man with a large scimitar raised. The man fell back and Thukuli slashed at him, a red mark appearing across the man's neck. Blood poured down from his throat in a thick stream as he collapsed.

Thukuli grinned at Kasai, but he just turned away. Kasai barely hid his disgust. Thukuli's frown did not go unnoticed by Kasai. He headed towards the captain's cabin by habit.

Kasai used the end of his cane to bust down the door, but the man inside just cowered. Kasai suppressed a sigh, attempting to ignore him.

"Take whatever you want!" The merchant captain cried, trying to hide behind an ornate desk. He was dressed richly, his clothes tasteful to the point of being tacky. Outside, screams were heard and some cut off quickly.

Kasai looked around the room; books, figurines, a stack of recent newspapers, and a strange square of glass with a metal pad sitting atop a thick book. He picked it up, but shrugged and set it back down. He didn't know what these were, but never asked anyone. They had been appearing on almost every merchant ship in the last year. He looked for an en-crys, but saw none and quietly cursed.

Thukuli came through the door as the sounds of fighting died down. "Finding anything?"

Kasai nodded and grabbed a few books. "I have a few things. I'll sell most of these in port, but I'm keeping one or two." He ignored the clothes, though he would've liked some of them. He usually just wore the same sleeved tunic and flare-ended coth pants.

He missed having new clothes, but he didn't want to keep much on the ship.

"I still don't know how you understand those." Thukuli scoffed.

Kasai barely glanced at the books. Science books, a few on animals, and a book about medicine. Stuff Brinar may have liked. Kasai had a small collection under his cot, but Thukuli didn't know how many he really had.

Some he was genuinely interested in, but a few were more because of the author.

Kasai knelt as best as he could by the desk, heating the lock on the drawer enough it melted. The captain flinched, both from the heat and Kasai's proximity, but Kasai ignored him. The drawer held only a strange metal contraption, which might fit the glass and metal square, and Kasai glanced at Thukuli.

Thukuli didn't see Kasai put the wires into his bag, too busy staring outside. "Come on. There's enough junk in here." Outside was quiet, the merchant crew subdued finally.

Kasai nodded and when Thukuli left the room, he turned to the captain, still cowering behind the desk. "What are those wires for?"

The captain shook his head, pointing at the glass square, but said nothing.

Kasai grabbed it, pocketing it carefully, and decided he would figure it out later. Outside, the crew were already taking their spoils over, with Bek noting everything. While Kasai told him about the books, but kept the strange pad and wires to himself.

KASAI GRUNTED WITH effort, the wrench screeching against the bolt. The engine creaked, and Kasai jumped back when he felt a jolt through his left arm. "Dammit..."

He sat back, panting, and flexed his hand experimentally, but there was no lasting damage. The engine shuddered, but suddenly ran smoothly.

Kasai glanced up and sighed. "Sibra, enough. I don't need your help." A bolt was floating above the engine.

There were footsteps, and Sibra stepped out from behind the doorway. "Sorry. But it's fixed now!" Her hand was raised, palm facing upward. She shrugged and gave Kasai a sheepish smile.

He frowned, the heat rising. "I almost had it. And put that down before someone sees you." There was a fleeting ache in his head, which he ignored.

The bolt dropped slowly; Kasai reached out but cursed when his hand reached past it. The bolt bounced off his arm and clattered to the floor. Slowly, he bent down and grabbed it before dropping it into a nearby bucket.

"Is your sight bothering you again?" Sibra's voice was quiet.

Kasai tried not to glare at her. "It's fine," he snapped. He stood quickly and limped to the bench against the wall. "I just missed, that's all." It was, but not that much.

Gripping his head, he groaned in pain as a sharp agony shot through the left side. Sibra's footsteps darted away and a few minutes later, a thickly built woman appeared at the edges of Kasai's vision.

He barely had time to notice her when she slung him over her shoulder, then carried him to his cot. "Those headaches are going to kill you, you know."

Kasai couldn't answer as intense waves of pain surged through his head. From behind his left eye to the back of his skull, radiating randomly. His pulse echoed in his ears, his vision wavered in jagged colors.

"Can't you give him anything?" Sibra's voice was dim in his ears.

"Just what I always do." Feluna's deep voice sounded muffled. Kasai felt a mask over his face and a sickly-sweet scent rushed over his nose.

As he breathed in, his headache faded slowly. When it was gone, he ripped off the mask and sat up. "Thanks..." There was still pain, but it wasn't bad. His vision was a tad fuzzy, but better.

"Did your vision change again?" Feluna asked.

"He tried to catch a falling bolt and overshot," Sibra told her quickly.

Kasai shot her an annoyed look, but nodded. "She's right." The ache was receding. Barely. Slowly.

Feluna raised an eyebrow and sat down on the floor; even sitting, she was tall. "You've had this problem for two years now and it's getting worse. Are you sure you don't remember how you got hurt?"

Kasai grunted, closing his eyes. He had never revealed to them his struggle against Blacksmoke, and he genuinely couldn't remember what happened after. He tried not to think about that day.

Feluna was staring at him. "Those headaches are getting worse, Kasai. Anything you could tell me about how you got your injuries would help me figure out how to treat you better." Her eyes were hard.

He knew part of this was because without a medical history, it was hard to treat him. But he had also refused to tell her the origins of *all* his injuries. Some were too painful to think about.

He stared at the floor. "I don't know how I got hurt. But I had loads of injuries before that, including some head ones I *did* tell you about." He only told her about that he got his facial scar in a fight, but not how. But not about his fractured skull, or the brain damage.

The pain in his head was almost gone thankfully. He focused on breathing.

Sibra cocked her head. "We can tell you're lying. You remember how you got hurt."

Heat suddenly flared out, and Feluna and Sibra flinched back. Kasai growled, "I don't remember."

Feluna glared. "You do, but you won't tell us." When Kasai said nothing, she shook her head. "I won't pry. That's not my style. But if you don't get to the bottom of whatever's bothering you, you'll never heal. I'm the ship's doctor. It's my job to help." And she was annoyed he wouldn't be honest with her, but he knew she wouldn't admit that.

"Does it have anything to do with that shifter guy in Sedgeliss?" Sibra asked suddenly.

Heat flared out again, making the air almost crackle, and Feluna struck out without warning. She pinned Kasai against the wall by his shoulder. "Knock it off!"

A sharp throb shot through his shoulder; his right arm spasmed involuntarily.

Kasai pulled fire from the air and suddenly knocked her back with a thick staff. He didn't think, didn't even register the once familiar form. "Don't. Ask. About. Oxe." He shut his jaws with an audible snap as they stared at him.

"Whose Oxe?" Feluna finally asked after a few tense moments.

The staff dissipated in a flash, and Kasai sank back on his bed. "I don't..." His head ached again, but a different kind of hurt.

They exchanged a look, and Feluna stood. "I won't ask, at least for now. But get some rest. And during our next raid, use that staff. It's a useful weapon and you clearly know how to use it." She grabbed the tank and mask she had used on Kasai, avoiding his eyes.

Kasai chose to disregard the warning in her voice and merely nodded.

Sibra watched Feluna leave, then looked at Kasai. "I'm sorry."

Heat lashed out in an arc, and Kasai didn't flinch as Sibra was knocked back by a tongue of flame.

But as she ran off, her hand on her face, Kasai felt a single tear roll down his cheek.

Chapter 5

Oxe

OXE SHIFTED NERVOUSLY as he waited for North. North stood a few feet away, facing a woman in front of him. Nakan.

She glared at North. "North, just leave." His twin sister stood with her arms crossed, a tool belt around her waist.

In the two years since Oxe had seen her, she had not aged well with her attitude towards pyrates, even if her brother was one.

Not that he blamed her.

With a sigh, North shut his eyes momentarily before fixing a steady gaze on her. "Please. Just for a few days at least. We can work if you need us to, but we're waiting for Brinar and we don't know when he'll be here."

Nakan grit her teeth and her lips curled in a snarl. "He's already here. Remember the hospital? You'll find him there. Now get out and take your crew with you." Her voice was brittle, like jagged stones through the air. Behind her, a man crossed his arms and looked over the pyrate crew standing back from them.

Oxe stepped forward. "Nakan, when did he get here?"

He resisted the urge to react to her glare and the frosty tone in her voice. "Yesterday. He was dropped off by a merchant from Witch Island. He stopped by yesterday afternoon, told me where he would be and to let you know, which is the only reason I'm talking to you."

Oxe nodded, and she stalked off. The man glared at them, but he didn't seem angry.

North sighed and glanced at the sky. "I don't think she'll ever forgive me."

"You can't blame her," Arat said as they began walking down the road. The rest of the crew trailed behind, letting the three men walk ahead of them. "I'm just glad they were able to restart the business."

Oxe nodded in agreement. They had sold the remains of the shipyard after Sonus' crew had fought Blacksmoke three years ago, but luckily, they had rebuilt a new shipyard after months of hard work on the Surval Dockmarket.

But Nakan had given up her animal healer work to run the business, and Oxe could empathize with that. He gave up his tribe, or at least living with them, to stay with Kasai. While he would've had to do that anyway because of their customs, it would have been more than unpleasant if he did not enjoy the person he was bound to.

The hospital came into view after several minutes. It hadn't changed since they were last here.

Brinar met them outside and Oxe was surprised to see Amalia and their kids with him. "North, you brought your crew?"

North nodded. "There were Seaborne in the harbor." He explained.

Brinar nodded and waved his hand to them. "Just hang around here. The Seaborne have an agreement not to attack or capture anyone on hospital grounds."

They looked relieved and scattered around. North, Arat, and Oxe followed Brinar over to a seating area where Amalia was watching their kids.

At almost two years old, Bronwen resembled Amalia greatly. Her blonde hair was tied back and Oxe smiled as she suddenly got up and ran to Amalia. "Ma!"

River looked up from his toys, little wooden blocks with writing on them, and watched the men approach. He looked more like

Brinar, except he had one blue and one green eye. His dark brown hair was cut short.

Brinar picked him up and sat down. "Oxe, explain everything again." River watched Oxe and he felt a little unsettled by the toddler's keen gaze.

"I wanted to look for Kasai one more time while we were on Veridey's Island." Oxe started.

Amalia smiled. "It's a good thing you did."

Oxe grimaced, remembering the village. "I had actually just decided to give up on him..."

Everyone exchanged concerned looks, but he ignored them.

"I was going to head back to North's ship when a girl came running from Sedgeliss. She asked me for help then ran for the Seaborne tower. When I got there, the town was under attack. I only had enough time to move one child to safety before I heard someone." He hung his head, closing his eyes.

"What are the odds that Kasai would be the one to spot him?" Amalia murmured to Brinar.

"Honestly? Not all that high," Brinar responded quietly.

Oxe looked at him. "Kasai has changed. He recognized me immediately, and I think he wanted to leave, but something held him back. I saw it in his eyes. And when Ironwood showed up, he was scared."

North and Brinar exchanged a look, then North's gaze met Oxe's. "How did Kasai act?"

Oxe thought for a moment. "He had trouble walking, and I noticed he only moved away from a building when his cane touched it. I know he could see me, but I do not think he could see well. He said only what I told you before."

There had been a man in the tribe like that when Oxe was little, but in the tribe, someone had always been there to care for him. And even then, it wasn't exactly like what he witnessed with Kasai.

Brinar regarded him carefully. "Anything else?"

Oxe cocked his head. "When Ironwood showed up, he was afraid. But more like he was afraid of Ironwood attacking me. Ironwood kicked the ground and a...thorn shot out."

"A thorn?" Amalia looked at him, then at Brinar. "A genetic?"

Brinar nodded, his face grim. "Yes. I had heard rumors of Ironwood a few years ago. He's a plant genetic, or something related."

Oxe growled, his features shifting. Bronwen cried a bit and Oxe forced his features back to human. "Sorry. But it would make sense. He tried to attack me before I even entered the village, and he did the same thing, but smaller. He did not see me shift though."

Amalia held Bronwen tight. "Oxe, do you think Ironwood is keeping Kasai prisoner somehow?" Bronwen looked afraid of Oxe, but Amalia's grip seemed to help her.

Oxe shrugged.

"How would he do that? Kasai would be the first of us to fight back against something like that." Arat glanced at some of the crew lounging nearby.

"It might have something to do with the girl who followed him." Oxe told them.

Everyone stared at him, then River climbed down and played with his toys. Brinar watched him for a moment, then looked up. "What girl?"

Oxe shrugged. "I saw her only once, but she smelled strongly like Kasai. I think she spends time with him." And she had been hidden mostly, only part of her face was visible. Oxe had smelled more than seen her.

Amalia nodded slowly. "Kasai was always protective. Maybe he's protecting her somehow?"

North frowned. "But if Ironwood has a hold on Kasai, what can we do?"

"We need to get close to Kasai, talk to him. Maybe he needs help." Arat suggested.

Brinar snorted. "Remember his reactions when people suggested that before? I believe Kasai's changed, but not *that* much."

He clearly hadn't forgotten the few months before the fight against Blacksmoke. Brinar had been afraid, or mad, enough that he hadn't talked to Kasai for two months; Sonus had even been angry with him for a bit.

Oxe growled again, his face shifting. "But maybe he would if it would mean being free of Ironwood. I do not believe he enjoyed being there, and using his fire to destroy homes."

Bronwen's fear grew and he forced his features back.

"Maybe not, but remember that he was a pyrate before...before the last time we saw him." Arat hesitated. "I don't know if any of you noticed, but I think Kasai enjoyed it."

Oxe nodded. "He did, but not for the reasons you think."

North shot him a look, then turned to Arat. "I think Oxe is right. Kasai never enjoyed hurting people or destroying things, but I know he loved being with us."

"Oxe, do you really think Kasai wanted to leave?" Amalia asked.

Oxe shot her a dark look.

She glared back. "I'm serious. I'm not trying to doubt you, but we have no idea what he went through. Mentally or physically. It sounds like he healed badly, or got other injuries since then, but why would he be with Ironwood? Especially willingly?"

No one answered her. Oxe watched River playing, but there was a loud crashing of metal and everyone turned in time for a young girl to come bursting through a window in a shower of wood and glass.

Oxe shifted his legs and grabbed River. He raced out of range of the glass, then waited for Brinar to reach him. His skin itched as the fur immediately receded, the paws changing shape, but he ignored it.

"What happened?" He asked the older man, handing River over. The child was quiet, watching Oxe and the other shifter. Oxe felt his skin prickle but ignored it.

Brinar waited a minute, checking River over quickly before answering. "Shifter genetic. I was treating her earlier, but she has no control over her abilities yet."

Oxe looked towards a cloud of dust, barely able to make out a tangle of limbs and fur. North was wrestling with someone. After a few moments, the dust cleared and North had a girl pinned on her stomach.

Oxe stepped forward as her features changed. A long, narrow muzzle, a short fuzzy tail, thick fur with a striped pattern sprouted all over her body. North was suddenly thrown clear and Oxe didn't hesitate.

His bones ached from the speed of his shift; paws hit the ground, fur sprouted almost instantly, his muzzle shoved forward. Blood touched his nose, and he locked jaws with the stranger as she rose to meet him. A strangled yowl tore from her throat, thrumming against his snarl.

He snapped, snarled, and clawed at her, standing between her and Brinar and his family. Her eyes had locked onto Bronwen and Oxe recognized that look.

Sometimes, when shifters in the tribe first changed, they had a few months of bloodlust that was pure animal. It took time to win against the animal side of the mind and he thought maybe she was new to this.

She seemed comfortable in her movements, but there was nothing human about her reactions. She had locked her sights on something that an animal would have hunted, and wouldn't back down unless she had no choice.

She growled and hissed in his face, pacing back and forth in front of him. She was a true shifter, like him, but he knew he was human. He didn't think she did.

"Oxe!" Brinar's voice called out and Oxe flicked an ear back. "Try to corner her."

Lashing his tail, Oxe flew at her. His paws met hers in midair. He knocked her back, though she was much bigger than him now. He recognized her as a colf, albeit without the second set of front legs.

With a hiss, she opened a gash along his muzzle with a deft paw and he clamped his jaws around her ankle. He crunched down, the taste of blood in his mouth, and she yowled in pain. Maybe not a colf? Colves didn't hiss like that, nor were they that agile.

He let out a snarl as she sank her fangs into his shoulder and shoved her roughly against the wall. There were rapid footsteps and a quiet *pop*. Oxe stepped back as a red feathered dart appeared in her flank. His ears rang, but he didn't look away from her.

She growled and hissed, pawing at it, but slowly she sank to the ground.

Oxe backed off, panting, and shifted back to human. He felt blood on his cheek and wanted to wipe it away, but he couldn't take his eyes off her.

Her eyes met his as she lost consciousness, and then she was asleep. Her features slowly melted back; short black hair, ebony skin, long gangly limbs. Except for the darker skin, she could've been from the Nuveri tribe.

"Oxe, are you okay?" Brinar touched his arm, taking in his face. "I'm surprised she got close enough to hurt you."

Oxe nodded, still out of breath. "I am fine. She was fast."

"I'll say." Amalia came up, holding both kids. "I've never seen anyone fight that quickly, even real animals."

Bronwen was shaking, but River was silently watching Oxe and the girl still.

"Get her inside." Oxe noticed a doctor he recognized, who was giving orders to a small group of white clothed people. "Oxe, come get that gash treated." He was surprised the doctor recognized him, but followed slowly. Brinar was on his heels while everyone else stayed outside.

Oxe walked slowly as they carried her into a large room. Sitting at a small table, he watched the doctor treat her.

Brinar sat down next to him, a medical kit in his hands. He opened it, sending out a small scent of antiseptics, cleaning coth, and revealing some needles and thread.

Oxe didn't flinch as the peroxi touched his cheek. "What do you think we should do?"

"About her?" Brinar asked.

"About Kasai." Oxe responded.

Brinar was quiet for a few moments, his expression unreadable.

Oxe winced as Brinar pulled a needle through his cheek. He didn't think it had been deep enough to need stitches.

"I'm not sure," Brinar said after he was done. "This is a difficult situation, and we don't know the entire story."

Oxe waited for him to continue.

Brinar paused, taping a piece of gauze over Oxe's cheek. "I think we should figure a way to contact Kasai. Maybe someone can get a message to him, like another pirate who could meet on neutral ground. Or we can capture him, force him somewhere we can talk to him."

Oxe frowned. He felt the new stitches pull immediately. "I do not think he would trust even us if we did that."

"But if we have no other ideas, then I'm not sure what else we can do." Brinar told him.

Oxe didn't want to agree to that, but he had to admit it might be preferable if nothing else worked, or if they couldn't think of anything else to do.

It was quiet for a few moments. Oxe glanced over at the girl. "What will they do with her?"

She was unconscious on the table, straps over her legs, hips, and chest. Oxe guessed this was a precaution in case she shifted again. He wondered if it would be enough, but said nothing.

Brinar glanced at her. "No idea. Most animal shifters don't live that long after their abilities manifest, but she's survived four years so far. I've thought about sending her to Witch Island, but we wouldn't be able to help her any more than someone here."

"We could send her to my home." The words were barely out of Oxe's mouth when he regretted the thought. She was not one of them, an outsider.

But how else could she learn?

Brinar raised an eyebrow. "Would they accept her?" He knew almost as well as Oxe about the tribe's customs. While not a member, he was considered an ally. He was the only outsider the island allowed to come without reacting with hostility.

"I have yet to contact them. I can ask." Oxe flinched away from Brinar's gaze.

"They need to know about Kasai. He's one of you now. They had rites for him." Brinar nearly growled, his brow furrowing slightly.

Oxe nodded, his face sheepish. "I know. But I am away from him, and have been for two years. I know he has been...missing...but will they understand that?"

Brinar watched him for a few minutes, thinking before he spoke. "I think given the circumstances...they are more likely to be understanding than angry."

Oxe sighed. "I know you are right, but I do not know what to say to them."

Brinar gave him a sympathetic look and stood up. "Call them from the hospitals en-crys. They won't mind." He paused for a moment, then looked at Oxe. "No shifting until the stitches are out."

Oxe nodded and stood, looking for a healer. Spotting the doctor from before, he mentally braced himself for the call back home.

Chapter 6

Kasai

"FILTHY PYRATES!" KASAI stepped back, and the sword sank into the wood by his foot. The Seaborne mate drew a pistol and aimed, but he was too close and Kasai just knocked him away with his bow.

"Kasai, hurry up. We have goods to get rid of," Thukuli called over.

Kasai nodded and whipped the bow around. It slammed into the man's temple, and Kasai watched as he crumpled into a heap at his feet. He looked away, noticing Thukuli's grin. Kasai hated when the captain looked happy when Kasai used more force than necessary.

Sibra stepped up to his side. "Kasai? Do you need my help?"

Kasai shook his head, not wanting to look at her. The burn across her face sickened him; he should've never flamed her. It was fading a bit, but still.

She frowned and stepped back as he crossed the deck. She stood by the mast, her eyes never leaving Kasai. He tried not to look guilty.

"Thukuli, where are we dropping these goods off?" Kasai asked.

Thukuli drew his sword from a man's back and looked around. "I'm not sure. Maybe Aromere Port?" His cloak was ripped and blood was splattered over his boots.

"Aromere is a Seaborne port captain." Bek called over. "So unless we want to deal with more of these idiots, we need to go elsewhere."

Kasai frowned and thought about the maps he had studied. "We can go to Surval. I've been there before. They don't mind pyrates in a few places. There's also a northern port we could try. I've never been to the Brimna Atoll, but I know they're supposed to be welcoming to pyrates."

It was a strange spot, a tundra atoll. Only one other, found in the Southern Ice, existed in the world. He had wanted to go there for a few years now, since he first read about it, but he hadn't been in that area of the seas yet.

Thukuli frowned for a minute, then grinned. "That's a good idea. I'm sure they'd love what we found." He turned and vaulted over the railing easily.

Kasai breathed a sigh of relief when he leaped back over to their ship, stumbling only slightly. Sibra met him and handed him his cane. He gave her a nod and took it, leaning heavily on it for a moment. The ship was rocking slightly, but he was used to that by now.

It helped that his vision was better today, too.

Thukuli tapped his arm. "Can you take care of that?" He jerked his thumb over his shoulder.

Kasai looked and grimaced. "I can, but why?" He immediately regretted his question.

Thukuli gave him a hard stare. "Because we shouldn't leave any evidence that we can attack the Seaborne yet." His lips curled into the beginnings of a snarl, his eyes glittering.

Kasai wanted to protest, wanted to argue against this, but he knew it would do no good. He had already attracted Thukuli's ire by questioning him.

Sibra flinched as the heat rose and Kasai fired an arrow into the ship's sails. She knew just as well as him that trying to argue against Thukuli was not a good idea.

Kasai stepped back as the sails caught fire, but Thukuli stopped him. "Not there."

Kasai looked at him, then narrowed his eyes. "They won't be able to go anywhere. Anyone left will die soon anyway." He knew this was risky, openly defying Thukuli's order, but he wasn't wrong.

And he was beginning to feel sick at the thought of killing people. Enough that he couldn't ignore it.

Thukuli growled, and the bag at his side shook. "I said I wanted no evidence."

Kasai glared back, but after a few tense moments he dropped his head. Pulling fire from the air, he shot an arrow without looking. He didn't bother using his bow either, not having to shoot that far.

Thukuli nodded as the power magazine exploded. The ship rocked, and he placed a hand on Kasai's shoulder, keeping him from falling over. When the ship finally stopped rocking, Thukuli let him go.

Kasai rolled his aching shoulder, not meeting Thukuli's eyes. "I'll be down by the engine." Thukuli said nothing, just glared. "Sibra, stay above deck for now."

She nodded, but suddenly everyone stepped back from the wave of heat that spread out as Thukuli stepped in front of Kasai.

"I'm more than happy to call your debt even if you want to end it now." Thukuli kept his voice low and even. His eyes glittered darkly, and he alone didn't recoil from the heat. "But until then, you're part of my crew and you follow orders."

Kasai stayed silent, leaning on his cane. He didn't look up. From Thukuli's painful grip on his shoulder, he knew already he had pushed too far. The words just dug the reprimand in deeper.

"Stay below. I'll send food down at the next bell." Thukuli jerked his head toward the door leading below.

Kasai limped down the stairs heavily, hearing footsteps behind him. It wasn't Thukuli, but he didn't care who it was right now. He was in no mood to talk.

He tapped his way through the dark room, dropping into his cot with a sigh.

"You're really testing him lately." The voice was quiet. A lamp was lit nearby, the flame fluttering softly.

"Leave me alone Velu." Kasai closed his eyes. Beside him, the engine was silent. They didn't need it yet, but for once, he wished he could turn it on. The sound might help clear his ears.

Maybe drown out his thoughts.

Velu appeared in the lamplight. "Easy, I just wanted to make sure you were alright." There was a cut on his arm, and his shirt had blood on it.

Kasai swallowed his growl. "I'm fine. Everyone needs to stop treating me like I'm some fragile being, like I'm made of glass or something." The words surprised him, but more because he openly admitted this to someone he didn't particularly care for. Not that he didn't like Velu, but he didn't really care for anyone anymore. Not since...he shook his head, clearing the thoughts away.

Velu cocked his head, waiting a few moments before speaking. "Thukuli and Bek may care because you're valuable to them."

Kasai scoffed at this, but he knew Velu had a point. Thukuli had never been more powerful since Kasai had come aboard.

"But some of us genuinely care." Velu sounded a tad hurt.

Kasai sat up, looking at him.

Velu looked hurt too, his eyes tight. "I'm serious. I've been trying to look out for you since day one, and even after you recovered, you've just spent most of your time down here. But this is the first time you've been sent here by Thukuli in months."

He was standing against the wall, his hands at his sides but held taught.

"So?" Kasai couldn't see what he was getting at.

"Why now? Why say something about what we've been doing now?" Velu let out a breath, clearly bothered.

Kasai frowned. "He's never had me sink a ship before. We've also never attacked a Seaborne ship."

"You've never ended a life before us?" Velu asked. He didn't sound judgmental, only curious.

Heat flared out. "Twice." Kasai's voice deepened to a growl; his fists clenched against his legs. He could feel his hands beginning to shake.

"But I'm guessing those weren't in a situation like this," Velu stated. "I won't ask about those times. It's none of my business, but I should warn you that Thukuli told Bek they need to keep a closer eye on you. You've been acting odd since Sedgeliss and they noticed."

Kasai frowned. "So has everyone else. Not exactly like that can be helped. Most of the crew knows I want to leave by now." If they didn't before, they might guess after today.

Velu's gaze hardened. "I'm serious. Whatever's going on, either talk to Feluna or someone about it, then get your head back on straight before Thukuli decides you're no longer worth the trouble."

Kasai felt uneasy at this. Everyone on the crew remembered Briss, the former second mate. She had questioned Thukuli once, and not long after, she had been tossed overboard. Or at least what was left of her.

Thukuli said she had disobeyed him, but everyone knew all she had done was question attacking a child.

Not that anyone blamed her, as the only person onboard who would willingly attack children was Thukuli, but no one had stood up to him before. Not over something like that especially.

Velu was still glaring, so Kasai shrugged. "I'll back down, okay?"

Velu relaxed and leaned back. "Can I ask about something? About before us, I mean?"

Kasai shot him a heated look, but nodded.

"Were you a pyrate before us?" Velu asked.

Kasai waited a moment before answering. "Yes. For about a year and a half, close to two years maybe. Why?"

"But you never ended lives?" Velu pressed.

Heat flared out softly. "No. The crew I sailed with didn't agree with ending lives unless it was necessary." He felt an itch under his skin. Why was Velu asking this?

Velu contemplated something before continuing. "Who did you sail under?"

The heat built until Velu broke out in a sweat. Kasai growled. "It doesn't matter."

He didn't want to think about that. He couldn't. He wasn't ready to think about what he had done.

Velu backed off, fear flickering in his eyes briefly. "Alright, I won't ask."

Kasai laid back on his cot, his voice bordering on harsh. "Please don't." He closed his eyes. He felt guilty for scaring him, but he wouldn't show it.

It was silent for a few moments, then he heard receding footsteps as Velu left. The lamp flickered out.

He sighed and sat back up, speaking aloud quietly. "I'd explain if I could...but I don't know how."

The ship creaked. Footsteps echoed above him.

"Maybe I could jump ship at the Brimna Atoll. Find a way to Surval, contact Doux." He mused.

The ship rolled, and he braced himself against the engine.

"Who am I kidding? Thukuli would kill me if he ever saw me again and I don't want to go into hiding." He frowned, trying not to think about the last time he ran. Look how that had turned out.

Footsteps and a light ahead of the engine room told him that someone was below decks and he laid back again.

He thought about what it would be like to not have to run, to stay in one place or even just travel without fear, and waited for sleep.

Chapter 7

Oxe

"BRINAR, NICE TO HAVE you onboard again." North stood at the helm, Brinar and Oxe leaning against the railing nearby.

Brinar snorted. "And here I thought I had given up the life of a pyrate."

North laughed, shooting him a wide grin. "You know it's not that easy to leave. And you have to admit, you're not bored."

Brinar shook his head, grinning. "Alright, I will admit you've got a point there. It's nice to collect books again."

Oxe frowned slightly. A month out of Surval and heading north, he wasn't yet used to attacking merchants and the few other pyrates in the area. So far, no one had heard of Ironwood being in the area, and Oxe was getting restless.

North glanced over. "Sorry, Oxe. I know this isn't exactly what you planned on doing with your life. It's better than sitting around doing nothing though."

Oxe grimaced. "Yes, anything is better than that."

"What did your people say, by the way?" North asked.

Brinar glanced at Oxe, curious.

Oxe thought for a minute, thinking how to translate it. "They were understanding about me not being with Kasai and not angry at all. They worry that he's been touched."

"Touched?" North looked at Brinar.

Brinar nodded. "They don't have the words to describe when someone loses their mind from mental illness." He crossed his arms, watching the sails for a moment.

Oxe growled softly. "They told me we must find him and help him. They have released me from the tribe until that time, but I am free to return once we have him."

Brinar gave him a slightly shocked and sympathetic look. "Well, they do have to follow their own customs, Oxe."

North nodded in agreement, though Oxe knew he didn't understand Nuveri customs, turning the wheel slightly as a ship appeared on the horizon. "Hold on, Seaborne ship coming up." He looked up. "Crew, belowdecks for everyone not essential. Brinar, Oxe. Act as captain and first mate for now."

Brinar assumed command, though Oxe sensed a certain reluctance. The rest of the crew scrambled down the ropes and lines, disappearing through the hatch. Oxe moved briefly to put on a simple tunic, covering his tattoo, and leaned against the railing again.

"We'll ask about Ironwood," Brinar said.

Oxe nodded. "They will not know it has been us attacking the merchants nearby?"

Brinar shook his head, glancing at a man standing by. "They shouldn't. Sioco, can you take the wheel? I'm still not comfortable up here."

Oxe wasn't surprised at this. For one, Brinar had sent his family back home, so he was separated from them. He knew the older man was uneasy being away from them. Another thing was Brinar was not a navigator of any kind; he was a doctor, but he couldn't take over the position currently as the crew's doctor was less of a fighter than Brinar was.

Not that Brinar couldn't fight. In fact, he could beat North in a fight with his staff alone, but he didn't like to. And Oxe knew that ever since that fight against Kasai, Brinar had been more reluctant than ever to hurt someone.

Sioco nodded and took the wheel happily. Oxe admired the second mate of North's crew, who took great pride in his role. He had been a friend to Kasai on Sonus' crew, and he understood better than the newer members of the crew about why they kept looking for him.

Brinar stood next to Oxe and watched the Seaborne ship get closer.

When they were close enough, someone waved, and Oxe was surprised to see Doux dressed as a captain. He exchanged a look with Brinar, and they waited until the ships were closer.

"AT LEAST HE'S ALIVE." Doux leaned back and closed his eyes. In the two years since they had seen him, he had filled out and radiated power. He had joined the Seaborne, which they knew, but they were surprised that he had already been made a captain.

Brinar gazed around the cabin, looking a little uneasy. "We were hoping you had heard about Ironwood lately, like if he's in the area." Mostly charts of the various seas, labels pinned to various spots to signify routes, and a plain but comfortable looking bed against the wall.

Oxe played with the hem of his shirt. They had told Doux about meeting Kasai, but not who he was with.

Doux slammed a fist down on the table suddenly, making them jump. "That bastard sunk one of our ships, somewhere southwest of Surval! We couldn't find any wreckage, but one man survived thankfully." Oxe was suddenly glad they hadn't mentioned that Kasai was with Ironwood. Doux's eyes were almost blazing.

Oxe pricked his ears. "He sunk a ship?"

"Yes." He turned and spoke into the brass tube by his table. "Send in Uvaag."

They waited a few moments, then a skinny man with glasses came into the cabin. "You called for me, sir?" He was bandaged around his head and left arm.

"Tell us what happened when Ironwood attacked. Everything you can remember." Doux told him.

Uvaag nodded, clearly uncomfortable, and paused for a moment before speaking. "We were patrolling west of Surval, along our usual route, when the captain spotted a known pyrate ship nearby. He ordered us to attack, but I didn't know it was Ironwood. The flag didn't match."

Doux nodded. "That's not surprising. He doesn't always use his own flag. Continue."

"We got close and suddenly the air was filled with fire. Someone was shooting arrows at us, but I didn't see anyone in the crow's nest. And I swear the flames didn't move like fire should." He shuddered and Brinar held up a hand.

"I just have one question before you can stop. Did you see a young man with black hair, a scar across his face, probably using a bow?" Brinar asked him.

Uvaag nodded. "Yes. He shot an arrow into the powder magazine. That's when the ship sank."

Oxe snarled, and Uvaag flinched back from his fangs. "Are you sure it was him who shot the arrow?"

Doux cuffed Oxe's shoulder. Hard. "Oxe, enough. Uvaag, out." His expression was cold, his fist clenched against his leg.

Uvaag nodded and fled the room. Oxe rubbed his shoulder, surprised at the strength behind the blow.

Brinar sighed and gave Oxe a significant look. "This matches up with everything we know so far, unfortunately."

"You *knew* Kasai's been with Ironwood?" Doux said, his face incredulous, his tone barely hiding his rage.

Brinar nodded. "Yes. We don't think he's willingly with him, if that makes a difference."

Doux frowned, relaxing back into his seat. "You think Kasai is being held against his will or something?"

Oxe shook his head. "Maybe. He wanted to leave when he saw me, but he feared Ironwood too much. We do not know what happened, but Kasai would not leave him."

Doux leaned back, thinking hard for a few minutes. Finally, he looked at them. "Alright. We're on the lookout for Ironwood anyway, and we were already looking for Kasai ourselves."

Oxe shot a look at Brinar. "What will the Seaborne do if they find him?" He wasn't sure if Leil would uphold her promise, not after this.

"Unfortunately, Kasai will probably be jailed for a while," Doux told him. "Even our grandmother can't get him out of this mess, but if he didn't attack willingly, maybe the sentence can be lighter."

Oxe growled, fur fuzzing over his body and bristling. His jaw shifted, and he saw Doux flinch slightly. "If we can get him away from Ironwood, will the Seaborne leave him alone?"

Doux sighed and shook his head. "It's not that easy, Oxe. If he hadn't sunk the ship, even if he was forced, I could've called in a few favors and gotten him off the hook. But now..."

Brinar gave him a sympathetic look. "But remember that Kasai may have thought the Seaborne caught him. Why else would he have run?"

Doux's eyes widened. "But North is the one that tranquilized him. He remembers that, I hope." He didn't sound as confident as his tone suggested though.

Brinar shrugged. "Maybe, but he woke up when none of us were in there with him. We don't know what he was thinking, or how much he knows about the two weeks following his fight. It would be better for everyone if we found him first."

Doux glared at him, but finally closed his eyes and nodded. "I agree. If we catch him, and that's why we're out here, more or less, it will be bad. With you, he has a chance to escape."

"But it doesn't change what he's done." Brinar added after a moment. "I just hope he hasn't started doing this because *he* wants to."

Oxe nearly growled, but swallowed it. "Will you be on this ship, then?"

Doux looked at him. "Yes. This is my first ship as captain, and I haven't been doing this long, but I can't promise we can go light on Kasai if we catch him, Oxe. He might be my brother, but I'm Seaborne now. I think Leil requested I come here though."

"That's not surprising. Another captain, or a commander, would be far harsher on Kasai if they caught him," Brinar mused.

Doux gave a reluctant nod. "I think Leil is hoping Kasai disappears so we don't have to capture him. But what will you do now? I'm guessing that's North's crew?"

Oxe nodded. "We did not know it was you, so he hid. Are you the only captain out here?"

Doux looked at his desk; papers were scattered across it. "Yes, for now. If Ironwood isn't caught within a year though, or sinks more ships, I think they'll send more. It's just us right now. We were only sent out because the other ship was destroyed."

Brinar nodded to himself, listening, but he was lost in thought.

Oxe looked out the window, noticing the red tinge to the sky. "Is there a safe harbor for pyrates?"

Doux looked at him sharply. "Brimna Atoll, why?"

"I think we should try there." They knew Ironwood was in the area now, but Oxe felt uneasy about looking for them on the waves. Especially if the Seaborne had already gotten this close.

But if there was a safe spot where pyrates could meet without fear of the Seaborne, it might be worth a shot.

"I don't know, Oxe. While North and his crew will be fine there, we'll stand out." Brinar looked a little uncomfortable at the idea.

"But it's a good idea." Doux gave him an odd look. "But unfortunately you'll fit in a lot better than you think, Brinar. The Seaborne remember you from the epidemic in Cernu, but mostly they recognize you as the doctor aboard a pyrate ship now."

Brinar frowned at this.

"But, Oxe, you'll stand out more than you might like. I hate to ask, but you might need to stay hidden, or shift into something other than a wolf while you're there." Doux finished.

But he flinched back as Oxe shifted into an anthropomorphic wolf. Oxe stood to his full height, towering over the other man almost threateningly. "I cannot shift into another form. I would not want to." The words growled out through his teeth, his lips pulled back in a snarl. His ears were shoved forward and his claws were curled into fists.

His tail stood straight up and he kept his gaze on Doux.

Brinar touched Oxe's elbow. "He wouldn't know that, Oxe. Only me and Kasai know about your tribe's restrictions. Doux wouldn't have suggested that if he had known."

Doux nodded, his eyes wide. "I'm sorry Oxe. I really had no idea. Remember, we didn't get a chance to really talk after Kasai was hurt."

Oxe nodded and his features shifted back to human, but he didn't sit down. "I will not hide." He felt bad about scaring Doux, but it couldn't be helped.

Doux tried not to flinch, but the fear rolling off him stung Oxe's nose. "Fine, but you'll have to go in disguise. While few people know about the Nuveri warriors, you stand out."

Oxe reluctantly had to agree with him, but had no answers to what he could do to disguise himself at the moment.

"Now, unfortunately, I can't entertain you any longer." Doux stood up quickly. "While we are friends, or at least allies, I am also

Seaborne and I feel that some of my men are a little uncomfortable about this."

Brinar frowned but stood. "One more question, and this is for Kasai's sake. Did you ever find Naomi?"

Oxe wished he had met their younger sister, but she had gone missing before he had even met Kasai. He knew Kasai still missed her, or at least he did before he disappeared.

Doux shook his head. "No. Leil had the Seaborne check Anvilcloud Island extensively, but the only lead we got is that she was not seen leaving Cloud Village. No one ever found her body, however, so it's possible she's elsewhere."

Oxe thought he sounded a tad upset at that, but said nothing.

Brinar gave a single nod. "At least there's no proof she's dead. Maybe she escaped then and went somewhere else."

Doux lips twitched in a strangled smile, but he closed his eyes. "When you find Kasai, do me one favor, Oxe."

Oxe looked at him expectantly.

"Tell him I miss him, but I never want to see him again. We might be brothers, but I also have a job now and I don't think either of us could take fighting each other." Doux's eyes said much more though.

Oxe nodded once, then followed Brinar out.

Chapter 8

Kasai

"SIBRA, HOLD IT THERE." Kasai reached into a crevice and flicked the wrench. It was a tight spot, but the engine shuddered and suddenly ran smoothly and quietly. Kasai sat back, wiping his forehead.

Sibra released her hold, and the engine shuddered again. After another moment, it ran quietly again. "I almost lost it." Her arms fell to her side, trembling.

"You did fine." Kasai assured her. "You just have to practice here whenever you can, and helping me with the engine gives you something to do away from Thukuli."

She grinned and sat on the bench. "Yea, but I don't think he would like it if he knew I was reading." The burn mark on her face had mostly faded, leaving an almost invisible scar. She had forgiven Kasai for it, even if he hadn't forgiven himself.

Kasai snorted, looking into a cracked mirror on the wall. Lamplight from a small el-turn cast small shadows across his face, but he grimaced when he saw the black streak across his forehead. "Which book do you have this time?"

He saw Sibra glance at the slim book next to her. "Um, *Oceanic Currents of the Old World*, by someone named Brinar."

Kasai's eye twitched at the name. Grabbing a rag from beside his cot, he spoke without looking at her. "Didn't peg you for someone interested in something like that."

He glanced at his face briefly, trying to hold back a tear as he took in the changes he noticed. He had let his beard grow out, and it was normally twisted into a braid, but his hair was down for once and suddenly he had a flash of a different face.

Dark blonde hair and green eyes flashed in his mind, and he turned away before the memories fully surfaced. He wouldn't think about him, and Kasai realized that he might have to get rid of the mirror. He wiped the dark smudge from his face without looking back.

Sibra hadn't noticed his reaction, flipping through the book. "I'm not really, but you don't get story books. Just science stuff mostly."

Kasai sat down next to her, handing her a different book from the shelf. "Here, this one is about animals. It's mostly informational stuff, but better than reading about ocean currents."

She flipped through it happily, and Kasai stuck the other one under his cot. He had grabbed this one because it was newer, released a year ago, and many copies were being delivered to Surval when they found them. It helped when planning routes, so Thukuli hadn't complained.

"When do you think we'll get to Brimna Atoll?" Sibra asked after a quiet moment.

"Maybe a day? The winds keep pushing us back, and the currents aren't favorable towards the atoll right now. It'll be winter there, at least late winter." Kasai thought about overhearing Bek and Thukuli earlier that day, but they had noticed him and clammed up, unsurprisingly.

"Will you leave when we get there?" Sibra's voice held no inflection, but Kasai jerked his head up and saw her hide a sad look.

He spoke automatically, though the hurt in his voice couldn't be hidden. "I can't. I still have to pay Thukuli back."

She looked at him. "But if you could?"

Kasai met her gaze evenly. "Yes. If I could, I would gladly leave. I want to get back to my family."

She closed the book, frowning. "I thought you were a pyrate before all this though?"

Kasai grimaced; Velu must've said something. "Yes, but that doesn't mean I don't have family." He looked away and stared at the floor.

"Where are they at?" Sibra asked.

Kasai thought for a minute. "I know my brother and his family were somewhere near Erith, and my sister is probably is Nimbus." And he knew Oxe was out there somewhere looking for him, but didn't mention his mate.

"What about your parents?" Sibra tilted her head curiously.

"Dead," Kasai said bluntly.

She must've realized he wouldn't elaborate, so she changed the topic. "If you leave, what will you do?"

Kasai eyed her warily. "What would *you* do?"

She shrugged. "I can't go home, so probably find somewhere new to live."

"What would you have done if we hadn't taken you in?" Kasai asked carefully.

Sibra shrugged again, turning at the sound of footsteps.

Velu appeared. "We just docked. Come on."

"That was fast," Kasai remarked. He grabbed his cane and followed them above deck. His vision seemed better outside, and he didn't need the cane to make sure he didn't bump into anything. But he still kept it hooked over his arm.

Velu shrugged. "You fixed the engine. It gave us the extra push we needed. And an hour ago the wind changed. Make sure you grab warm clothes, Sibra."

Kasai didn't notice the change in temperature like they did; he felt a chill wind, but the other two grabbed coats as they reached the deck.

"Kasai, wait for me." Thukuli met him at the railing. He was bundled up heavily, shivering even in his coat. "I'm waiting here for the dock merchant. They'll take our haul off and give us what we're owed in a while."

Thukuli didn't do so well in the cold, probably because of his powers. If they landed somewhere cold, he usually had Kasai nearby to help him stand it better.

Kasai nodded and turned to Sibra. "Do you want to wait for me?"

She glanced at Thukuli and shook her head quickly. "I'll stick with Feluna."

Feluna glanced at Kasai, then quickly left. Sibra scrambled to follow her.

Thukuli snorted, watching them. "Why do you stick with her so much?"

Kasai shrugged. "You told me to look out for her. That's what I'm doing. Plus, she keeps me company." And it kept her away from Thukuli.

"Better than your books?" Thukuli shot at him.

Kasai ignored that. He knew it bothered Thukuli that he read so much, but since he couldn't work in the rigging, it helped him pass the time. And it's not like many people on the crew were friendly. At least before he could've talked to – he cut the thought off with a barely audible growl.

Thukuli glanced at him, but said nothing.

They waited while a ruddy faced merchant, a former pyrate Kasai guessed, boarded the ship with a handful of helpers and talked to Thukuli. He took the moment's respite from comments to look at the port.

Thatched stone buildings, old brickwork, salt-stone, and wooden houses were jumbled in a mismatched arrangement across the streets. They twisted, turned, and rarely went straight for more than a few houses long. The air was chilly, even for Kasai, and he saw many people wore coats here.

Several blacksmiths, a tattoo artist, and a chandler's shop could be seen nearby, though it looked there were many other shops further away. He noticed many of the people around here were rough looking, and lots of other ships bore unusual flags that he now recognized as pyrate flags. His previous experiences told him that a few pyrates didn't always use the skull and crossbones, but most tended to. The trend had risen recently, and it was getting harder to find pyrates that *didn't* use some sort of flag.

Thukuli's was a skull in profile, with a strand of thorned ivy snaking through and around it.

Many of them stopped and watched Thukuli's ship with interest, probably wondering what kinds of goods they had brought, but Kasai noticed one man stare at him in particular. Tall, white hair streaked with darker grey, and almost yellowish eyes, he stood out among the other people. He was huge compared to them.

Kasai ignored the shiver down his spine and turned away, leaning heavily onto his cane. He watched Thukuli take a bag of coins and walked over. "Can we go yet?"

"Eager to get onto land, are we?" Thukuli asked, grinning.

Kasai grunted. "It's easier to walk on land."

Thukuli chuckled. "Alright, I can try to understand that. Come on." He headed down the gangplank but stopped at the bottom. "Well, this is an honor!"

Kasai ignored the nervous feeling in the pit of his stomach as the tall man approached them.

"Ironwood, nice of ya to drop by. I don't recognize yar friend here." Although his voice was nearly squeaky, Kasai held back his laughter. It seemed at odds with his gigantic frame and muscles, which, while hidden under his coat, were clear from his size alone. His head was shaved along the forehead and halfway back, and Kasai saw the edge of a tattoo crawling up his jaw.

"Cifius! It's nice to see you still here." Thukuli took the man's hand, his own nearly disappearing in Cifius' grip. "This here is Kasai."

Cifius' gaze sharpened, taking in Kasai. The man's stare made him uneasy. Cifius looked at Thukuli. "I think ya better tell me how ya found this one. Last I knew, he was sailing with Lightning."

Kasai felt his heart drop to his stomach and barely kept his face from blanching. Cifius observed him for a long moment, clearly aware of the flinch Kasai tried to hide.

"Lightning?" Thukuli's brows furrowed, then his eyes went wide, and he stared at Kasai. "You sailed with Lightning Sonus?!"

The surrounding air blistered suddenly and everyone but Cifius and Thukuli flinched back.

"Knock it off. You never mentioned him before, so it's kind of surprise," Thukuli snarled. Sweat beaded along his face.

Everyone watched Kasai, some with fear and a few with curiosity. Cifius stepped forward and raised his hand to cuff Kasai, but was stopped by a thick staff of condensed fire.

Kasai could see Cifius eyeing the swirling reds and oranges in the staff's center. Kasai hadn't moved anything but his arm, and he glared at the larger man.

"A genetic?" he asked Kasai, his hand still raised.

Kasai tightened his grip on the staff. "Heat genetic."

Cifius nodded and stepped back and lowered his hand. "Well, don't burn down the town. We may be pyrates, but we have rules here." His voice was cool, but his eyes betrayed his curiosity.

"Cifius is the leader here, or at least who everyone defers to for any issues," Thukuli explained, his gaze narrowed. "Now please, put away the fire."

Kasai stepped back, the staff disappearing in a flash. "I sailed with Lightning's crew for over a year, but then I left."

"More than left," Cifius scoffed. Flames bubbled along Kasai's skin, though no one noticed them, as Cifius continued, "He took down Blacksmoke and somehow Sonus died, then Kasai up and disappears."

Thukuli glared at Kasai, standing close enough that he was surprised the captain didn't catch fire. "I think you remembered more than you let on." His tone had taken on a dark edge. He eyed the brief flickers along Kasai's arm.

Kasai's fierce glare made Thukuli flinch and step back.

He held his hands up. "I get it, I won't ask. Not right now. But I have business in town. Go off and enjoy yourself for a while." He left quickly, and Kasai had a feeling that Thukuli was going to find out about some of his connection with Sonus through his contacts.

A tremor shook his body. Thukuli was powerful, and Kasai knew some of it was because of his ability to manipulate people. He found out secrets easily and exploited them however he could.

Most of his crew were only there because Thukuli had threatened them.

Cifius watched Kasai for a few moments as the other people faded away, heading to homes or shops elsewhere. When they were alone, he jerked his head. "Follow me."

Kasai glared but saw no polite reason to refuse, and he didn't want to run into Thukuli anywhere, so he limped after the large man reluctantly. His hand curled around the top of his cane, his knuckles white.

"WHAT HAPPENED WHEN ya left Lightning's crew?" Cifius pulled out a chair for Kasai, then sat down across from him.

Kasai sat down slowly, leaning his cane against the table. "I was hurt. Then Thukuli's crew found me. They took me in while I healed, and I've been with them for about two years now."

He glanced around, looking at the smokey interior of the bar with veiled interest. A long bar crossed the far wall, several empty tables were scattered around the room, and many cushioned booths crossed the wall where they sat. But this table stood apart from the others.

Thick, ancient, with gnarled chairs made of the same wood, Kasai wondered if this table was from the old world somehow. Worn grooves showed where plates and cups had been moved across it, or knives or bullets had grazed and pierced it.

Kasai absently ran a finger through one of the grooves in front of him.

Cifius narrowed his eyes. "I'm not surprised ya were hurt when fighting Blacksmoke, but what happened to Sonus? I asked his crew when they stopped here once, but they never answered me."

"North was here?" Kasai looked up.

Cifius shook his head. "No. Fayde, before she became a big shot in Western Region last year. She said ya killed him."

Kasai flinched. "She wasn't wrong." Why did Cifius have to ask about this? Kasai hated thinking of that day; the nightmares would probably start up again now. After almost three months without them, his sleep was going to be hell again.

Cifius tilted his head, then leaned back. "I didn't think his kid would be torn up about an accident."

It took Kasai a moment to process what he had said, then his head shot up. "You know?" Accident or not, though, Sonus' death was his fault. But how did Cifius guess Sonus was his father?

Cifius nodded. "Ya look just like him. Even sound like him. Well once he fought that brat Blacksmoke, that is. But what are ya doin' with Ironwood though? He's not the same kind of pyrate as yar father."

Kasai shrugged. "I have a debt to pay back," he said simply.

"Powerful debt to run with that kind of pyrate. He's almost as bad as Razora." Cifius shook his head and motioned at the man behind the bar. "But if ya owe a debt, it has to be repaid."

"How did you know Sonus?" Kasai asked. He didn't want to think about his father. It was still painful, but he couldn't resist the idea that someone knew him before everything went to hell.

"He was on my crew for a number of years." Cifius said cryptically.

The man brought over two tankards, setting one in front of Kasai. Cifius took his and drank half in one gulp, but Kasai didn't touch his drink.

He still had no taste for le, but it also affected his vision sometimes. "Were you the one he left home with?"

Cifius nodded. "Taught him everything he knew. Was sad when I heard what happened, but never knew what." He glanced at Kasai's scar and grinned. "I'm not surprised one of his kids ended up pyrate themselves."

Kasai shook his head, trying not to grin. "Not what our mother wanted, but that's how it turned out."

"So what are ya doin' here, then?" Cifius asked, finishing his drink.

"Thukuli wanted to sell some goods we got from various ships. It's been building up in the cargo space for a while, and I suggested here." Kasai shrugged. There was a slow ache creeping along his head.

Cifius nodded. "Glad ya did. We could use the business. I won't speak for the rest of Ironwood's crew, but yar welcome to stay here during yar shore leave. It's on me."

Kasai managed to smile despite the building headache. "Thanks, I appreciate that. And I hate to be rude, but I might turn in and explore tomorrow."

"Headache?" Cifius asked suddenly. Kasai gave a single nod. Cifius sighed. "I thought so. Used to plague me too, and yar father got them when he was yar age. It's past noon, though ya can't tell from through the clouds right now. Go find the doctor about a mile north of here and they might give ya something."

Kasai thanked him and headed for the bar. The barman just pointed up the stairs. "First door on the right."

Limping up the stairs, Kasai felt Cifius' gaze on him, and opened the first door on the right.

A simple bed, washstand with piping, and a small bedside dresser greeted him. Kasai sank onto the bed gratefully and only when he made sure the window and door were shut tight did he let the tears finally escape.

Chapter 9

Oxe

"IGNORE THE RUNDOWN part of town for now, Oxe," Brinar called to the wolf at the bow. "A lot of pyrates hang there, and while that's what we are-" Oxe growled. "-except for you, of course, we want to find Cifius. He's an old friend of Sonus', and if anyone here can find Kasai's whereabouts, he can. But there's no guarantee he's here."

Oxe put his paws on the railing briefly, watching the ship drift slowly against the dock. The smells coming from town were muted because of the cold. Hot metal, faint scents of fish, and people who didn't bathe regularly touched his nose. He didn't want to imagine how much worse it was in summer.

He backed away and stood by Brinar as the crew finished mooring. A month since they had met with Doux, it had taken longer than usual to get here. A strong wind had switched a few days prior and pushed them back, but North was skilled enough to crab, or go in a zigzag sideways pattern, to let them reach here without forcing their way into the headwinds.

"You could have put on a coat, you know," North told him. He was watching the men come down and handing out coats to anyone who needed one.

Oxe shrugged. He knew being a wolf now wasn't exactly the safest right now, but so few people could recognize what he was, and fewer would know where he came from, that it was better than wearing something that felt uncomfortable for him.

And probably a better disguise, too. Hopefully.

Brinar nudged him. "There's Cifius. He must've been out in town. He rarely greets the incoming ships."

"I actually called him yesterday. He knew to expect us," North said unexpectantly. "I didn't explain why we were coming in, just that you needed to talk to him."

Brinar frowned briefly, then shrugged. "Saves me the trouble of looking for him, at least." When Oxe gave him a curious look, he explained, "Brimna Atoll is huge, and he could've been anywhere. He's sort of like a leader here and takes care of any disputes."

Oxe gave a low huff, letting Brinar know he understood. He waited until Brinar was down the gangplank before following, feeling strange on land for once.

"Brinar, it's good to see ya," the large man greeted Brinar enthusiastically. Oxe tilted his head in confusion. This man looked much older than Brinar, but he had never seen someone so large and powerful looking before. Even in the tribe, once someone reached even close to this age, they never looked so strong.

"Cifius, I'm glad I didn't have to hunt you down." Brinar smiled.

A jolt shot through Oxe as he smelled the man. He inhaled deeply and whined, nudging Brinar excitedly.

"What?" Brinar glanced at him. "I'll ask." He turned to Cifius. "Sorry, but we're here on business for once. We're looking for a young man-"

Oxe yelped, then jerked his head at Cifius. He could smell something familiar. He wagged his tail a few times.

"He's not having some kind of fit, is he?" The large man didn't seem concerned though.

"No, but I might guess what he wants right now." Brinar shrugged. "Have you heard of someone named Kasai? He's tall, has black hair, walks with a cane."

Cifius grinned widely. "Friends of his? Ya, he's stayin' down at the Drowned Bird."

Brinar smiled, and Oxe nearly danced on his toes. He wanted to head off, but he wasn't sure if he would know the place on his own. Brinar glanced at Oxe again. "Can you point us there? We've been looking for him for a while."

Cifius suddenly looked at them sharply. "Why? Doesn't have to do with Sonus' death, does it?"

Brinar glanced at Oxe, who whined and flattened his ears. "We should probably talk in private. It's...hard to explain."

Oxe tucked his tail between his legs, lowering himself a bit.

"I know he killed Sonus," Cifius told them.

Brinar and Oxe exchanged looks. Oxe had never dreamed that Kasai would remember that, or want to, let alone admit it out loud.

"He admitted that what Fayde told me was right and got upset. I saw Kasai yesterday at the doctors. He had a lot of injuries." Cifius glared at Brinar. "But I would like to hear the story from ya, if ya can tell me."

Oxe whined loudly and nudged Cifius. He didn't want to shift, and he couldn't out here on the street, but he needed to find Kasai.

"Down the street. Look for the sign with the bird lying on its back," Cifius told him, and Oxe darted off at once. He didn't question how an animal could understand him, or act so human. Oxe was grateful for that.

"Bring Kasai to the ship if you can," Brinar called after him.

Oxe raced along the cold road, the dirt and gravel biting into his paws. Quickly, he spotted a sign of a bird lying on its back and dripping, and skidded to a stop outside. He sniffed around and nearly howled when he found Kasai's scent. He had been coming here often lately.

He sniffed around more, ignoring the curious looks he could feel coming from the few people out, and moved as quickly as he dared after the trail. Kasai's scent, a warm, subtle, almost clove-like and spicy smell, was strong. He had been here recently and moved quicker than Oxe would have expected.

The indentations on the ground, what few there were, told him that Kasai was leaning heavily on his cane. He walked straight at least, so Oxe didn't think he had any fresh injuries. Or at least none that affected his walking.

He followed the trail deeper into town, but lost it when the road turned to stone. He growled and looked around, but didn't see Kasai anywhere.

What he saw, however, was a familiar face, and a scent mingled with Kasai's touched his nose. They were pointed right at him, their head tilted. He ducked into an alley and shifted, then quickly approached her.

She looked up and stared. "You're Oxe, aren't you?"

"SO THAT IS WHY HE CAN'T leave with me," Oxe growled, his fur bushing.

Sibra stared, then looked away. "I didn't know you were mates, but maybe you can join with us so you don't have to be separated anymore." Her voice was hopeful, but ther was a touch of fear.

Oxe glanced at her and sighed. "No. I do not wish to be a pyrate. I want to return home and bring Kasai with me."

But there were no words to show how much this bothered him. Sibra didn't know exactly what Kasai had to pay back, but she knew that in the year before she joined, he had been recovering from the wounds received, and badly healed, from his fight before.

What bothered Oxe most though was the fact that Kasai had killed so many though. It was tempered by the fact that Kasai was reluctant, but he couldn't ignore it completely. Sibra had told him about the Seaborne ship, so Oxe couldn't blame Kasai for that. Ironwood had threatened to kill him, and Kasai couldn't have attacked him alone.

Not that Kasai would have attacked him at all, at least that's what Oxe hoped.

"I wish I could tell you more about what happened, but I don't know." Sibra looked upset at this, and Oxe gave her a sympathetic look. "You could ask Feluna, but I'm not sure where she is."

"Is she the doctor?" Oxe asked.

Sibra nodded. "She was the one who took care of Kasai when he was hurt. She knows about his injuries better than anyone."

Probably not everyone; Brinar would know more. At least how he got them, if nothing else. Oxe had the feeling that Kasai had told no one about how he got hurt, based off what Sibra had told him. He shifted a bit, his fur itching in the cold. He would prefer to be a wolf right now, but at least his fur kept him warm while he talked to her.

"Why not leave with us?" he asked her. "We could take you somewhere safe and take Kasai away with us as well."

She gave him a sad look, clearly wishing she could. "Thukuli would hunt us down. Especially Kasai. I guess before he joined, Thukuli couldn't attack ships often."

"Can he not fight?" Oxe was confused by this.

She shook her head. "Not very well. He can use a sword, and can shoot pretty well, but he's much better on land."

Oxe nodded, filing this away for later. If he ever had to fight Ironwood, he would make sure they fought on water.

"But he's crafty." She grimaced. "He uses trickery, and fights a lot smarter than almost anyone. Kasai could beat him in a fair fight, but he won't hurt him."

This surprised Oxe. "Why not?"

Sibra shrugged. Far off, they heard a roar but ignored it. "Not sure. He's scared of Thukuli, I think. But you'd have to ask him why. He won't tell me."

Oxe pricked his ears. Something was running around nearby, something large. "Do you know where he is?" The ground was shuddering beneath his paws.

Sibra hesitated. "Maybe-"

With a deafening roar and the crack of shattering wood, a nearby house exploded as an enormous beast came crashing through.

Oxe barely had time to glimpse a narrow jaw, two sets of black eyes, and a scaled hide before the beast burst into the street in a cloud of dust.

"Run Oxe, that's a tucowary!" Sibra yelled out.

Oxe didn't recognize the name, but that meant little. He shifted and ran between the beast and Sibra. It was snarling, shaking its head, and pawed at something around its neck.

As the dust cleared, Oxe got a better look at the creature. The head was similar to his, but more massive. The jaw itself was not much larger than Oxe's, but the teeth were longer. Four black eyes focused on him, and surprisingly small triangular ears flicked forward in aggression. A chain around its neck was clear, a broken link hanging from its neck caught his eye; it had pulled itself free, snapping the iron.

Oxe's mouth went dry. *What kind of strength does that thing have to break iron?*

It flexed its front paws, showing off claws almost the length of Oxe's leg, and snarled at him. Fresh scars were dotted along its hide, and missing scales from several places showed a dull grey skin underneath.

Oxe snarled, but he knew he stood no chance at something three times his size. Several people were chasing the beast, but they hadn't caught up yet.

The tucowary paused, sniffing, and two of its eyes focused on Sibra.

"Oxe!" Sibra screamed as the tucowary lunged forward. Its jaws closed around her neck before Oxe could react. There was a strangled gasp and a *snap!*

He was shocked at its speed, but he howled a challenge and leaped at its muzzle. The small end would be sensitive; most animals' noses were. He bit and clawed as much as he could, trying to sink his teeth into any spot he could reach.

The tucowary howled with pain. It released Sibra and swiped at Oxe. It sent him flying into a wall and he slammed into bricks with a *crunch*.

Oxe whimpered, but got up quickly. Another bruise, maybe a cracked rib, but he couldn't just back down. People were yelling and trying to shoot feathered darts at the tucowary, but the darts just bounced off its scales. More people were clambering over the house, some with chains.

Sibra was laying still, but no one was helping her. Oxe raced over to her, feeling his ankle give, but he didn't stop until he reached her side. He held his back leg up, keeping weight off it as much as he could.

Behind him, the tucowary growled a challenge; there was a scream as someone was sent flying. It had turned away from him at least, though he felt bad for the others.

He sniffed her over and whined. No breath could be felt, and her scent had become sour already. With a glance at the people nearby, who had finally gotten a dart stuck in a scaleless spot, he shuffled his paws nervously.

He had to move her. Even if there was nothing to do, he couldn't just leave her here.

The tucowary roared; Oxe wondered if the single dart would even have an effect. It swiped at the surrounding people, its gaze darting around wildly. The people stood in a loose ring around it, chains at the ready. None of them were watching Oxe.

Carefully, he clamped his jaws around her throat. It was the only way he could grab her without shifting and began dragging her away. If he could just get somewhere where he could shift back human and carry her elsewhere, it would be far easier.

He tugged gently, trying not to tear her skin. It was difficult with his injuries, but he got to the entrance of an alley and was forced to stop. With his jaws around her, it was difficult to breathe, and there were shooting pains in his paw.

There was a shout from behind him and the ground shuddered as the tucowary thundered off. Most of the people followed it.

He whined and lowered Sibra gently to the ground. The few people left on the streets were staring at him. In the tucowary's absence, there was now silence and nothing to keep their attention away from him.

"What is that?"

"Did it kill that girl?"

"Catch it!"

Oxe flattened his ears. Didn't any of them see the tucowary had her in its jaws?

"Kasai, thank goodness you're here! We really need your help." A woman's voice caught his attention, but then he smelled Kasai before he saw him.

He whined, his belly to the ground and tail between his legs as Kasai limped up to him. His ears flagged, torn between shoving forward and flattening against his skull.

"Everyone, leave." Kasai's voice rang out, with an unfamiliar authority Oxe didn't recognize. "Go after the tucowary before it kills someone."

Oxe lowered his ears, flashing the whites of his eyes. Did Kasai really think *he* had killed Sibra? But then he glanced at Sibra and saw the fang marks were no different from his own. Despite being larger than him, the jaws and teeth were similar to Oxe's, and the marks did not stand out against his own easily.

A feeling of unease washed over him when he realized unless Kasai was willing to listen or had become an animal expert, he would believe Oxe had done this.

But had Kasai changed enough to really believe Oxe had done this? Oxe whined and looked at him, flattening his ears to his head and tucking his tail completely.

Chapter 10

Kasai

WOULD OXE REALLY HAVE killed her? Kasai didn't think so.

Thukuli appeared behind Kasai. "Another one? Are they some new species?"

Kasai wanted to glance at him, but kept his gaze on Oxe. "No." He tried not to stare at Sibra. His leg trembled from the recent run and the fights of the past few days. He stood as straight as he could, but somehow...the sight of her made him sick.

He recognized the marks on her neck, and they matched Oxe's teeth too well. A tad deeper, but that meant little.

Kasai looked around at the people beginning to crowd around them. "Did anyone see this creature attack her? Or maybe the tucowary grabbed her?"

Several people exchanged looks, but no one spoke.

Kasai flared some heat, frowning. "Is there any proof that this creature attacked her?" He met a few pairs of eyes, but no one met his gaze for more than a second. They weren't used to him yet.

Five days ago, Cifius had announced to the people that Kasai would learn some skills in leadership and would oversee the animal pens while he was in port. But none of them really knew him. A few had shared drinks with him at the inn, but he was unknown to most people here still. Those familiar with him knew him mainly from the fighting ring where he trained with his staff in the evenings.

A man stepped forward, frowning. "The tucowary didn't get close enough to attack her." His gaze dropped, his voice shaking.

A woman next to him nodded quickly. "I saw the creature dragging her away. It was next to her when we chased the tucowary here." Her voice was steady but high-pitched.

"It started dragging her off while we dealt with the tucowary, sir," a younger woman added, scuffing her feet as she spoke.

Kasai frowned and looked back at Oxe. He couldn't believe that Oxe would do this, but there was no proof otherwise.

"You might have to make an example out of it, Kasai." Thukuli murmured.

Kasai shot him a glare, but looked back at the others. "No one saw anything that says this creature didn't attack her?"

Oxe flinched.

No one said anything, and Kasai sighed. "What should I do then?" he asked Thukuli quietly. There were too many unknowns here, too many people that weren't being entirely honest, and he didn't have the experience yet to just make an order. Not confidentially, at least.

Thukuli regarded Oxe carefully, then shrugged. "It killed her. You need to kill it."

Kasai closed his eyes. He couldn't do that. He wished he and Oxe were alone. Then he would ask Oxe himself, but he couldn't do that with everyone crowding them. If he let on that he knew what Oxe was, or that he *knew* Oxe, it would create many more problems than what he could deal with right now.

A thought occurred suddenly; if Oxe were here, was Brinar? North? Or did Oxe get a ride here from some other pirate? He glanced around, but saw no one familiar.

"Kasai, if you don't take care of it now, it'll get away!" someone called out.

Oxe hadn't moved; his gaze locked with Kasai's.

Kasai groaned inwardly. He didn't have a choice. "Fine." With a quick burst of heat, he pulled flames into his hand and formed his staff.

Oxe's eyes grew wide. A low growl, more of a throaty whimper, escaped. Not challenging, but afraid.

"I'm sorry." Kasai's whisper was nearly silent, but he hoped Oxe heard. He swung the staff. It connected with Oxe's ribs.

There was a terrible howl.

Kasai struck again, but he felt each blow, both physically but also in his heart. His arm shook, and he forced himself not to look away. If he did, someone else would kill Oxe. Or worse, Thukuli would. He could already feel the weight of Thukuli's gaze on him and he couldn't risk the captain getting involved.

People behind him cheered.

Oxe shuffled back on three legs, and Kasai stopped. Blood coursed through his fur in thin rivulets, dripping onto the ground.

Thukuli placed a hand on Kasai's shoulder. "Finish it." His voice was nearly a growl, and Kasai almost turned on him.

Oxe snarled, startling him, and Kasai was shocked to see him shift back to human. "I did not do this." His arm was held against a large bruise along his ribs. His voice was pained, hurt dulling his gaze.

Everyone went quiet.

"Do you really think I could?" Oxe's voice broke. He coughed and blood dribbled from the corner of his mouth.

"It's a shifter..."

"But what was that animal?"

"We can't have a killer among us!"

"Kasai, he needs to be held accountable." Thukuli's voice was iron. His grip on Kasai's shoulder painful.

Kasai couldn't take his eyes off Oxe. "How can I believe you?" How could he believe Oxe would do it? It made no sense, but one man's word alone meant nothing here. He wished Cifius was here.

He wanted to tell Oxe he didn't believe the others. He wanted Oxe to tell him what had happened. And ask why he risked shifting in front of others.

Thukuli struck out, a giant thorn shooting out of the hard ground like a bullet. It stopped only a few inches from Oxe's chest. "Kasai, we have rules here." The threat loomed over them.

Kasai met Oxe's eyes. He didn't want to do this.

"Kasai!" Thukuli cuffed him.

Kasai recoiled and struck out. He flinched from Oxe's scream and turned. "Just leave him." He knew what he had just done.

Oxe would be scarred from it.

He fell with a heavy thud, and Kasai forced himself to not turn back. He couldn't, not now. Yet, a profound ache settled in his chest.

"But..." someone stepped forward. "What about the body?"

Kasai resisted the shudder that threatened to wrack his frame. "Have someone get it later. Let him die in agony." The real agony was going through his mind, and probably Oxe's, and Kasai limped away.

Thukuli walked with him. "That was hard for you, wasn't it?" His voice sounded sympathetic, but Kasai knew it wasn't real.

He grunted, his ears ringing.

Thukuli waited a few moments; a short and lean man raced past them, heading for the crowd. "That was the man from Sedgeliss."

"So?" Kasai asked. He had glimpsed brown hair and glasses, but the man moved too fast for him to identify. He had seemed familiar, but Kasai pushed it out of his mind.

"You knew him. That was a friend of yours, from before us." Thukuli looked at him. "But you really are one of us now. I wasn't sure you could do that, but you did."

And it made Kasai sick. But he knew something Thukuli didn't. He knew the power behind his flames, and he had not killed Oxe.

At least, he hoped not.

But guilt racked him. And he couldn't race back, apologize and help him. If he did, Thukuli would think him weak and probably kill them both. Or worse.

"We should leave port. I still have to pay you back, then I'm done." Kasai couldn't hold the words back any longer.

Thukuli's face turned dark, then he gave Kasai a wide grin. "We were leaving tomorrow morning, anyway. That's why I was out here, gathering everyone up. Only temporarily though. We'll be back in a few months."

"And I'm guessing you need me to return to the ship now," Kasai growled.

Thukuli nodded. "Yes. But after that display, hurting your dear friend that way, I think I'll let you off the hook for the hesitation with that Seaborne ship."

It wasn't worth it, but Kasai wouldn't say that out loud.

"We'll burn Sibra tonight. She deserves that," Thukuli said, surprising him. When Thukuli made a statement like that, it meant he would ask for something else later.

Kasai closed his eyes. He didn't want to think about her right now. Not with Thukuli next to him.

"But return to the ship. I'll round up the others. We leave on the morning tide." Thukuli told him as they stopped on the street just before the docks.

Kasai nodded and limped up the gangplank. Feluna took in his face and nearly walked over to him. However, when he glared at her, she immediately stepped back.

He limped down the stairs and disappeared into the darkness, not bothering to light the el-turn for once.

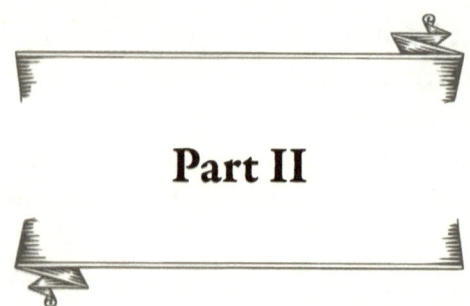

Part II

Glow

Chapter 11

Oxe

"YOU GOT LUCKY." BRINAR was leaning against the wall, his face drawn.

Oxe shrugged, not trusting his voice yet.

"Or Kasai knew what he was doing," Cifius responded. "Give the kid some credit; he knew he had to do something, but he was smart enough to make it look like he killed Oxe."

Brinar sighed, shrugging. "It's hard for us to tell what he was thinking though. I wasn't there and Oxe was trying not to go against his homeland's customs."

Oxe's gaze flicked to Cifius, who eyed him warily for a moment.

The older man turned to Brinar. "What will you do now though? Ironwood said they're coming back in a few months, so we might have about three or four months."

Brinar stayed silent. He turned a page, but Oxe could tell he wasn't paying attention to it.

North had left. The main reason was that the crew didn't want to stay for an extended time, but he also wanted to find Kasai himself first. It was a slim chance, but he thought if he could get to Kasai first, then maybe Brinar and Oxe wouldn't have to worry about getting him away from Ironwood themselves.

That maybe it would be safer for everyone.

"I need to talk to Kasai, away from Ironwood," Oxe croaked. His throat spasmed, the blisters in his mouth smarting from the movement.

Cifius gave him a long look, then shrugged. "I can try to get him alone when they come back, but that's going to be hard. Do ya know about his deal with Ironwood?"

Brinar and Oxe shook their heads. Oxe knew a little, but nothing specific.

"After Kasai escaped from the Seaborne, with no memory of you helping him, he told me that Ironwood's doctor treated him. Under Ironwood's order." Cifius explained.

Brinar exchanged a glance with Oxe, then looked at Cifius. "I want to talk to Ironwood's doctor when they return."

Cifius shook his head. "Won't be possible. She only leaves the ships to get supplies, and that's rare. It's usually brought to her by someone else."

There was silence for a few moments, then Brinar looked out the window. "Does Ironwood ever take on new crewmates?"

Cifius suddenly glared at him. "Don't. Getting onto his crew is a good way of putting a target on yer back."

"But would he?" Brinar shot back.

Oxe waited, his eyes on Cifius. He understood Brinar's intentions, but remained apprehensive. Kasai would recognize him and Brinar easily. But if it was the only way to get close to him, Oxe would risk it.

Cifius squeezed his eyes shut and didn't speak for several minutes. When he opened them, he looked at Oxe as he spoke. "It's a tremendous risk, but if ya can disguise yourself, it might work. And ya would need someone to vouch for ya, or show yer worth immediately."

Oxe nodded. "What kind of disguise would I need? Kasai would recognize us both." A blister burst, making him flinch, but his gaze stayed steady.

Brinar eyed him nervously. "With a change of clothes and some hair dye, he might not recognize me. But for you? Oxe..."

The silence stretched out, Cifius and Oxe watching him.

Brinar coughed. "He knows you too well and won't let you on the ship. You need to change yourself completely."

Cifius narrowed his eyes. "How could he do that?"

Brinar's hands fidgeted a bit against the wall. "I can... There's a procedure I can perform. But it's...well, it's risky."

Oxe had never seen Brinar so nervous before. He even smelled nervous, and almost a little afraid.

"Would it kill me?" Oxe rasped.

Brinar didn't meet his eyes. "No. If I do it myself, I know you won't be at risk of dying. And the materials I would use...they would be absorbed into your body over time. It's not permanent; you would only have about six months before it would need to be redone."

Oxe thought about that. Six months could be a long time, or short, depending on how things went. He would need to get close to Kasai, and quickly, and get him away from Ironwood. Or at least learn about his debt, escape, make his way back here, and go from there.

"Are ya sure he's worth the risk?" Cifius' question broke into his thoughts. When Oxe glared, his fangs bared, Cifius didn't back down. "I just mean, would there be a safer way ya can think of being disguised?"

Brinar shook his head. "No. Kasai is Oxe's mate," Cifius' eyes grew wide; he hadn't known this apparently, "And Oxe needs to look as different as we can make him for him to have even the smallest chance of this working."

Cifius stared at Oxe for a minute, his brow furrowed. He turned towards the door. "I'll leave that up to you two. But Brinar, if there's anything you need, just let me know. We have almost as many supplies of just about everything that Cernu does."

Brinar nodded. "I appreciate it, Cifius."

"Why are you helping us?" Oxe asked before Cifius could leave.

Cifius paused in the doorway, then spoke without turning around. "Kasai is in a position that even most of the pirates living here don't agree with. If I can do anything to help him be free of that bastard, I'll help however I can. And I'll do anything to help my grandkid."

He left without another word, and Oxe exchanged a shocked look with Brinar.

OXE TOOK THE NEXT WEEK to let his throat heal, then approached Brinar in earnest about the...procedure.

Brinar was not happy about it. He tried to talk Oxe out of it at first, but finally relented when Oxe all but threatened to bite him. Oxe felt bad about it, but he was willing to even fight Ironwood himself if it meant getting Kasai away from him.

And he knew he wouldn't win if he did that.

Two weeks after his "death", Brinar approached him with a young woman. "Oxe, this is your last chance. Are you sure you want to do this?"

Oxe nodded. "Yes."

Looking uneasy, the woman asked, "Brinar, have you done this before?"

Oxe waited, the silence charged.

Brinar took a deep breath before speaking. "No, but it was done on me years ago."

Oxe and the woman stared at him; the former with a glare, the latter with barely disguised fear.

Brinar's voice sounded professional, something Oxe hadn't heard often. "Oxe, we're going to move you to a more...private area for this. You'll be knocked out for the operation, but when you wake up, it's going to be painful."

Oxe nodded, expecting this. "What will this do to me exactly?" he asked.

"The...plastic will be implanted along areas of your face, and along your collarbone and shoulder areas, and give a different shape to your general appearance." Brinar paused, his eyes staring at the wall without seeing it.

Oxe tried to imagine this but couldn't.

"You also wanted me to change your hair color, which is easy usually, but at the root, which is not. It might burn for a while, but over time it will grow back to its original color. Because of the nature of what you're going to be doing," at this, Oxe wondered if the woman knew, but continued listening, "you have only six months, maybe a little more. After that, you'll look like yourself again."

"How different will I look?" Oxe asked.

Brinar paused, eying Oxe critically. "You'll have lower cheekbones, a broader neck, and the hollow at your throat won't be so defined. Your jawline might be sharper, but I can't use much of the plastics in that area without causing permanent damage. Your hair will be lighter; more like mine." He gave a sardonic grin. "You'll essentially look like a teenager again, going through puberty. Just without the hormones and...unpredictability."

"What will happen if this goes wrong?" The woman asked this, and Oxe felt a twinge of nervousness. He hadn't allowed himself to think of that.

Brinar shrugged. "I'm not sure, honestly. If it goes wrong, you'll more than likely have an allergic reaction." He said this casually, but something about his face made Oxe think that something worse could happen. Maybe it would kill him.

But to get Kasai back, the risk was worth it.

He didn't look away from Brinar. "Do what you need to."

Brinar nodded and held up a sack of woven fibers. "Forgive us Oxe, but you'll have to wear this to where we're going."

HIS FACE STUNG WITH more force than anything he could've imagined. It had been a week since the procedure, and he still couldn't move without some pain.

Brinar looked up from the paper he was reading. "I think you're clear for allergies by now."

Oxe gave a noncommittal grunt.

Brinar gave him a sympathetic face, turning towards the door as it opened. Cifius walked in, bundled in a thick coat. A dusting of flakes following him and melted on the floor.

"Warning, there's a blizzard out there. I almost got lost on my way here." He shook snow off his shoulders. "I hate these late season snows."

Brinar shook his head, smiling. "Glad we've been staying inside then."

Cifius grunted, then looked at Oxe. "Healing alright?"

Oxe shrugged.

"He should be fine in a week or two. The healing is going much better than expected. Maybe because he's a shifter." They had revealed to Cifius early on about Oxe's abilities, though not where he came from, and Cifius had admitted to knowing already thanks to Kasai. "As long as he doesn't shift his bones, he'll be okay."

"And if he does?" Cifius asked.

Brinar gave Oxe a hard look. "It'll reverse itself, probably cause lots of damage, and who knows how the plastics will react to being moved around like that." Oxe nodded in understanding. "I'm serious. If you shift, only shift anything elbow or waist down."

Cifius looked at Brinar. "Ya said before he can't change into anything but a wolf. Is there a specific reason?"

"My people would disown me." Oxe's voice came out higher pitched than usual, an extra effect from the operation that had been unexpected, but helped with the disguise. He swallowed heavily, his throat hurting a tad. "But I can grow claws or paws if I need to. There are lots of animals that have those features; they won't stand out."

Brinar nodded in agreement. "I wouldn't grow fur though, unless you can do a different color. While it's not enough to show who you really are, Kasai knows you too well and might ask questions. At the very least, he'll get suspicious."

Oxe nodded, turning away to blink back tears. He didn't want to hide from Kasai; he didn't even think he could, at least for long. But it couldn't be helped.

"I came by to pass along a message. From North." Cifius pulled out a piece of paper. "There was a girl ya met in Surval, a shifter? She's with his crew now. He says if they meet with ya again, he wants Oxe, er, I mean Tamotsu, to give her some help."

Oxe still felt weird going by a different name, but that also couldn't be helped. He couldn't go by any name from his tribe, so Brinar suggested it. Kasai hadn't learned his language yet, but he might recognize the sounds of it.

"Is she in control of herself yet?" Brinar asked.

Cifius shrugged. "He didn't say. The only other part of the message was that he's heading north of Surval, trying to look for Kasai. For now, Tamotsu, stay here and rest-" there was a snort at that, "-and when ya can, start exploring the town. Brinar, ya won't stand out, so ya'll be fine. But when Kasai makes port, ya'll need to hide or disguise yourself."

The other two nodded as Cifius turned and left. They didn't question why he went out into the blizzard, but they also weren't that worried.

Brinar waited a few moments before speaking. "It'll be alright, Oxe. If North finds him before the Seaborne, we know he'll be okay."

Oxe just gave him a sad and worried look but didn't respond.

Chapter 12

Kasai

"YOU'VE BEEN QUIET." Kasai didn't look up when Thukuli appeared. "Wishing you had stayed in port?" The captain smirked, his eyes on Kasai.

Kasai didn't respond, knowing that Thukuli was baiting him. His cane leaned next to him. His hair was braided for the first time since leaving port, but stray strands kept getting in his face.

"But hey, maybe we'll get a big score out here and your debt will be repaid." Thukuli was dangling the bait in front of Kasai's face now.

Kasai raised an eyebrow, but still said nothing.

"Hey, come on, stop moping. I know Sibra's gone, but now she's not bugging you." Thukuli just grinned at the wave of heat that blistered the air. Someone in the rigging fell behind him, and the heat dissipated.

Kasai didn't look at the man who fell, or the two people that came and dragged him off, or at their looks of worry. He merely flicked to the next page in his book.

Thukuli frowned and ripped the book out of Kasai's hands suddenly. "Seriously. I know she's gone, but *move on*. It happens." He didn't have his sword currently, and his belt pouch was gone for once.

Kasai felt every nerve in his body screaming at him to hurt Thukuli, to scream at him, to *fight back!* He pushed the feelings away, merely grabbing the book back. He shoved it in his bag, away from where Thukuli would grab it.

Thukuli gave a sarcastic grin as Kasai pushed past him without a word. "I see you're still not speaking. Perhaps you'll feel better after the next raid." He didn't follow, only stood still.

Kasai stopped, turning the side of his head towards Thukuli. The end of his cane thudded onto the deck; Kasai barely noticed the sparks.

An electric tension crackled in the air, despite the ship's silence.

"We're going hunting for more prizes for the next few months, then returning to Brimna Atoll. After that, I'll tally up your shares and we'll talk about your debt." Thukuli's grin widened when Kasai turned to look at him. "I'm serious. With your help, we've gotten more prizes than ever before, and that means a lot to me."

Behind him, Bek didn't seem to disagree, but he glared at Kasai where Thukuli couldn't see. He leaned against the railing with a few others, watching the exchange with barely disguised animosity.

Thukuli's grin faded, replaced by a thinly veiled concerned look that set Kasai's nerves singing. "If we can bag enough ships, and get enough prizes, I'll consider your debt repaid and you can leave."

Kasai raised an eyebrow, but just turned and headed for the stairs leading below deck. The ship rolled slightly and a stiff breeze blew across the deck for a moment.

No one stopped him, though there was an almost visible tension in the air that felt even thicker below deck. He let his palm glow, a new technique he was working on, lighting his way to his bunk. Despite carrying it, he hadn't been using his cane to help walk. But not by his own choice. Feluna requested he try walking without it in clear weather. He didn't want to argue with her, but still carried it when above deck.

He closed the door to his bunk, a fresh addition to the ship that Thukuli had strangely allowed, and let out a strangled sound and cracked his fist against the wall. There was a flash of pain, but he ignored it.

He sank to the floor sobbing. He didn't believe Thukuli would ever let him leave. His words about considering the debt repaid meant nothing. He would find another reason to keep Kasai aboard, even if he had to make one up.

Footsteps sounded outside and Kasai quickly rose, wiping his face and swallowing the remaining sobs as Feluna came through the door. The ship creaked, and the door swung slightly before she closed it.

She raised her eye at the scorch mark from his punch, and his bloody hand, but sat down on the bench next to the door. "I heard about what happened up there."

Kasai just glanced at her, sitting on his cot.

"I think you should leave the next time we make port," she told him bluntly.

He shot her a glare.

"Debt repaid or not, leave." Her voice stayed hard, but her eyes took on an unexpected softness. "*I* consider your debt repaid, since I'm the one who treated you."

Kasai shook his head. He rolled his right shoulder, flinching as an opening appeared.

Feluna moved to help, but his glare sent her back. She watched as he quietly adjusted something under his sleeve. "That's one reason you need to leave. You need that seen by someone else."

He snorted in response, flinching at the movement his arm made as he adjusted it. The ship rolled sharply; the waves slapping loudly against the hull.

Feluna gazed at his arm thoughtfully. "I know of one doctor, sometimes roams with pyrates, who could help. He's considered a medical miracle. Brinar-"

She didn't flinch at the staff that appeared next to her head with a deep *thud*. As soon as it made contact, a crack in the wood appeared and started smoking. Kasai glared at her, the air crackling.

"You know him." It wasn't a question. "I won't ask how, but I think you need to find him." She gazed at him coolly, not moving.

"No," Kasai croaked, his voice strange after two weeks of being unused.

Feluna's glare pierced him, sharp as a dagger. "Why not?"

Kasai turned away. "Can't." The staff disappeared in a flash.

"Why. Not." She growled.

Kasai shook his head, but couldn't hold it back anymore. He sank against the engine, tears streaming down his face. "He won't help me."

Feluna sank to her knees next to him. She held her hand up for a moment, but seemed to think better of it. "Does he hate you?" Her hand twitched against her thigh.

Kasai's body shuddered, gasps ripping through his chest. "I think so."

Her eyebrow raised. "Why do you think so?"

"I nearly killed him. All because I was angry." The words gasped out unevenly; his left arm clutched around his chest.

"Why were you angry?" She asked.

He paused before answering. "Secrets. He kept secrets from me. Lied."

She nodded to herself, then picked him up. Setting him on his cot, she sat on the floor next to him. "I met him many years ago, when I was a little kid in Cernu. I lost my parents to the sickness that plagued the city, but he saved me. I remember him. Kind, caring, he worked tirelessly for days to heal the sick. I truly doubt he could hate anyone."

Kasai buried his face in his hands. "He didn't save me."

Feluna stayed quiet, not moving.

"He promised he would be there, but he wasn't." Heat flared out, making Feluna flinch and the walls, even below the ship's waterline, smoked.

Feluna grabbed Kasai's shoulders and forced him to look at her. "Kasai. Listen to me. If Brinar didn't help you, it was because something literally kept him from it. I saw that man nearly collapse over a patient and other doctors had to *physically drag him away* because he hadn't slept in days."

Kasai didn't respond; flashes of memories scorched through his vision. The arena, the exploding arrow, Brinar's avoidance of him afterwards.

Feluna kept her hold on him until he focused on her, then slowly released him. "I understand why you're hurt, but you can't let that stop you from getting the care you obviously need."

Kasai nodded numbly. "But where would we even find him?" He didn't want to admit that he *didn't* want to find him. He was scared that Brinar wouldn't help him. Wouldn't want him there. He truly believed that Brinar had abandoned him, as what would have kept him from not being there after his fight against Blacksmoke?

She sat back, her eyes flicking over Kasai. "I'm not sure. When we stop at Brimna Atoll, we'll talk to Cifius about using an en-crys. If he has a face-crys, even better."

"A face-crys?" Kasai blinked, the confusion enough to bring him completely out of his memories.

Feluna nodded, looking a tad relieved. "It's a square object, with a glassy surface and a metal pad across the bottom."

Kasai turned around and dug in a bag tucked behind his cot. He pulled out the slim pad and a wire contraption, then showed it to Feluna. "Like these?"

She nodded, her face suddenly solemn. "We get back, you tell Cifius you need to contact him. Tell him it's an emergency. But until then, you need to be at least a little more honest with me about your injuries so I can help better."

Kasai nodded, but inwardly shuddered as he thought about the origin of some of them.

"ALRIGHT CREW, WE'VE got enough space for one more prize. What do you say we go south for a while and find someone else to get?" Thukuli grinned as the pyrates in front of him nearly roared in agreement, their excited faces shining in the noonday sun.

Two months at sea and it had been steady raids, usually two a week.

Only three people stood out, but they were where Thukuli couldn't see them clearly. Feluna stood by Kasai's side, her eyes shaded as she gazed out behind them, her eyes on the sea. Kasai was leaned against the railing, itching to go back inside and sleep. Velu was sitting on the railing, one eye on Kasai and the other on Thukuli.

Kasai shook his head as Thukuli started giving out orders to change direction. "Do we really have enough space for even one more prize?" He crossed his arms, his cane in his hand.

The question was rhetorical, but Velu snorted. "If he has to store things in his own bunk, I think he will."

Kasai couldn't find it in himself to argue with that, but sighed. "Well, at least it'll be warmer when we get back."

Feluna cracked a grin, chuckling lightly. "Warmer? For who?"

Kasai snorted, but stayed quiet as Thukuli leaped down to them.

"So Kasai, ready for a final ship before we head back?" His tone was light, but his eyes gleamed darkly.

"Do I have a choice?" Kasai couldn't stop the words before they came out, but continued before Thukuli responded. "Yeah, but I don't think I'll keep anything for myself from the next ship." He mentally cursed himself for speaking without thinking.

Thukuli frowned. "Really? Have enough books?" His brow lowered and he cocked his head.

Kasai ignored the mocking edge to his tone and shrugged. "It'll probably be nothing of worth to me. I have everything I would be interested in, and just keep finding copies of what I already have."

Thukuli waved the other two away. "Feluna, check your stores in case we get injuries. Velu, check with the cook for work. If he has nothing, get some sleep before the midnight watch."

They nodded and left quickly, Velu shooting a concerned look at Kasai as he passed.

Kasai inwardly sighed. The wind blew across the deck, a bite to it. He didn't move, knowing the captain would speak when ready.

"I know about Sonus." Nothing Thukuli said could've shocked Kasai more.

Kasai glared at him, the air growing cold.

Thukuli tried to hold back his grin. "That you killed him and Blacksmoke. That you sailed with him for over a year, but also that he trained you himself."

Kasai tried to control his breathing, to control the heat that threatened to break free and burn everything around him. "I didn't know Blacksmoke was dead until you mentioned it. I sailed with... Lightning," he couldn't say his name, "for a while, and he wasn't the only one who trained me. He merely helped me hone my own powers."

And taught him about running a ship. How to take care of the sails. About the finer points of fighting. How to temper his strength so as not to kill people he fought. And most importantly, what having a father could be like, even if Kasai hadn't known the truth until it was far too late.

Thukuli snorted. "But I guess you got pissed at him, even hurt him a few times. And I guess when you saw your chance to get back at him, you took your chance and brought him down."

The blood roared in Kasai's ears, nearly drowning out Thukuli's voice.

Thukuli didn't bother to hide his grin now. "Apparently you're more blood-thirsty than you let on." He leaned closer, nearly touching Kasai.

Kasai shut his eyes, struggling to hold back the heat. His hands shook, his chest hurt, and he could feel a burning rising in his throat.

Thukuli's voice grew dark despite the teasing tone. "Maybe you *wanted* to take him down."

Kasai's eyes snapped open. He nearly ran down the stairs, slamming the door shut behind him, and collapsed on the floor. A lantern had been lit and left in the hallway, the flame waving erratically as Kasai stumbled past.

He held his chest, sobbing heavily, barely breathing through his rage. Thukuli had *no right* to say that! Kasai hated taking lives. It gnawed at him deeply. He hated himself for it, even though he knew he had no choice now. He had the image of Sonus' face the moment he died burned into his brain, and he hated himself every day for it.

The heat rose, but condensed around him until his clothes were smoldering.

There was a clatter next to him, but he didn't notice the bindings to his arm had been burned through. His right arm, scorched and a little melted, lay on the floor as he sobbed.

Eventually, he got ahold of himself and slowly sat up. He blinked when he saw his arm and groaned. Dents he could fix, but melting? He picked it up and got out his repair kit.

He refused to think about Thukuli's taunts and tried to focus on his arm. It was awkward doing this one-handed, but he braced his arm between his knees as he worked.

And it forced his mind shut for a while; a small respite, but welcome.

The ship creaked, rolled, and water moved against the hull. Footsteps, rapid and faint, could be heard on deck. A bird cry echoed quietly below deck.

He didn't notice Feluna and Velu until he was done, thoroughly engrossed in his work. He didn't meet their eyes, but saw the concern on their faces when he finally stopped.

"Thukuli sent me down," Velu started, but his voice trailed off and he didn't finish.

"But I came to make sure you were alright enough for a raid," Feluna said.

They both stood there, one awkward and one angry but uneasy, until Velu coughed.

"We heard what Thukuli said." His voice was low, even. Scared.

Kasai tried to ignore that, tried not to show how guilty he felt.

"We don't believe him." Feluna's blunt words were followed by silence.

Velu shot her a look, but spoke to Kasai. "We know you aren't like that." When Kasai just stared at him, he continued, "Blood-thirsty I mean."

Feluna nodded. "I can understand why you took down Blacksmoke, regardless of how he was ended, but I know you wouldn't have killed-"

"Don't." Kasai's voice came harsher than he meant. He tried to soften it. "Don't say his name." He squeezed his eyes shut. "I didn't mean to. He wasn't..."

"You don't have to finish, alright?" Velu reached out hesitantly, then laid his hand on Kasai's shoulder. "We can tell it hurts."

Feluna nodded. "Get your arm back on, then meet us on deck. Thukuli spotted a ship and we're closing in."

Kasai nodded, but then set his arm down on his bed. "I need to get more straps for it, the others...snapped." He glanced at it for a second, then sighed and set it under his cot with the repair kit. It would have to wait for a while.

Feluna and Velu exchanged a glance, but said nothing.

"Come on, before *he* comes down here." The words were bitter, though true. They followed Kasai as he quickly led the way above deck. He blinked as they came out; the sun had lowered and was glimmering across the waves harshly.

Another pirate ship was nearby, within Kasai's range, but just out of reach for the cannons. It wasn't trying to escape though.

Strange.

"Kasai, there you are. I need you to send them our greeting." Thukuli said nothing about earlier, only jerked his head at the other ship.

Kasai nodded, but paused. "Sir," when on raids, he rarely called Thukuli by his name, "I should tell you, I was in the middle of replacing the straps on my arm when Velu got me."

Thukuli raised an eyebrow, but shrugged. "Still, I know you can shoot an arrow one-handed. You've done it before." The words were said lightly, but Kasai knew he was reminding him about the Seaborne ship.

Kasai nodded and formed an arrow easily, but had to boost the flares to get it to reach the other ship; the foresail went up in flames. He was about to fire a second one when something made him pause.

Did someone over there look familiar? He couldn't tell from here.

Thukuli glared at him. "What's wrong? Shoot!"

Kasai immediately shot it, not wanting to piss Thukuli off.

The crew cheered as the mainsail turned black, then fell with a loud *snap!* to the deck.

Unease unexpectedly gripped Kasai. There was no figurehead, but something about the ship looked familiar. He must be imagining it.

Grappling hooks were thrown, lashing the two ships together. Kasai's breath hitched; everything felt strangely slow, and he couldn't grasp the reason. The waves slapped against the sides. A bird screeched, almost deafening in the moment. His heart was pounding, but he didn't know why.

"Kasai, what the hell?!" He wasn't prepared when North suddenly leaped over the railing and slammed his fist against Kasai's jaw.

Chapter 13

Oxe

OXE GRUNTED AS HE LIFTED the beam, the strain of his muscles a pleasant distraction. For the past week, he had been helping with some minor construction, errands, labor, and general help around the docks. Two days prior, the blizzard had let up finally, but not before it took down a warehouse. The wood, old and partially rotten in a few unprotected spots, gave easily.

Luckily, no one was hurt. And the supplies within were protected inside crates and barrels.

"Tamotsu, once that beam is in place, you can go." A woman walked by, two buckets hanging from a short pole against her shoulders. "Seriously. You've been working harder than anyone here. No one's going to complain if you take a break."

Oxe gave her a sideways glance, but sighed. "Fine. But only for a short while."

She grimaced as she set the buckets down and rolled her shoulders. "Tamotsu, it's getting late. Take the rest of the night off and come back in the morning. I heard there's a fight tonight." She grinned, clearly looking forward to it.

Oxe knew she meant the small fighting arena at the edge of town. Pyrates, or others, who wanted to test their skills would sign up for a chance at the ring each weekend, sometimes even nightly.

He had heard about how Kasai had wiped the floor with their best fighters in three days, using only a glowing staff of fire. Each fight had lasted less than five minutes; even for Kasai, that was impressive.

Brinar had asked Cifius about it, but Cifius was surprisingly tight-lipped about it. Only when Brinar pressed him did he answer.

He wanted to give Kasai a chance to find something else to do, something that could keep him off the ocean permanently. One option was to be a resident fighter, which Kasai excelled at, but seemed to not really enjoy. Another approach was to eventually assume leadership of the animal pens, which proved to be somewhat successful but ultimately failed.

Oxe had signed up, but not been called yet. They didn't take well to newcomers, especially ones that didn't seem to have any fighting experience.

The woman picked up her buckets and walked off, giving Oxe a smile as she left. Oxe fitted the beam into place, then grabbed his bag. To look and seem as different as he could, he had taken to carrying around a side satchel, wore a cap, and dressed warmer than he liked.

He nodded at a few people as he walked out, reluctantly putting on a coat and gloves as he walked out into the cold. Snow crunched under his shoes, and he sighed. He missed the feeling of the ground under his paws.

His breath came out in a cloud, but the air was already feeling a tad warmer than the day before. He resisted the urge to fluff out his fur.

"Tamotsu, there you are." Gir, a local man who had more or less taken Oxe under his wing, appeared in the doorway of a shop nearby. "Come on, join us." He smiled and waved his hand at Oxe.

Oxe walked over, attracted to the warmth and at the summons. "Hey Gir. I was just heading back to the Inn." He and Brinar shared a room at the Drowned Bird, though Brinar slept at the local doctor's office more than the inn.

Gir shook his head. "You still can't find a place of your own?" Without waiting for Oxe's response, he quickly brought him inside.

Oxe gratefully shed his coat as he stepped inside. Three people sat at a large table near the back wall. Along the other walls were shelves of carvings; colves, birds, fish, every kind of animal that had been seen it seemed like.

"This is Tamotsu, the new guy I was telling you about." Gir pulled a seat out for Oxe, then sat down in the last empty chair.

Oxe sat, his hand on his bag.

The woman sitting across from him grinned. "Don't worry. We might be pyrates, but we won't take your bag. Cifius says no stealing within the town."

Oxe nodded, feeling a tad more relaxed, as she pushed an extra tankard towards him. "Orlani let me off for the night, told me there was a fight going on in the arena tonight. Are any of you going?"

The other man snorted, his seatmate grinning. "No. Not interested enough. Haven't you heard who's fighting?"

"Who?" Oxe asked.

The other person answered. "Some old dude named Eaden."

Oxe pricked his ears. Brinar was fighting? That was surprising. "Old dude? I've...met him. He didn't seem that old to me." He almost didn't catch himself in time. He didn't mind letting on that he knew Brinar a bit, but if he admitted to bunking with him, someone might ask questions.

"Yea," the person snorted. "You say you've met him, but have you actually *seen* the guy? He looks kinda young, or at least not old, but the way he talks, the way he walks, there's no way he's getting out of there without a scratch. Plus, he's a doctor. Even for a pyrate, why would a doctor want to fight?"

Why indeed? Oxe frowned and sipped his drink. He stopped himself before he made a face; spiced le, not something he could tolerate much of.

"I guess it could be good for a laugh," the woman giggled, covering her mouth. "I mean, no one enjoys watching someone who probably never fights go into the ring, but this dude sounds determined."

Oxe murmured an agreement, staying quiet. For one, they had no idea who he was. For another, Brinar could be almost lethal when pressed. Oxe still shuddered when he remembered the calm radiating from when Brinar fought Kasai. While that fight hadn't been long, or that many blows, and ended badly, Oxe had never seen anyone seem so dangerous.

The others talked and drank for a while, trying to get Oxe to join in, making crude jokes as they got drunk. The woman even flirted with him, and he left them singing some dirty song in time to leave for the arena.

BRINAR SHRUGGED, TURNING his back on Oxe. "I only did this because the guy I'm fighting is a current member of Ironwood's crew. He told me that if I win, he'll tell me anything I need to know about him."

Oxe felt his hackles rise. "And if you lose?"

"Then I get beaten up for nothing. You're already taking a risk, and Cifius said they should be back within a week or two, so I thought I would help while I could." Brinar grabbed his staff and stood behind the poorly latched gate. He was refusing to meet Oxe's gaze.

Over the top of the gate, they could see the high seats around the arena. The air smelled sour, like spilled le and sweat and blood and who knows what else. But here, it was easy for them to talk and no one would hear them over the sound unless they were in the small entrance with them.

Oxe growled, resisting the urge to shift his face like he normally would. "And you are okay with that?" His claws grew and fur prickled along his arms.

Brinar shot him a black look. "O – Tamotsu, I'm stronger than I look." Brinar's voice hitched as he caught himself. "This is too good of a chance to waste. I want to help when I can, because the sooner we get Kasai back, the sooner we can all head back to our homes."

Oxe stared at him with a mixture of incredulous and sadness. *Of course.* Brinar was missing his family. And it was warring with his concern about Kasai. Oxe understood that; he missed his home, and tribe, and hated that he was technically not even a Nuveri warrior currently.

He swallowed, his voice low with concern. "But is it worth possibly getting beaten up enough to not get back to your family?" His fur slowly receded and his claws shrank.

Brinar stopped, his hand on the door. His shoulders shook, the only evidence that what Oxe said had got to him. "I can do this, you can't." Though the words were a quiet growl, Oxe sensed a hint of fear.

With that, he pushed open the doors enough to slip through, leaving Oxe alone.

Oxe sighed and made his way to the stands, looking for a suitable spot to sit and watch. The announcer, an ancient woman with almost none of her snow-white hair left on her head, called out the fighters and welcomed them into the arena.

Despite her age, her voice was powerful and carried easily. It was helped by the silence that was followed as soon as the fighters were noticed. Oxe found a spot on the edge of one of the seat rows, with a decent, if not good, view of the arena. He cast a wary gaze towards the arena.

A roughly circular, more wavy-sided oval, area marked out by a crude wall made of driftwood planks. Oxe initially thought it had been painted red, but after a few moments, realized it was stained with blood. Two rough doors, facing each other from opposite sides of the arena, were roped closed at the top.

Brinar stood in front of one of them, while a large, muscular man stood in front of the other. Bald, or shaved, with a dirty tank and thick, baggy pants, he wielded no visible weapon.

He looked so much stronger than Brinar, visibly stronger at least, that Oxe felt a stab of concern.

"Fighters," the woman's voice broke into his observations, making him focus on the arena better, "Remember that the only rule is to not purposely kill each other. This is an all-weapons, no holds barred fight. As always, grenades are forbidden. By agreement beforehand, the fighters have made a deal so this fight will not be for personal money. Any bets made will be given to the betters, but the winners have their own prizes decided."

Unease settled over Oxe. What had Brinar promised if he lost?

The larger man shot forward, startling Oxe. He hadn't expected someone that size to move so fast.

Brinar slammed his staff down on the sand floor, kicking up a cloud of sand. The watchers saw Brinar calmly walk out of the blinding cloud and slam his staff into the other mans back with enough force to propel him against the wall.

The audience went quiet. Oxe saw quite a few people with wide eyes and suppressed a grin. He expected some fight from Brinar, but this exceeded his expectations, although he wasn't shocked.

"You bastard, that was a dirty move!" The big man turned, blood pouring down his face from his now crooked nose.

Brinar shrugged. "I thought there were no rules tonight?"

A series of chuckles sounded. Oxe held his breath.

The big mans face turned red, almost as much as the blood on his face. "Fine then."

There was a loud bang, a blinding flash, and a massive cloud of sand. Then Oxe was shocked to see Brinar lying flat on his back, gasping for breath. Oxe had been momentarily blinded and hadn't seen what had knocked Brinar back.

There was a throaty chuckle and the cloud settled, revealing the other man. His arms shone brightly, the thousands upon thousands of little facets gleaming bright enough to be blinding.

He was a genetic.

It took all of Oxe's willpower to overcome his instincts and not jump into the ring to rescue Brinar.

The older man coughed, struggling to his feet. In the silence, the words could be heard clearly. "I should've guessed you had some trick up your sleeve. The flashbang was a bit much though." He calmly dusted himself off, but barely had time to dodge as the man barreled forward.

Oxe struggled to stay still as he watched the large club come out of nowhere and swing towards Brinar. There was a collective gasp.

Brinar held up the staff, but it snapped like a twig as the club hit it.

There was a collective groan as Brinar was sent flying, rolling to a stop near the edge of the ring.

There was a tense moment while everyone waited, but he didn't get up.

"It seems that the winner is Jonzu." The woman's voice rang out. "Those who have made bets, go to the money bar to collect your winnings."

The fight had barely last five minutes. Oxe felt a tad sick as he heard the sarcastic laughs and whispers around him.

He made his way to one of the doors leading into the ring, arriving in time to see two people propping Brinar up. There was a large gash along his forehead, and his arm stuck at an odd angle. He had one hand on his head, so at least he was conscious.

"I'll help him from here," Oxe told the two girls as they stood Brinar up. "I can get him to the doctors quicker than you can." Brinar was blinking, looking disorientated.

One girl gave him a skeptical look, but the other nodded. "It's okay, I know Tamotsu. He's a lot stronger than he looks." She smiled at him with a nod as Oxe knelt next to Brinar.

The other girl nodded, frowning, as Oxe lifted the older man onto his back.

Brinar didn't react, didn't even seem to notice, as Oxe carried him out. The shorter man was heavier than he looked, but it didn't bother Oxe. The streets were mostly empty. The only people out were the ones at the arena. Some of them shot Oxe and Brinar sympathetic looks, while others tried not to laugh when they got near.

The snow crunched loudly and Oxe had a moment of concern; should he have grabbed Brinar's coat? Despite the short distance, Oxe had previously noted that the cold bothered him much less than it did others. But there was no time to go back.

Only when they arrived at the doctor's office, where Brinar and Renela worked, did Brinar finally notice anything. Oxe could feel the blood, which had soaked his coat, beginning to dry. He flicked the light on, revealing an empty office.

"Oxe? What happened?" Brinar groaned as Oxe gently set him on a cot.

Renela came running out, her hair still mussed up from being asleep. "Tamotsu? Eaden? What's going on?" She had been appraised of the need for alternative names and was at ease with them.

"He fought in the ring tonight, against someone with some kind of shiny and hard skin," Oxe explained. "He got hit with some kind of club." Sitting on a nearby cot, he kept his eyes fixed on Brinar. His shirt crackled softly from the drying blood.

"It was Jonzu, wasn't it?" Her voice was low, but unsurprised. When Oxe nodded, she cursed and looked like she wanted to smack Brinar. "You idiot! If you had told me who you were fighting, I could've prepared you for this!"

Oxe didn't realize she had known about this, though her anger was a shock. And it sounded like she knew Jonzu well, or at least about his powers.

Brinar grimaced, and Oxe visibly blanched as the doctor grabbed his own arm and shifted it back into position. The sound of bones rubbing together beneath the skin reached his ears, and he could only imagine the agony Brinar must be experiencing.

But he had to admit, he had to admire how Brinar stayed calm.

After a few tense moments, Brinar let go with a loud gasp, startling them. "Renela, get the splint. And maybe something for the pain. I need you to look at my head though."

She nodded as the door opened, then grimaced and disappeared into the back room briefly. Oxe wondered what she had seen, but ignored it. A chill wind blew in, scattering a few stray snowflakes across the floor. There was a smell of blood, too.

Oxe turned in time to see Jonzu squeezing his bulk through the door. He was large enough, and the doorway narrow enough, that it was a tight space for him. "I came here to talk about our...arrangement." His nose was bandaged, but the blood hadn't been cleaned off very well.

Oxe gave a low growl, shooting a glare at Brinar.

Brinar glared back, then looked at Jonzu. "I'm a man of my word. When Ironwood comes back, I'll take your place on his crew."

Oxe snarled, only the fear of undoing the plastics stopping his jaw from shifting. "You traded places with this man?" His hackles rose.

Jonzu grinned. "I'm guessing you're the partner Eaden mentioned. He said he needed an in with Ironwood and had a friend who wanted on the crew as well."

Oxe merely glared, not trusting his voice.

"Seriously, there's no bad blood here. Eaden here wanted information, so I...found a way to get the best possible way to get it." Jonzu's grin got wider.

Brinar glared at Jonzu as well. "You nearly killed me. I didn't know you were a genetic."

Jonzu frowned. "Sorry about that, but I had to make it convincing. If I had gone easy, it would've been much harder to convince Kelin. And if you knew how to counter me to easily, it would've made him too suspicious."

"Kelin?" Oxe turned to Brinar, confused.

Brinar nodded. "Kelin is a scout for Ironwood's crew. I knew you wouldn't go easy, but *I had no idea you were a diamond genetic!*" Clearly this bothered Brinar a lot, but Oxe couldn't blame him. Not when his arm had been broken clean through and he was bleeding badly from the head.

Oxe glanced at Renela, who had come back in and began treating Brinar's forehead, then turned to Jonzu. "Would he speak for me as well?" With the ease of decades of practice, Brinar set his arm in the splint.

Jonzu nodded. "Kelin's already agreed to vouch for you both. Eaden as a fighter, of course, but you were harder to convince for him. You're an anomaly here; not a fighter. New, unknown to most people, appeared almost out of nowhere. But he's seen you work, recognizing you from the labor workers lately. Can you fight?"

Oxe didn't answer, only turned to Brinar. "Why did you try to get onto the crew?"

"Because at least one of us needs to. This way, if he declines one of us, the other has a better chance," Brinar explained. He looked better with his wound stitched, but still a tad disorientated.

Renela gathered up the kit and left the room.

Jonzu looked between them, frowning. "Wait, are you saying that you *need* to get on his crew? Why?" His tone turned wary, cautious, and his expression bordered on angry.

Oxe froze and Brinar closed his eyes as they realized their mistake. Brinar finally looked at Jonzu. "We...know Kasai. And we need to talk to him. But we haven't found any way of getting close to him. This was all we could come up with."

Jonzu snorted, surprising him. "Fat chance of that."

"Why?" Oxe asked, shocked at his certainty.

"Kasai hates others. The only people that have ever gotten close to him were Sibra, Feluna, and Velu, but that was because Feluna's our doctor, Sibra was his responsibility, and Velu...well, he might feel responsible for Kasai because he's the one that brought him aboard." Jonzu shrugged.

Oxe leaned back. Kasai *hated* others? That didn't sound right.

"Course, Thukuli's always trying to get onto Kasai's good side, but hasn't worked so far," Jonzu mused.

"Why are you here?" Oxe asked.

Jonzu looked at him warily.

Oxe met his gaze evenly. "If you were on Ironwood's crew, why are you not here now?"

Jonzu shrugged. "Doctor's orders. I had a nasty infection and Feluna made me stay here while they went out raiding for a few months."

Brinar snorted. "So when I came to you, looking for information, you saw your chance to be rid of Ironwood for good."

Jonzu nodded a tad sheepishly. "Can you blame me though? Few people join his crew willingly."

Oxe was a little astonished at his openness, but wasn't surprised when Jonzu opened the door to leave. He leaned back, his head spinning as he tried to think about what could happen.

"When they get back, which should be soon if Thukuli only meant about three months, I'll vouch for you both. But just to warn you, if you go after Thukuli himself, there won't be anything left for either of you two to worry about." Jonzu laughed as he made his way out.

Brinar sighed. "Well, this just got...interesting."

Chapter 14

Kasai

KASAI DIDN'T EVEN TRY to defend himself. For one, he was caught completely unaware. For another, this was *North!* He had sailed with him for long enough, known him well enough, that he could've never imagined North would hit him. Especially like that.

He fell to the deck, his face stinging. It also felt like a tooth had been knocked loose.

North was only stopped from punching him again by Thukuli slamming his sword down between them. "Back off, Fatal, you came over here alone."

Not alone. Arat, his look a mixture of horror and sadness, stood behind North. A few other pyrates were at the railing, some leaping over to protect their captain, some on the other ship, ready to protect it.

Kasai struggled to his feet; he was shaking but couldn't react.

North snarled at him, "You took down our sails and killed one of our crew!"

Kasai blinked, the words settling slowly into his ears. The sails he knew about, but someone was killed? The blood drained from his face but quickly shook himself, not wanting to show how much this bothered him.

Arat set a hand on North's shoulder, but spoke to Kasai, "We need to talk to you." His voice was steady, his gaze dark with worry.

Thukuli snorted, causing almost everyone to look at him. "No. We are here for a raid, and you were the ship we picked."

If those words were a signal, no one listened.

His calm expression was more unsettling than his anger. "Crew, I think we'll have some resistance from them."

No one moved.

Kasai met North's glare; he could see hurt and disbelief warring in his eyes.

Thukuli swung his sword at North, but was shocked when the older man stopped the blade with an en-pist. North had only moved his arm. His expression was unreadable. Thukuli backed off a few steps, then glared at Kasai, looking bothered. "Can you explain what's going on here?"

With a blink, Kasai's face was an impassive mask. "North was one of my mentors."

Thukuli shot a glance at North. "Oh right. The navigator for Lighting's crew." He turned his dark gaze on Kasai. "But you're not on his crew anymore. You don't owe any allegiance to North." The dark edge of his tone made Kasai's uneasiness rise.

North didn't look away, didn't respond. Arat opened his mouth to say something, but the words never came out. The silence deepened.

Velu stepped forward, trying to break the tension. "But sir, if Kasai was taught by him, it stands to reason that Fatal is stronger and Kasai can't beat him."

Kasai flashed heat towards him, warning him to shut up. North's eyes narrowed.

Thukuli growled and a strange vine snaked out of the bag at his waist, wrapping around his arm. "But it's been more than two years since he left Lightning's crew. He's gotten stronger."

Kasai stared at North, silently urging him to flee.

North took a few steps back. "You wanted to raid us? How about a deal?" He didn't look away from Kasai as he spoke.

Kasai inwardly cursed. No matter what he said, Thukuli wouldn't agree to any deal. Not even if he said he would.

Thukuli glared at North. "What kind of deal?" Everyone on his crew would've heard the warning in his voice.

Kasai forced the heat to flare out briefly, enough to touch Arat, and the other man gave him a curious look. Kasai risked darting his eyes at Thukuli and gave a tiny shake of his head.

Arat blinked and whispered to North, who tore his gaze from Kasai to look at Thukuli. "You let me fight one of your crew, one-on-one, and if I win, you leave us alone. If you win, you can take any of our prizes."

North's crew looked unsettled, but no one argued.

Thukuli gave him a thoughtful look, then turned to Kasai. Behind his back, where North couldn't see, he made a motion to Bek and spoke to Kasai. "Then *you* fight him."

Kasai felt his throat tighten. If Thukuli wanted him to fight, he would expect Kasai to kill North. And he couldn't do that. And what had he motioned to Bek for?

Kasai shuddered inwardly, feeling like something was about to happen.

Bek raised his en-pist and fired. Chaos erupted, and Kasai cursed under his breath.

North's crew scrambled back to their ship, the ones who were over here at least, and the others took up defensive positions along the deck.

Thukuli's crew roared and chased them over, the sounds of gunfire, en blast, and the *clang!* of sword against sword rushing through the air.

Kasai hesitated, an automatic reaction, and Thukuli was suddenly behind him. He grabbed Kasai by the back of his neck and whispered in his ear, "you fight them, or you will *never* be free of me."

He shoved Kasai forward, his eyes black, then leaped over the railing. Kasai stumbled, landing on his knees.

Velu appeared and helped him up. Velu took in Kasai's face and grimaced, speaking just loud enough for him to hear, "Fight, but don't hurt anyone. Just put on a good show."

Kasai nodded, his heart in his throat, and leaped over the railing to join in the attack.

He didn't see Sioco's body until he tripped over it.

The man's head was split open, hit by a falling spar.

Kasai felt sick, but didn't hesitate to send out a wave of heat.

Many of Thukuli's crew fell back, but strangely, none of North's crew seemed to notice.

Velu met Kasai's gaze briefly, then disappeared into the fray.

Kasai wasn't surprised when Arat appeared, a sword in hand. He formed his staff and blade met fire as they clashed.

"What are you doing?" Arat hissed. Not normally a fighter, he had clearly practiced. Unfortunately, he was no match for Kasai.

But Kasai held back his strength, unable to hurt one of the men who had taught him so much.

"We looked for you. We know Oxe saw you," Arat said as quietly as he could.

Kasai frowned and knocked the sword away with a practiced move. He said nothing.

"Do you even remember us?" The anguish in Arat's voice was so palpable that it hit like a physical force.

Kasai opened his mouth to speak, but was stopped by North.

"You bastard! We just wanted to talk to you!" Kasai had never seen North in such a rage before. It reminded him of Nakan, the day she had slapped her brother.

Kasai glanced around him, barely noticing the battle raging between the two crews. He dodged and blocked North's furious punches, barely holding his own as North's anger escalated.

Thukuli was watching him, fighting off two people at once with his sword and the vine around his wrist; a backup weapon. He could harden it in a flash but control it well as long as he was in direct contact with him. But it was limited.

Kasai waited, continuing to struggle, holding back North's heavy blows, until Thukuli was forced to turn away.

He saw his chance.

And took it.

He shoved North and Arat away hard, sending them crashing against the railing, and rose the heat higher than he ever had before. There was a cry from someone as they hit the rail, but Kasai ignored it.

A wall of flame rose around them, cutting the three men off from everyone else. The flames rose to half the height of the mast; the roar blocked out sounds from beyond the wall.

Kasai kept his hand raised, controlling the flames by sheer will alone, and stepped forward. "I am not doing this by choice!" His voice cracked, his throat spasming.

North and Arat, briefly dazed, froze.

Kasai groaned, the pressure of the heat difficult for even him to stand. "I don't want to hurt you." His legs shook, his arm aching.

They stared at him as tears streamed down his face.

"Just escape. If you don't, he'll make me kill you." Kasai fell to one knee; the flames lowered a fraction.

North suddenly lunged forward as if to attack, but held Kasai up in an embrace. "I knew you hadn't changed."

Kasai smiled weakly, then everything went black and cold.

"WHEN HE WAKES UP, I want to see him. In my cabin." Thukuli's voice was faint, but loud enough it woke Kasai.

He stayed still as the footsteps receded.

There was a growl, and the sound of a fist against the wall echoed dully. "That idiot...I told him to put on a good show, but he just risked everything!"

A snort; Feluna. "Can you blame him? You saw his face. He was devastated when he saw who hit him."

Velu growled; another punch against the wall. "I don't want to be throwing his body overboard! And I'm sure we will soon!"

Silence for a minute, then Feluna let out a sigh. "No. If Thukuli...punishes him, he'll leave his body for the crows. We have maybe three hours until we're docked, and one chance to get Kasai out of here...safely."

Kasai shifted his hand, letting them know he was awake. Light filtered through his closed eyelids. He must be in the surgery; his room had no portholes.

Feluna was there, her hands roaming over his body gently. "Good, you're awake. Can you speak?"

Kasai let out a groan and sat up. Everything was sore, and there was a pulsing kind of pain in his stomach to his hip, but nothing was broken. He could feel a bruise across his jaw. "I'll be fine. Just...give me a minute."

Velu didn't hesitate. "What did you do?"

"What I needed to." Kasai responded automatically.

"What did you need to do?" Feluna asked.

Kasai paused, holding his head for a moment. He finally looked at her. "I saved their lives."

They paused, staring at him. Velu exchanged a glance with Feluna, then looked at Kasai. "I hope you did."

Kasai didn't register the words at first, but then his head shot up. "What do you mean?"

Feluna hesitated, then spoke slowly. "After you collapsed, the flames went down, and we all saw Fatal laying you against the railing. A lot of people thought you were dead and..."

"Thukuli lost it." Velu interrupted her, his voice blunt and direct. "He...well, he went nuts and cut down everyone in his path, then used that vine to destroy their ship."

Kasai felt sick. "Did anyone survive?"

Feluna watched him carefully. "We don't know. One of their crewmembers is with us now, chained below until she agrees to join the crew willingly, but the rest fell into the water."

"Thukuli took a crewmate?" Kasai was momentarily confused by this.

Velu nodded. "She said her name is Linota. She's a shifter, but she's...unstable."

Kasai raised an eyebrow. "Will she really join us?" He doubted it, especially since she was taken and chained.

Feluna snorted a laugh. "No. Not unless Thukuli finds a way to blackmail her, like he has most of us."

Velu walked over to the table. "I saw what happened between you and Fatal."

Feluna stared at him.

"How?" Kasai asked.

"I was in the rigging, chasing one of their sharpshooters." Velu shrugged. "I saw you say something, but then...it looked like he...hugged you."

Kasai closed his eyes and dropped his head.

"Whatever you did nearly killed you," Feluna told him.

Velu laid his hand on Kasai's shoulder for a moment. "Thukuli's going to ask that you do that again sometime."

Kasai shook his head. "I...I don't think I could...I've never done anything like that before."

Feluna waited a moment, then nudged Kasai. "I need to ask you something, and I want an answer."

Kasai looked at her; he knew he must look terrible, but she didn't react. "What?"

"What is your connection to Lightning's crew?" She was blunt, but there was no malice behind the question.

Kasai glanced at the door, which Velu closed, before he answered. "I...joined them after my home was destroyed by Razora." He knew there was no reason to hide it from them now.

Feluna nodded. "But it was more than that, wasn't it? You didn't have to stay with them, didn't have to be a pyrate." There was a moment of silence as she paused. "Why do you get upset whenever anyone brings them up?"

Kasai's first reaction was not to answer. Memories flashed through his head, and it took several minutes for him to shake them away. "I...he was my father."

Velu, leaning against the door, fell.

Feluna's eyes grew wide. "North?"

Kasai swallowed heavily. "Lightning."

They stared at him with wide eyes. Velu braced himself against the door, then whispered. "That means you're a generation genetic." He blinked. "That explains the amount of power you showed."

Kasai felt a flash of surprise that Velu understood what that meant.

"And why you get upset whenever Lightning's mentioned." Feluna was gazing at him thoughtfully. "But...and forgive me for asking, didn't he die alongside Blacksmoke?"

Kasai nodded, unable to speak.

Feluna closed her eyes. "But it was an accident, wasn't it?"

Kasai nodded again.

"I won't ask any more about it then. I'm sorry I brought it up now, but I always thought you were angry with them. The kind of all-consuming rage that Thukuli has towards others sometimes." Feluna watched him for a moment, then grabbed something from the counter.

Kasai stared as she handed him a bowl of thin gruel. He took it, but didn't eat. "No. I was mad, for a long time, but now I just..." His voice trailed off.

Velu gave him a sympathetic look. "I get it."

Kasai and Feluna looked at him in surprise.

Velu looked uncomfortable as he explained, "I killed my brother years ago. By accident. I still hate myself for it, even though I didn't mean to. It took a long time to recover from that, and I miss him every day."

Kasai wiped his face, not looking at them.

Feluna waited a moment, letting Kasai collect himself, then spoke. "Thukuli said he wants to speak to you when you're ready, but if you want...I can tell him to wait. He won't like it, but after that...well you need to rest."

Kasai nodded. "I don't want to face him. Not yet."

Feluna nodded and left the room.

Velu was silent while Kasai ate.

Once the bowl was empty, Kasai set it to the side. "What happened after I collapsed and Thukuli...reacted?"

"Like I said, he used his vine to destroy the ship. We fished out any of our crew in the water, got rid of the dead, and chained up Linota. Everyone else, he just left them in the water. I think a lot of them were dead." Velu told him.

"North? Arat?" Kasai's voice cracked.

Velu waited a moment before answering. "I don't know. I'm not sure who Arat is, and I saw North on a piece of driftwood. I couldn't tell if he was alive or not, sorry."

"S' okay." Kasai said thickly.

Feluna came in a few minutes later. "Thukuli wants you in his cabin now. I tried to tell him you needed rest, but he refused to hear it."

Kasai groaned, but stood a little unsteadily. He looked at his arm; the right arms straps had been repaired and attached, but the melted spot was still there.

Feluna kept a hand on his shoulder until he was steady, then let go. "Good luck."

Kasai nodded, then left the room. He barely noticed the simple tunic and pants he wore, but knew Thukuli never commented on his clothes.

The captain was sitting on his hammock when Kasai came in, staring out the back window. "Glad you survived that." His voice sounded normal, but there was a tightness that made his words vibrate in Kasai's ears.

His cabin was surprisingly spare; swords, guns, various weapons that were trophies from other pyrates hung on the walls. But most of the space was taken up by a series of garden beds.

Taking up almost half the room, the waist high beds had dark soil and several kinds of vine plants were sprouting all throughout them. One vine, recently trimmed, looked tiny compared to the others, but still healthy.

Stone vines were a variety only Thukuli grew. Hard as steel, these vines could even burrow through mountains if given the chance. But they reacted unusually well to his powers, so he had only saved a few seeds and destroyed the rest so no one else could use them. Outside of this room, they were extinct.

Kasai grunted, sitting on a stool nearby.

Thukuli turned to him, his eyes glittering in the dim room. "I was beginning to doubt your loyalty there for a while."

Kasai remained silent, his gaze unwavering.

"But then those flames...you took out most of Fatal's crew for me, so that made up for your...hesitations." Thukuli's voice grew to a snarl, but he took a deep breath before continuing in a calmer voice. "I want to ask what happened behind that curtain of flames."

Kasai hesitated briefly, as if trying to think. Really, he didn't want to say, but he knew Thukuli would make Kasai tell him if he didn't answer. So he lied as well as he could. "I told them I was on your crew now. They attacked me. I got knocked out by North, I think, and the power I used took more energy than I expected."

Thukuli nodded. "I have to admit, I'm not sure if I could ask you to do that again."

This surprised Kasai, but he didn't let it show.

"If it does that to you, then there's no point in doing it again. Save it for emergencies." Thukuli gave him a strange look, but continued. "But since you fought, even if you were beat, you're off the hook for hesitating before."

Kasai raised an eyebrow, but stayed silent.

"Don't give me the silent treatment." Thukuli shot him a glare, then rose and walked along his plant beds. "I'm serious. I'll let you off the hook, since you fought against an old mentor, but don't think I'm happy about that."

"I wouldn't expect you to be," Kasai muttered.

Thukuli glared at him for a moment, then ran his fingers through the soil. "But you're on watch for a while. Anything like that happens again, I won't let it go unpunished." The threat hung in the air for a few minutes while he checked his plants.

"Feluna told me we were docking at Brimna Atoll soon. How long was I out?" He could've asked Feluna this, but forgot.

Thukuli didn't answer for a few minutes, pruning a vine and adding water to a smaller sprout. Finally, he sat down, turning to Kasai. "About four days, give or take. We've had a good wind, and the current is pushing the right way."

Kasai nodded, mentally calculating how far they had gone.

"But I should tell you, we're making some changes to the crew when we dock. Well, most likely tomorrow now, but I left Kelin in Brimna to look for more crewmates." Thukuli gazed at him thoughtfully.

"Do we have room for more?" Kasai knew they were using every available spot for hammocks lately, so how many new crew members was Thukuli taking on?

Thukuli shook his head, grinning. "No. But it's time we...expanded our fleet."

KASAI GROANED SILENTLY as he sat near the two captains. They were discussing Kelin's choices deeply, and Kasai had to admit he was bored for once.

A somewhat large group of people, all new crew members, stood nearby. Kelin, a small man with a good nose for potential, had been gathering them since their last visit to the port. Jonzu, one of their best fighters, was sitting with him nearby. He was grinning, so he had definitely recovered, but there was a strange air about him.

Feeling a gaze on him, Kasai saw a tall, tanned young man looking his way. Short hair, recently shorn, muddy brown eyes, and dressed somewhat less warmly than everyone else. There was something oddly familiar about him, but Kasai didn't think he had seen him before.

When he noticed Kasai looking at him, he flushed and turned away, speaking to an older man with his back to Kasai next to him. Kasai narrowed his eyes; something about the other man's stance, his braided hair, his clothes, was maddeningly familiar.

Before Kasai could dwell on it anymore, Thukuli's voice broke into his thoughts. "Alright everyone. I've talked with Bek here, and he'll pick out who he wants on his crew."

Bek nodded. "I'm taking some of Thukuli's members with me, because I need at least a few experienced sailors, but most of you newbies are coming with me."

The younger man flicked his gaze towards Kasai, but looked at the captains.

Thukuli nodded. "Kelin, you'll stay with me. Jonzu-"

"Hold on Captain." Everyone stared as the large man stood and walked up to Thukuli and Bek. "We have a...problem with me. I found someone to trade places with me on your crew."

Bold. Stupid, but bold. For both him and the other person. Kasai frowned.

Feluna nudged Kasai suddenly and whispered, "Do not react to the man he's about to bring forward, whatever you do." He hadn't seen her approach.

Kasai shot her a confused look, then watched Jonzu with interest.

Thukuli's expression turned stormy. "That's not how your contract works."

Jonzu didn't flinch or back down, and Kasai felt a bit of respect towards him. Jonzu shook his head. "But someone took over my contract when I beat him in the arena, part of a deal we made beforehand."

Thukuli cursed and spat at his feet; a major insult. "Why would you do that?"

Jonzu shrugged. "It was the only thing I could offer. He wanted a pirate crew to join. I wasn't sure if I could return to the sea yet. I didn't have any money to offer, so I gave him the one thing I had."

Thukuli glared at him. "And who is taking your place?"

Kasai watched the strange calmness on Thukuli's face with a growing sense of dread. Whoever was taking Jonzu's place wouldn't last long.

There were footsteps and the crowd of new members parted to let a somewhat older man through.

A long nose, dark red-brown hair in a braid, short stature. Kasai felt a twinge as he took in the staff at his side, but when he saw the rose-tinted glasses, a snarl ripped through his throat and he shot to his feet.

The people around him, except for Feluna, backed off in surprise. A wave of heat rose out, making everyone break out in a heavy sweat. Steam rose from the ground.

"Captain, I wouldn't recommend letting him on the crew." He didn't realize it was him who had spoken until Thukuli turned his black gaze to Kasai.

"Do you know Eaden?" Thukuli asked calmly.

Eaden. That was not his name. Despite the different clothes, and the hair being darker, Kasai knew who he was.

And no disguise could hide the painfully familiar hurt look in Brinar's eyes as he met Kasai's gaze.

Chapter 15

Oxe

OXE MADE HIMSELF FLINCH, though the heat didn't bother him. Brinar was staring at Kasai, not bothering to hide the hurt on his face. His shoulders drooped and he took a step back. Most of other new pyrates recoiled more than Oxe did, though a few didn't respond as badly.

"Kasai, it's nice to see you again." His voice was calm, but Oxe could smell nervousness radiating off him. Brinar shifted slightly, his movements hesitant.

He could also smell Kasai's anger, shockingly strong. Was Jonzu right? Did Kasai really hate people now? Or was this personal? Did he know Brinar had saved him after the fight with Blacksmoke? Or did he believe he had been abandoned? Or was this something else?

He slowly made his way to the side of the crowd to get a better view. Brinar didn't glance at Oxe, but he knew the doctor must've seen him. The road crunched under his feet, the remaining frost still holding onto the ground.

Kasai's eyes were blazing, his fist clenched at his side. He was wearing simple clothes; had he been hurt recently? Oxe could tell his hair had been hastily tied back. It was how he used to look when he was getting treatment from something bad.

"Kasai, how do you know Eaden?" Ironwood's voice oozed through the air, the condescending undertone thick enough to taste.

His expression was unreadable, but Oxe resisted a shudder at the look in his eyes.

Kasai gritted his teeth, his eyes not moving from Brinar. "We sailed together at one point."

"Part of Lightning's crew?" Ironwood gazed at Brinar with renewed interest.

"He hired me as an extra hand on a relatively short voyage once," Brinar explained. He and Oxe had designed a believable backstory for him in case something like this came up.

Ironwood regarded him for a moment, then shot a dark look at Kasai. "But why shouldn't he allowed on the crew?" Oxe could smell a touch of anger rolling off Ironwood. Aside from the black look in his eyes though, he appeared calm.

Oxe shuddered inwardly. People who became angry but did not show it could never be trusted.

Kasai paused, and Oxe saw a moment of pain cross his face. "He can't be trusted."

Oxe felt a stab of disbelief, but stayed silent. He couldn't speak out, even though he wanted to. But did Kasai really mean that?

Ironwood gave Brinar a questioning look, tilting his head but remaining silent.

Brinar shook his head. "There was a...misunderstanding...and it didn't go well. I can understand why you think I'm not trustworthy." He watched Kasai, his unease evident in his half-truths.

Kasai snorted, sitting back down. The large woman beside him was staring at Brinar curiously, a deep frown etched on her face.

Ironwood gave Kasai a thoughtful look, but turned to Brinar. "Well, as much as I want to question you about that, I'm afraid I have to decline you being on the crew." He leaned back on his heels, his gaze unreadable.

Oxe clenched his fist in his pocket, feeling his claws prick his skin through the fabric.

Kasai looked away and met Oxe's gaze again. Oxe looked away quickly. He had expected relief, but not the pain and regret in his eyes. Nor the curiosity; did Kasai recognize him? Or was he thinking about Brinar?

"Why not? He lost the fight. He has to follow our deal," Jonzu said. His face fell, his voice hitched up an octave. Oxe knew Jonzu wanted to leave the crew, but he hadn't expected the desperation in his tone.

Ironwood shrugged. "You're not wrong, he has to follow the deal, but unfortunately I can't let him on the crew if Kasai has that bad of a problem with him. You know the rule: no bad blood on the ship. If I let him on, and he and Eaden get into a fight, you know what will happen." A few of Ironwood's original crew, standing on the dock, shifted and Oxe saw looks of fear being exchanged.

Oxe frowned, wondering what he meant. Jonzu clearly did though and said nothing more. He stepped back and didn't meet anyone's gaze.

"But I'll release you, Jonzu. You accepted the deal and beat him, so I'll consider our original contract moot now." Ironwood's voice was even, but Oxe's nose stung at the almost overpowering scent of fury issuing from him.

Jonzu gave him a nod, clearly uneasy, and left quickly.

"If you're still interested in joining a crew, you can join Bek's," Ironwood continued after Jonzu was out of earshot. He didn't sound reluctant, but his expression was almost cold. His hand twitched against his leg.

Brinar cocked his head for a moment, but shook his head. "I think I'll pass, if that's alright. I was told I would join Ironwood's crew, not someone else's."

Ironwood's scent grew earthy, and Oxe noticed a thorn poking through the soil at his feet. "Understandable. Unfortunately, unless

Kasai can get over his...issue with you, I can't let you join." Oxe heard the frost crackling as the thorn pushed up through the road.

Brinar shot a look at Kasai, but spoke to Ironwood. "If we can come to an agreement, can I fulfill my end of the deal?"

There was a tense silence as everyone waited for the answer. Some people looked at Kasai, most watched Ironwood. A chill wind blew through, sending many people shivering.

Oxe held his breath, almost quivering from the invisible pressure.

Ironwood stared darkly at Kasai for a few moments. "I'll leave that up to you two. If Kasai want's to, that's his decision. If not, then let it go." He turned back to Brinar. "But I admire your commitment to your end of the deal." He sounded as if he meant it, but looked disinterested already.

Brinar looked briefly at Ironwood before stepping aside. He stood still, but Oxe could see him fingering the beaded bracelet around his wrist; a nervous habit.

The woman left Kasai's side and made her way behind the crowd to Brinar's side. She whispered something to him, then they both left.

Ironwood watched them briefly, but then turned to the crowd. "Alright, the rest of you. Let's get you squared away."

"TAMOTSU, THIS IS FELUNA." Brinar was sitting at a corner booth with the large woman when Oxe returned to the inn. It was warmer inside and he was glad to shed his jacket. He grabbed a tankard of something weak and sat with them.

She raised an eyebrow at Oxe, but spoke to Brinar. "Know him?"

"We met here, and occasionally share a drink after his day job," Brinar told her.

Oxe nodded, agreeing with him silently. He sipped his drink; jra, weaker than le. He could tolerate this better.

Feluna eyed him suspiciously, but said nothing to Oxe. "So Brinar," this surprised Oxe greatly, "Now that you can't get close to Kasai, what will you do?" How did she know him? As far as Oxe knew, Brinar had been with Sonus' crew for many years, probably since he met him.

Brinar shrugged. "Go back home, I suppose."

"Hm. Well, I bet that will be a nice change for you," Feluna said, a bitter edge to her tone. "It's a shame though. I could use another doctor, especially when Kasai won't let me treat him."

Brinar groaned and covered his eyes. "He's still like that? I should've guessed." Oxe resisted a smile.

Feluna grinned. "So that's not new then? I figured." The ship's doctor. That explained why she was with Kasai earlier.

Oxe watched carefully. He hoped she would continue talking about him.

"So what's your story?" He wasn't prepared when Feluna turned on him.

"I'm here for Kasai." He immediately regretted his choice of words, but he had been caught off guard for once. Brinar stayed silent, but Oxe could smell the anger from him.

Feluna's eyes pierced him. "What do you mean?" Her tone was dark, wary, angry.

"I just mean...I've heard about Kasai before." Oxe scrambled with his words; he tried to come off as a youngster-admiring-a-role model instead of missing-his-mate-like-crazy. "I want to learn from him about how to fight, how to be a pyrate."

He ducked his head a bit, fingers drumming on the table nervously.

Feluna snorted. "You got guts, kid." It still felt weird that people saw Oxe as a teenager now, instead of a 25-year-old. "But you won't have much luck with that."

"Why not?" Oxe asked.

Feluna glanced at Brinar, who shook his head sadly, and looked at Oxe. "He's damaged, hurt by others. Doesn't let anyone get close to him."

"Anyone?" Oxe found this hard to believe, no matter what he'd heard by now.

"Anyone. He won't even open to me, and I'm the ship's doctor." She looked out the window thoughtfully. "But if you're persistent enough...you might get lucky."

Oxe didn't comment on this. "Ironwood said we leave in a few days. Should I stay on the ship for now? Or wait?"

Feluna shrugged. "It's up to you, but he has no quarrels about leaving someone here if they're late."

Oxe wanted to ask what Kasai was doing, but didn't want to push his luck. He turned to Brinar. "I'm going to head to the ship then. I hope I'll see you again, Eaden."

Brinar's lips pressed together, but as Oxe shut the inn door, he heard Brinar warning Feluna, "Keep an eye on him, please."

OXE PAUSED IN HIS SCRUBBING when a pair of black boots appeared at the edge of his vision. The sea was calm and luckily most of the new crewmembers had gotten over their motion sickness; Oxe was glad he had been on a ship for the better part of four years now.

"You've done enough Tamotsu. I have another job for you." It was Kelin. When Bek had left, it left Geralf free to become the first mate and Kelin was offered the newly freed position of second mate.

He reveled in it, and Oxe was a bit tired of his arrogant attitude.

Oxe tossed his holystone brush in the bucket of water next to him. "What do you need?" His shirt was still on, despite doing heavy work, but he had rolled his pants up to his knees and removed his shoes. He rarely wore his shoes, but it was still cold, so he wore them to keep others from questioning him.

Kelin waited until he stood. "Leave the bucket. I'll get someone else to finish."

Oxe followed him below deck, unease settling over him as he saw Kasai's door ahead.

Kelin nodded towards the open door. "I need someone to keep an eye on Kasai for a while. Feluna's concerned about headaches or something, and doesn't want him being alone for the time being. She suggested you might be up to the task."

Clever. So she had found a way to get him close to Kasai without raising suspicion. She had no idea the truth, though, had no idea of how well this was working out.

But concern shot through him. Could he keep quiet about who he really was? It wasn't safe to reveal himself yet, and it had been a month already. Ironwood continued to observe him, as he was still deemed too inexperienced to be left unsupervised.

"Do I need to do anything?" Oxe asked. The hallway was lit by a single el-turn on the wall; shadows danced slowly on the walls, matching the movement of the ship.

Kelin shrugged, his dirty blonde hair hanging down his back. "Whatever Kasai needs, barring you leaving until the captain says so. Or Feluna."

Kasai cursed as they walked in, rubbing his chin. He had recently trimmed his goatee, and it looked a little strange. Uneven. He spotted Kelin, then Oxe, and grimaced. "What?"

Oxe almost flinched from the harsh tone.

"Feluna doesn't want you alone for a while, wanted one of the new guys to keep you company." Kelin didn't back down from the wave of heat, but Oxe made himself even though every part of him was aching to run forward.

Kasai curled his lip in the beginnings of a snarl. "Fine. Don't get in my way." He turned back to the engine. Aside from an el-turn hanging from above a bench, the room was dim.

Kelin turned to Oxe. "Warning, he has a bad attitude, but he won't hurt you." Oxe made a face like he didn't believe him, though he really did. "Someone might come to relieve you in a while. I have no idea who or how long it'll be though. So get comfortable." He gave a harsh bark of laughter and left.

Oxe gingerly sat down on the empty bench against the wall, afraid to speak. The air smelled heavily of salt-soaked wood, Kasai, and engine grease. He watched Kasai for a few minutes, studying him.

His hair was braided again; with a flash, Oxe realized it was braided the same way Brinar did his. Did Kasai realize that? Or maybe he did that as a reminder?

His clothes were different today. A dark woven tank, loose pants, and thin shoes. Different from how he used to dress. Oxe knew Kasai was one of the few pyrates who regularly washed and changed his clothes, but pushed the thoughts away as Kasai spoke up.

"Tamotsu, right?" Kasai didn't stop in his work while he spoke, startling Oxe.

He nodded, then realized he would need to speak aloud. "Yes." His voice hitched, and he flinched.

Kasai paused, then continued without turning around. "Hand me a wrench, will you? Bucket under the bench, size four...no, three."

Oxe pulled out a large bucket full of tools, taking a moment to find the wrench with the right number on it, and handed it to Kasai's outstretched hand. While he couldn't read well, he knew basic numbers at least.

Kasai took it with a grunt, moving a tad. Oxe was surprised to see his palm glowing softly; that was new. It gave off a soft illumination. Useful, but Oxe wondered how hot it was.

He waited several moments before daring to speak. "So...you work on the engine?"

Kasai stopped, but still didn't turn around. "Yes. What's to you?"

This was wrong. So very wrong. Kasai sounded hostile. His scent didn't change, but Oxe could feel the bite of animosity from him. He had tensed up, his stance becoming wary.

"I just... I'm just getting to know the crew." He said, letting a bit of honesty into the statement. He could feel his hands shaking and gripped the bench, trying to still them.

Kasai set down the wrench and turned to face Oxe fully. "What made you think you could join this crew?" His eyes were hard, guarded.

Oxe thought he had cut his beard without looking. Why?

Kasai watched him expectantly.

"I wanted to go to sea. This seemed better than a merchant." Oxe shrugged, trying to play it off as being naïve. He tried not to stare, to drink in every little detail that he missed.

Kasai snorted, sitting on a cot Oxe hadn't noticed before. "Yea. Better. Get this through your head though. I don't make friends, I don't enjoy talking to anyone. Feluna gets a pass because she has to treat me, the captain because I don't have a choice."

Oxe tried not to show how deeply this hurt him. But he reminded himself that Kasai didn't realize he was speaking to his mate; he thought he was speaking to a stranger. "I'm...sorry."

Kasai glared at him for a moment, then leaned back. His expression relaxed and he looked remorseful. "Alright. I know you're new, and I'm sorry. I just don't want you thinking we can be friends now so you aren't hurt later."

Oxe nodded, his throat constricting. What had happened? Sibra flashed through his head; had her death changed Kasai?

Kasai grabbed a book from under the cot. "I understand Feluna wants you to watch me, but just...don't bother with anything unless I need you to, okay?"

Oxe nodded again, trying to hold back a tear.

Kasai really had changed. Become harsh, even mean. Untrustworthy. Oxe started to wonder if he could get Kasai to talk to him, especially if he saw Oxe as a stranger, and sat on the bench, watching his mate quietly.

Chapter 16

Kasai

TAMOTSU WAS STRANGE. He sat quietly on the bench, looking around the room with interest, while Kasai pretended to read his book.

Really, he was watching the new crewmember silently. His clothes were still fairly fresh; a dark cream shirt made of thickly woven fibers, pants of dark leather that looked snug despite being baggy, but no weapons hung at his side.

Probably not a fighter. But he looked strong, lean, probably a labor worker before this. But young. Maybe 16? Couldn't be younger than that. But he didn't look older than 19 or 20.

He had a flash of Sibra and grimaced.

Why would Feluna request this guy watch him? Was she trying to help him fit in? Give him something to do that would help ease him into this life? Or did she think he could be another ear for Kasai?

He snorted, making Tamotsu look at him curiously, and flipped a page.

He read several pages before he noticed movement. Tamotsu had noticed the mirror, tucked behind the bench with the reflective side towards the wall. Kasai saw a look of sadness cross the boy's face briefly before he replaced it with mild boredom.

Kasai sighed, relenting. "Bored?"

Tamotsu started, then gave him a sheepish grin. "A little."

Kasai sat up and pulled out a couple of books from his stash. "Can you read?"

"A little." This surprised him. Very few people he had met had a hard time reading. Oxe, of course, because his tribe didn't have a written language. A few of...North's crew couldn't. Sibra had difficulty as well, but she said the letters didn't look right to her, like they got mixed up.

Tamotsu took one of the books gingerly, flipping it open.

Kasai waited a moment. He didn't want to get close to anyone, not anymore. It seemed like lately, anyone he was close to got hurt, or worse, and he couldn't handle that again.

His hand spasmed; Tamotsu gave him a concerned look.

"I don't have a large variety, and unfortunately most of what I have is scientific, but there's not much else to do down here." Kasai picked up his packet of repair tools for his arm and set them to the side.

Tamotsu nodded, then opened his mouth but hesitated. Kasai raised an eyebrow at him, and he tried again. "If I need help...is it alright...can I ask you?"

Kasai had a brief flash of someone; Naomi, when she was little. She was shy about asking for help too. "Yea, but not right now. I have to work on some repairs."

"Repairs?" Tamotsu looked curious, but he blanched as Kasai undid the straps on his arm and took it off.

Seeing the look of horror on his face caught Kasai off guard. "Hey, it's alright. It's mechanical. I lost my arm a few years ago and found a way to...replace it."

Tamotsu nodded weakly. "Sorry...it's just......"

"Unexpected?" Kasai offered.

Tamotsu nodded again, his face ashen.

Kasai shrugged and took out some tools. He couldn't fix the melted part, not in here, not with another person present, but he could fix a creaking joint, the neural connector, and other small bits.

He worked in silence for a while, keenly aware of Tamotsu watching him.

He bent the joint, listening for any creaking, and added a bit of oil to a few spots.

A rustle made him look up; Tamotsu was leafing through the book. It was a book on genetics, one of the most recent ones he had seen in a while, written by Brinar.

The heat rose as Kasai thought about him; a faint sizzling from the waterline could be heard. What had Brinar been doing in Brimna Atoll? Research? Looking for him? Then he had a thought. *Was that why he tried to join Thukuli's crew?*

He stopped working on his arm for a moment, thinking. It took him a few minutes to realize that Tamotsu hadn't reacted to the heat. Strange. Tamotsu was still flipping through the pages, seeming completely unaware of the torridity.

Kasai shook his head and went back to work.

"I heard there was a shifter on board," Tamotsu said suddenly, not looking up from his book.

"What about her?" Kasai asked.

Tamotsu paused, a brief look of alarm in his eyes. "Her? I haven't seen many women aboard."

Kasai shrugged, uncomfortable now. The heat rose. "She's...kept below deck. She's been...hostile, and her powers aren't under control."

Tamotsu looked up. "What do you mean?" He sounded wary.

Kasai glanced up; there was definitely a look of alarm on the boy's face. "She's a true shapeshifter, one of the only two I've ever met. And unfortunately, she can't control her mind when she shifts."

Tamotsu nodded, a troubled look on his face.

"She won't hurt you." Kasai said automatically, the words slipping out before he could stop himself. While it was expected for the crew to protect one another, he couldn't understand the sudden sense of protectiveness towards Tamotsu.

Maybe he was lonelier than he wanted to admit, even to himself. But he truly didn't want to get close to someone again. Not when bad luck seemed to follow anyone close to him.

He sighed quietly and reattached his arm before putting away the repair kit.

Tamotsu closed the book, and Kasai was curious when he held out his hand. "I...might be able to help."

His fingers had sprouted claws, and dark gray fur.

"LINOTA, CAN WE TALK to you?" Kasai was glad they didn't have to go above deck to reach her, but he still felt nervous. If Thukuli found out he had been to her, there would be lots of questions.

He used his cane despite being indoors; his sight was bothering him again. Tamotsu had almost reached out a few times when Kasai tapped along the wall, but backed off from the dark glare.

Linota snarled, looking up from the shank of raw meat in her claws. She swallowed loudly, her voice a throaty growl. "What about? I'm busy?"

With a jerk of his head, Kasai encouraged Tamotsu to come forward.

The boy nodded, but strangely seemed...familiar with this.

Linota's reaction was immediate - her nostrils flared, her eyes widened, and she lunged towards him. The manacle around her ankle clanked loudly.

Using a nearby lamp's light, Kasai called for his staff, but was astonished to find his worry was unfounded. It had happened so quickly, in less than a heartbeat. So quickly that Kasai hadn't seen him move.

With Linota trapped beneath him, Tamotsu growled something in her ear. In response, she let out a fierce snarl, but he quickly pinned her by the throat. There was nothing savage about this. Kasai had seen this before.

Tamotsu was showing his dominance.

He waited quietly, not wanting to interrupt. He had seen Oxe do this once with Vrai. She had been bugging him, trying to get him to play when he wasn't able to. He had pinned her almost exactly like this, though this moment was far more intense. Oxe had also pinned Kasai once, though not quite the same way.

After a few tense moments, Linota sat back and grabbed the meat.

Tamotsu, his claws out and his feet like oversized paws, watched her warily. "Will you listen to me?"

"Like I have a choice," Linota growled, ripping away a strip of meat. Her claws were dug into the meat and blood stained her fur. Her tail twitched, but she hadn't shifted anything else.

Kasai eyed Tamotsu warily. Who was this boy? There was something almost...painfully familiar about him.

"Kasai told me that if I help you learn how to control your shifting, he might be able to convince Feluna to let you out." It was really Thukuli they needed to convince, but Kasai had to admit that Tamotsu had a point.

If Feluna could speak about her, it would go further, and raise fewer questions, than if Kasai spoke out about Linota.

He felt a touch of respect towards Tamotsu. He hadn't suggested mentioning Feluna, but in hindsight, it was smarter.

Linota eyed Kasai with a strange intensity. "Do you mean it?"

Kasai nodded. "I can talk to her, and we can go from there. Trust me, not many of us are easy with you...like this." He didn't bother hiding the pained look on his face. He leaned back and let his staff go back into the lamp.

Linota flared her nostrils and huffed. "Fine. But I want to practice outside."

Kasai gave a slow shake of his head. "I don't think you'll be allowed. Not yet, at least. Give it time, show everyone you have at least enough control to not attack anyone, and maybe the captain will let you out."

"Why should I trust you? You..." She bared her fangs, her jaw elongating. Her tail swished. "You destroyed my captain's ship."

"That wasn't me," Kasai said quietly. "I tried to save them." He dropped his head and clenched his fist around the cane.

She growled quietly, the sound just on the edge of his hearing.

Tamotsu gave him a curious, alarmed look.

Kasai shook his head, trying to ignore the tears that were threatening to show up. "I'll talk to Feluna. Just...work with Tamotsu."

He backed up and all but ran back to his room. He would forever feel guilty about wiping out North's crew. They may not have reacted as badly to the heat itself, but the flames he had made were another matter.

The weight of Sioco's death, caused by him directly, hung heavily on him.

He didn't notice Tamotsu had followed him until there was a hand on his shoulder.

He reacted instinctively, flaring his heat out. But Tamotsu didn't react like he expected. Most people flinched, or screamed and backed off if they were burnt, but Tamotsu merely looked concerned.

Kasai sank onto his cot. "Sorry. Habit."

Tamotsu nodded and curled up on the bench, looking strangely vulnerable.

Leaning his cane against the wall, Kasai laid down and closed his eyes. He tried to relax into the cot, but the knots in his muscles wouldn't unwind.

"Kasai..." Tamotsu's voice was quiet, "You're not like the others here, are you?"

Kasai furrowed his brow, giving Tamotsu a perplexed stare.

"I mean...you don't seem to like to hurt others." He sounded strange. Almost...relieved? He was tensed up though, his knees to his chest. He looked lanky like this, and Kasai sighed internally.

Looking up, he met Tamotsu's gaze. It was several moments before he spoke. "I don't."

Tamotsu gave him a sad look, not speaking.

"I..." Kasai's voice died in his throat. He didn't know Tamotsu, but something about him made Kasai want to talk. He dropped his head, trying again, "I can't stand hurting others. I've done it enough."

Tamotsu nodded. He got up and sat closer, closer than almost anyone had dared.

Despite the stifling heat in the room, he remained oblivious to it.

Kasai wiped his face. "When I hurt someone, it's always an accident."

With a hesitant gesture, Tamotsu reached out his hand, but then changed his mind and dropped it onto his lap.

"Just...stay on the bench, okay?" Kasai couldn't go on. Today had drained him. "I need to sleep." All his energy vanished in an instant, leaving him feeling completely exhausted.

Tamotsu nodded and sat on the bench quietly. He picked up the book from earlier, but didn't open it. He looked concerned, like he wanted to come back, but thankfully he stayed there.

Kasai sighed and laid on his cot, his back to the boy. He didn't want Tamotsu to see the tears on his face or the pain in his eyes.

Chapter 17

Oxe

OXE ALMOST VISIBLY fought himself as he heard Kasai crying. It was nearly silent, but he remembered all too well the quiet gasps and hiccups he could hear now. He wanted to go comfort him immediately, as he had done in the past, but it was too early to do so.

He waited until Kasai had fallen asleep, then quietly sat down closer to the cot. He couldn't help it.

Asleep, Kasai looked strangely vulnerable. Oxe wished he knew what had happened after he ran from the medical facility. He wished he could ask Kasai, but he couldn't. Not without revealing himself.

He thought about the way Kasai had acted towards Brinar at the port. Brinar had obviously been nervous, but while Kasai had looked angry on the outside, Oxe remembered the scent of fear coming off him.

Oxe suddenly had a flash of insight; Kasai didn't trust *himself*, not others. He was still dealing with everything that had happened over two years ago, and he had never really recovered.

Oxe shuddered as he pictured the empty spot where Kasai's arm had been. When did he lose it? Was it after the fight? He remembered Kasai's arm had been badly infected, resisting the medications Brinar had given him. Maybe it never healed and got worse? That could explain the reason for the amputation, and possibly the need for a mechanical arm.

Kasai shifted slightly, causing Oxe to freeze, but he remained sound asleep. He sighed a bit.

Oxe watched him for a few moments, then looked at the closed door. He thought about Linota.

She had recognized him; he knew she did. And when he warned her not to reveal that, she had resisted. Only at first, but after he asserted his dominance, she surrendered. She wouldn't give him away. For now, at least.

With a sigh, he cast a longing look at Kasai, desperately wishing he could be by his side right now. But if he tried, he didn't think Kasai would react well.

He laid down on the bench, feeling the rough texture of the wood against his back, and closed his eyes.

"Oxe, you realize what will happen if we accept this? Right?" His grandfather's voice came through the face-crys softly. It felt good to hear his language, even considering the circumstances.

Oxe nodded, his face blank.

"If you cannot get him back, you can never call yourself one of us again." The elder said. This was now Elder Wolf, not his grandfather.

Oxe took a deep breath. "I accept the consequences, Elder Wolf. If I cannot get my mate, and my charge, back, I will no longer be a Nuveri Warrior. I will no longer be a protector of our tribe, and I will mark myself as is custom."

The words were dust in his throat. His heart thudded dully in his chest.

Elder Wolf was silent for a minute. "Protector Oxeanukatahishi. The wolves have heard your howl. If you shall fail, your name shall be struck from the tribe. If you return, but have failed, your skin will be marked by the pack."

Oxe nodded, his face like stone. Each word was a knife in his heart. In his very soul.

"But if you succeed, then you will be restored to your rightful place in the pack. And if you return, and have brought you charge and your mate back, he shall be considered one of us, as is his right and claim." Elder Wolf finished.

A formality, as Kasai had already been made one of the tribe, but the words had been spoken. There was no taking them back.

Oxe resisted the urge to drop his gaze. He would not do that.

The elder spoke, his grandfather once again. "He has been Touched, Oxe, but maybe you can reach him."

The connection went blank, the face-crys dull now.

Oxe carefully set it back down and rose. He was no longer one of them. And he wasn't sure if he could ever return. And it hurt more than he had words for.

The creaking door jolted him awake.

"Tamotsu? Are you keeping an eye on him?" It was Feluna. From her expression, he could tell that she had caught him sleeping, yet there was no trace of anger in her eyes.

Oxe nodded.

She motioned for him to follow her and closed the door before leading him a few steps away. "How has he been?" They knelt against the wall.

Oxe glanced at the door. "Difficult. Sad. Distressed." The pain in his voice was too much to hide.

Feluna gave him a long look. "Tamotsu...why are you really here?"

Oxe froze, then looked at her. "I wanted to learn from Kasai, and I heard he was with Ironwood."

Her eyes were daggers. "Is what you say true?"

Oxe nodded, a lump in his throat.

She relaxed a bit. "I'm sorry, but it just seems like you know him. I mean better than from papers."

Oxe swallowed hard, thinking quickly. "I, um, come from Verideys." It was the first place that came to mind and partially true, sort of. "I saw him years ago with Lightning's crew."

Feluna narrowed her eyes.

"It was before his fight with Blacksmoke," He rushed the words out. Most people had heard where Blacksmoke had been caught, and Sonus died, so hopefully this wouldn't seem too suspicious.

"What were you doing in Brimna Atoll then?" She asked quietly.

Oxe couldn't look away from her. "I heard it was a place for pyrates. I hadn't been there more than a few months when I heard about Ironwood's crew being there. But then he left, and I, um, heard Jonzu talking to Eaden about joining the crew and asked."

This felt wrong. There were details that wouldn't add up, too many inconsistencies. He silently begged her not to connect the dots and start asking questions.

She didn't believe him; he could see it in her eyes. Her voice was dark when she spoke next. "You're lying."

Oxe waited, his heart pounding a tattoo on his ribcage, eyes wide.

"But I won't rat you out as a fake. I respect Brinar, and he spoke pretty highly about someone he claimed to barely know. But it's clear you won't hurt Kasai. I don't think you want to learn from him, not really, but I can tell you're no threat to him." Her words were like ice.

Oxe dropped his gaze, his hands trembling. No one had ever frightened him like this; but then again, he'd never been in this kind of situation before.

"I'll tell the captain that you're my assistant now." Her tone remained firm, but there was a slight hint of relief in her voice. "Your job is to stay with Kasai. Bunk with him, don't leave his side."

Oxe cast her a wary glance. "What if he asks?" He didn't know if he meant Kasai or Ironwood.

Feluna didn't respond immediately. The sound of footsteps echoed through the stairs, and she patiently waited for them to fade away. "Tell him it's by my orders." She stood quickly and glared down at Oxe before walking off.

It took Ox several minutes to regain his composure and return to the bunk he now shared with Kasai.

Chapter 18

Kasai

KASAI CURSED AS THE bolt bounced out of reach. He sat back, sighing. "Stupid engine..."

Tamotsu, lounging on his cot, looked over. "Need help?"

"No, I've got it." Kasai still wasn't used to him being in here. He didn't exactly question Feluna, but made it known to her, albeit silently, that he wasn't happy about it. It had only been a week, but still.

Tamotsu frowned, but watched as Kasai got another bolt from a bucket.

Kasai grunted as he pushed down on the wrench, trying to tighten the new bolt, and his hands slipped. He gasped as he fell, his cheek rubbed raw against the metal.

There was a gentle creak, but no movement.

Kasai sat up, hand on his scraped cheek, and reached for a rag he knew was nearby.

"Let me." Tamotsu was suddenly kneeling beside him, the rag in his hand.

Kasai took the rag, turning away. "I can do it." He ignored the hurt look in Tamotsu's eyes and sat on the bench. He held the rag to his cheek. He closed his eyes, trying to ignore the sting.

"Why won't you let me help?" There was a strange pain in Tamotsu's voice.

Kasai opened his better eye, watching him.

"If you'd let me help, it might be...well, better." The words sounded a little lame in Kasai's ears, but Tamotsu seemed a little nervous.

Kasai sighed. "Maybe, but I don't like others touching me."

Tamotsu nodded, a sad look flitting across his face. "I'm sorry."

Kasai closed his eye again. "Long experience as a pirate has convinced me that most people who touch me mean to do me harm." His chest throbbed, the scar over his heart aching. He resisted the urge to touch it; both it, and the memories associated with, too painful.

"How long have you been a pyrate?" Tamotsu asked.

Kasai was silent for a minute, thinking. "Maybe four years now? I know it doesn't seem that long, but..." he paused, unsure how much he could say. "I've...gone through a lot. More than some pyrates ever deal with."

Tamotsu nodded. It was silent for a few minutes, then he asked, "If you could, would you stop being a pyrate?"

Kasai shot him a sharp look, sending a wave of stinging pain through his cheek.

"Sorry." Tamotsu held up his hands as Kasai sent out a wave of heat.

Kasai watched him curiously. "How can you stand that?"

Tamotsu looked confused. "Stand what?"

"The heat." Kasai said.

Tamotsu shrugged. "It doesn't bother me, that's all."

Kasai grunted, but was surprised when he felt something warm trickle down his cheek.

Tamotsu was suddenly very close, another rag in his hand. Without a word, he wiped away the blood.

Kasai froze, hardly breathing.

Tamotsu suddenly froze, as if realizing what he had done. He backed away quickly, looking down. "I'm sorry!"

Kasai felt his heart thudding quickly. No one had gotten that close in over a year. And then, well... Thukuli was still sour about it.

Tamotsu sat on his own cot, his face in his hands. "I just...reacted."

Kasai nodded. What was it with this kid? Kasai knew Feluna had ordered Tamotsu to stay near him, but it was like Tamotsu was...he didn't know, infatuated with him? Adored him? It differed greatly from Sibra; with her, Kasai knew she adored him, sometimes bordering on worship he felt like. But Tamotsu was much different.

And Kasai couldn't ignore the strangely familiar musk that had come from him. "You're Nuveri, aren't you?"

Tamotsu froze, his expression...scared? Wary? He was hiding something, and he didn't want Kasai to know.

"It's alright," Kasai said quickly. "I know about them already. I've...met one before."

Tamotsu slowly regained his composure, his face blank when he turned to Kasai. "Yes..."

Kasai nodded thoughtfully. "You just... You remind me of someone, though he's older than you. But they don't leave their island. What are you doing here?" Oxe had never mentioned someone going missing, but maybe he hadn't known. Or maybe Tamotsu had left after Oxe.

But he looked at Tamotsu strangely.

Tamotsu wouldn't meet his gaze, his words unsteady. "My...mother was a warrior, but she left the island many years ago. She never told me why, but she met my father and they had me. She told me about them."

Kasai frowned. That explained the name then. "Where are you from?"

"Verideys Island." Tamotsu's answer was curt. Nervous, uncomfortable. His next words sounded unsure, almost rushed, "I wanted to be a pyrate and found a way to Brimna Atoll. I heard there was a captain looking for crewmembers and joined then."

"So you chose Thukuli's ship?" Kasai couldn't keep the bitterness out of his voice. "You could've done better, you know."

Tamotsu shrugged. "He was the only captain there, at least the only one wanting crewmates."

Kasai frowned at this, but turned away as the door opened. Thukuli stepped inside, his gaze narrowing as he took in Tamotsu's uncomfortable face and Kasai's grazed cheek, and glared at them. "Ship spotted. Get above deck."

Kasai exchanged a look with Tamotsu, but they said nothing and followed the captain out.

"ANOTHER PRIZE AND WE'LL find a port." Thukuli chuckled, smacking a man in the head with his blade. The man sank to the deck, blood trickling from his mouth.

Kasai kept one eye on Thukuli, and another on Tamotsu. The younger man, and he was definitely a man, was looking uneasily at the quivering merchant crouched at his feet.

It had been another month since leaving Brimna Atoll and the boy had started looking older. His cheeks looked a little higher, his frame slimmer.

But it was painful to Kasai, as he was beginning to look like Oxe. Tamotsu was already the same height, and his hair was growing out, thick and curly in the same way. His skin was almost the same shade too, though darker from being out in the sun a lot.

Kasai shook his head and turned to Thukuli. "Captain, where will we go? It's a little far to Brimna Atoll."

Thukuli gazed over the waves thoughtfully. "I'm not sure. I know Witch Island is around here, but I don't want to go there. I don't know anything about them, except that they don't like trading with most people."

Kasai almost let out a sigh of relief. He didn't think Brinar was there, but even if he was, Kasai knew Amalia would be, and he was almost more afraid of her than Brinar. But he didn't want anyone knowing his connection to the island. It would raise some very uncomfortable, and possibly painful, questions from Thukuli.

"We could head to Locke Island, sir," Velu called out. "It's a little further south, but I know it's a pyrate friendly port."

Locke Island? Kasai wasn't so sure. He had heard about it being a Seaborne base, though a small one, when he passed through here a few years ago. But before he could speak up, Kelin spoke out. "Captain, problem below."

Thukuli's lip twitched and he walked over to Kelin. "What's going on." Not a question, a demand.

"We may have a...complication to deal with." Everyone noticed his eyes dart to Kasai, and Thukuli's look darkened. Kelin didn't look concerned, but he looked uneasy with Thukuli's reaction.

Thukuli whipped his head around until he found Kasai. "Come with me. It sounds like you might be involved...somehow." The darkness in his tone made everyone flinch, and Tamotsu gave Kasai a concerned look as Kasai passed him.

The hallway was dark and stank. Kasai wrinkled his nose, glad he didn't have Oxe's sensitivity to smells. Thukuli made a face. "Kelin, what did you find?"

Kelin hesitated outside the door to the brig; the door was iron, not wood, and a heavy padlock hung broken from a hook. "Um, Captain, you remember the crew you fought before you returned to Brimna Atoll?"

Thukuli glanced at Kasai as he spoke. "Fatal North's crew. What about them?"

Kelin paused, wringing his hands. "There were survivors."

Thukuli   snarled,   startling   Kelin   and   Kasai. "Someone...*survived?!*"

Kasai's heart pounded against his ribs.

Thukuli kicked the door open and they all recoiled back as it crashed to the floor, half out of the doorway, as the hinges squealed and broke.

Kasai had to force himself to walk after Thukuli; Kelin stayed in the hallway.

"Well, I'm a little surprised at this. Arat, is it?" Thukuli clicked his tongue.

Kasai held his breath, trying his best to keep his face calm. Or at least controlled. He stepped in and his heart stopped.

Arat and North were both chained to the wall by their wrist. They had been cared for, at least somewhat, but what were they doing on a merchant ship?

Thukuli kicked North's leg and snorted. "Been brought low, have we?"

North bared his teeth and spat at Thukuli; the captain smacked him across the face, the sound echoing in the small space.

Arat caught Kasai's eyes. "Please..." His voice was weak

Thukuli glanced at Kasai, then turned to Arat. "What happened? This isn't a Seaborne ship." His words echoed Kasai's thoughts.

North jerked against the manacles. "It is. Or at least it had a Seaborne captain onboard. They found us a while ago and have kept us down here for weeks. Said they would take us to the base at Locke Island."

So it was a base. Kasai couldn't look away from Arat, feeling sick.

Thukuli frowned at this. "I have to admit, this is low of them. Keeping you chained like animals in a place that's not suited for it." He glanced back at Kasai for a moment.

Rich coming from the man who ordered Linota to be chained below.

Kasai felt even sicker as Thukuli slowly grinned, then turned to the chained men. "I'll make a deal with you. If I release you, you'll be loyal to me from now on."

Arat looked at Kasai, not at Thukuli.

North barely glanced at Kasai, glaring at the captain instead. "And if we refuse?"

"Then Kasai here will sink the ship..." Thukuli shrugged, pausing as if for effect, "the moment he leaves it."

North looked at Arat, who still hadn't looked away from Kasai, then dropped his head for a long moment.

The silence was thick, the room cold.

"Fine." The word hissed from between North's teeth.

Thukuli nodded, turning around. "Kasai, Kelin, stay here and get our two newest crewmates free. When they're aboard our ship, we'll sink this junk. There's nothing of worth here."

Kasai kept his face blank as Thukuli stalked out of the room.

Kelin nudged North, getting his attention. "Where's the keys?"

North jerked his head to a spot behind Kasai. "They were hanging there earlier, but they dropped when you started your attack."

Kelin nodded, looking at the chains. "I supposed we could rip these from the wall. It would be easy enough, but you'd still be chained."

"We'd be free of here though," Arat almost whispered.

Kasai had never seen him like this before. Morose, almost glum usually, and enthusiastic and cheerful when it came to cooking, Kasai had never seen him so...beaten.

North glared at Kasai. "Well?"

Kasai looked at him, but not meeting his gaze, and spoke. "I could melt the chains. You'd have the manacles, but you technically wouldn't be chained anymore."

Kelin raised his eyebrows. "Can you do that?"

"Yea, but it'll get pretty hot, so open that window." Kasai nodded at the single porthole above the chained men's heads.

Kelin reached up and opened it, then stepped back.

Kasai stood next to North's chains first, not looking at him. "I'm sorry, but this might hurt."

North just glared; Kasai wondered if North forgave him for attacking his ship before. While Kasai had done his best to save them, it hadn't worked and North had lost almost his entire crew, and his life, because of Kasai's failure.

Kasai pushed his thoughts away and heated his palm, similar to when he just created light. But this time, he forced the heat out and wrapped his hands around the thick chains as much as he could.

There was a growing heat, a sizzling noise, and North cursed as the red-hot chain ends landed on his head briefly.

"Sorry." Kasai repeated it with Arat's chains, and Arat dodged the ends.

Kelin nodded in approval. "Come on."

North stood on his own, but Kasai helped the other man up.

"Thanks," Arat whispered. He looked thin, which wasn't surprising, but Kasai was surprised to feel how weak he was.

Kasai helped him down the hallway and outside, North at his heels.

Tamotsu came over, but froze when he saw the other two.

North's eyes widened, but he said nothing.

Kasai looked between them, wondering what that was about, but mentally shrugged. "Tamotsu, get Arat to Feluna. North, come with me." He wasn't sure if North would listen, but the older man followed him closely as they crossed to Thukuli's ship.

"Kasai, where are you going?" Thukuli stopped him, placing a heavy hand on his shoulder. He eyed North warily, a cruel glint in his eyes, but spoke to Kasai.

"I'm taking North below so he can rest. He needs it after that. I sent Arat to Feluna; he's weak." Kasai told him. He spoke easily, but his hand trembled in his pocket. Fear, anger, nervousness. Kasai was a little surprised he could sound so calm; he expected a fallout later, when he was alone...well, as alone as he could get.

Thukuli didn't speak for a moment, looking at North for a moment. "Fine. But I want to see you tomorrow, North, and we'll talk about what you'll do here."

North nodded, but said nothing. Kasai could see him shaking with rage as Thukuli walked away.

Kasai rolled his shoulder, which was aching from Thukuli's grip, and led North down the steps. He didn't lead him to the crew's quarters, at least not yet, and headed straight for his room.

"SO YOU'VE BEEN JUST following orders, trying not to get killed, and saving who you could." North closed his eyes and leaned back.

Kasai nodded, looking at the floor. "I...I hope you know I would never-"

"I get it," North said.

Kasai didn't look up.

"But you...we thought you were dead, Kasai." North's voice cracked a bit.

Kasai didn't move, didn't look at him.

"Oxe...he never gave up. But watching him..." North's voice trailed off for a moment. "Wait, where is he?"

Kasai looked up, confused. "Oxe?" He felt his breath hitch.

North gave him a strange look. "Yes. We left him and Brinar at Brimna Atoll with Cifius, then came back to sea to find you."

Kasai squeezed his eyes shut. "I...I don't know. I did something...horrible."

North narrowed his gaze. "What do you mean?"

Kasai shook his head, his throat tight.

"Kasai...what happened?" North sounded both concerned and...angry.

"I think I killed him." The words choked out and North shot to his feet.

"Explain." He towered over Kasai, his face unreadable.

Kasai flinched back. "Cifius was teaching me how to be more of a leader. He told me to take over some of the duties he did for a few days."

North just glared at him.

"There was an accident. A tucowary escaped from the pens at the edge of town. And Sibra..." Kasai struggled to stay together. "Something killed her. The tucowary's jaws were not much different from a wolfs, and there were fang marks in her neck. Oxe was dragging her, and people kept saying he did it."

North hissed through his teeth, "So you believed them?"

Kasai shook his head. "I don't know. I...I didn't want to, but they gave me no chance to talk to him. He...he shifted in front of everyone."

North blinked in surprise, stepping back.

"He told me it wasn't him, but everyone was pushing me to...to deal with a murderer." Kasai held back a sob as he spoke. "I flamed him. I only meant it to *look* like I had killed him. But then we left."

"And ran into us," North clipped.

Kasai nodded, wiping his face. "And then we went back to port, and I thought he would be there. But...I saw Brinar and...I messed up, North."

North seemed to deflate. No longer angry, but the pity on his face hurt more than his anger.

Kasai turned away, not wanting to look at him. He froze at first, when North knelt next to him, but glanced at him sideways.

"Kasai, I don't think you messed up." His voice wasn't gentle, but it wasn't hard like before. "I'm sorry I was so angry, but...you don't know how scared we were. How much we've missed you. How...happy we were to see you, even after we...got lost."

Kasai didn't move.

"I don't think you killed Oxe. Maybe you hurt him, maybe bad enough he was still recovering," North said. "But I don't think you messed up." He was hiding something, but it didn't matter.

Kasai began crying as North hugged him.

Chapter 19

Oxe

OXE STRUGGLED TO GET Arat over the railing and was glad when Velu came over to help. The older man was incredibly weak and sick, unable to even walk on his own.

"I heard we have new crewmates. This one of them?" Velu asked.

Oxe nodded. "Arat. But he's weak. They've been in the brig since they were picked up weeks ago."

Velu curled his lips in disgust. "Damn Seaborne..."

Feluna didn't seem too surprised when they brought Arat in, though Oxe knew she wouldn't recognize him. At least, as one of their crew. "What's wrong with him?"

"Weak, sick. He's been chained for at least two months, maybe longer," Oxe explained.

Feluna nodded. "Lay him on the table. I'll take it from here. Tamotsu, go check Linota."

Oxe nodded and quickly headed below deck. Almost every night he was there, trying to help her gain control of her abilities, but she was struggling. She had yet to show any progress, at least with her ability to keep a human mind when going full animal, so she hadn't been allowed on deck yet.

Oxe paused when he heard quiet sobs from Kasai's room, but he wasn't surprised this time. He knew North was there. He glanced at the closed door briefly, then made his way to Linota's area.

"Have some fun?" She was lounging against a post, her tail curled around her legs.

Oxe shrugged. "As much as I could." None, really. The acrid smell of fear still lingered in his nose, and there was blood under his nails.

She snorted. "Maybe I can join next time." Her lips curled into a snarl.

"Can you stay human yet?" Oxe shot at her.

She responded by sprouting fur and leaping for him. Almost in slow motion, she shifted her limbs, elongating and changing to a fully feline form.

Oxe snorted; she had horns this time, resembling a druxe. He struggled to keep his face from changing, but brought his front claws up to meet hers, his hind ones digging into the wood beneath him.

She still wasn't human.

He flipped her onto her back, glad she was chained around the ankle still.

She was jerked to a stop midair, both by the chain and Oxe's attack.

He pinned her by the throat. "Stay. Human." He stared into her eyes, making it known that he wouldn't back down.

She snarled, struggling underneath him. Yowling and thrashing around, she couldn't make him budge.

He didn't move, keeping his body still, his claws dug into her throat enough he could feel them prick her skin.

She growled and quieted.

He could see something struggling, something trying to break free in her eyes. Silently, he willed her to break free. She *wanted* to be human, and he knew that would be enough.

But the animal was strong in her, stronger than he had ever seen before. It didn't help that she wasn't bound to a single form like his people were.

Maybe she should be.

Her eyes shut tight, a low growl vibrated in her throat. There was a huffing noise after a moment and Linota turned partially human underneath him. "I...can't..."

Oxe nodded and stepped back. "It's alright. I could see you were trying, and it was closer than you've come before."

She snorted. "Poor best."

"Why do you change forms?" Oxe asked her unexpectedly.

"Because if I don't, I don't feel me," she shot at him.

He shook his head. "I mean, why don't you stay in a single animal form?"

She didn't answer at first, staring at the floor. "I'm still not sure how to keep from changing into something different each time."

A common problem, one that the young shifters in his tribe struggled with for the first year. For Oxe, the only True Shapeshifter aside from his grandfather and mother, who had been shifting for years already, it was a harder struggle and took almost three years to master staying with a wolf form only.

He cocked his head, studying her. "You always keep your tail out. Why?"

She shrugged. "It's more comfortable that way."

He could relate; he missed his wolf form terribly. "What other parts feel comfortable?"

She frowned at him; he could tell she didn't understand what he was getting at yet. "Claws. Teeth. The horns actually felt pretty good, though heavy."

A druxe. "Try staying in one form for now. Maybe that's why you have so much trouble."

Her frown deepened. "You mean, maybe changing into a different animal each time is what's keeping me from being human?"

He nodded. "I...well, you've seen me shift before."

She nodded slowly. "Yes. Into something I've never seen before."

"It took a few years to stay in one form, but that was the form I felt most comfortable in." Not entirely true, at least at first. "Once I stopped changing into something different, staying the same with every shift, it helped me remember I was a human, not an animal." He couldn't think of a better way to describe it, not as a human at least.

"Why don't you shift then?" She asked.

He looked away uncomfortably. "It's..." He struggled to come up with a believable explanation for her.

"It's Kasai, isn't it?" The question caught him off guard.

He nodded; his throat tight.

She looked at him, her face both curious and almost...haughty. "You don't want him to know."

He nodded again.

She shrugged. "I won't give you away. I didn't the first time, I won't with this. I won't ask why you're hiding that from him. It's not my business."

Oxe relaxed, grateful, but said nothing.

"But seriously, I miss the sun. Get me out of here, at least for a few hours." She settled back against the post, closing her eyes.

Oxe stood. "I'll talk to Feluna." She didn't respond, but he was sure he saw her smile as he left.

"ARE YOU SURE YOU CAN'T help him?" Oxe shot Arat a sympathetic look.

The older man was asleep in a spare cot; it was more comfortable than the exam table and Feluna didn't want him near the others yet.

She shook her head sadly. "It's aqualungia, Tamotsu. There's no way I could treat it without a hospital."

Oxe couldn't hide the fear on his face as he looked at Arat. Kasai had been sick with that once and nearly died. Oxe had felt his heart dying with him, but thankfully, Kasai recovered. Barely in time, too.

"Do you know him?" Velu had noticed his face.

Oxe didn't think before he spoke, his thoughts tangled in his memories. "I sailed with him for almost four years."

Feluna and Velu's heads shot up.

Too late, Oxe realized what he said.

"Tamotsu." Feluna's voice was low. Calm. Cold. Fury flowed from her like a flood; Velu's anger stung his nose.

Oxe tried not to meet either of their gazes.

He wasn't prepared when Feluna suddenly slammed him against the wall by his throat. She snarled in his face, "How. Do. You. Know. Him?"

Oxe didn't struggle; he knew he was caught. Maybe not entirely, but enough.

Velu cocked his en-pist, his expression grim. "You have some explaining to do."

Oxe struggled to nod, finding it hard to breathe now.

Feluna stepped back, releasing him.

Oxe fell to the floor, gasping, hand on his throat. "Please. I promise. I'm no threat!"

Velu aimed the barrel of the short en-pist in his face. "Start explaining, or I get Thukuli."

"Please! Give me a moment!" Oxe gave a cough. They waited until he had caught his breath, their expressions black. "Just...I don't want to be overheard is all." Not entirely true, but honest.

Feluna's gaze darkened. "It's secure in here. Start talking."

Oxe nodded, glancing at Arat. "I was with Sonus' crew before."

"Lightning?" Velu's eyes widened. His anger dissipated a bit.

Another nod. "Yes. He...well, Kasai, saved my life." He knew he couldn't lie to them. Not now. "I...I wasn't really one of their crew, but I sailed with them for almost two years before Kasai confronted Blacksmoke."

Feluna relaxed a bit. "Why did you hide this?" Not any less angry, but she didn't look as ready to kill him now.

"Kasai." Oxe looked at the floor. "I came here to get him."

Velu and Feluna exchanged glances. Velu lowered the en-pist. "What do you mean?"

"I...he...after Blacksmoke, he disappeared. We didn't know where he was." Oxe struggled to explain, his voice shaking. "We thought he was dead. I stayed with North and Arat sometimes when they went to Verideys Island, trying to find him."

Velu nodded slowly. "That explains a lot, actually."

Feluna shot him a quick look. "What do you mean?"

"Remember when I found Kasai? How injured he was? They must've been from Blacksmoke," Velu told her.

Oxe pricked his ears, but said nothing yet.

"Why wouldn't he say anything though?" Feluna glared at Oxe, as if blaming him.

Oxe shook his head. "Kasai's not had an easy life since he joined Sonus' crew, some weeks before he saved me. He's gotten several injuries, nearly died many times."

Feluna's eyes widened, her anger gone.

Velu looked sick, and sympathetic. "He never told us."

"That's not surprising." They turned to see Arat propped up on his elbow.

"You should be resting." Oxe could tell Feluna's words were automatic, but she made no move to keep him from sitting up.

Arat kept an arm on his lap, but used the other to hold himself up. "Kasai's faced worse than most pyrates do, especially in such a short time, and he's barely made it out alive too many times. That changes a person."

Velu nodded. "Understandable." He turned back to Oxe. "But that doesn't explain why you want to get him."

Oxe shrugged. "I just want to take him home." A simple statement, but truer than anything else he could say.

Arat coughed, then looked at Oxe strangely. "How do you know Kasai? I don't recognize you."

Feluna's gaze sharpened and she glared at Oxe.

Oxe felt his mouth go dry. It was several minutes before he could speak. "Well...I look different right now."

Arat frowned, then fell back onto the cot, jerking a bit.

Feluna rushed over and began checking him over. "Both of you. Out. Now."

Velu and Oxe didn't argue, only left quickly.

Oxe was stopped from leaving by Velu's hand on his shoulder.

"This isn't over Tamotsu." He hissed, but there was no anger in his voice or expression.

Oxe nodded, and Velu released him. He sighed and thought about how he was going to tell Kasai about Arat.

"NORTH, STAY HERE." Oxe came through the door slowly, making sure they saw it was him first.

He nodded, looking nervous for a moment, but sat back down on the bench.

Kasai, his eyes red, looked at Oxe. "Is Arat okay?"

Oxe hesitated, shooting a glance at North. "Not...really."

The other two men froze. North was the first to react. "What's wrong with him?"

"How long has Arat been sick?" Oxe asked him first.

North paused for a moment. "Maybe two weeks. Why?"

Oxe closed his eyes. "Feluna thinks he has...aqualungia."

Kasai gasped and North lowered his head.

Oxe kept his eyes on Kasai. "Feluna is keeping him away from everyone but her right now."

A tear fell down Kasai's cheek. "She won't be able to help."

Oxe nodded, struggling not to rush over.

North looked at Oxe strangely, glancing at Kasai for a second. "Thanks for telling us."

Oxe nodded and sat down on his cot.

"Sleep in here?" North asked him, startling him a bit.

"Feluna asked him to keep an eye on me," Kasai told him.

North raised an eyebrow. "Why?"

Kasai shrugged; they could see he was upset. Oxe answered for him. "Kasai...has headaches and still struggles with a few injuries. She told me to watch him, make sure he's not alone."

North snorted. "I doubt there's anyone better than you she could've asked."

Kasai shot him a confused look, but didn't ask.

Oxe wondered if North knew who he was. He hadn't glanced at himself in the mirror; he had no idea how much of the plastic had been absorbed yet. His voice was deepening already, but that was easier to ignore.

"North, you can stay here for a while if you want," Kasai said suddenly, "but I need to sleep. If you two talk, just please keep it down."

Oxe and North nodded, both knowing they would, and watched as Kasai laid on his cot.

North waited until they knew Kasai was asleep, then came over to Oxe. He sat down, then cuffed Oxe across the head. Hard. "Idiot! When I said find Kasai, I didn't mean like this!" he hissed quietly.

Oxe shrugged, his head smarting. "We couldn't think of a better way. Brinar tried to join the crew by exchanging places with someone else, but Kasai recognized him and refused to even talk to him.

Ironwood didn't want bad blood on the ship, so we left Brinar back in Brimna Atoll."

North sighed, hanging his head for a moment. "I'm guessing Kasai doesn't know who you are?"

Oxe shook his head.

"Didn't think so." North shot him a glare; partly exasperated, partly cross. "But you're playing with fire, you know that, right?" He snorted at the lame joke.

"What would you have done?" Oxe's voice rose a bit, and Kasai shifted. They waited a moment, but he didn't wake up. "Brinar suggested we try to kidnap him or something, but we didn't think he'd take that too well."

North nodded reluctantly. "Yea, that would've made things worse. And put a target on our backs from Ironwood."

Oxe watched Kasai for a moment, sadness etched on his face.

"How's he been?" North asked after a bit.

Oxe shrugged. "He's...difficult. Doesn't interact with much of the crew. Feluna and Velu mostly, and Ironwood trails after him sometimes." He caught North's amused look and shoved him a bit. "Not like that! But I think Kasai's been resisting him for a while and Ironwood doesn't like that."

North nodded. "I can see that. When they...attacked my crew a while ago, Kasai wasn't too keen on attacking us."

"He *attacked* you?" Oxe hadn't heard it was North's crew they had attacked. Only that Kasai had let out an incredible power and Ironwood destroyed the ship afterwards.

North shook his head sadly. "I couldn't believe it at first. At first, we thought it was Ironwood heading towards us, but then an arrow made of fire took out our sails. We were hoping to talk, but then attacked."

Oxe looked at Kasai, wondering what had made him attack North. Maybe he had been forced?

"I won't lie, Oxe-" North stopped as Oxe waved his hand.

"Tamotsu. Don't use my real name on this ship." Oxe glared at him, fangs bared slightly.

North nodded in understanding. "Sorry. But I hit him. I just couldn't believe he had attacked us. I just reacted."

Oxe gave him a sympathetic look.

"But then...I don't know how he did it, but there was this wall of flame and he told us to leave. Said Ironwood would make him kill us. But he held off me and Arat alone." North let out a breath. "I've never seen him so powerful, but he was terrified at the end. He only attacked because he had to."

Oxe glanced over at Kasai. "He doesn't hurt people needlessly. He tries to keep from killing them if he can." He was quiet for a moment. The ship creaked, rolling as it turned. "But he's harsh."

"Harsh?" North sounded confused.

"He gets angry, loses control occasionally. Not with his powers, but his temper. He seems...not happier, but more...I don't know. Relaxed? Calmer? At ease down here." Pain crept into Oxe's voice. "I think he's afraid to interact with people now."

North watched Kasai for a moment. "That's no surprise there. The kid's a bad luck magnet." He leaned back. "How much does he talk to you? Considering...well, you know."

Oxe shrugged a bit. "Bits and pieces. He's quiet a lot, but at night sometimes he talks in his sleep."

North snorted. "Somehow, I expected that."

"Do you know about his arm?" It still made Oxe sick to think about it.

North nodded. "Yea. I noticed that, but never had a chance to ask. But it happens sometimes." He held out his hand and pressed against his wrist.

Oxe couldn't hide his shock when his left hand came off.

"I was younger than him when it happened. That's why I always wore a glove on this hand before. But this is newer, I have better control, and it's nearly undetectable." North seemed amused by Oxe's reaction.

There was a murmur from Kasai's cot, but he didn't wake.

Oxe watched him for a moment, then glanced at North. "We have Linota here."

North relaxed. "I'm glad she's alive."

"She's chained in the hold." Oxe flinched back as North growled. "She's too unstable. Ironwood doesn't trust her with the others yet."

"But *chained?!*" North hissed hotly.

Oxe glanced at the manacles still around North's wrist. No wonder he was so angry. "For now. She can move around though, and has a bed. It's just by her ankle."

North looked like he wanted to rush out and free her.

"She still isn't human when she shifts." Oxe spoke quickly.

North looked at him, his eyes nearly blazing. "Still?!"

Oxe nodded. "I've been helping her. I meant to tell Feluna that Linota wants to come above deck sometime, at least for a while, but then Arat..."

North nodded, looking at the ceiling. "Ironwood's a monster."

Oxe shifted an ear, flicking it towards Kasai; he was quiet, but Oxe wasn't sure if he was asleep or not. He nudged North, nodding towards Kasai.

North nodded. "I'll find a hammock with the rest of the crew. I'll try to come talk to Kasai when I can. Just...take care of him, okay?"

Oxe nodded and watched him leave, then sighed and curled up on his cot.

Chapter 20

Kasai

KASAI LOOKED UP FROM the book in his hands as he heard Geralf's voice. "Captain, we should head back east for a while."

The black-haired man, the first mate now, had been in town until a few moments ago. He held a large bulging pouch; Kasai could hear a faint clinking noise as the coins shifted with the movement.

Thukuli glanced at the rest of the crew on the dock; most had taken the chance to come onto land, even if they didn't go into town. His eyes landed on North and Kasai, sitting together on a barrel, and he shrugged. "Fine with me. Too many Seaborne here as it is."

Kasai sighed, flipping a page over.

"Is this mostly what you do?" North asked.

Kasai shrugged. "Usually. They sell the goods, I sit and read."

North snorted. "You haven't changed, have you?"

Kasai frowned but didn't respond. He knew North was sort of teasing, but it still stung.

"Kasai, North, get aboard." Thukuli walked over. "Here's your share." He handed Kasai a bag, but not North. "North, this outing's share is being withheld to repay the treatment we tried to give your friend."

North hung his head; Kasai gave a sympathetic look. Arat had only lasted two more days, then died from his sickness. Even a month later, it still hit North pretty hard.

Thukuli took a few steps towards the ship, but stopped and turned back to them for a moment. "North, you'll be the navigator for a while. You're...ability is far better than our current navigators skill."

North nodded and headed aboard. Kasai followed, but was stopped by Thukuli.

The captain's gaze bore into his. "I want you above deck for a while. Help with some duties for once." There was a dark bite to his voice.

Kasai nodded, tucking his book in his bag. He knew Thukuli wasn't pleased with his friendliness with North, but what did he expect? That Kasai would treat him like an enemy? "What duties?"

Thukuli appraised Kasai silently, then grinned. "Bowsprit, clean the barnacles off."

Kasai resisted the urge to growl. It was difficult getting down there, and back up, and dangerous to do while the ship was ripping through the waves. After a second, he gave a single nod and headed aboard, grabbing the bucket and scrapper before lowering himself over the side.

Velu's surprise was evident when Kasai joined him in the bowsprit netting. "What are you doing here?"

Kasai held up the bucket, grimacing. "Barnacle duty."

Velu gave a short bark of laughter. "Same, but I'm port side. Get started. Let me know if you need help."

Kasai set to work, the scrapper easily popping off the little creatures with a bit of force. After a while, he found that sending out some heat made it easier.

He started when Velu joined him; they held tight to the rope as the ship turned, picking up speed, sending up large splashes of saltwater in their faces. He resisted a groan as he thought about his book getting wet. The bag was waterproof, but still.

Velu swung himself to Kasai's other side. "Sorry. I finished pretty quickly, so I thought I'd help."

Kasai grunted as he unstuck a large barnacle. "It's alright. I think I've got it though."

Velu clung to the ropes as Kasai worked in silence for a bit, then glanced up. "So you're still in trouble." Not a question, just a fact.

Kasai grunted in response.

"I think it's unwarranted this time." Velu said.

"Like it hasn't been before?" Kasai retorted.

The ship turned again; the wood creaked. Another wave came up, threatening to drag them into the sea.

Velu chuckled. "I'm just sayin', you push his buttons sometimes."

Kasai snorted, trying not to laugh. "Not my fault it's so easy."

Velu laughed this time. "Yeah, I don't know why it's that way, but I have to admit, it's almost funny sometimes."

"Yea. Real funny." There was a shout on deck, but Kasai didn't look up. "Especially when he all but acts on his threats."

There was a deep *boom* and they started as a cannonball splashed into the water not five feet away.

They shot up the ropes hanging over the ship's side, Kasai much slower than Velu, and were met by Kelin. "Seaborne ship. Get to your stations." He didn't stop to ask why Kasai was grimacing, just ordered them about.

Velu shot off into the rigging, Kasai limped to the quarterdeck.

"Hurt your leg again?" Thukuli asked as Kasai limped up to him.

"You try climbing up the ropes quickly with a bad leg." Kasai knew it was a bad idea to snap, but his leg was smarting. He hadn't moved that quickly in a good while, and he wished he had taken his time.

Thukuli glowered at him for a moment, but brought the teleglass back to his eye. "North, where's the nearest island?"

Kasai glanced to where the teleglass was pointed and spotted a Seaborne ship heading towards them; there was a puff of smoke and the water sent up a plume of water as it landed close to their starboard side.

North didn't hesitate. "At least 60 miles out. It might take us an hour to reach it though. They're chasing us into a tailwind."

He may not like being on Thukuli's crew, but Kasai knew he would do anything to avoid being caught again. And while the tailwind would help them, the Seaborne ship had more sails to catch it.

Thukuli cursed. "Gunners, man the stern chaser, fire if they get within distance."

"They're already within distance, Captain." Kasai said. "That cannonball was only five feet from hitting me and Velu."

Thukuli let out a snarl, turning to the crew below the quarterdeck. "All hands to stations, shift the sails, catch as much of that blasted tailwind as you can, but keep us moving."

People scrambled about, racing up the rigging or running to ropes along the mast.

"Kasai, get below. Fire up the engine." Thukuli ordered.

Kasai nodded, limping down the steps. "Tamotsu, help me with it."

Tamotsu, his hands on the halyard, let go and raced over; behind him, someone grabbed it and pulled.

Kasai nearly fell down the steps going below and stumbled into his bunk. "Get the engine started. I'll check the charge." He was too focused on getting the engine working right now to feel the pain coursing through his leg.

Tamotsu nodded, flicking some switches along the casing at the bottom.

Kasai glanced at the three energy readings; steady, steady, and flickering. He cursed, grabbed his cane, and raced outside for a moment. He called up to Thukuli, who was waiting for him, "Two steady, one flickering."

Thukuli snarled, turning to face the approaching ship. "Fine. Get it running as long as you can."

Kasai shot back down, crashing against the wall as the ship turned. He ignored the pain in his shoulder and raced to the engine. It was quietly humming already.

"What do you need me to do?" Tamotsu asked.

Kasai glanced over at the engine. "Stay here. I won't be able to watch this alone, and I'll need a messenger."

Tamotsu nodded, then looked concerned as Kasai crashed against the wall. The ship had taken another sharp turn; they heard a splash as a cannonball missed the ship. Tamotsu took a step towards him, but stopped at Kasai's expression.

Kasai waved him off. "I'm alright, my legs just acting up again."

They listened to the sounds of running feet, a scream from someone falling from the rigging, more cannonballs landing on both sides of the ship.

There was a sharp burning smell leaking under the door. Something was on fire.

Kasai hissed through his teeth as he was slammed against the wall again; the ship had taken a sharp enough turn that they could feel it beginning to keel over.

Tamotsu leaped to his side, wrapped an arm around Kasai tightly, and braced himself between Kasai and the wall.

Kasai felt himself flush, but didn't tell the other man to let go. For one, the ship was still leaning and slowly righting itself, so there was still a chance Kasai could fall.

And something about the touch felt...comfortable. Familiar.

Kasai felt awkward suddenly. He didn't like this. He didn't *not* like it, but he didn't like it either. He was Oxe's mate, and wanted no one else.

But he couldn't ignore how warm Tamotsu's arm was.

Tamotsu didn't relax his grip as the ship began turning again.

The engine sputtered briefly as the first charge emptied, but began running smoothly again as it pulled from the second.

Tamotsu froze; he didn't seem to have realized he was holding Kasai until now. He let go as soon as the ship was righted. "Sorry!"

Kasai knew his face was red, as was Tamotsu's, but he shook his head. "It's alright. You probably saved me from a bruised shoulder."

Another cannonball sounded; there was a splintering sound from above.

Another scream, more than one it sounded like, sounded from above.

Tamotsu glanced at the door, at Kasai, flicking his gaze between them nervously.

There was another scream. The two men exchanged uneasy glances, but no one came through the door.

Kasai braced himself against the wall, kneeling to give his leg a break.

"How did you hurt your leg?" Tamotsu asked quietly.

Kasai glanced at him briefly, then looked back at the engine. "A few years ago I got struck by lightning. It...did some damage that didn't quite heal."

Tamotsu's widened.

Kasai shrugged. "I never told my...friends. They were worried enough." He had never told Oxe, or even Brinar, how much it still hurt even months afterwards. If they had known, they would've been concerned and possibly angry with him for keeping it from them.

Kasai resisted a snort. Knowing Brinar, he would've forced Kasai to wear a brace...*after* chewing him out.

"Why? Maybe they would have understood." Tamotsu said.

Another crash, more splintering. The ship rolled heavily again.

Kasai braced himself against the engine, unable to feel the heat he knew it was emitting. Tamotsu was crouched by the opposite wall now.

Kasai shook his head. "Brinar...might have. He was my doctor. But...not..." He swallowed. "Not my mate."

Tamotsu regarded him quietly. "You have a...mate?"

Kasai nodded. "Had."

He heard the pain in Tamotsu's voice. "Where is he?"

Kasai didn't want to say it. He shook his head, wiping away a tear.

There was a tremendous crash, sending the entire ship shuddering. The door burst open and Feluna barged in. "Both of you. Out. The ships sinking."

They didn't hesitate, their conversation forgotten for the moment. Kasai headed straight for the hold, not listening to Feluna's shout behind him. He knew no one would save Linota, not unless they were already there. And he knew she was alone.

Linota was an animal, her eyes wide and frightened. The chain around her ankle clanked as she tugged it. She gave a plaintive whine as he approached.

Kasai didn't hesitate, he grabbed the chain and burned through it. "Follow me!"

She raced at his side as he ran up the steps, bursting out through the broken door onto the deck. He stumbled heavily, nearly falling to his knees, but Linota caught him and let him lean on her.

Around them were bodies. Blood. No one was moving.

Tamotsu waited nearby, his eyes wide. "We have a lifeboat. Come on."

Kasai nodded, but hesitated when they reached it. "What about Linota?"

"Can she shift back?" Feluna called to him.

Cannon fire, falling and crashing wood, flames. The sounds were becoming deafening.

In the boat, there were very few people. Thukuli. Feluna. Velu. Kelin. North. Two others Kasai weren't familiar with. But there was little room.

"I don't think so." Kasai glanced down at Linota, who was huddled against his legs. His heart ached as he took in her form; a pale grey colf, nearly identical to Vrai except for the extra legs, who had died years ago. He would've saved Linota anyway, but this made it harder yet better.

He remembered how to handle a colf.

Thukuli snarled. "Make her or leave her. Get in."

Kasai flinched as a burning spar nearly hit him. He jumped in and held his hand out to Linota, still cowering on deck. "Come on. Even if you can't be human, you can still get away."

She flashed the whites of her eyes, but leaped into the boat.

Kasai gasped as she knocked the wind from his lungs, wrapping his arms around her.

North watched the burning ship with a grim expression. "We have to go. Now. I can get us to the island, but if we don't go now, we'll either die or get caught."

Thukuli nodded and slashed at the ropes holding the lifeboat to the davit.

Tamotsu held onto Kasai and Linota as they dropped into the water, keeping them from being knocked overboard.

Thukuli gave them a dark look, making Kasai shudder, but quickly grabbed an oar. "Everyone helps. Now get rowing."

Kasai glanced at the ship, a mixture of regret yet relief as it suddenly cracked in two and began to sink.

But he froze when he heard a scream echo across the water. "KASAI!"

If he didn't know better, he could've sworn it was his brother.

KASAI STARED INTO THE fire, stressed enough to not worry about passing out. Beside him, Linota whined, her paws twitching in her sleep. Except for the extra pair of front legs, she looked exactly like Vrai, especially with her fur having fluffed out.

He kept a hand on her fur, giving her comfort and taking it as well.

There was the sound of shifting sand and Thukuli dropped next to him. "Those bastards will pay for destroying my ship *and* my crew."

Kasai said nothing.

"What happened with the engine?" Thukuli shot at him.

"It worked fine, but they must've had their own engine going," Kasai said. It wasn't the first time Thukuli had asked, but Kasai didn't have a different answer, no matter how often he heard the question.

Thukuli snarled and picked up a branch sitting nearby. He flung it into the dark. "I'll make them pay for that," he repeated.

There was a soft crackle from the fire in the silence that followed.

Some kind of animal cry came from the forest behind them.

"Why did you not leave her like I said?" Thukuli growled quietly, sending a dark look at Linota.

"It would've been cruel to leave her chained up like that while the ship was sinking." Kasai said evenly.

Thukuli snorted. "So? As useful as she could've been as a human, she's just an animal."

Kasai swallowed his growl. "But she has been useful. And combined with Tamotsu's hunting ability, we haven't gone hungry yet."

Thukuli sighed, leaning back into the sand. "You've got a point there."

A breeze made the flames waver briefly, but Kasai made them stay within the stones.

"Tomorrow we're moving on. There's got to be someone on this island." Thukuli twitched his hand and a small strand of ivy came poking through the sand, snaking around his wrist.

Kasai gazed out over the waves further ahead on the beach. He knew the fire was well above the tide-line, but he still got a little nervous when the waves crept higher.

He glanced over when Thukuli stood up, brushing the sand off his pants. "Wake Feluna in an hour. She'll be on watch til morning."

Kasai nodded and watched the flames while the captain returned to where the others had set up makeshift beds and a shelter.

He laid his hand on Linota's head and rubbed her ears; an unconscious action he had developed with Oxe.

She woke with a small whine, flicking her tail.

"I'm alright. Just..." Kasai sighed.

She nudged his hand. She hadn't been able to shift back in the five days they had been here, and Tamotsu was getting a little worried it might be permanent. Kasai didn't ask why he thought that, but Linota didn't seem unhappy like this.

He gave a small smile, giving her ear a scratch. "Just tired."

She huffed. She may be an animal right now, and not with a human mind like she should, but she showed more intelligence than a true animal would have.

"I just wish I knew what to do is all." He said the words quietly, not wanting them to reach the others.

Linota whined quietly, cocking her head. He guessed she was asking what he meant.

"I can't leave the crew, or Thukuli will hunt me down." Kasai knew he would. Thukuli had been holding Kasai's life by a chain for almost a year, more than he had before that. "I want to find...find my friends, go home."

She flattened her ears and licked his hand. She shifted around, laying her head on Kasai's lap.

He absentmindedly scratched her as he watched the flames. "I had a mate before...all this."

She looked up at him expectantly.

"I don't think he's around anymore and...as painful as that is, I don't want to be a pyrate any longer." His voice caught in his throat.

A log fell with a loud crackling noise, sending up a shower of sparks and ash.

Kasai watched as one burning ember landed on the sand, being snuffed out almost immediately. "I know someone I might be able to turn to, but I'm afraid he'll reject me."

Linota wrapped her tail around Kasai, a curious growl rumbling in her throat.

"No, I'm not sure where he is exactly. But...I don't want to tell Thukuli because I don't want to lead him there," Kasai explained. "I mean, it would difficult to hurt his home, but I don't want to risk it."

Linota blinked, sympathetic. She laid a paw on Kasai's leg, removing it when he flinched.

"Sorry. It still hurts." He had left his cane on the ship, not thinking to grab it during the escape.

"Then go rest." Kasai and Linota jumped as Feluna appeared in the firelight. "Sorry. I woke up a few minutes ago and thought I'd relieve you early."

Kasai nodded. "That's fine, but I'm not sleeping tonight. Mind if I stay here?"

She shrugged, sitting down on the other side of Linota. "Still not human?" She asked her.

Linota whined, flicking her tail.

Feluna shook her head. "Just asking." She gave Kasai a sideways glance. "Anything to report?"

Kasai shrugged. "No. It's nearly midnight, the sea is calm, and there's no weather to speak of yet. It's still pretty warm here, but can't figure out why."

It was strange. The sea, the sand, the air, it was much warmer than a northern island should be. Even North wasn't sure why; he had never been to this island before. He didn't recognize it from any maps and had never heard of this island being here before.

He knew they were only a month or two away from Brimna Atoll though, if they could find a ship.

Feluna looked at Linota while she spoke to Kasai. "Tamotsu's offered to help you around if you need it, at least until we can find something to use as a cane."

Kasai nodded, expecting that. "Captain says we'll be heading on in the morning. He wants to figure out where we are, see if we can't get a ship out of here."

She nodded. "Makes sense. Will you be alright walking around then?"

"I should be fine," Kasai shrugged.

Linota yipped, nudging Kasai's empty right side.

"If you try to replace that, you know he'll consider your debt unpaid." Feluna said quietly.

Kasai nodded. "I figured, but I won't replace it through him again. If we can get to Brimna Atoll, I'll ask Cifius for help." He gripped his right shoulder tightly. The scar burned under his touch.

His arm had fallen off on the way here, dropping into the water before anyone could catch it.

Tamotsu had looked sick; Kasai had thought he was used it by now.

They watched the fire for a while in silence.

The water glinted as dawn broke, and Kasai sighed. "Do you think I'll ever be free of Thukuli?"

Feluna frowned at him. "No. Not really. But if you can find somewhere he couldn't reach, maybe you could escape."

Linota opened one eye, her ear flicking.

"Do you know where you could go?" Feluna didn't seem that confident in his ability to get away despite her words.

Kasai nodded. "Yea. My mate's family..."

Feluna looked at him sharply. "Mate? You have a partner?" Her gaze flicked over to the shelter then back.

Kasai nodded, shutting his eyes. "Had."

Feluna exchanged a glance with Linota as Kasai stood.

Linota whined, standing.

Kasai shook his head. "Just...stay here, okay?" But as he walked away, he felt their eyes on him.

Chapter 21

Oxe

OXE GAVE KASAI A SYMPATHETIC smile as the other man groaned, sinking to the bench.

They stood among the ruins of a crumbling village. Long abandoned houses in various states of decay, rotten stalls from a marketplace, tattered cloth hung from doorways and on poles along the stalls.

An old well, with stagnant water and a broken bucket, stood nearby. The frames of a long-since-rotted roof loomed over it. North had already checked the water, but didn't think it was safe to drink.

Ironwood raged at the decrepit docks at the edge of town. No boats, no ships, just the remains of an old rowboat and some ratty sails. When he had seen the old frame, the area erupted into a tangled mess of ivy and thorns, too dangerous for the rest of them to stick around, so the couple people that had gone with him came back to the village's center.

"Tamotsu, come help us search some houses for anything we can use," Feluna called out. Velu stood at her side, his expression unreadable.

Oxe ignored the stab of unease he felt, looked at Kasai. "Will you be alright?"

Kasai nodded, a tad annoyed. "I'm not alone here, Tamotsu. Don't worry about me."

Oxe heard North's snort and ignored the older man's grin, and walked over to Velu and Feluna. "Where are we checking?" He knew the nearby homes had been checked, but not more than the first ring around the well.

Feluna just jerked her head for him to follow, leaving him between her and Velu.

Oxe suppressed a sigh and followed her without complaint.

They rounded on him when they were well out of earshot of the others.

"Who the hell are you?!" Feluna's face twisted into rage as she glared.

Oxe rubbed his arm self-consciously. "I'm not sure how to explain."

Velu didn't seem as angry, just greatly annoyed. "You said before that Kasai saved your life."

Oxe nodded, leaning against the wall. "I was...injured. Badly."

"How badly?" Feluna asked.

"I nearly died," Oxe said. "I had a bad wound for months. It wouldn't heal." He didn't bother explaining why, or how, he had it. "Kasai saw me in a cage and rescued me, nursed me back to health."

Feluna nodded slowly, looking more curious now.

"But that doesn't explain your protectiveness." Velu stated.

Oxe made a sheepish face. "I'm his mate."

They both stared at him for a moment, then Feluna laughed. "I knew it! I knew there was something you weren't telling us!"

Maybe more than something, but Oxe stayed quiet.

Velu's eyes were wide. "Why doesn't he know about you yet?"

Oxe shrugged, his face twisted with sadness. "I don't want Ironwood finding out."

Feluna stopped chuckling, her face suddenly grim, and exchanged a look with Velu. "He can't find out. Ever."

"If he does, he'll kill you. He won't even hesitate." Velu added.

Oxe nodded in agreement. "I figured."

Velu's gaze was sympathetic. "This must be hard for you then."

"I'm glad I assigned you to watch him then," Feluna said dryly. "I doubt anyone could watch him better."

Oxe gave a short bark of laughter. "That's what North said."

"Does he know who you are?" Velu asked.

Oxe nodded. "Yes. He recognized me when we brought him and Arat aboard. I think Arat had trouble because he was sick."

Feluna grimaced. "I'm surprised he could even sit up that one time."

Oxe sighed. "I got...I don't know how to say it, but I got some kind of disguise that is supposed to wear off after some months, but I don't know how much I've changed back yet."

Velu glanced around, then suddenly reached for something gleaming in the rubble. Oxe was surprised to see a mirror shard in his hands. Velu handed it to him after wiping it off with his shirt edge. "Not very clean, but maybe this will help."

Oxe's hand trembled at first, but then he caught his reflection. It wasn't often he looked at himself, but he had seen himself in clear streams at home, and a few mirrors since meeting Kasai. But the face in the mirror hardly looked different.

Aside from the thin beard that was growing, he looked more or less like himself.

"Is it wearing off?" Feluna asked when Oxe hadn't moved for several moments.

Oxe nodded, setting the shard down carefully. "Yes. It's almost gone. My face is...hardly different. If Kasai isn't wondering about me now, he will soon." It had been a little over six months now though. Oxe thought he would be lucky if this lasted another month at most.

"Would Kasai act different if he knew who you were?" Velu asked after a moment.

Oxe shrugged. "I don't know. He's not the same man I knew. Some things, yes, but enough is changed that I don't know how he'll react. He thinks I'm dead."

The other two exchanged alarmed looks.

Oxe held his hands up. "He burned me back in Brimna Atoll, but I don't think he wanted to."

Feluna nodded. "I remember that. I didn't know it was you. How could I? But I remember when Sibra died, the people there said someone who could turn into an animal did it."

Velu tilted his head, thinking. "But wouldn't it help him if he knew you were alive?"

Oxe didn't have an answer for that.

They turned as North appeared. "Come on, Ironwood wants us to move on."

Velu grabbed North before he could disappear around the corner. "Wait. We know about...Tamotsu."

North shot Oxe a look, who nodded. "When are you telling Kasai?"

Oxe shrugged in response, his throat tight.

"It's too dangerous. If Thukuli learns who he is, he'll kill him." Feluna told him. "He doesn't like being tricked, or especially lied to."

North took a deep breath. "Alright. I can understand that. And there's no telling how Kasai will react either."

"How do *you* think he'll react?" Velu asked him.

North looked at Oxe thoughtfully. "It's hard to say. Kasai's really changed. I remember when it came out that he and Oxe loved each other."

Oxe closed his eyes, the other two listening intently.

"Kasai...he wasn't a happy-go-lucky person before all this, but he was happier at least. Liked to hang around a few others, played music, badly," North gave a bitter chuckle at that, but it died in his throat. "But he was never...hard." He looked at Oxe. "But he was like...well, a lighthouse, after Oxe got hurt."

"A lighthouse?" Feluna asked.

Oxe was a little confused by this. But he also hadn't seen Kasai during the time he was in a coma.

"I can only describe him as a lighthouse without a light," North explained. "He was there, he used his powers, spent time with another crewmate at the time, was fine with raiding merchants with us, but there was something missing. Sonus talked to me shortly before Oxe got hurt."

Oxe pricked his ears at this.

"He said something had sparked in Kasai, and he thought it was Oxe." He gave Oxe a small smile at this. "Said that Kasai finally had someone that he could connect to, help him through...well, everything he had gone through before. Now, Kasai's like the ruins of a lighthouse."

Velu gave Oxe a curious look.

"I told Kasai that he probably hadn't killed you," North said to Oxe, "but I think we need to wait to tell him. We need to make sure he's more..." He trailed off, looking unsure of how to finish his sentence.

"Stable." Feluna said. "The word you need here is stable. Kasai's sort of a time bomb lately. Something like this could set him off, though I'm not sure how, and the aftermath would be too much right now."

Oxe was reluctant to agree with her, but he felt he had to. "Maybe if we can get to Brimna Atoll."

North shook his head. "We'll just have to keep an eye on him, and if the time seems right, just go for it."

Oxe gave him a nervous look, not sure if that should be left to him.

"THIS EXPLAINS THE WARMER air," Kelin remarked.

Oxe felt Kasai falter and helped him sit on the raised stone edge of the hot springs.

He glanced at Kasai with a worried look. Kasai wasn't one to ask for help, so it was strange when Kasai asked Oxe to help him walk today. His eyes were closed; his left arm wrapped around his chest. He was breathing somewhat heavily, his skin damp with a sheen of sweat.

Thukuli gave them a dark look, but turned to Kelin. "It does. But it's no help in finding a way off this island."

North was walking around, looking at a few huts nearby, trying to see if there was anything of use.

Feluna and Velu were with the other two crewmembers, exploring the edges for edible plants or anything of interest.

Linota was sniffing around the edges of the stone walls, her tail swishing slowly.

"Kelin, anything of interest here, you think?" Thukuli asked.

Kelin shook his head. "No idea, sir. I've never heard of an island with hot springs before."

"That's no surprise." Everyone turned to North as he spoke up. "There's only a few of them as it is. There's three in the Northern Waters, one in the Eastern Region, and another in the Western Seas."

Thukuli's lip twitched. "So do you have an idea where we are?"

North shook his head. "No. I've never heard of an island with natural hot springs. The others are all manmade or enhanced somehow. These are natural, with only that stone wall added to fortify it."

Linota started whining, nudging Kasai. Oxe gave her a strange look, letting out a strange growl at her. She turned to him, her ears flat against her head.

He let his ear shift, the one not facing Kasai, and twitched it.

Linota let out a whine and he felt his hackles raise.

"Is everything alright?" Kasai looked up at him.

Oxe gave a terse nod. "Stay here." He followed Linota into the tree line and immediately huffed, his jaw shifting, his teeth bared in a snarl.

There was a long-dead body here. A man, or an older boy, dead for a few years at least. Probably when the village was destroyed. Linota gave him a harsh growl and he snarled back, understanding what she was asking.

But he couldn't do a full shift here. Not now.

Linota whined, flashing the whites of her eyes in submission.

Instead, he walked around the small area, looking at the body, the ground, anything that might give him an idea of what happened. It might've been years, but he could at least try to learn something.

He inhaled deeply, trying not to gag on the strange scent of decay that still hung here. He had never heard of that kind of smell lasting this long, but maybe there was something in the soil here.

There was the scent of decay, of course, and the trails of small animals and insects. A floral scent of some nearby flowers touched his nose, and the acrid smell of the hot springs almost made him sick when he took a large breath again.

But there was something underneath it all.

Oxe knelt, sinking his claws into soil, and breathed deeply again. A musk, not unlike mushrooms, but meaty. And alive. A creature, a carnivore? Or an omnivore? His tail swished behind him slowly, sending up a cloud of the scent from behind him. His ears shifted and he caught the sounds of birds, people talking at the springs. Little stirrings among the underbrush.

Linota yapped, catching his attention. She whined and looked at the body.

Oxe took a step closer, then noticed the marks along the bones. Something had eaten part of it, maybe when it was fresh, or not long dead. But nothing recent. But as he glanced around the body, something gleaming in the grass caught his eye.

He used a stick to move the fetid grass out of the way, then nudge the open bag towards him. Using the tips of his claws, he upended the bag and poured out the few items inside.

A handful of pistol casings, old fashioned ones that were used with ash-powder guns. A broken compass, the glass shattered and turned to crystal dust. A badge, a key, and a broken ash-powdered pistol cap.

There were footsteps, and he turned to see Ironwood glaring at him.

"What are you doing over here?" The captain asked, his voice low. Dangerous. Anger, suspicion, they rolled off him in waves.

Oxe stepped to the side, out of Ironwood's view, hiding his nervousness. "Linota found this and showed me. Since I'm a shifter, she thought I could make sense of this."

Ironwood didn't look at the body. His glare pinned Oxe to the spot. "What's your deal with Kasai?"

Oxe flicked an ear back.

Ironwood took a threatening step forward. "You've been hanging around him an awful lot since we got here."

"Because that's my job," Oxe stated. "That Feluna gave to me." He didn't bother to hide his confusion.

A tendril of ivy snaked up Oxe's leg, catching him by surprising and wrapping around his body. Ironwood's fingers were twitching. "No. There's something else."

Oxe tried to suppress the whine building in his throat. Behind him, Linota snarled, but he glimpsed the vines holding her down from the corner of his eye. "I swear, that's all it is."

Ironwood stepped up to him; the captain was shorter than Oxe, but not by much. "I'm not sure if I believe you...Tamotsu."

Oxe whined in pain as the ivy tightened, creeping towards his neck.

Linota snarled, attacking the vines around her legs.

"I did some digging about Kasai on our last visit to Brimna Atoll. Kasai didn't just sail with Lightning, he also had a partner. Apparently put the crew in danger because of him a few times." Ironwood growled. "And after Kasai killed Lightning, he went missing."

Oxe gritted his fangs as a sharp thorn dug into his neck.

"But then, I heard rumors of some kind of savage man running with Fatal's crew. Every time they were seen on Verideys, there would be questions about Kasai's whereabouts." Ironwood circled him slowly. His hand motioned down and Oxe fell to his knees, the vines digging into his body. "Then, closing in on a year ago now, Kasai runs into a strange man in Sedgeliss. And that same man appeared in Brimna Atoll months later. In the company of a young girl from my crew."

Oxe was forced to look up at Ironwood as a thorn pressed against his throat.

"And the strangest thing was," Ironwood paused, standing in front of Oxe again, "he could change into the same creature I saw in Sedgeliss."

"That wasn't me," Oxe bluffed. He refused to show how terrified he was right now. "I can't shift like that." He didn't move his gaze from Ironwood.

Linota desperately snapped at a vine trying to wrap around her muzzle.

Ironwood flicked Oxe on the nose, making him yelp. "Awful big coincidence. And then Kelin told me something strange."

Oxe felt a cold chill go down his spine.

"That man that Kasai had a problem with? The old dude with the glasses? His name wasn't Eaden." Ironwood's voice darkened, his eyes glittering. "That was Brinar. The famous doctor from the mysterious Witch Island. The doctor for Lightning's crew for years. *And you had been seen with him!*" His hand spasmed.

Oxe let out a gasp as the thorn shot up, skimming his neck, barely missing the jugular. A bead of blood slowly dripped along his skin.

"If I find out you're lying..." Ironwood snarled, "there won't be anything left of you for him to mourn."

He flicked his hand and the ivy tendrils retreated into the soil quicker than they had come. He stalked off without another word, leaving Oxe and Linota gasping and whining in pain.

Chapter 22

Kasai

THERE WAS A MOMENT of worry when Thukuli disappeared after Tamotsu, but it wasn't too long before he was back, looking angry.

He stalked to the center of the clearing. "Alright, we're moving on from here. Kasai, get up and walk on your own for a bit."

Kasai nodded, trying to ignore the heaviness in his chest and the surrounding air. It was too hot here. This wasn't his heat, which he was accustomed to. This was muggy, a little like crossing the Expanse but thicker.

Everyone watched as Thukuli stalked down the path, no one daring to say a word.

North came over and helped Kasai up, but walked at his side. "Are you alright?"

Kasai nodded. "Just hot. This is sort of like the Expanse, but worse."

"I remember you didn't take that too well." North grinned grimly.

Kasai shook his head, giving him a push. "Oh please. You know it wasn't the heat that made the crossing bad."

They joked, but he knew North remembered him nearly dying, and a fair few of the crew not making it, and most everyone else getting sick, including North himself.

Kasai stopped after a moment, looking around. "Where's Linota and Tamotsu?" He hadn't seen them since Tamotsu had followed her into the trees.

North looked behind them uneasily. "Can you walk on your own for a bit? I'll find them and catch up."

Kasai nodded, though he didn't feel too confident, and watched North lope back a bit, disappearing into the trees. He waited a moment, then walked after the rest of the crew.

He tried not to breathe through his nose; that just made it worse. The path was smooth, with very few bumps despite not having been used for years. He saw the telltale marks of a cart or wagon occasionally, but they were old. He got the feeling they were originally much deeper, but time had smoothed them out.

Small flowers dotted the border to the forest on their left, in various shades of white, cream, ivory, and pale pinks and purples. On the right, smaller hot springs, none big enough for a person, dotted the surface and Kasai saw they stretched up the steep mountainside. They poured into the next lowest pool, fed by some higher and unseen source, until they reached the bottom. Kasai didn't see where they let out, but it was mildly interesting.

He didn't react when he noticed Thukuli walking next to him.

"Missing Tamotsu?" There was a sneer embedded in voice.

Kasai didn't rise to the bait. "Just admiring the springs."

Thukuli glanced at him but they kept walking in silence for a while.

Kasai saw North pass him, Linota and Tamotsu at his heels. He frowned as he took in the tense air around them. "I wonder if they found something."

Thukuli snorted. "Who knows? If they aren't telling me, then probably not."

Kasai cast a sharp glance at the captain, hearing the scorn but also the threat in his tone.

"I wanted to let you know that when we find a way off this island, we're heading back to Brimna Atoll," Thukuli said.

Great. "How long will we stay?" Maybe Brinar was still there. Part of him wanted to talk to him, but he was still afraid the old doctor hated him. He wanted to believe what Feluna had said once, that Brinar *couldn't* hate someone, but she didn't know what Kasai had done to him. He felt himself caught between hope and fear when it came to Brinar currently.

Thukuli shrugged, stopping for a moment to pull a flower up. "Not sure. We need a good ship, and a crew, so maybe a month or more. Depends on how long it takes." He crushed the flower in his fist.

Kasai raised an eyebrow, but stayed silent.

"But I wanted to talk to you about Tamotsu." Kasai didn't expect this from Thukuli. "You're always around him. North too, but I can understand why with him. Being old crewmates and all." His voice became a tad scornful, but Kasai gritted his teeth and ignored that. "But with Tamotsu...you have no prior connection with him, right?"

Kasai nodded, keeping his gaze on the path ahead. "I'd never met him before he joined the crew."

"Even though he knew Brinar?" Thukuli taunted.

Kasai stopped, glaring at Thukuli. "What are you talking about?"

Thukuli was grinning. "He knew your old friend Brinar before he joined the crew. Kelin saw them together multiple times while he was there."

Kasai hid his shock. "So? Brinar tried to join the crew. Tamotsu had been in Brimna Atoll for a few months. They probably met while they were both there, maybe stayed at the same inn."

Thukuli's grin disappeared. "Maybe. But why do you spend so much time with him? And don't give me that crap about 'Feluna told him to watch me.'"

They had stopped in the middle of the path; none of the others had noticed they stopped.

"It's mainly that, but he's the only one besides her and Velu that's *wanted* to stay around." Kasai shut his jaws with an audible *snap*. If he said anything more, he would say something that would give Thukuli some kind of ammunition. And he didn't want to put a target on Tamotsu's back.

Thukuli frowned darkly. "Don't trust him." The captain turned and stalked off quickly, leaving Kasai behind.

Kasai stared after him, but followed a moment later. What had he meant? Or was he jealous? Kasai shook his head. Thukuli had shown interest him at the beginning and Kasai had turned him down. And he had been spending a lot of time with Tamotsu, but he didn't like him like that. He followed as quickly as he could, wondering what Thukuli had meant.

"HERE." KASAI GLANCED up at the cup in front of him. Tamotsu sat down when Kasai took it. "Feeling any better?"

They had walked past the rest of the hot springs and the air had grown cooler.

"Yea, thanks. I just couldn't take that heat." Kasai sipped the water and made a face. It tasted of musty stone.

Tamotsu gave a sheepish shrug. "Sorry. There's another well here, but the waters barely good enough to drink."

Kasai made another face but downed the cup. "What had you found the other day?" He wanted to question Tamotsu about the wound on his neck, something that looked like a thorn scratch, but he had deflected Kasai almost harshly when he mentioned it before.

It didn't help that his face was partially bandaged either.

Tamotsu looked a little uncomfortable, glancing towards the others sitting around the well. Linota walked over, shoving her head under Kasai's hand. "We found an old body, someone who had died some time ago."

Kasai gave him a sad look. "Was it bad?"

Tamotsu shook his head. "The smell was strong, a lot stronger than I expected, but it looked...eaten."

Kasai shuddered; Linota whined and he scratched her ear. "Sorry. That just sounds...disgusting."

Tamotsu laughed. "Yea, it was. But that wasn't the most interesting thing. There was an old bag, an old-fashioned one made of silk I think, with ash-powder bullets, a broken compass, and a few other items."

Kasai noticed Thukuli glowering at them, but ignored it. "Those haven't been seen for, what, fifty years?"

"200, actually. At least, that's what North told me." Tamotsu cast a nervous glance at North. "But something about this place made it look like the body had been there for a few months at most."

Kasai blinked. That was very unusual, and interesting, but he didn't think he could study that. But he'd try to remember where this island was for later. "Was that all?"

Linota yipped. Tamotsu nodded, agreeing with something. "There was the smell of some kind of animal, but it was hard to detect. I haven't smelled it since then either."

For six days? That was unusual too, unless the smell was from a long-ago animal preserved in the unusual soil.

"Everyone up, we're moving on. Kelin thinks there's a settlement ahead," Thukuli stood up, speaking to everyone but looking at Kasai and Tamotsu.

Kelin had run ahead, trying to find something of help, earlier that morning. Kasai hadn't seen him come back, but was glad he seemed to have found *something*. He was tiring of forest, cliffs, and walking so much.

The cane Feluna made, formed from a sturdy branch, certainly helped, but Kasai hadn't walked this much for a long time. And it was a little short for him.

He staggered for a moment, then readjusted himself with the cane. The others started off quickly, but he struggled to follow at their pace.

Tamotsu kept pace with him, but strangely kept his distance. He had been like since they had stopped at the springs but hadn't said why. Kasai wondered if Thukuli had said something to him.

"Kasai..." Tamotsu started, but trailed off.

Linota nudged him, walking between him and Kasai.

"Yea?" Kasai didn't slow down, though he wanted to.

Tamotsu was silent, his feet scuffing the dirt with each step.

Kasai glanced at him, stumbling a tad. "Is everything okay?"

Linota growled, startling them.

Tamotsu matched her growl, making Kasai immediately grow wary. He stopped and watched them.

The others had stopped, but looked tense when they caught sight of the two shifters growling and staring in the same direction.

"Kasai, get behind me." Tamotsu snarled, shoving Kasai roughly behind him.

Kasai stumbled back, barely keeping his footing, as the others ran up.

North caught him, his gaze fixed on Tamotsu. "What's wrong?"

Linota moved in front of Kasai, shoving herself against him.

"There's some kind of animal following us." Tamotsu sprouted grey fur over his body, his tail bushed out and raised straight up.

Kasai watched him curiously. He shifted more than he let on. Kasai thought it was limited to his limbs, but the tail, the ears, the fur, that was new.

Did he know he could do that?

Or...was Thukuli right somehow? Could he be trusted? Was he hiding something?

There was a heavy snuffling noise, then a glimpse of dull scales in the trees, high up. Everyone froze, then backed away slowly.

Linota and Tamotsu kept themselves between whatever was following them and the others, though Kasai noticed they stayed close to him especially.

Thukuli growled softly, "That's an adult tucowary. I didn't know they were found here."

That was an *adult*? How old had the one in Brimna Atoll been? They had told him it was a year old, maybe a tad younger.

North leaned closer to Kasai and whispered, "If we have to run, don't be alarmed if I grab you."

Kasai nodded. He knew he couldn't outrun anything right now, especially something that size.

"Linota. Tamotsu." Thukuli spoke quietly but forcefully, "Could you lead that thing away from us?"

Linota glanced at Tamotsu, who had frozen.

"Tamotsu," Thukuli snarled quietly.

Tamotsu flagged his tail and bolted, startling everyone. A crashing sound was heard as the tucowary turned, paused, then chased after him. They didn't see it, except for glimpses, but a few trees fell as it turned around.

Linota whined, dancing on her paws. She nudged North, who nodded, and kept pace with him as he easily slung Kasai onto his back and ran. Kasai knew this was going to happen, so he didn't protest, but it didn't stop the surprised gasp from escaping.

Feluna and Velu brought up the rear, Jen and Daro at the sides, and Thukuli and Kelin leading the way.

Kasai felt guilty that he was, literally, a burden on North right now, but he knew he had no choice.

They saw the edges of a settlement after a few moments, but before they reached it, Kasai knew it was abandoned.

Kelin didn't hesitate, leading them down a tight alleyway. There was a quiet rumbling and Kasai glanced back to see a barrier of ivy and thorns blocking the entrance as everyone made their way through. Thukuli was stopped at the other end and waited until everyone had come through.

"Find the most intact building you can and hide. I'm going to the end of town to look for another path, a dock, something that could help us get off this godforsaken island," Thukuli said quietly.

No one argued, though Kelin immediately followed him; he wouldn't let Thukuli go alone, and no one could blame him.

Kasai was glad when North set him down, though he kept a hold on Kasai's shoulder. They walked in silence, looking for somewhere to hide.

"Kasai." He turned his head towards Feluna as she walked up. "I know you read. Have you read about tucowary's before?"

He nodded, his face grim. "Once. There wasn't much though, few of them have been found."

Everyone listened as he talked, though they each kept an eye out for a suitable building.

"I knew they would be large, but that thing was almost twice the size of the one in Brimna Atoll." Kasai paused as Jen checked a house, grimacing when she came out shaking her head. "Hard scales, thick skin, and semi retractable claws."

"Can they be taken down?" Velu asked.

Kasai shook his head. "No. At least, not easily by any means. Remember how they tried to dart that one in town?" Velu nodded. "It would've taken at least five darts, with longer needles, to just make it drowsy."

Feluna hissed. "So we don't stand a chance then."

"Maybe we do. Tamotsu is fast, and he's smaller than it," North responded.

Kasai glanced at him. "That won't be enough. They have four eyes, with their only blind spot being on the back of their necks. Their tail is nimbler than it looks too."

"Was all that in the books you found?" Daro asked, his voice low. He had joined when Tamotsu did, and he was a decent sailor and gunner, but slightly annoying. He had tried to get close to Kasai early on, only to be shot down when Kasai didn't respond to him.

He felt a little bad, but Daro was...persistent.

"No. Not everything. The blind spot, the appearance, and their diet was in the book, but no one knew about the thick skin or how fast it was until I got a chance to study the other one," Kasai told him.

He shuddered as he remembered the beast they kept in a flimsy cage, scarred and half starved. They couldn't figure out how much it ate; Kasai had begun to wonder if it was sick when it broke free. He had been almost glad to see it dead in the end, freed from the torment it had endured.

There was movement from ahead and they saw Thukuli running towards them.

They stopped, waiting, as he approached. He looked a little excited, though apprehensive.

"I found a ship," He panted.

Chapter 23

Oxe

THE SECOND HE WAS OUT of sight, Oxe shifted fully. His paws met peat, leaves shook as he burst through them, his fur itched as dust tried to settle, his ears flattened to his head, his tail flowed out behind him.

He heard a pause, then heavy footsteps as the tucowary began chasing him.

He *knew* that had been a tucowary's scent before, but it wasn't tainted with the smell of human and metal, so he hesitated. A fleeting fear gripped him, but he ran on, ignoring it.

The tucowary must've caught sight of him, as it roared and pounded after him.

Oxe flitted through the trees as fast as he could, leaping, dodging, ducking, even springing into the trees a few times in an effort to break the creature's sight. He hadn't seen it fully, but it looked bigger than the one from before. That one had been three times the size of Oxe, so how big was this one?

He flicked an ear, his tongue lolling from his jaws, but it was gaining on him. He was panting heavily, his lungs beginning to ache.

He didn't see the log until it was too late.

Partially buried in leaves and vines, it was sunk into the forest floor, nearly undetectable.

Oxe yelped as his front paw snagged on a low branch, bending it sharply and painfully.

The tucowary appeared a moment later, its jaws gaping.

Almost twice the size of the one before, this one had no missing scales, no chains, though one eye was scarred. Its jaws weren't much bigger than the younger ones, as this one had to be an adult, but the teeth were far larger. The front canines were long enough that they stuck out from under its lip at both the bottom and top, though the bottom were larger.

So it was a digger. Oxe was reminded of the ash boar from his home island, a thickset creature with a wide but short snout, with tusk that could resemble the tucowary's fangs, only set to the side instead of the front. It dug through leaves and snow to find something to eat.

The tucowary paused, fixing its three good eyes on Oxe. It snorted; the meaning clear.

Oxe twitched an ear in response. Not a challenge, a recognition that he was in its territory.

The tucowary swung its head from side to side, bashing the trees.

Oxe lowered his tail, not quite tucking it, but trying to signify he was no threat. The tucowary from before had been enraged because it had escaped from a cage and was being chased, but this one was wild. Maybe it would listen.

Or maybe it would charge.

Oxe barely dodged the outstretched claws, longer than his leg and almost thicker, landing heavily against a tree. He whined, pinning one ear back. His paw was twisted. Any pressure sent a stabbing pain through it.

The tucowary paused for a moment, but then its good right eye caught sight of him and it sprang with surprising speed.

Oxe snarled and shifted his legs longer. He sprang to the side, then shifting them back. A trickle of blood could be felt in his fur along his hip; the claws had almost caught him.

The tucowary snorted, its jaws around the tree where Oxe had been a moment before. With a snap, it bit clean through and the tree toppled.

Oxe felt a trickle of ice along his spine. That tree had been wider around than Oxe, and the tucowary's jaws weren't able to close around it fully, but it had bit through like it was a twig.

It roared, rearing up briefly before crashing down.

Oxe rolled out of the way, howling as the claws ripped along his leg.

The tucowary paused again; Oxe was on its right side.

He edged slowly backwards, trying to move as little as possible. He suppressed a whimper of pain. Blood trickled down his leg, soaking his fur. He felt dizzy for a moment, but blinked to clear it.

The tucowary sniffed around, but somehow it couldn't seem to smell him. Maybe it couldn't smell very well. Its good right eye, the only one he could see, was darting around as it looked for him.

He froze as it focused on him, but then it skipped elsewhere. The tucowary turned, snuffling through the leaves on its left side, using its fangs to move them aside.

Oxe crept back a few steps, keeping his body low. A whine threatened to escape, but he bit it back. Another step; the tucowary moved further away.

But Oxe forgot about its tail.

It turned and lunged the second its tail touched him and Oxe let out a hoarse, choked off yelp as it slammed its claws into him, sending him backwards into the log.

HE AWOKE WITH A QUIET, pained whine. He couldn't move, not easily at least. Stabs of pain came with every breath, his fur felt caked with blood.

There was a snuffling noise nearby; an animal was nosing around.

The forest was black. A blank moon at midnight he guessed.

He closed his eyes, trying to think through the pain. He tried to move his hind legs, but the movement sent a burning pain through his body and he let out a weak whine.

The snuffling stopped.

Oxe tried to hold his breath, but it was no good. There were light pawsteps, leaves crunching under...boots?

"Thank the stars...can you hear me?" North and Linota.

Oxe didn't see them until they were almost on top of him. He let his tail wag once, but stopped when it hurt.

"Don't move. Let me see how bad it is." North knelt next to him, running a rough hand over Oxe's limbs; he was no doctor, his touch alone proved that.

Oxe whined through his teeth, flashing his eyes at Linota. She crept forward on her belly and began licking his face, washing away some of the blood he felt stiffening his whiskers.

"Can you shift back? Or would that be too much?" North asked.

Oxe closed his eyes, trying to focus on his body, trying to shift as slowly as it could. He let out another whine as the pain intensified, but slowly the fur melted back into his body, the limbs changing shape, the bones moving under his skin.

He bit his lip to keep from screaming in pain as he lay there, completely human. He panted heavily after a moment.

"Damn..." North muttered, his eyes wide. "Will you be okay while I get help? Or make a stretcher?"

Oxe couldn't move. It hurt to speak, so he just blinked.

Linota lay next to him while North scrounged around for something to help.

Oxe twitched a finger, getting Linota's attention. "Kasai?" He gasped; some teeth felt loose.

She whined, but swished her tail over him gently.

He was fine. Good.

North came back. "Oxe, this is going to hurt, but I need to move you."

Oxe nodded once; he let out a hiss of pain.

He cried out as North shifted him onto the makeshift stretcher, unable to keep quiet any longer. His chest was aching, his legs felt like fire, his left arm was strangely numb.

"Sorry. Linota, come here." There was movement as one end of the stretcher was lifted. Oxe heard Linota grunt, but couldn't look. North took a few steps to the end and lifted it. "Sorry, Oxe, we're trying to be careful."

Oxe gasped at the strange, almost jogging-like movement as they started walking. The end where his head was lifted him higher than his feet. Linota had a series of vines around her chest and neck; she was pulling him along, and North was keeping his end from dragging along the ground.

It took them a few hours to reach the others. Kasai and Jen were asleep, while everyone else looked up as the strange procession appeared.

Thukuli narrowed his eyes, but Feluna gasped and shot to her feet. She rushed over as they reached the fire that was burning in the center of the clearing and whispered, "Get him over here so I can look better." She darted her eyes to Kasai. "But can you put up some kind of barrier?"

Oxe felt confused at this, but groaned as quietly as he could as they set him down on a stone ledge. Once still, he blinked and tried to take in the surroundings.

They were in the remains of a large stone building. One wall was halfway down, the entrance they had come through, and the other walls reached maybe a foot or so above Oxe's height.

A partial roof, covering only where Oxe was laying, looked to be made of some kind of tile. A window opening above him had been covered by a scrap of fabric, but it was blowing gently at a breeze he couldn't feel.

The fire was positioned in the center of the old stone floor, and Oxe could see where they had set up a temporary sleeping area.

Some old crates had been set around the fire for them to sit at, but only Thukuli was there now, watching Oxe with thinly veiled suspicion. Velu stood along the wall, gazing outside; Oxe realized he was standing guard, making sure nothing snuck up on them.

He flinched as Feluna began examining him, breaking his concentration.

"Four broken ribs, a broken leg, your left wrist is sprained, and that gash worries me. I'll need to stitch it, but I'm not sure how without my kit," she barely murmured the words, her eyes flicking over him. "Bruises all over."

Oxe grunted, "A splinter. Take a splinter, some sinew or vine, and use that." It was how the healer fixed open injuries within the tribe.

Feluna nodded and disappeared for a moment. North appeared; Oxe hadn't seen him leave, and prop up some sticks. He didn't understand what North was doing until he draped a large ratty piece of cloth across the top stick. A barrier.

"Keep that open a bit so I can see. Bring me some water, and see if there's some clean fabric nearby." Feluna told him, coming back.

"Moss," Oxe grunted. "Use moss."

North nodded and disappeared for a few minutes before coming back with a gray kind of moss that was unfamiliar to Oxe. "Will this do?"

Oxe took a sniff, flinching at the pain, and nodded. It smelled sharp, but a little like the moss his tribe used.

Feluna waited until North returned with a cup of water, then dipped the moss into it. "I need to wash this as best as I can, then I'll stitch it."

Oxe blinked to show he understood, then hissed as she gently ran the wet moss over his arm. It stung like hell, feeling like little stabs of ice along the open flesh, but he gritted his teeth. It was harder to keep from crying out as she stitched along his arm, but he kept quiet by sheer willpower.

Feluna worked quickly, thankfully, but paused when she came to his leg. "Tamotsu, I'm not sure how I'll be able to set this."

Oxe blinked in confusion. "Is it bad?"

She shook her head. "It's not that, but I'm not sure if you'll be able to stay quiet while I set it."

"I told her about your tattoo," North explained quietly. "If Kasai wakes up and sees it before we can get you covered, he'll figure out who you are." He gazed darted to Thukuli and Oxe realized it wasn't really Kasai he was worried about discovering Oxe.

He nodded stiffly. "Give me something to bite." He wasn't sure how bad his leg was, but he guessed it was bad enough to worry about this. He could handle pain usually, but he had already reached his limits.

North handed him a tough strip of old leather. "I'm going to hold you down while she does this, in case you jerk."

Oxe nodded, the leather between his teeth, and mentally prepared himself.

He screamed against the strip as he felt Feluna jerk his leg into place. The bones scraped under his skin, sending jagged pain shooting through his leg and hip. North's hands were iron, keeping his jerking to a minimum as his body reacted to the pain.

He wasn't prepared for the second jerk though, and blacked out for a few minutes.

"Get him covered. I'll keep Kasai away." North's voice, faint, roused him.

He felt movement and blinked his eyes open.

Feluna glanced at him, not stopping in whatever she was doing. "Sorry. Your leg was also dislocated, and I had to set it back quickly so the damage wasn't permanent. Your scream woke everyone."

Oxe nodded, gasping at the movement. The leather strip dropped. "Thanks."

Feluna said nothing as she finished, then glared at him. "What happened?"

"The tucowary," Oxe gasped out, trying to move his shoulder.

"Don't move. We found a ship, something big enough to get us to Brimna Atoll, but we need to stay here for a few days and gather some supplies." Feluna told him.

Oxe closed his eyes. "How long will that take?"

Feluna paused, looking behind her. "North thinks maybe a couple weeks, maybe a month if the winds are bad. It'll take a lot of food and water, but we can set up water catchers on the ship and fish if we need to." She gave a snort. "Kasai said he'd rather starve than eat fish though."

Oxe gave a small chuckle, but it turned to a groan. "That's no surprise. He almost died from bad fish."

Feluna shot him a look. "You're going to have to tell him soon, you know."

Oxe nodded. "I know." He wanted to tell him now. He wanted Kasai to come over and see him like this. But he understood how dangerous that was.

She was quiet for a few minutes; they could hear the others talking quietly on the other side of the barrier. "North says that whatever you had done to disguise yourself has worn off completely."

Oxe held his breath. He forgot. He wasn't supposed to do a full shift until well after it had worn off.

"You'll need to hide your face for a while." She held out some bandages. "You'll need to wear these over at least part of your face.

The scar on your cheek is a good enough excuse for these for now, but you'll need to figure something else out later."

A scar on his cheek? Maybe he blacked out for more than a few minutes.

"What should I do then?" Oxe asked. The bandages from earlier had fallen off in the shift, but he had only agreed with those at first because they couldn't think of anything else at the time.

Feluna regarded him carefully for a moment. "As soon as we get back, tell Kasai and get the hell out."

Chapter 24

Kasai

THE SHIP ROCKED UNSTEADILY, a stiff breeze blowing from the west. Kasai perched on a crate, his hands on the railing, watching the sails. A fishing pole lay next to him.

Tamotsu was still injured, so everyone else had to watch the winds and water. Kasai typically took the morning watch with Feluna and North, while Thukuli, Kelin, and Jen took the afternoon, and Daro and Linota shared the night watch.

Thukuli wasn't happy having an "animal" on watch, but he understood that there was little choice.

"Any news?" Thukuli asked Kasai, startling him. He hadn't heard the captain approach.

"Nothing yet. North thinks it'll be another day at least before we see anything," Kasai reported.

Thukuli grunted, walking off.

Kasai watched the waves for a while, the water shimmering as the sun rose. After another hour or so, he stood and stretched, then walked along the railing until he reached Feluna at the bow. "How's Tamotsu?"

"Grousing." She snorted. "Might be getting some cabin fever."

Kasai felt a stab of sympathy. Three weeks stuck inside was a bit much. "How's his arm?" There had been an infection scare at first, but the swelling went down the next day thankfully. But Feluna had told him it was hot to the touch still a few days ago.

She frowned, keeping her eyes on the waves. "I'm still worried about infection."

"It's still hot?" Kasai asked, surprised.

She nodded. "There's no swelling, and no signs of gangrene or anything, but I can't keep it cool."

Kasai watched the waves for a moment, thinking. "Well, he's a genetic, right? Sometimes genetics don't respond to the same healing a non-genetic needs."

Feluna's lip twitched upwards a bit. "You some kind of doctor?"

Kasai snorted, trying not to laugh. "No, but I've been sick or injured enough that I know about that." Plus, Brinar had tried to teach him medicine at one point, though it hadn't interested Kasai and was quickly dropped. Only a few things could he remember.

"But even if that's true, we don't have medicines to treat him with." Feluna said bitterly.

Kasai sighed, knowing she was right. "I might sit with him for a while after my watch."

Feluna gave him a strange look. "Might be a good idea. He needs someone other than me checking on him."

Kasai laughed and walked back to his spot. He understood that feeling well. He had tried to sit with him a few times once Tamotsu managed to stay awake, but he had become quiet and a little withdrawn. Kasai had used the time to doze often, but Tamotsu didn't seem to mind.

He stopped when he saw a dark smudge to his left. Crossing the deck, he grabbed the old teleglass and brought it up. Smiling, he set it down and headed up the few steps to North. "I just spotted the Atoll's cliffs."

North grinned. "I can feel them. It'll be another couple of hours until we reach the main port though. Go let the captain know."

Kasai nodded. He was glad North wasn't bitter about being on Thukuli's crew, though he could tell North was going to bolt the moment he could.

Entering the hall, Kasai heard muttering coming from the captain's quarters at the far end. Heavy footsteps echoed through the door, and he wondered how agitated the captain was.

Kasai paused just before opening the door. There was a broken section at the top, a hole just big enough for sounds to drift through. Thukuli mutters grew distinct. "Stupid, I knew they would retaliate!" More words, indistinct, then silence for a moment. "...take my ship...crew...need to get back..."

Kasai took a deep breath and rapped on the door loudly. "Captain, the cliffs were spotted. We'll be at the dock in a few hours."

There was a crash and the door opened. Thukuli was shirtless, his eyes wide, a snarl on his face. His pants were messy and unbuttoned, his hair in disarray. There was blood on his hand; Kasai noticed the glint of broken glass on the floor.

"What?" Thukuli's voice was strange; slurred but sharp. He'd been drinking, but then went into a rage. That explained the broken glass at least. He usually broke things when he was drunk or angry.

"We spotted the cliffs. We'll be at the docks in a few hours," Kasai managed to get out. He had never seen Thukuli like this before, and it frightened him. He was used to angry, drunk, a mixture of both, but never had he seen the wild look that currently shadowed the captain's face. He took a step back, but Thukuli reached forward and grabbed his arm.

"Stay in here for now." Thukuli growled.

Kasai felt the hairs on the back of his neck stand up. Thukuli had shown a romantic interest, or what *he* perceived as romantic, when Kasai was recovered enough to join with the crew fully, but that had been incessant flirting, innuendos out of hearing of the others, and hints as to what Kasai could have.

It disgusted him.

But this...this was so much worse.

Thukuli had never made a move like this, let alone when drunk.

Kasai jerked his arm, but Thukuli kept his hand around Kasai's wrist. "My watch isn't over yet." He flared out heat, knowing that Thukuli couldn't stand it in close quarters; it's why he developed that skill in the first place.

Thukuli growled, his eyes glittering, and twisted Kasai's arm a bit, making him cry out. "It'll be over soon, anyway. Just stay with me for a while."

Kasai made the surroundings hotter, bracing himself against the wall and jerking again.

"You-" Thukuli stopped, his eyes blearily focused on something behind Kasai.

Or someone.

"Let him go." The snarl echoed darkly in the short hallway. There was the soft scratch of claws on wood.

Thukuli silently snarled and shoved Kasai away roughly.

Tamotsu wrapped his unbandaged arm around Kasai, catching him easily. He limped, one hand against the doorway to steady himself, his right leg held off the floor, into the hallway. "Don't ever touch him again." His fingers had claws, and one foot was a large paw; the claws were digging into the wood, leaving furrows.

Kasai had never heard anyone sound this dangerous before, but strangely, he didn't feel afraid. Not of Tamotsu.

"Threatening me?" Thukuli asked. His lips were curled, and he was standing against the wall. He swayed slightly, but it could've just been from the waves.

Tamotsu only rumbled; the sound vibrated through his chest, low and deep.

Kasai glanced up and saw his muzzle had shifted, his teeth bared.

Thukuli slowly shook his head but backed away. He stepped into his room and slammed the door shut.

Tamotsu slowly released his grip on Kasai. When he had let go completely, he asked, "Are you alright?" His eyes were hard, his muzzle wrinkled slightly.

Kasai nodded. Shaken, obviously, but otherwise okay.

The door leading outside opened and North stepped in, looking a tad confused. "I felt some heat. Is everything alright?" The watch must've ended.

Tamotsu bared his teeth, looking towards the captain's cabin. "Ironwood tried to take Kasai."

The alarm, and anger, on North's face reddened it. He took a few wide steps towards them. "He *what?!*" He looked over Kasai quickly, his hand on the en-pist at his side.

Kasai nodded. "He's drunk."

North looked ready to bust down the door and attack Thukuli, but Kasai stepped in front of him. North glared at him.

"Don't. It's not worth it." The words stuck in Kasai's throat, but he choked them out roughly.

"Kasai, I'm not leaving your side for a while." North's tone left no room for arguments. He shot a look at Tamotsu. "At least until Tamotsu is better."

Tamotsu nodded.

Kasai looked at him and opened his mouth to speak, but something caught his eye. What was under his bandage? He could see the edge of a tattoo on Tamotsu's chest, a straight edge that disappeared under the cloth. It looked...unusual. But this wasn't the time to ask. "Okay." He'd ask about it later.

North gripped Kasai's shoulder and pushed him lightly towards the outside. "Come on. We're going below deck for now. I'll get Kelin and tell him the captains...drunk."

Kasai didn't argue. If he couldn't have Oxe here, then North was the next best person he could trust.

He resisted the urge to look back at Tamotsu though. Something was nagging at him; he could feel there was something about the man that felt...off.

Outside, he caught Feluna's alarmed gaze, but he shook his head and followed North below.

"KASAI, COME WITH ME," Thukuli called over to him.

Kasai, sitting on the ground against a crate, glanced at him nervously.

Thukuli frowned. "Come on. Cifius is waiting for us."

North watched as Kasai join Thukuli, but unfortunately couldn't follow them.

The first day back, he had confronted Thukuli and threatened him. Thukuli had knocked him flat, nearly blinding him with a thorn, as a response. He warned North that if he tried that again, he wouldn't just end up blind.

Kasai had quietly begged North to back off a bit after that, not wanting him to get hurt.

North reluctantly relented, but warned Kasai that if Thukuli tried that again...North wouldn't hesitate to kill him.

Tamotsu, already heading for the local doctor's office to finish his recovery, hadn't been there for that, and Kasai was glad. He wasn't sure if Tamotsu would've been able to hold himself back like North managed to.

Thukuli glanced back at Kasai, a few steps behind him. "I'm not drunk enough to try that shit again."

Kasai didn't trust that. He hadn't needed to be drunk to come onto him before, though never that strong. At least Thukuli was easier to fend off when he was sober. And he didn't get drunk often thankfully. He took a few steps closer, but stayed an arm's length away.

Thukuli glared, but said nothing about that. "Bek's in town."

Great. More of the Ironwood crew.

"I'm meeting with him at the large bar in town. We're going to figure a way to get back at the Seaborne." Thukuli kicked at an empty cup; it clattered down the roadway and stopped against a drunkard laying against a building.

Kasai glanced at the slumped figure, but said nothing.

"Cifius is there, too. He wants to offer us something that can help." Thukuli continued.

Cifius had something that could help? Kasai frowned, unsure of what to make of that.

Thukuli glanced back again. "We'll be here for a few months probably. I need a new crew, a new ship, and some time to...relax."

Kasai suppressed a shudder. He didn't like the look on Thukuli's face. But there wasn't a way to detach himself from the captain right now. He didn't like the sudden interest, but wasn't sure how to respond. In the past, this had never been an issue.

He had a flash of Oxe, but pushed it away. That was wanted, that was between mates. But that wouldn't happen again.

Thukuli pushed through the rough door of the Hanged Dur, the largest bar in town, Kasai only a few steps behind him.

"Captain, over here." Bek was sitting at a large corner booth, several pints in front of him and a few others Kasai didn't recognize.

Cifius was sitting with them, his eyes hard. By the look he gave Thukuli, he knew what had happened. Kasai wouldn't be surprised; Cifius knew North, who had disappeared for a few hours the second they got back. It was when North came back he had threatened Thukuli.

"Ironwood. I heard about your crew." Cifius' tone erased any doubt about him knowing. "But attacking the Seaborne is foolish."

Thukuli slammed a fist down on the table, making the pints rattle and spilling le over the wood. "They owe me a ship! And it was that damn new captain!"

Bek snorted. "You got beat by the newest Seaborne captain?" He laughed, but stopped when a sprig of ivy appeared around his neck.

"That bastard got cocky and got lucky. If it weren't for that tailwind, we could've made it." Thukuli shot at him, his fingers clenched into an open fist.

Cifius' voice broke in. "Ironwood. You know the rules."

Thukuli growled, but the ivy retreated, probably into his bag.

Cifius met his gaze evenly, but turned to Kasai. "What happened that day?"

Kasai looked down at the table, thinking. "We had just left a port; I think they were waiting for us." He had given it some thought on the days they spent walking afterwards. "They attacked only when they really thought they were within range, and the first cannonball landed almost in front of the ship."

Bek was trying hard not to grin, despite the black look Thukuli gave him.

"I tried to get the engine started, but we didn't have a full charge and they caught up enough to blast the ship. I managed to get Linota out from the hold, and we escaped on the lifeboat," Kasai told them.

Cifius kept an eye on Thukuli as he spoke, "Ya can stay here for as long as ya need, but don't expect any free food or board. Find work or make deals, I don't care. Just follow the rules of the town." He stood. "Kasai, come with me."

"With all due respect, he's to stay with his crew." There was no respect in Thukuli's eyes despite the halfway polite tone.

"With *no* respect," Cifius towered over him, "*Captain*, Kasai is my charge while in this port. And I don't take kindly to people like ya." With a sneer, he spat at Thukuli's feet and stalked out.

Kasai hurried after him, not wanting to see Thukuli's reaction.

"THAT RAT BASTARD'S becoming a problem." They sat in the Drowned Bird, the inn Kasai had stayed at previously. Cifius leaned back in his chair, his anger almost visible in the air. The air crackled softly, making Kasai uneasy from its familiarity. But he pushed the memories aside and tried to pay attention.

Linota huffed, nudging Kasai as they sat across from Cifius.

North, his cheeks slightly red from too much le, shook his head. "I promised Kasai I would kill him if that bastard tries that again."

Cifius gave him a half-hearted scowl. "While I want to agree, ya know the rules here, North. If ya kill him without being provoked, I'll have to either kill ya or have ya banished." But Kasai could tell he would try to avoid that.

North grimaced, downing another drink. "I don't care. I promised Sonus I'd watch out for his kids if anything happened to him."

Kasai flinched.

North frowned. "S'rry. Forgot. It's still hard for you, isn't 't?"

Kasai shrugged, rubbing Linota's ear absentmindedly. "Yea."

North was quiet for a moment, then looked at Cifius. "When Brinar was here with...did they have a logbook with them?"

Cifius shook his head. "No idea where it is. I know the other one had it, the tall man that came with him, but no idea where he stashed it. Brinar might have it."

Brinar. Who was back on Witch Island. *Of course.* Kasai had no idea what was so special about a logbook, but it must be important.

"Ya could call him." Cifius' words jolted Kasai a bit. "Use a face-crys. He's got a personal one, special hookup."

"I don't have one, and don't know how to use one," Kasai told him. He had one under his cot before the ship sank, but hadn't thought to grab it in the escape.

Cifius motioned to the bartender, a larger woman with a kind but hard face. "Use Kelli's."

Kelli nodded, walking over. "Yer welcome to use it any time, love. Anything fer family."

Kasai paused and looked at her. "Family?"

She nodded. "Aye. Cifius is me cousin, and yer father was his youngest grandkid."

Kasai's eyes widened and he looked at Cifius, who nodded. "Aye, she's right. But out here, family is more than blood."

"He's right about that Kasai," North said, grabbing another drink.

Kelli smacked his hand with a spoon. "Yer drunk already. Ya don't need more."

Kasai suppressed a grin at North's frown. Linota yapped, her tongue hanging from the side of her jaws in laughter. Even Cifius looked amused.

North snorted and stood, though he seemed unsteady. "Guess I'll find nicer company then." He glared at Kelli, though there was no heat in his look, and disappeared out the door.

Kasai couldn't help it; he burst out laughing. Kelli and Cifius joined and it took a few minutes for them to calm down.

Kelli wiped a tear from her cheek. "Never thought I'd see that one drunk. Didn't think that could happen."

Kasai smiled; he could remember North getting into a drinking contest with Arat and the others before. He snorted another laugh as he recalled North getting drunk enough that he started badly singing some shanty once. Or more than once, really. Or a lot, actually.

Kelli returned to the bar, and Cifius watched Kasai for a moment.

"I heard ya've got a crewmate at the doctors," he said, taking a drink.

"Tamotsu. He was one of the people that joined the last time we were here," Kasai told him.

Cifius was quiet for a moment. "Funny. I don't recall anyone by that name from here." He said this calmly, slowly. Holding something back, maybe hiding something.

Kasai ignored the chill he felt down his spine. "He said he was from Verideys Island. He heard this was a place for pyrates, wanted to be one, and came here."

"Hm," was all Cifius said for the moment.

Linota whined uneasily, nosing Kasai's hand.

"What is she, by the way?" Cifius asked.

Kasai shrugged. "A shifter genetic. But she can't shift back human and Tamotsu thought it might be permanent now. She has trouble keeping a human mind like this, but seems happy as an animal."

Linota gave a quiet yip; Kasai wondered if she sensed his uneasiness.

"Kasai, I see every passenger manifest that comes here. I don't remember every name of course, but I think I would remember a name that...unusual." Cifius frowned at him. "I think we should pay your crewmate a visit." A nudge, trying to hint at something.

Kasai felt a trickle of ice through his body now. "No." Cifius stared at him, but Kasai continued. "If it's alright, I'll go see him alone."

Cifius nodded, looking a little relieved.

Kasai stood. "Linota, go find North. Make sure he doesn't fall off the docks or something."

She whimpered, but didn't follow him as he left the inn.

Tamotsu's name didn't show up on any ship coming here? And he wasn't a native?

Kasai stalked past some late night drinkers, some stumbling around, some on the ground, a few singing drunkenly outside a tavern.

He could've used a different name.

But he had been seen with Brinar, if what Thukuli said was true.

Kasai shoved past a rowdy crowd along the docks, turning down the street towards the doctors.

He was a Nuveri warrior too, though he claimed it was through his mother. But their people never left their island. It wasn't a taboo, but they had no interest in the outside world. Willingly leaving was something none of them would think of doing, and how would his mother had survived if she had been washed out to sea by the tide?

The doctor's window showed she was awake.

Kasa hesitated, his hand raised to knock on the door. If he accused Tamotsu of lying about his identity, he may not trust Kasai for a while, if ever again. Cifius had sounded odd about him, but maybe it was nothing.

But if Kasai was right...he wasn't sure if he could handle this.

He took a breath and opened the door.

"Hey Kasai, is something wrong?" It was Reoko, one of the few actual doctors here. She had trained down in Surval, but wanted to come here after training was finished.

Kasai ignored the startled look on her face. "Is Tamotsu awake? I need to talk to him."

Her eyes darted to the side; her voice hitched. "Now's not a good time."

Kasai pushed past her. He saw someone with their back to him and froze.

"Did you need something?" Tamotsu asked, not facing him.

Kasai couldn't form the words he wanted to say. He couldn't take his eyes off the scar on Tamotsu's...no.

On *Oxe's* back.

Blacksmoke had given him that wound. It was a near perfect crescent, usually undetectable unless Oxe got pale.

And he had been wearing a shirt over his torso for over six months now, so only his arms, neck and above, and below his knees were tanned. He didn't even know he had it; Kasai had never told him.

"Kasai?" Oxe turned and met Kasai's eyes.

A wave of heat flooded out, making him flinch, and Reoko moaned in pain behind Kasai. There was a soft *thud* as she fell.

"You..." Kasai started, but his voice failed.

Oxe's eyes widened slightly and his hand rose, touching his cheek. His eyes widened more, pain creeping into his expression. The bandages on his face were gone, and except for a scar along his cheek, Kasai couldn't understand why he didn't recognize him sooner.

Maybe he had just convinced himself that Oxe was dead.

That the person following him around only looked like Oxe due to a coincidence.

Oxe scrambled to his feet, wincing as he put weight on his right leg. On his chest was a single geometric design. The mark of his tribe's protectors. "Wait, I can explain-"

"You...lied...to me." Kasai hissed out. His eyes stung. His hand curled into a fist. He could feel himself shaking.

He hadn't killed Oxe.

But he had been sailing with Kasai for months.

And.

Said.

Nothing.

Oxe took a step forward, flinching against the heat. "Please...listen-"

"No." Kasai took a step back.

Oxe froze, his hand out.

"I can't..." He couldn't deal with this. This was too much.

He thought if North had been right, Oxe would be here, alive. Or with Brinar. Or gone back home.

Kasai raised his hand; it was trembling badly. "Don't..." He squeezed his eyes shut. Something wet dripped down his face.

There was too much that added up now.

There was a footstep and he felt someone grab his hand; gentle, slow. Familiar.

Kasai jerked and pushed him away, then streaked out the door.

Chapter 25

Oxe

"HAVE YOU FOUND HIM yet?" Oxe limped over to North, the crutch making his gait awkward.

North shook his head, grimacing. "No. Sorry Oxe, I was drunk last night, I didn't think he'd come looking for you, or that it would turn out..." He took a deep breath. "I should've made you tell him sooner."

Oxe could see the guilt in his face. He laid a hand on North's shoulder. "No. You left it up to me, and I am the one who made the mistake of not saying something sooner." He turned as rapid footsteps approached.

"We found the beach up north turned to glass." Velu panted. "There's no blacksmith up that way, no houses, no glassworkers."

North nodded. "How far?"

Velu shrugged, catching his breath. "Not sure. Maybe five blocks?"

"How much glass?" Oxe asked. He remembered the arena's floor turning to glass when Kasai faced Sonus and Brinar.

Velu looked away for a moment. "A big crater. Enough for a neixe to stand nose to tail from either side in the center and barely reach the other. It's kind of...I'm not sure, but it looks like a flower opening in a great big circle."

North exchanged a worried look with Oxe, then looked back at Velu. "Show us."

Oxe hated that he couldn't move faster, but Velu and North didn't leave him behind. His leg would be well enough in another week, or at least that's what Reoko told him. Until then, he was told not to shift and put as little weight as possible on it.

His skin itched with impatience.

Unfortunately, Reoko was still passed out. Feluna had offered to keep an eye on her while they looked for Kasai, and Cifius and the owner of the Drowned Bird had said they would help them search the town.

Velu wanted to help too, and he watched out for Thukuli as well. The last thing they needed was for him to find out.

It took longer than Oxe liked for them to reach the edge of the town, but he and North were forced to a stop when they saw the glass along the beach.

The center of the crater was a perfect circle, like someone had stood or crouched there, but there was an almost perfect ring radiating outwards, with waves of glass rippling slightly upwards, reaching up in a gentle, dilating motion.

The glass reached thirty feet out, completely smooth. They could see no rough edges. It was beautiful.

But painful.

Oxe let out a breath and limped towards Cifius and Kelli. "Any sign?"

Kelli shook her head. "We tracked some footsteps north, but then we ran into stone and lost him." Her face was calm, but Oxe could sense the concern.

Cifius gave him a sympathetic look, then looked out towards the cliffs.

"Can you track him?" North asked, looking at Oxe.

Oxe nodded. "As long as the scent holds."

He took off as fast as he dared, shifting his muzzle to make it easier.

Kasai's scent was erratic, weaving back and forth for a great distance before they reached a field of stone. Ahead of them, the cliffs loomed upwards. Oxe knew Kasai was heading this direction; Kasai's scent was gone, but Oxe could feel it.

North sighed. "I'm guessing the scent's gone?" Oxe nodded and North gazed at the slope ahead of them, leading up gently before becoming steeper towards the top. "Unless he changed direction, he's probably at the top of the cliff."

Oxe looked at him.

"There's an outcrop up there, a kind of sheltered half-cave. I swear I've been following Sonus," North said unexpectedly.

Oxe stared. Cifius and Kelli, standing nearby, nodded in agreement.

North glanced sideways at Oxe. "After Sonus returned to sea, the last time he saw his kids, we came here. We stayed here for, I don't know, a month? Maybe two?"

Oxe looked at the cliffs, listening.

"I found Sonus on the beach, almost in the same spot at that crater, actually. But when I tried to talk to him, he got really upset, filled the air with lightning, took out my hand, and ran off," North explained.

This startled Oxe; he had injured a crewmate with lightning long before Kasai had been hurt? Maybe that was part of the reason Sonus had been so upset when it happened to Kasai.

"I found him on the cliffs," North continued. "I was maybe fifteen or so, and hot-headed, but I couldn't leave my captain alone."

Cifius snorted. "Annoyed the hell out of him, too!"

North shot him a glare, but there was no anger behind it. "Can you blame me? I learned everything I know from him!" He sighed, his voice growing sad. "But I followed him up and found him in that shelter. I've only ever seen him that upset one other time."

Oxe looked at him. "When?"

North looked back. "When he thought Kasai would die on the Expanse."

"Not when he hurt him before?" Oxe asked.

North shook his head. "No. He knew Kasai would survive then; he had a lot of faith in Brinar. But when Kasai got sick and people started dying..." he paused, taking a deep breath, "it wasn't the same sickness the rest of got that made Sonus so bad afterwards. He blamed himself for letting Kasai come to sea, for putting him in danger all the time. He stopped eating, didn't sleep."

A pang shot through Oxe at this. He remembered the gaunt look Sonus had during that time, but he had assumed he had been sick like the rest of the crew. He hadn't smelled sick, but Oxe hadn't thought there was anything more than that at the time.

Cifius stepped forward. "That was after Kasai killed Grimshaw, right?"

Oxe nodded. "After I tried to protect him."

North gave Oxe a sympathetic look. "Considering everything going on, you did fine." He turned to Cifius and Kelli. "We'll follow him up. Cifius, can you call Brinar and let him know what's going on?"

Cifius nodded. "'Course." He turned and walked off.

Kelli laid a hand on Oxe's shoulder. "Cifius explained a little bit about what's been going on."

Oxe felt a shudder go through his body; not of fear, of regret.

"He's been through a lot, Oxe. Give him time." She patted his shoulder once and followed Cifius.

North waited until they had disappeared, then jerked his head towards the slope. "I'll head up first. He might be more inclined to talk to me right now."

Oxe nodded. "I will follow as fast as I can, but I won't come to the shelter in case he...doesn't want to see me."

"I'm sure he does, Oxe, but last night was a big shock." North gave him a small smile, then headed up.

Oxe took a deep breath and followed.

"YOU DON'T GET IT NORTH! He lied to me!" Kasai's voice, cracked and desolate sounding, drifted down from the shelter.

Silence for a tense moment, then North's voice. "I do get it. I was on the ship for a time with him too, remember? But he couldn't reveal himself. Not yet."

Oxe hadn't been too far behind, but North made it up the steeper part quicker while Oxe struggled not to stumble.

Quiet breathing, a sniff, then Kasai's voice, "Because of Thukuli..."

Oxe stopped before he reached the top of the cliff; small stones smattered the open area. If Kasai didn't see him first, he would hear him. Oxe fingers the edge of his shirt, then opted to sit against a scraggly brush nearby. It was wind torn and thin, but sturdy.

"Yes. And I wanted to ask you about that. Why does he have such a hold on you?" North kept his voice low, but Oxe could hear them clearly.

Another sniff. "After I ran from the Seaborne, I don't know what happened."

"The Seaborne? Is that what you think what happened?" North broke in.

A pause. "Then what happened?"

North sighed. "I had to...shoot you."

Oxe flinched.

A touch of fear, Kasai's, touched his nose. "But it was you who got me out?"

"Yea. But the Seaborne...that's hard to explain right now. But there wasn't a better place to take you regardless. But it was Brinar who was treating you," North explained.

A sob echoed out. "I thought he hated me...I thought he abandoned me."

Stones shifted. "No. Never. None of us did, or would." North sighed deeply. "But then Oxe said you were gone, and we couldn't find you."

A pause. "I ran. I don't remember how, or where, but I got out and made my way elsewhere. Someone found me, I guess, but I don't know how long I was out." There was a soft *crack* as a stone hit the ground; Kasai had tossed it. "Next thing I knew, I was waking up on Thukuli's ship."

"Is what why you owe him?" North asked.

"More or less. He had Feluna treat me, Velu watched out for me, and it took about six months for me to feel better. Thukuli found a way to get me the tools to make an arm, but it was...expensive," Kasai explained bitterly.

North didn't speak for several minutes, his voice dark when he finally spoke. "That would've been around the time we heard reports of a vicious pyrate in the Eastern Area, one that used fire. Kasai...you killed people."

Not judgmental, just stating a fact. Oxe had been almost wild with grief when he heard the reports. Hardly ever human, an animal trapped on a boat. They weren't even sure it *was* Kasai, but it still got to Oxe terribly. It had been too much of a coincidence.

Oxe didn't blame them for locking him in the makeshift brig they made. It was the only way to keep him safe.

"I didn't want to." Kasai's voice was almost a whisper. "I never meant to kill anyone. But Thukuli...I had to do whatever I could to pay him back so I could leave."

"I can understand that." Stones shifted as North leaned back. "Don't get me wrong, I'm still upset, but it helps that you weren't doing it because you wanted to."

Another sniff. "I nearly left that day when Oxe showed up." The pain in Kasai's voice cut through Oxe like a knife.

Silence for a minute. "I won't lie Kasai, I thought you were...well, a lost cause. I didn't believe he would find you."

Oxe flinched. He knew North and Arat had given up, but it still stung.

"But then he came back, frantic...I've never seen him lose it like that," North said.

A flash of heat came from the outcrop; the ground sizzled slightly. "I thought Thukuli was going to kill him. I didn't even realize it was Oxe at first, but the wolf was just too...familiar. And he was helping a kid, something that I knew he would've done, anyway." Oxe was touched by Kasai's view of him. "But then Thukuli threatened him, and me, and I had no choice but to leave."

"I understand. But you've been taking ships with him for, what, two years now? Surely you've paid him back." North sounded a little skeptical, though a tad hopeful.

Another flash of heat, stronger. "No. Even if I have, he won't let me go. If I leave, he'll hunt me down, kill everyone I love, anyone connected with me," Kasai growled, the heat rising, the ground smoking in a few spots. "And as much as I despise him, I don't want to take another life ever again."

Oxe felt a wave of sympathy. He remembered how much Kasai struggled to deal with killing Grimshaw, and how reluctant he was to kill Blacksmoke, even though the captain had taken his brother and family.

Kasai spoke softly, but Oxe couldn't make out the words.

North snorted. "I don't think you'll have to worry about *that* with Ironwood. Either me or Oxe will probably kill him at this point." His voice was dark, threatening, but he continued, "Has he done anything like that before?"

Oxe pricked his ears, gritting his teeth.

Kasai didn't answer for several minutes, but Oxe could taste the fear in the air. "No. I mean, he's shown interest, flirted, made a lot of jokes, but he's never outright acted like that before."

Oxe resisted the urge to go hug Kasai, but he wasn't sure if he should. Yet.

"I'm glad Oxe was there," North said quietly.

"Is he... I'm afraid he's mad at me." Kasai's words were almost a whisper. "I think I hurt him last night."

North let out a laugh, startling Oxe. "No Kasai, he's not mad. He's just worried. But I think we all understand your...reaction."

Kasai groaned; Oxe couldn't help but smile.

"We really are sorry we didn't tell you sooner. I was surprised when I saw him on the ship with you, but then I realized soon after why you didn't know." North chuckled softly. "But I think you should find him and talk with him."

"What about Thukuli? If I'm not in town today, or he hears about what I did at the beach, he'll start to ask questions." Kasai sounded...not reluctant, but wary.

"We'll keep him busy if he ask," North said.

"We?" Kasai sounded confused.

A brief pause. "Me, Velu, Feluna, Cifius, and Kelli are all in on this. Well, Velu and Feluna didn't know at first, but they found out Oxe somehow, so we had no choice but to tell them. But I trust them; they haven't exposed him so far, so I doubt they will at any point after all this," North told him.

Oxe heard Kasai take a deep breath before he spoke. "Do you know where Oxe is?"

Movement; North appeared, standing and facing down the slope. "Stay here. I'll tell him where you're at."

Oxe waited until North passed him; the older man jerked his head towards the outcrop but said nothing, just giving Oxe a small smile as he left.

Oxe paused just before he reached the outcrop, just out of Kasai's sight. He had heard Kasai and knew he felt bad, but the anger from last night was burned into his head.

But he couldn't stay away any longer.

Chapter 26

Kasai

KASAI STARTED AS OXE slowly sat down, moving awkwardly. He hadn't expected Oxe so quickly; had he been nearby?

Oxe set a crutch down; he had managed to make it up here despite his injuries. He looked tired...no, wary, upset, maybe sad?

Kasai looked away, not wanting to meet his gaze. "I'm sorry."

"There's nothing to be sorry for." Exhausted. Relieved? Relieved at Kasai finding out, or the apology? Oxe's voice was lower than usual, almost hoarse.

Kasai couldn't hold himself back, even if he wanted to. He flung himself at Oxe, burying his face in Oxe's chest, his arm wrapped around his waist, sobbing heavily.

Oxe wrapped his arms around Kasai tightly, his cheek on Kasai's head. "I'm here now."

It was several minutes before Kasai was composed enough to speak. But now he was mad. "Why did you come here?"

Oxe looked confused. "When you ran out last night-"

Kasai shook his head. "No, I mean, why did you join Thukuli's crew? If he finds you, he won't just kill you, Oxe!" As glad as he was to know Oxe had found him, and been protecting him, he was terrified for him.

Thukuli had literally torn someone apart for defying him, for talking back to him.

But this? Thukuli would *torture* Oxe, just to keep Kasai from doing anything against him.

And Kasai wasn't sure if he could fight back, not before Thukuli destroyed Oxe.

"We couldn't think of a better way to get you," Oxe said soberly. "Brinar had the thought of kidnapping you, but we didn't think you'd react well to that."

Kasai chuckled dryly, shifting so they were more comfortable. He laid his head on Oxe's shoulder, closing his eyes. "I probably would have burned you both before being relieved."

Oxe's shoulder shook as he laughed. "We quickly abandoned that plan."

It felt good to hear his laugh. When he had been Tamotsu, he hadn't laughed often, but when he had, it was different. Restrained, low. Here he was freer, happier. Lighter.

Kasai froze for a heartbeat. "Is that why Brinar tried to join the crew?" He remembered that day with a pang; he had gotten angry, flashed Brinar with heat that he didn't react to, treated him... Brinar had tried to speak to him once after that and Kasai had turned his back on him.

"Yes. We needed to get close to you, talk to you, try to find a way to get you away from Ironwood." Oxe explained, rubbing Kasai's arm. "But he didn't realize you would be so..." His voice trailed off, uncertain.

"Hostile?" Kasai offered bitterly.

Oxe nodded. "But it's nice to know you haven't changed...much."

Kasai felt the hesitation more than heard it. "I hope you understand why...why I've changed."

He had meant because of his current situation, not from before.

"After the fight with Blacksmoke..." Oxe started, pausing when Kasai flinched, "He explained to everyone about everything. It made me understand why you got so upset."

Kasai felt tears falling, stinging his eyes.

Oxe tightened his grip. "I also...saw how you were injured. Both then...and in the other fight."

Kasai shut his eyes. "What happened after that?"

Oxe took a deep breath. "After North shot you with a dart, we took you to the nearby Seaborne base. We had to take Blacksmoke there, and they were the only place nearby that had what Brinar needed to take care of you."

Kasai buried his face in Oxe's neck. It hurt to think of that day, and it was almost worse hearing the aftermath.

"But about two weeks after that, I went to check on you and you were gone. I tried to find you for over a week, but then we had to go." Oxe tightened his arm around Kasai tight enough it hurt, but Kasai didn't mind. "We came back every once in a while, but it wasn't until a year ago, well more than that now, that we found you."

Kasai sighed. "I should've just left with you then."

Oxe nodded and opened his mouth, but a clatter of stones stopped him.

Velu came skidding into sight. "Captains called the crew together. In the Hanged Dur." He paused, seeing them together, and grinned. "Nice that you two made up, but come on or he'll come looking."

Kasai got to his feet and helped Oxe up. "Thanks, Velu." He grabbed the other man's arm briefly before he dashed away. "Did you know?"

Velu nodded. "Some of it. Me and Feluna figured he had been hiding something and found out when we were on the tucowary's island. Seriously though, he's already looking for you both. He's mad."

Kasai and Oxe exchanged concerned looks, then Kasai looked at Velu. "I'll head down myself; it'll be better if I'm not seen with Oxe."

The other two nodded, and Oxe leaned forward, kissing Kasai softly. "We'll be there soon. Just...be careful."

Kasai felt his heart pound, but pulled away quickly and headed down the slope.

He had a feeling of what Thukuli might be planning, and didn't like it.

"WE'RE HAVE YOU BEEN?" Thukuli sneered as Kasai approached.

Kasai shrugged. "Went for a walk." The frantic beating of his heart long since calmed, his features giving nothing away. "What's going on?"

Thukuli jerked his head towards the crowded bar. "Wait with everyone else. We're still waiting for a few people. I sent Velu to get Tamotsu, but they aren't back yet."

Kasai nodded and made his way over to a less crowded spot, spreading out his heat to make sure no one got too close.

Despite the new...revelation about Oxe, he had to keep up his show of hating everyone else. He knew what the crew had said about him, heard the whispers in the night. He didn't want to ruin that, not with *this* crew.

He sat down heavily, grimacing a tad, next to the remains of Thukuli's crew. Daro glanced over, then gazed back out over the other pyrates and muttered to Kasai quietly, "Have you met Bek's crew yet?"

Kasai shook his head. "No."

Daro's gaze darted around. "They're bloodthirsty."

Kasai shot him a look. "Bloodthirsty?"

Jen, on Daro's other side, nodded. "Ruthless, they don't hesitate to kill. They took out three Seaborne ships in a week."

Kasai shuddered. Three Seaborne ships within a *week*? Even Thukuli had never dared that.

One woman looked over, flashing sharp teeth at them. "We'd be happy to do it again."

Kasai met her gaze coolly. "Interesting approach though, provoking them like that."

She lunged forward, lifting Kasai up by his shirt. She was tall, even taller than Oxe. "Listen here you little shit. We handled them when *you* couldn't!" Her teeth were sharpened, not through shifting, but through filing. Her eyes were so pale they were nearly white. Dark freckles were smeared unevenly across her face, standing out starkly thanks to her nearly white-blonde hair.

The room went silent.

Kasai stared her down, not moving. She hadn't lifted him off the ground, only stood him up; he was on a raised section of the floor, raising his height closer to hers. The surroundings cooled dangerously and several people shuddered.

Kasai felt the heat condensing around himself, almost making his skin glow.

She hissed at him through her teeth. "We can do better than Ironwood's little flame any day."

"Delta, back down." Bek ordered, clapping a hand down on her shoulder.

She didn't flinch, though she slowly released Kasai.

"You're first mate is certainly an asset," Thukuli mused, easily heard from across the silent room.

Bek hadn't removed his hand. "Oh, she certainly is, but her temper is going to get her burned if she's not careful." He glared at Kasai as he spoke, "Delta, sit elsewhere."

She jerked herself from his grip, shooting daggers at Kasai before sitting on the other side of the room. She grabbed a full tankard from the bar and downed it while a low buzz started up.

Thukuli's gaze raked the room. "We're just waiting-" The door opened and Oxe and Velu walked on; Linota slipped in behind them and made her way over to Kasai's side. Thukuli's face twitched. "Nevermind." Oxe's face was bandaged again, making it difficult to recognize him.

Not that Kasai would ever make that mistake again.

Linota curled against Kasai as much as she could, shivering. Kasai frowned and placed a hand on her as he listened.

"I've talked with Bek and learned about his crews...achievements." Thukuli stated. There were cheers from Bek's crew, but Thukuli cut them off with a wave. "Which is good because he told me something interesting."

Kasai felt uneasy at the look on their faces.

Bek spoke up. "We found out that Locke Island is under construction. It's being turned into a prison for the worst pyrates in the world, or other offenders."

Other offenders? Kasai couldn't imagine anyone worse than a pyrate, but no matter.

"But they have several ships being stored at the bay until further notice," Bek continued. "Big ones, including something called a man o' war."

A man o' war? That was unusual. It was an old-fashioned style of ship. And utterly terrifying in its supposed manpower.

Thukuli nodded, taking over. "They owe me a crew, and a ship, and I know several pyrates of...ill-repute are being kept there. I figured that if we can get inside, free some of them, maybe they'll be willing to join us in exchange for their freedom." A nasty grin stretched across his face.

Kasai could see several things wrong with that plan, but said nothing as everyone else gave their approval.

Thukuli gave a dark chuckle, still grinning. "Now it will take some time, and we'll have to pass ourselves off as a legitimate construction crew, so we're going to take two months to learn that trade and learn how to act as un-pyrate as possible."

Several people exchanged uneasy looks.

Velu spoke up from near the door. "How long until they finish the construction? Might they be finished before we get there?"

Thukuli motioned to Bek, who grinned. "It wasn't set to start until a month from now. But the crew we caught was more than happy to give us any information we asked for."

Several of his crew chuckled cruelly; Delta grinned, showing her teeth.

"We planted someone in there as well, someone who could infiltrate easily and send out information," Bek told them. "He'll be our contact while there, already having established himself as a person in charge of construction."

"So...we have to act like normal people?" someone asked, earning a few grins.

Thukuli chuckled, shaking his head. "Just enough to fool the Seaborne is all. Be able to lift beams or stones or whatever a construction crew is required to do. That's why for the next month and a half, at least, we're taking over all the construction in town."

Some people groaned; some seem excited.

"I became a pyrate because I was sick of that job!"

"Better than working with livestock!"

"Good chance to get stronger, I guess."

"This is gonna be so boring..."

Kasai tried to tune out the comments swirling around. Staying here could be a good thing. Maybe.

Oxe could recover, Kasai could lie low and avoid Thukuli easier, maybe even find a way to escape.

Maybe he should talk to Brinar.

He shook his head, trying to pay attention as Thukuli started up again.

"I know this means taking a "break from pyracy" for a short bit, but I want everyone learning their job, getting stronger, preparing for the assault on Locke Tower." Thukuli grunted. "Meanwhile, I will be talking to someone of the crew and figuring out how to hide some of our more...noticeable figures."

Most of the pyrates glanced at Kasai, who was probably the most well-known on Ironwood's crew, aside from Thukuli himself. North, sitting at the bar, also got a few looks, but there had been no sign from the Seaborne that they knew North was one of them yet.

Kasai knew he would have to hide, but at the moment he had no idea how. He was too well known, too recognizable by his powers alone. Looking exactly like – he shook his head, not wanting to think about that.

"Get gone, find your own places to stay." Thukuli waved them away. "Kasai, North, Bek, Delta, you four stay."

The others all filed out quickly, an undercurrent of excitement and apprehension in the air. Kasai caught Oxe's gaze, but looked away quickly.

Kasai kept his hand on Linota, warning her to stay.

She whined, wrapping her tail around his waist.

"Linota, get out." Thukuli walked over, his expression hard.

"She stays," Kasai said.

Delta looked thunderous, but Thukuli held up his hand. "Whatever. We need to discuss what we'll be doing."

He led everyone to one of the private rooms in the back. No windows, only one exit, and sort of cramped once all six of them were inside.

Thukuli stood leaning against the back wall. "All of us are well-known faces to the Seaborne. A change of clothing and a few bandages or eye patches won't be enough to fool them."

"Would we need to stay on Locke Island while the others pass themselves off as workers?" Delta asked.

Thukuli regarded her silently. The pause stretched out, the tension palpable, but then Thukuli nodded. "Yes. We can debark on a smaller boat, row around the shore, and meet our contact there. He can take us somewhere to hide out while the others get to work."

"What will they be doing?" North asked. He crouched on the floor near Kasai, his expression dark as he looked at the captain.

Thukuli curled his lip a bit. "Getting intel. Weak spots, guard schedule, patrol routes, anything of interest. Every few days, someone will bring us all that and some food."

"So we'll be hiding out, depending on someone else to get literally everything?" Delta scoffed.

Thukuli snarled at her, "If any of us five are seen, we can forget about *everything!*" He stepped forward, a vine wrapped around his arm. Thorns studded the stem and it curled around his fist.

Delta snapped her jaw shut, looking at the floor.

It was quiet for a minute, then Thukuli looked around at the rest of them, his expression cool. "The five of us don't need to join the others in the construction jobs unless we want to. Just don't leave the port, don't even leave town. I'll have someone always watching." He looked directly at Kasai and North as he finished.

North glanced at Kasai.

Linota whined softly.

Kasai just grit his teeth, his hand clenched around a clump of Linota's fur where the others couldn't see.

Chapter 27

Oxe

OXE KNOCKED AWAY THE hand that reached for him. "I said back off."

The woman frowned, swaying on her feet. "Jus' want some company, love."

Oxe glared and she shrugged before walking off, a tad unsteady. He set off down the street, ignoring some stares he got.

Despite Brimna Atoll being a northeastern island, it was hot out. Oxe had taken to wearing a tank, and the recent work he had been doing showed. He sweated more, but that couldn't be helped.

Already tall, he had always been lean, but the constant lifting for the past month had defined his muscles well. It showed along his arms especially, and he knew his shoulders were a tad broader.

He had earned his reputation as a hard worker rightfully...but he hated it.

He was a fighter, a warrior, a *protector*.

Not a laborer. But he had to fit in with the crew's activities or find a way to disappear. And Ironwood, along with Bek, Kelin, and Delta kept too close an eye on him to do that.

Kelin sat outside one of the smaller inns nearby, his face red. The crew was celebrating the coming voyage, eager to steal a ship from the Seaborne. They would leave in the morning, and it would take another month to get to Locke Island, at least. They were taking a different ship from Bek's; smaller, but faster. They would be cramped, but that couldn't be helped.

Most of the crew were celebrating by getting drunk, spending the night with a local, or having some kind of fun.

Oxe would've shifted into his wolf form if he could, race along the beach or find Kasai, but he knew that if he did Thukuli would kill him on the spot. He wished he could relax.

He wished he could join Kasai tonight, but he was elsewhere.

Oxe sighed, thinking about his mate. Oxe and Cifius, and North when he was around, had been trying to get him to call Brinar, but he kept putting it off.

Cifius was getting exasperated, but Oxe had defended Kasai. He knew of the problems between his mate and the doctor, and it wasn't something they could force Kasai into.

Oxe stumbled to a stop when someone appeared in front of him, blocking his path.

"Tamotsu, right?" It was Delta, Bek's first mate. A bottle of something sweet was in her hand, on her breath. She might have been drunk.

Oxe gave a curt nod.

She snorted. "No need for silence. I'm not going to threaten you."

He somehow doubted that. Her eyes held disdain, her stance confident and arrogant.

"It's nice to see one of the newbies settling into what we're doing." She smirked. As if she hadn't joined the same day he did.

Oxe tried to step around her. "I have somewhere to be." Not really, but he had no desire to talk with her. He had seen her grab Kasai, smelled her metallic, almost harsh scent flare with excitement when it nearly came to a fight.

She grabbed his arm, falling into step with him, flinging her arm over his shoulders. "Seriously. You're a powerhouse. You'll be a huge asset during this...moment."

Oxe resisted the shudder he felt at her tone.

She revolted him.

She grinned, matching his slow, wide stride. "I mean it." She took a swig of whatever she was drinking; some splashed down her shirt, staining it with a strong, strangely bitter smelling liquid.

Where was the sweet smell coming from then?

"You know, I saw something interesting the other day," she prattled on, Oxe only half listening. "I saw Kasai with someone...at the inn by the docks."

Oxe almost froze, keeping his stride just barely, his face blank.

"I mean, I didn't *see them* see them, but I heard them." She laughed; a cruel sound, hollow and dead. "Up in his room?" She grinned at him, her nails digging into his shoulder.

Oxe forced himself to shrug. "So? Sounds like Kasai found someone to spend the night with." He cursed inwardly; they had risked one night together, sharing a bed until morning. None of the others came close to the Drowned Bird. It was too far from the larger bars and more...choice inns.

Her grip tightened and she whispered hotly, "I think he wasn't the only one. Oxe."

Oxe froze, his eyes wide, his chest pounding. He cut a sideways glance at her.

Her eyes were like diamonds, hard and icy. "Oh yes, I know alllllll about you and him." She barked out a harsh laugh. "You think you two were the only ones to sail with Sonus?"

He took a step back.

Delta grinned, showing her teeth. "I was usually in the rigging at the time, you two never noticed me."

Oxe had no idea. Nothing about her was familiar. Looks, scent, attitude, none of it.

"Oh, don't worry, I won't tell." She wagged a finger, shaking her head. "I don't really care if Thukuli finds out or not. That's not my business."

Oxe struggled to think. "Then why confront me?"

Delta paused, taking a long draught from the bottle. When she was done, she threw the bottle against a nearby building. It shattered with a strangely muffled tinkling noise.

Blood roared in Oxe's ears; his heart seemed to hammer inside his chest slowly.

"Because if you and Kasai try to escape, if you fuck this up for everyone," she drawled, her nose almost touching his; he tried not to gag on the sweet and bitter smell of her breath, "I will hand him over to the Seaborne and that bastard brother of his. Just his head though."

She laughed cruelly and walked away, pulling another bottle from inside her vest.

Oxe tried not to bolt, to run to Kasai and take him away. He watched Delta greet a scantily dressed person outside an inn and disappear inside with them, but he couldn't move.

He forced himself after a moment though, not wanting someone to get suspicious and ask him what that was about, and hurried into a dark alley.

He sank against the stone and hung his head between his legs. "Shit."

"TAMOTSU, GRAB THE SHEET." Kelin was struggling with it, trying to get the boom to move.

Oxe ran over, trying not to slip on the drenched deck, grabbing the sheet just as Kelin lost his grip. He pulled hard, and the boom quickly moved, quivering against the force of the rain.

A stupid northern hurricane.

And he was forced above deck.

North, along with three others, were keeping the wheel from turning too much, trying to stay on course. They should reach Locke Island soon, provided the weather allowed them.

Oxe could see several others holding onto ropes, a few climbing into the rigging, and winced as someone was swept overboard.

That made the third person lost this week.

"Tamotsu, hold steady," North called out suddenly, his voice nearly lost in the wind. "Ports coming up. I can see them waiting."

Oxe looked, squinting through the rain running over his eyes, and barely made out some figures standing on the dock. "Can we dock in this?"

North grunted as the wheel tried to turn. "Yes, as long as we can get the ship tied down and the anchor dropped." He yanked the wheel hard; Oxe saw him narrowly miss the end of the dock. "Dina, take over."

The woman nodded, grabbing the wheel as North jammed a hat over his face and disappeared below deck.

He had only come up to help during the storm, his ability far too useful to justify sending him off early; he would join the others the second he could. The day before, despite the worsening wind, the other five had been sent off before the storm hit.

Oxe hoped they were okay.

"Everyone off, we have it now!" He looked to see a Seaborne mate approaching the quarterdeck. He took the sheet from Oxe. "Get ashore, the walls coming!"

Oxe nodded, not needing to be told twice. He was terrified of hurricanes, and it was worse this time because he knew Kasai had probably hit the edge of it. In a scanty little *rowboat*. The hurricane had hit a few hours after the others had set off; the tiny ship would be no match for the rough waves they had faced last night.

He stumbled on the dock, but quickly regained his footing and followed the crew as they ran towards the formidable stone fortress ahead of them.

Most the of the crew were already inside, finding places to dry off and sit while they waited out the storm. If they were unnerved by the amount of Seaborne mates and guards here, no one showed it. Oxe sat down near the entrance, grabbing an offered towel to dry off with. He knelt over and started rubbing his hair first.

A deep voice wrang out, "I understand you're the new construction crew hired by Oake. I'm sorry you arrived during our storm season though."

Oxe paused. Something about that voice was familiar.

"As you may understand, you might have some more work starting out. This storm isn't that bad, however, so we might come out okay." A pair of black boots appeared in Oxe's vision; they faced away from him.

Oxe drew in the scent, but while it was familiar, too much was strange. Ash-powder, salt, metal, the typical scents he had learned that came with Seaborne. But something subtler, almost spicy, lay underneath it. But the blasted rain had washed much of it away!

"We'll be by later to hand out food packets, which you can get from Hana once you begin working. Tents will be provided for you as long as you're here, as the barracks are for Seaborne only." The boots moved away.

Oxe wiped off his arms, not looking up.

"Who speaks for the crew?" The person asked.

"I do." One of Bek's crew, a man Oxe didn't know, stood up.

"I need you and one other member of your crew to come with me. Don't worry, we're not going outside. I just want to discuss rate of pay and such with you in a room just down the hall." The person walked around as they talked, but stopped in front of Oxe. "You, come with me."

Oxe nodded, laying his towel down. He kept his head down as he followed the Seaborne...captain? Commander? He couldn't remember the color codes, but he knew this man was one of the two.

The member of Bek's crew fell into step with them. "My name's Yizaan, sir. This is Tamotsu."

"Nice to meet you both." The man said. "My name is Captain Doux. I'm in charge of the construction and guard here."

Oxe wanted to hiss and barely kept his head from snapping up. Doux? Doux was *here*, of all places? Oxe thought he would be on a ship in the Eastern Area!

He was suddenly grateful for the bandages partially concealing his face.

"You're the newer captain, aren't you?" Yizaan asked.

Doux laughed. "You could say that. Two years as captain isn't long, but long enough." He glanced back at Oxe. "Your construction crew is interesting."

Yizaan nodded as they entered a large room. "We're from all over. Most of us come from the Western Waters, though we have some Easterners too."

Doux nodded, gesturing at the table. "I'm glad you were all able to come so quickly. We're hoping to get the construction done as quickly as possible."

Yizaan sat down quickly. "Well, hopefully we can work to your expectations." Oxe stood behind him, looking down.

Doux brought out some papers and a few pens. "The rate we're paying is 50 kinas per person up front. You'll get that as soon as the hurricane is over, once we can get to the other buildings safely. That will be paid per month, which you are free to spend however you wish in town."

Yizaan nodded. "That's a fair pay per person. How much for the rest of the job?"

Oxe was a tad impressed. Yizaan must've been a merchant or something before joining Bek's crew. He wasn't sure if he could be as calm as Yizaan seemed to be.

Doux tapped the paper for a moment, then scribbled something down. "Three thousand kinas upon completion, with an additional thousand if the job is done quickly."

Yizaan paused.

"Is something wrong?" Doux glanced up.

Yizaan shook his head. "Sorry, sir, that just seems like a lot for a general construction job."

Doux set down the pen with a soft *click*, then folded his hands on the table. "Now that you are here, I will divulge what the construction job is."

Oxe resisted glancing at Yizaan. When Oake had explained the job before, it had been described as a large construction job. Constructing a large, multi-roomed building for the Seaborne. They had all assumed it was an office, a new barracks, something like that.

Had that been wrong?

"We are building a new wing of the jail. We anticipate an influx of criminals before long, and want to be prepared. Your crew is not just be putting up walls and doors as you were told, you will be adding in various jail equipment that needs to be permanently installed," Doux explained, tapping the paper. "That calls for a higher pay. But we could not give details beforehand for safety reasons."

Oxe felt his heart thud. What had Doux meant? He forced himself to appear calm; if Doux got suspicious of the crew, all hell could break loose. It was one thing if he recognized Oxe, but another if he suspected any of the others were not who they seemed.

Yizaan nodded. "Understandable. Will my crew be told? Or just us?" He asked, indicating him and Oxe.

Doux waited a moment before answering. "They'll find out anyway, so you can tell them."

Yizaan nodded.

"I'll let you get back to the crew, but I'll take Tamotsu with me," Doux said, standing.

Yizaan frowned slightly. "Is everything alright?"

Doux nodded. "Of course. But I noticed the bandages and thought I'd take him to one of our doctors. He can work it out with them if, and when, he needs help with that."

Yizaan looked at Oxe. "Of course. Is that alright with you?"

Oxe nodded, his throat too tight to speak.

Doux waited until Yizaan had left, then beckoned to Oxe. "Come with me."

He followed, keeping a bit of distance between them. Doux's boots clicked against the stone floor crisply.

They walked down a short passageway in silence.

Doux glanced behind him, his hands clasped behind his back, as they walked. "Not much of a talker now, are you, Oxe?"

Chapter 28

Kasai

KASAI CRAWLED OUT OF the water, gasping for breath. He *hated* swimming! He never got in the water if he could keep from it anymore. But being dumped overboard in a storm while in a dinghy took it to a whole new level.

Thukuli came running up then. He grabbed Kasai's arm. "Thank the stars...are you alright?"

Kasai nodded once, coughing. "Have you found anyone else?"

Thukuli pulled him to his feet and then let go. "Bek is already up in the trees. Delta's getting to her feet now."

"Linota?" Kasai had refused to leave her behind and she had been in the dingy with them.

Thukuli frowned. "Haven't seen her."

Kasai coughed up a bit more seawater and looked up as a yip was heard. He smiled as Linota came running up, her fur plastered to her body and her tail dragging through the sand.

Thukuli grunted. "Let's get going. North will get here when he's able, but the rest of us need to get to the meeting place."

Kasai nodded, but groaned as he took a step forward. His leg buckled and his knee hit the sand.

Thukuli stopped and looked back. "Everything alright?"

"Yea, just my leg." Kasai tried to ignore the fire burning through his leg, sending stabs of pains up and down erratically. Had he hit any rocks? He didn't think so...but why else would his leg hurt so badly?

Linota whined and stood next to Kasai; she braced herself against him gently.

He pushed on her, but only enough to stand. Once up, she kept herself under his hand. Not as good as a cane, but he knew she could help him get to the trees ahead.

Thukuli watched him, his gaze unreadable. "You never explained how you got your leg injury."

"Because I don't like thinking about that," Kasai retorted instantly.

Linota whined and kept pace with Kasai as they slowly made their way up the beach.

Thukuli walked on Kasai's other side. When they reached the trees, Kasai sank against a tree and Thukuli leaned nearby. "I'm guessing it was a fight."

Kasai suppressed a groan. He hated when Thukuli started asking about him, because he pressed so hard that Kasai usually relented; more to get him to leave him alone rather than let Thukuli get pissy.

"Seriously. That's the only injury, aside from your arm, that you never recovered from." Thukuli's voice wasn't dark, or teasing, for once, only curious.

Kasai hadn't really recovered his vision either, but that came and went. His leg had been fine for months, since Feluna had been making him walk without a cane when possible, but anything like that storm or a fight made it worse for a while.

"I got struck by lightning, okay?" Kasai heaved himself to his feet as he spotted Bek and Delta coming towards them.

Thukuli's eyes widened, but said nothing.

"Captain, we spotted Oake," Bek said, clutching his ribs.

Delta nodded, a bruise on her forehead. "He's waiting for us."

Thukuli nodded. "Alright. Kasai's injured, so we'll need to ask him about shelter first."

Delta sneered. "Couldn't handle the swim?"

Linota growled, but Bek stood between them. "Enough. Thukuli, lead. Delta, follow."

Kasai limped after them as quickly as he dared, but he could tell there was something wrong. His leg had never hurt like this before. Linota walked with him, and Bek kept a few feet ahead, but the others were already talking when they walked up.

A short man with bright blonde hair and wearing the uniform of a Seaborne guard was speaking to Thukuli.

"Yea, it's protected and sort of isolated. He'll be fine there if you have to leave him," Oake told Thukuli. He turned as Kasai limped up. "Come on, I just told the others about a place that will be safe for you."

Oake kept pace with Kasai, forcing the others to go slowly, leading him around exposed roots, stones, anything that could trip him.

"I'm not sure what you can do about your pet," he said after a while, addressing Kasai.

Linota huffed, but Kasai shot her a look. "She's not a pet. She's a shifter who's living as an animal," he explained.

Oake grinned. "Never seen that before; apologies. But I wouldn't let her run around freely. Someone might see her as a threat to the livestock."

"Livestock?" Kasai knew this was a Seaborne port, but was there a town here still?

"Mhm," Oake responded. "Mostly the families of those stationed here, but a few others who lived here before or got permission. There's an animal farm and an orchard nearby."

That made sense.

"I'm taking you four," Linota growled and Oake grinned, "Sorry, five, to an abandoned post up ahead. No one goes there. It's pretty overgrown and they no longer have a use for it," Oake explained as they reached a partly overgrown road. "There's a river that runs past it, so you'll have plenty of water, and it turns towards the town so no one come up this far anymore."

Delta snorted. "So no surprise Seaborne?"

"No. The captain here is somewhat strict with the ones stationed here." Oake frowned. "I won't be able to get free as often as I thought, though."

Thukuli hissed at him, "So what should we expect then?"

Oake shrugged. "Not sure. Maybe I can assign a runner, someone who can come back and forth occasionally, every few days like I was planning on. I'd ask Feluna, but I'm sure she'll be busy."

"It can't be Yizaan. He's acting as the leader of the crew. Tamotsu and Dina are possible choices, but those two are the strongest workers." Thukuli glanced at the ivy trailing along the path as they walked. "How many Seaborne are in the town?"

Oake shrugged. "Not sure. Some of them are stationed here and have their families, so most of them live in town. There's new recruits occasionally, but mostly guards who are sent here from elsewhere, and they all stay in the barracks."

"What about villagers?" Kasai asked.

Oake paused, thinking. "No idea. I don't really go into town much; I can't get away as often as I like. And when I do, it's usually because they need an extra hand with the animals or food deliveries."

Delta kicked at a fallen branch. "You sure no one comes up this way?"

Oake glanced back as the outline of a building could be seen. "Pretty sure. Like I said, the captain's strict."

"How often do they leave the base?" Thukuli asked.

"Every few days. His family is in town; he's got four kids! But his wife is nice. I've met her a few times," Oake responded.

Kasai looked up as the building came into view.

It must've been a storeroom at one point. Windows, high up, were shattered but the roof looked intact. The walls were straight stone, and the large iron door stood strong.

"I'm afraid it's just one big room, but you can separate it if you need to. Use some old crates and just be careful not to let anything fall," Oake told them.

"Will the Seaborne need anything that's left?" Thukuli asked, his eyes roaming over the ivy spreading along the outer walls.

Kasai watched Oake pause and noted the uneasy flicker on his face. Kasai didn't think any of the others saw it.

"I doubt it. It's been years since they used this place." His voice was even as he spoke, but Kasai couldn't help but wonder why he looked nervous.

Thukuli nodded and pushed open the door; it was double sided but opened easily. "It'll be dry, or at least mostly, and we'll be out of sight."

Linota whimpered softly as Kasai followed them inside. He tried to ignore the pain but it was getting worse.

"I can send someone to check you over, if you'd like?" Oake asked quietly, startling him. He must've noticed Kasai struggling.

"I'll be fine," Kasai nearly hissed.

Oake waited until everyone was inside, then shut the door. He joined Kasai at a pile of crates nearby. "I'm serious. I can talk to someone about coming to see you. You can meet her at the river tomorrow, if you can, and she can check your leg."

Kasai gave him a sideways glance. "Why are you helping us? Betraying the Seaborne like this?"

Thukuli, looking around, came over when he heard this. "I'm paying him."

Oake shrugged. "He's right. He's paying me, and well...I used to be a pyrate. Not a big face like you two, but I joined when my crew disbanded after the Seaborne attacked us and left us for dead. I don't mind helping Thukuli get a new ship. I understand the reason."

Did he know Thukuli was also going to free prisoners, if he meant that? Kasai doubted it.

"But seriously. Get downstream, to the cluster of boulders shaped like an animals back, and I'll have someone come check you over at noon," Oake told him.

Thukuli looked at Kasai. "You might as well. I know Oake wouldn't suggest this unless he thought it was safe, and you've been in pain since you washed ashore."

Linota whined, nudging Kasai's hand.

Kasai made a face but nodded. "Alright, fine. Just one request though."

Oake raised an eyebrow. "What's that?"

"Get me something for a cane," Kasai grunted.

THE SUN WAS HIGH OVERHEAD when Kasai finally reached the boulders. They really did resemble an animals back; the largest boulder could be the shoulders, sloping down to the back along a long but shorter boulder, and a slightly higher boulder completed for the hindquarters.

Kasai reached a little niche with a gasp. Linota licked his hand, but he scratched her ear. "Don't worry, I'll be okay." He doubted it. His leg had went numb through the night, though he still had enough feeling to walk thankfully. And feel the stabs of pain.

A pair of voices caught his ear.

"I'm missing my lunch for this, so I'll need to leave as soon as we find him." It was Oake.

A murmur responded, softer, indistinct.

"I'm sure he's here, or will be soon. Maybe wait by the rocks?" Oake sounded a tad unsure.

Kasai nudged Linota. "Can you let them know where I am?"

She yapped and dashed out.

"Oh, there's his...friend. He said she's not a pet, that she's a shifter?" Oake sounded a tad relieved. "Can you take us to him?"

A yap and Linota appeared a moment later. A few seconds later, Oake appeared, someone tall hidden behind him; from the angle, Kasai couldn't see their face.

"Na'vira, this is-" He was cut off as the woman pushed forward.

"Kasai?!" Na'vira ran forward and pulled Kasai into a hug.

Kasai froze as she wrapped her arms around him. Na'vira?! But that meant... "Oake, what's the captains name?"

Na'vira let go. "It's Doux. He's in charge of the base now."

Oake nodded. "I...didn't expect this. I need to get back before I'm missed." His gaze darted nervously between them, then back towards town. "Na'vira, can you promise not to tell anyone? I didn't think you'd know him."

Na'vira nodded. "Of course! Get going, Oake. If someone asks, tell them you went to me for a stomachache or something. I'll cover for you."

Oake nodded, clearly relieved, and disappeared.

Kasai held his breath as Na'vira turned to him.

"What are you doing here? What happened?" She sat with her legs folded under her, hands in her lap. She looked very different from the last time he had seen her. Clean, no bandages, a faint mark on her neck from the burns. Her hair was brushed and braided in an intricate style around her head, hanging down in a pair of loops on each side of her head. She wore a simple but lovely dress of some kind of wool.

"I got shipwrecked." Kasai told her the first thing that came to mind; not exactly a lie either. "That storm swept me overboard and I tried to swim to the closest place I could find."

She frowned. "It's lucky you were so close to land." Her eyes flicked over him, appraising him. "You've been hurt badly though, haven't you?" Her voice grew softer.

Kasai winced as he moved his leg. "Just my leg."

Na'vira shook her head. "No, it's more than that. You've got a mechanical arm, and I can see many more scars than before."

He was surprised she could tell so much without even examining him.

She gave a sad smile. "It's alright. I won't treat anything you don't want me to, okay?"

He nodded and gasped as a sharp pain stuttered up his leg.

She gently pulled up his pant leg, gently running her hands up and down, poking at various points. "This is much worse than before."

"Before?" Kasai gritted his teeth at the pain.

She nodded. "You've got nerve damage; I know that from Brinar. But...did you hit any rocks when you fell overboard? Encounter any sea life?"

He shook his head. "Not that I recall." He relaxed a bit as a numbness took over his leg.

Na'vira suddenly lifted the edge of his shirt. "That's the problem."

His body port opening, how he took his medicine every six months, was leaking blood and fluid. Kasai hadn't thought to check it and hadn't felt the wetness; his clothes were stiff from his dunking yesterday, but there was a faint mark from where his jeans had soaked up the fluids. Despite all the injuries he got over the years, it rarely ever needed checking. Thukuli wasn't aware of it, but Feluna and Velu knew.

"Kasai, I need to get you to one of the other doctors. This is going to require surgery, or at least more care than I can give," she said slowly, lowering his shirt.

He laid a hand on Linota. "Why would this cause a problem? It never has before."

Na'vira shrugged. "I'm not sure. I still don't fully understand how they work. Have you done something big with your powers lately?"

A chill swept through his body. "You could say that..." The wall of flame on Norths ship months ago. The glass crater at Brimna Atoll. The constant heat he put out to keep Thukuli at arm's length.

"What happened?" she asked gently.

Kasai sighed, leaning against the boulders. "It's a long story. The short of it is, I got upset."

She raised an eyebrow at him. "Upset? Over what? And how long ago?"

Kasai shrugged. "Four months? Maybe four and a half. But...I found out someone lied to me and I kind of...lost control." He felt his face burn and looked away. "And a while before that I sort of...attacked North."

She gasped, her hand over her mouth. "Oh Kasai..."

He shrugged, scratching Linota's head. "I've made up for it. At least, I hope I have. North isn't mad anymore, not after we talked." And after North had seen how Thukuli was firsthand.

"Kasai, this could kill you." Her words caught him short.

He looked at her, detecting an edge of alarm. "What do you mean?"

"I mean, I think the intense heat you've subjected it to has damaged it and being knocked into the sea made it worse," Na'vira explained with a worried look. "This can't wait."

"No one can know I'm here!" Kasai said quickly, but immediately regretted it. Linota shifted closer to him, her gaze darting at Na'vira. He bit his lip against a wave of pain.

Na'vira's eyes narrowed. "Why..."

Kasai hesitated, unsure of what to say.

"Are you afraid the Seaborne will catch you?" she asked.

Kasai nodded. True, but not just for the reasons she knew. Linota laid her head in his lap, curling her tail around him.

Na'vira sighed. "Okay. I can understand that. I've heard from Doux about the trouble Ironwood, and you, have caused," Kasai flinched but she continued, "And I won't let them take you. But you and Doux saved me. I won't let you die."

Linota nudged him, her eyes nervous.

Kasai nodded then looked at Na'vira. "Someone else got washed up with me, but they're fine. I need to tell them about this though. Can this wait until tomorrow?"

Na'vira opened her mouth, but then closed it. She watched him cautiously, her gaze flicking over him for several long minutes before she answered. "I'm not sure."

Kasai sighed, but looked as she brought out some paper and a pen.

She handed it to him. "Can your...friend," she glanced at Linota, "deliver a note to them?"

Kasai nodded. "Yes. What should I tell them?"

"That you need to be seen by a doctor, but you need to go into town. And that you're safe." She waited while Kasai scratched the message out. "I promise, I won't let the Seaborne take you, Kasai. Doux took the position here because he didn't want to be the one to catch you. That would've killed him."

Kasai looked at Linota. "Can you take this to where they're staying? And stay with them."

Linota whined, flattening her ears.

"I know. But if you need to, come find me. Stay out of sight, hunt for yourself, but stay away from the town unless you have no choice." He gave her a hug and she dashed off, the note between her teeth.

"Who is she?" Na'vira asked when Linota was gone.

Kasai sighed. "A shifter, like Oxe. But she can't stay human, or not entirely. She's no longer a wild animal, not really, but she's far more intelligent than a real animal is. She hasn't been able to shift back to human for months."

Na'vira nodded. "I'll tell the doctor you have an animal companion who might show up then, so he doesn't hurt her."

"Will you tell Doux?" Kasai asked suddenly.

Na'vira looked at him sadly. "I might have to, especially if the doctor requires you to stay nearby for any kind of treatment."

Kasai sighed. "Is there any chance I could stay anywhere without him knowing?"

Na'vira shook her head. "I'm afraid not. Anyone else who would recognize you would turn you in immediately. But Doux won't turn you in, not if you stay with us and out of sight." She gave a wry grin. "But he may demand you stay with us, give up being a pyrate."

If only it were that easy.

Kasai sighed. "Alright. I can agree to staying out of sight." Thukuli would come looking for him, but not for a few days at least. "Just do me a favor?"

Na'vira tilted her head. "What?"

"Don't tell Brinar." Kasai closed his eyes.

Chapter 29

Oxe

OXE SET THE BEAM INTO the hole and backed off. "Think that will hold?"

Dina nudged it; it wobbled slightly. "Maybe, if we brace it somehow."

Oxe grabbed a few stones stacked nearby and set them around the post, keeping them tight against the wood. "Think that will help until we get the crossbeam up?" The post stayed steady.

Dina grinned. "Nice job. You're pretty good at this."

Oxe shrugged. "This is what I did before." Not a lie, not really. He had been working in construction for a month before joining Ironwood's crew.

"Has that cut still not healed?" She asked as they walked towards the rest of the crew working nearby.

The bandages across Oxe's face had been repositioned to be more comfortable, but he refused to remove them. Doux had been confused, but respected that Oxe was hiding his face for whatever reason and helped him figure a way to make it more comfortable for him.

Oxe shrugged. "It's taking its time."

Dina gave him a concerned look but said nothing as they reached the others.

"Tamotsu, the captain wants a word." Yizaan looked unhappy.

Oxe repressed a sigh. Yizaan had asked about Doux's interest in him before, and Oxe had told him they had met a few times before, well before he became a pyrate. He assured Yizaan that they were in no danger of being discovered and he relented.

But he had decided that Oxe could throw Doux off their trail completely. Yizaan encouraged him to tell Doux about the crew, to highlight their work as construction people.

Oxe wanted to tell Doux the truth, but he was afraid that if he told Doux now, things would go badly. He wanted to find Kasai first, then maybe he could tell Doux about what Ironwood was planning.

The captain was waiting at the farthest edge of the construction site, away from everyone else. He was dressed in regular clothes; it must be his day off.

"Tamotsu, I wanted to invite you over tonight." Doux smiled as Oxe walked up. "I cleared it with your boss, and he's fine with it. You guys have been working hard for a few days and done really well so far."

Oxe gave him a small smile. "That'd be great. Does Na'vira know?"

Doux shrugged, giving him a sheepish look. "No, I haven't told her who's coming. She just knows we have a guest tonight. I thought it would be a nice surprise."

Oxe shook his head, smiling. "How's Lastel?" He guessed she was around four years old now.

Doux laughed. "Happy, demented, the most insane child I've ever seen!"

Oxe waved to Yizaan, who was watching them with a grim look, as he followed Doux towards town. "I am glad you've all recovered from before."

Doux's smile faded. "I am too. It took a while for Na'vira to become relaxed around other people, but she works as a healer in town here. The other doctors, the three we have here, are more skilled overall but none of them know herbal remedies like she does. And not everyone wants their medicines, so she gets to help out plenty."

"I wish I had talked to her before, got to meet her better," Oxe said honestly. He'd gotten to meet her and their daughter, but he had been more focused on Kasai at the time.

Doux nodded. "You can make up for that tonight. But warning...the house is sort of full right now." He gave Oxe a strange look. "We have triplets at home now."

Oxe almost stopped in surprised. "Triplets?" The word was unfamiliar, but he think he understood what Doux meant. "You mean three-born?"

"Yes." Doux sighed, the sound deepening into a groan. "They just turned six months and Lastel is jealous."

Oxe couldn't stop the laughter that bubbled out. He hadn't met any of them, but he could understand. Sometimes older siblings got jealous of newer ones in the tribe.

Doux shook his head, grinning. "Kassi and To'mas are already little troublemakers, but Soni is...well I won't be surprised if she takes after her uncle, or her grandfather."

"Soni?" Oxe asked.

"I named her after Sonus. I know I didn't know him, but I talked with Brinar a lot after you went to look for Kasai," Doux explained. "He told me a lot about him. Despite him being a pyrate, he wasn't bad. And he did love us, even though he had to be away."

Oxe glanced at him. "To bad we can't tell Kasai."

Doux didn't speak as they rounded a corner, reaching the edge of the town. He led them past a few houses before he spoke. "Did you ever find him?"

Oxe hesitated. How much could he say that would keep everything quiet for the moment? "Once. When I was in Brimna Atoll." He knew he and Brinar had told Doux they were heading there, more or less. "But I never got a chance to speak to him. There was an...accident and I got hurt."

Doux frowned. "Did Kasai take off after that?"

Oxe forced a nod. "Yes. But after I recovered, Brinar left for home and I stayed there in case he came back."

Doux cut him a harsh look suddenly. "Did the construction crew come from there too?"

"No," Oxe said automatically. "I started working there, but went to Surval after a couple months."

Doux relaxed. "Sorry. But why not go home?"

Oxe didn't meet his gaze. "I can't." He hoped Doux wouldn't ask.

Doux shrugged and stopped in front of a two-story house. Brick instead of stone, with a large window looking inside, the door was made of wood with iron accents. Doux saw him staring and shrugged again. "Not my choice for a house, but it's one of the few this close to the base with enough room for my family."

Oxe followed him inside, feeling a tad awkward. He felt uneasy, though he wasn't sure why. The front room was big; a wide couch, several toys, a hand-woven rug, and a wide but low bookshelf. Paintings were hung on the north wall, giving splashes of color to the beige tone of the room.

Na'vira's voice drifted from somewhere ahead. "Doux, who's our guest?" Oxe smiled as she came through an opening. She was holding an infant; the child's eyes were wide open, bright green, and her hair was a pale blonde color. Na'vira looked a little better than he had last seen her, but the biggest change was how happy she was.

Smells of something cooking followed her; meat, herbs, some kind of earthy vegetables. He even smelled hot milk, a treat he rarely saw on Wolf Island.

Oxe coughed. "Hey, Na'vira."

Na'vira stopped. "Wait...Oxe?!" She cast a nervous glance behind her. "What are you doing here?"

"I'm with the construction crew," he told her.

Na'vira glared at Doux, surprising Oxe. "I think you should go in there. Kassi's being fussy."

Doux quickly stepped past her.

"I think you should stay here for a moment, Oxe." Her words were hard, but her expression was a little reluctant and confused. "Dinner's not ready yet. Would you mind watching Soni for a few minutes?"

Oxe nodded, taking the little girl. "Of course."

Soni cried for a second as Na'vira disappeared into the other room, but then got distracted with the toy Oxe handed her as he sat down.

He watched her for a moment, smiling as she banged around a few wooden rings of different sizes. She could sit on her own, and she looked strong and healthy.

Soni suddenly pulled on his sleeve. "Ga!"

"Ow!" He gently stopped her as she hit his arm with a toy. "Don't do that, that hurts." He handed her a post on a stand, showing her how to put the rings on. He hadn't seen this kind of toy before, but guessed what's what it was for.

Na'vira's voice startled him. "Sorry. She just started that with her toys and we aren't sure how to get her to stop." She stood in the doorway. "Why don't you come in and eat...but, Oxe?"

"Hm?" He looked up from Soni's toy.

"Kasai's here," she said slowly.

"SO YOU BOTH LIED?" It was late and the three-born were asleep, while Lastel was supposed to be asleep in her bed; Oxe could hear her playing in her bed. Doux was leaned over, his hands behind his head.

Na'vira laid her hand on his back. "Can you blame them?" They were sitting on a wide chair across from Kasai and Oxe. Na'vira was on the arm while Doux sat in the seat.

Kasai exchanged a look with Oxe. He could see his mate felt bad about revealing...everything, but it was too late now.

"What's stopping me from marching up to the old warehouse and arresting Ironwood right now?" Doux growled.

Kasai shot up, then leaned back with a wince. "Don't! Thukuli is a decent fighter on the sea, but he's deadly on land!"

Oxe shot him a look. "What do you mean?" He had never seen Ironwood fight on land before, and he had seen the pyrate slaughter people on a ship a few times with no problem.

"His powers? He's a plant genetic, remember?" Kasai said. His hand fluttered against his side for a second; his stitches must be bothering him. "On land, he can call any plant to help him, especially anything related to any kind of ivy. Stone ivy is his favorite to work with."

Doux groaned, leaning back and tipping his head against the chair. "That's the whole damn island then!"

Kasai gave a low hiss, the fury in his eyes shocking.

Na'vira gave him a sympathetic glance, then looked at Kasai and Oxe. "Locke Island is home to three kinds of ivy. Ice ivy, on the northern shores, is the only ivy that can survive in salt water for a while. Cave ivy, sometimes called shadow ivy, grows in the shady parts or in the mine to the south. But stone ivy is found everywhere with stone."

Kasai groaned and shut his eyes. "Doux, he's going to kill everyone."

Doux looked up, his face reddening. "No he won't! We're Seaborne here, we won't lose!"

"And he kills people with that same kind of ivy for the fun of it!" Kasai yelled.

Someone started crying, and Na'vira quickly left the room.

"Sorry," Kasai muttered.

Oxe squeezed his hand.

Doux sighed. "What do you suggest, then? You said he was going to steal a ship, because I blasted apart his and took out most of his flagship crew?"

Kasai was silent.

Oxe laid a hand on Kasai's leg; now that the body port device was gone, his leg was sore but fine. "Maybe wait until he's on the ship and attack then."

Doux frowned in conversation. "That's not a bad idea, but the means letting pyrates work on the prison in the meantime."

Na'vira appeared, feeding Soni. She sat down on the couch next to Kasai.

"If you let on you know about them, he'll strike now," Kasai said darkly.

Doux grit his teeth, his anger a sharp smell that overpowered everything else. "So what do you suggest?" he repeated.

No one spoke.

Oxe cut a look at Kasai.

Pale, tired, his waist-length hair was down for once. Oxe didn't think he was taking care of himself very well. Underneath the clean clothes, he looked unkempt. He probably wasn't sleeping either.

"Maybe we should talk more tomorrow," Oxe said carefully. "If I'm here much longer, they'll get suspicious." He darted his eyes at Kasai, looking at Doux.

Doux glanced at Kasai and gave a small nod. "You've got a point. Oxe, I won't be able to drag you away much, will you be okay with them?"

Oxe nodded. "Yes. They think I'm keeping you off their backs; I'll let them think that for as long as I can."

Kasai placed his hand on Oxe's arm; his hand landed over the scar from when he burned Oxe just before he killed Grimshaw. "Just be careful, please. I don't want to lose you."

Oxe wrapped an arm around him. "I will. And if I can visit, I'll come back."

Doux nodded. "I might be able to assign you as a runner, but unfortunately you really are one of the strongest workers. Yizaan isn't going to let you go easily."

Oxe sighed. "But at least I know you're safe." He kissed the top of Kasai's head. "That's better than nothing."

"Do you know who Ironwood's contact is?" Doux asked suddenly. "You never mentioned their name or gave a description."

Kasai shook his head. "No. I didn't get a good look at him, but I know that Thukuli's paying him."

Na'vira gave Kasai a sharp look, but said nothing.

Oxe wanted to ask her about that, but now wasn't time. He helped Kasai up. "I'll stay for another minute, then I'll go."

Doux nodded. "Kasai's room is just over there. We moved Lastel to the upstairs room for the time being; he's been having trouble walking."

Kasai shook his head but limped into his room, Oxe on his heels.

Oxe shut the door quietly, then turned to Kasai. "Why didn't you mention Oake?" He had met him the day before. Oake wanted him to run food to the others every few days, but Oxe declined. He wanted to stay on site and keep an eye out for Doux when he could, and now he was especially glad he had declined; he wanted to be free to come see Kasai if possible.

Kasai sat on the bed with a heavy sigh. "He's not a bad guy, and while he's helping Thukuli steal a ship, he doesn't know that he also wants to free some of the prisoners."

Oxe sat next to him. "But shouldn't they know?"

Kasai didn't answer, just laid down under the covers.

"Kasai, are you okay?" Oxe asked softly. He knew he wasn't, but there was something off about him right now.

Kasai nodded. "Yea, I'm just exhausted is all. The doctors removed my body port and I'm still adjusting to that."

Oxe knew about the port, but not that it was gone. He had never asked Kasai about his medicines; they were mates, but Kasai had always been quiet about that part of himself and Oxe respected that. "Will you be alright without it?"

Kasai shook his head, the blanket up to his shoulders. "I have to be. At least for now. They told me that when I can get to a place where I won't be in so much danger, I can get another one, but for now I have to go without."

"Can you still take your medicines?" Oxe asked.

Kasai shook his head. "Not easily, not with where I usually am."

Oxe stood up and set something on the bedside table. It was Kasai's bangles, the ones he got to match Oxe's bracelet. His bracelet was with Brinar; they wanted to make sure he hadn't lost it. But Kasai's bangles wouldn't stand out much and Oxe had grabbed them before Brinar left, just in case he could give them back to Kasai.

He leaned down and kissed Kasai's cheek. "Everything will turn out ok."

Kasai sighed again. "I hope so."

Oxe left the room and saw Doux waiting for him.

Doux met his gaze. "Oxe, you understand how dangerous this is, right?"

"Yes. But that's why you can't fight yet. You need to wait," Oxe growled, his jaw shifting. "Ironwood, Bek, and Delta are their strongest fighters. Those three alone are dangerous, but I believe Kasai when he said that Ironwood is deadly on land."

"Do you really believe we can't take him on land? Oxe, some of the guards here are the best Seaborne men in the world. A few might even be able to match Razora; not win, but last more than a few seconds." Oxe was surprised by the tremor in Doux's voice. His eyes were hard, but there was a glimmer of fear in their depths. "I'm not just speaking as the base's captain, but also as Kasai's brother. If it comes to a fight, and it will, we'll have to fight him anyway, and Kasai will probably be in the fight himself too."

Oxe glanced at the closed door behind him. "We need to trust Kasai. If he says we need to get him off land before fighting him, then that's what we need to do."

Doux nodded, lines etched into his face. "But if we wait that long, then what? What if they escape in that moment?"

Oxe snarled through his teeth, "Then sink the ship."

Chapter 30

Kasai

THREE WEEKS OF RECOVERY were a hell he never wanted to experience again. He knew something like this would happen again, eventually, but he wished he could catch a break. Na'vira had been kind to him, and never asked of him more than he could handle, but she had her hands full with the kids.

Soni had quickly attached herself to Kasai once he felt well enough to help watch them. He was the only person she wouldn't hit with her toys and she liked to pull his hair. She sometimes got angry when being told no, and it didn't help that she had already shown genetic abilities...in the form of en.

Na'vira had asked Kasai to feed her, which was messy but relatively easy. He had tried to give her a piece of softened carrot, but she didn't like it and shocked him. His arm was numb for the next half hour and Na'vira wasn't sure how to handle her now, but luckily it was only one time, so Kasai didn't mind watching her.

Kassi was quiet for an infant, watching Kasai with wide blue-green eyes when he was nearby. She played quietly, slept quietly, and even stayed quiet when they read a book. Strangely, she didn't laugh, and didn't complain when given something strange that she may not like, but she ate well and didn't cause a large mess like To'mas did.

To'mas not only made large messes, both with food and in his diapers, but he had flung food onto the ceiling multiple times. He splashed in the tub to where the floor was almost a puddle, and threw his toys everywhere. Kasai didn't enjoy trying to get him to eat, but still helped with his nephew.

Lastel was...an enigma. White hair, dark brown eyes, and a penchant for music, she got Kasai's attention once and gave him a wooden flute that Doux had made for her. Kasai tried to play it, but she immediately took it and gave it to Na'vira, who played a beautiful tune and tried not to laugh at Kasai's playfully hurt expression. Lastel didn't talk much, and got mad when Kasai wouldn't do what she asked, but never gave a reason.

"Here Kasai." Na'vira interrupted his thoughts, handing him a heavy bag. "I picked these up for you today."

Kasai took the mysterious bag. "Er, thanks." He pulled out the first package on top, wrapped in brown paper.

"Me!" Lastel came over and took it, but Na'vira stopped her.

"This isn't yours. Go play with your sister for a minute." Na'vira shoed her oldest daughter away and handed the package back. Lastel pouted but sat with Kassi, who was hitting blocks together.

Kasai unwrapped it carefully to reveal a smooth crystal pad. Purple and marbled black, the metal pad on the bottom shone brightly. "A face-crys?"

Na'vira nodded. "So you can call us when you need to. There's a codebook and a hookup in the bag too. It already has a few codes in it."

"I can't accept this, Na'vira." They had spent quite a bit on him already. The surgery and medicines for his recovery, the extra food they needed to buy, and the two sets of clothes they got for him.

Not to mention the medical care for Linota. She had shown up a week ago, a bullet in her shoulder and half starved. She was sleeping at his feet right now, her bandaged ribs moving slowly.

Na'vira smiled. "Yes, you can. Doux has missed you so much, and while I liked you already and considered you family before, it's been great to have you here and I'll be sad to see you leave."

Kasai wanted to sigh at that; they had all agreed that after this, Kasai and Oxe were to head to Witch Island, then to Wolf Island. "I appreciate this more than you know."

Na'vira hesitated for a moment, and Kasai felt the words before they were spoken. "Maybe you could call Brinar before the attack."

"I can't." The words came out hoarsely. "And I wish people would stop telling me to." Kasai was hurt, annoyed, and saddened by everyone's nudges to call Brinar.

"But how will you know if he's mad at you if you don't talk to him?" Na'vira asked him quietly, watching her daughters play.

Kasai couldn't answer.

"Are *you* mad at *him*?" Na'vira's question caught him off guard.

Kasai blinked at her. "Mad at Brinar?" Na'vira nodded. "No." An automatic answer. Was he mad at Brinar? He didn't know. He knew he was afraid, but mad?

"I know you think he abandoned you, Kasai." She met his glare calmly. "No one told me. I can just tell." She took the face-crys pad and set it down. "But I also know how you refused to speak to him in Brimna Atoll."

Kasai closed his eyes. "I was just so..." He couldn't find the words and trailed off.

"Angry?" Na'vira said. "Upset? Afraid? Kasai, it's understandable. But you need to talk to him, make things right."

Kasai opened his mouth to say something but was knocked down as a massive *thud* came from outside, shaking the house and sending things falling. Linota yelped as Kasai landed on her, but licked his face worriedly.

Na'vira didn't hesitate; she dove for the two kids on the floor. "Kasai, get the others!"

Kasai grunted and made his way upstairs. Soni and To'mas were crying and he grabbed them both. Na'vira met him at the foot of the stairs. He handed them to her and asked, "What happened?" His leg ached, but he ignored it. The kids were more important.

"Explosion at the tower. I know it's a risk, but can you find out what happened? Stay in the trees!" Na'vira explained. "I'm okay with the kids. Just go find Doux and Oxe!"

Kasai nodded and grabbed his cane from the floor and burst outside, Linota at his side.

A siren screamed from the base and Kasai could see several Seaborne running for the base. He dodged into the trees across the road as quickly as he could. "Linota, stay close."

She growled and led him through the trees, helping him avoid anything that could trip him as best as she could.

It wasn't long before the trees ended, and Kasai was forced to a stop. Ahead of them, the base was a disaster. The half-constructed walls were collapsing, fire licking along them greedily. Planks, stones, bricks, all kinds of materials littered the ground. As Kasai watched, another explosion went off nearby.

He was thrown to the ground and narrowly avoided a falling tree, staggering to his feet as quickly as he could manage. "Linota, can you see the crew?"

She yipped and flicked her tail towards some figures running towards the docks.

Kasai nodded and tried to run behind a building; his gait was awkward and he almost fell a few times, but slammed to a stop as a bullet hit the fallen stone wall ahead of him.

"Halt!" It was a Seaborne mate. At a quick glance, Kasai knew this kid was no threat. His uniform was too big and his long en-gun was shaking. A new recruit.

Kasai waved his hand and a tongue of flame licked around the kid immediately. A tremor of fear, cold and sharp as ice, shot through

Kasai. His ability had never reacted that easily before, or felt that unstable. The flames felt stronger, but Kasai was glad that he still had control of them.

He got behind the wall before the kid noticed and sent flames ahead of him; they responded instantly. Was this because his body port was gone? He wasn't sure if he liked that. These flames were higher, hotter, and more dangerous than before.

They snaked through the rubble like a guiding light, showing him where to walk. There were yells, the sound of falling stone, cracking beams, and the crackle of fires in the air.

Kasai tried to ignore them.

Another explosion sent him into a wall and Linota howled. His head rang, but someone pulled him up and saw Thukuli.

"Get up. Go to the docks with everyone else. I have to do something first." Thukuli gave him a shove towards the others. Hard. "And we're going to talk about where you've been!"

Kasai shivered at the look on the captain's face. "Linota, come on."

She limped up to him, her paw held off the ground. Her tail dragged and she lowered herself until her belly was on the ground, flashing her eyes at Kasai.

Kasai took off as quickly as he could, Linota at his side. Thukuli disappeared towards the base.

There was shouting as the Seaborne arrived in full and began grappling with the pyrates. Kasai was forced to a stop as three people surrounded him.

"Give it up, Inferno!" The middle woman yelled at him, her sword out.

Inferno? His nickname had been updated. Kasai frowned, leaning on his cane. "Give what up? I'm just heading to the docks." A bit of a bluff. He jerked his head, but was surprised when flames shot up between them. Linota fell back with a yelp.

With a sharp cry, the woman stumbled backward. The other two raised their en-guns and shot through the fire.

Kasai grunted as he felt a bullet hit his shoulder, making him stagger. "Linota, get to the ship!" He barely glanced as she limped off at a trot.

He was forced back when one of the Seaborne rushed him, their saber raised. His shoulder ached, but he barely felt it; a warm trickle ran down his arm.

Kasai called his staff, but it felt wrong. It was lighter, longer, and two prongs on one end, while the other end looked flatter and wider, yet thinner. He brought the pronged end up, blocking the saber...*but the blade melted on contact!*

The Seaborne mate fell back, visibly shaking. "What..."

His companions charged Kasai from both sides and he froze, but flames shot up and he heard screams. The staff dissipated in a flash.

He stepped back, horrified, as he saw them drop to the ground, their skin on fire.

The woman wasn't moving, and the other man stopped quickly.

He had killed them.

With no effort.

The remaining mate yelled and slashed the remains of his sword, but Kasai dodged, barely missing the gleaming stub. The mate waved it wildly, unbalanced by the changed weapon.

Kasai brought his cane up to block the metal end, not wanting to risk his fire now.

"You'll pay for this!" the mate hissed, bringing the hilt down on Kasai's hand.

Kasai gasped and fell back, unbalanced. His cane clattered away, catching fire before he could react. He called the flames away, but the thin wood was already weak and he knew it wouldn't hold any weight before snapping.

"Kasai, get back!" A wild strand of ivy suddenly shot through the ground, wrapping around the mate in a heartbeat. Thukuli appeared, his shirt on fire. "And get this off me!"

Kasai scrambled back on all fours, willing the fire away; it disappeared with a *snap!*

Thukuli twitched his hand and Kasai flinched at the mate's screams. "Most of them are on the ship. Get yourself over there. I brought Velu to help."

Velu shot out from behind a nearby wall, helping Kasai to his feet. "Come on, we need your help."

Kasai didn't want to, but there wasn't a chance to get away. Not without hurting Velu at least, and he didn't want to do that. He had one arm over Velu's shoulder, the other man supporting him, but gasped at both the pain he felt and what he saw at the base.

Thick vines, some black, some a pale green, and many of them streaked with red, covered most of the walls. Doors were held fast by walls of ivy, and Kasai could see several forms, some struggling and some still, wrapped head to toe in dark, spiked strands.

He knew Thukuli was more powerful on land...

...but this was far beyond anything he had seen before.

The ground suddenly burst apart and ivy began crawling like a horde of snurves towards Thukuli.

Velu helped Kasai around some rubble, but they both turned as they heard a piercing scream.

Kasai glimpsed a hilt fall, the short blade fragment glinting, and the ivy-wrapped figure slump to the ground.

Velu let go of Kasai with a yell.

Thukuli turned calmly, his face cool, and began walking towards them. "I just saved your life, so you can head to the ship safely now."

Kasai barely heard Velu gasping.

Oxe appeared several feet away. In a flash, he turned and took a few steps towards them but stopped, his eyes wide. Kasai met his gaze for a second, but glared at Thukuli.

Doux, in full uniform, his skin dark and metallic, came running from the base. "IRONWOOD! BACK OFF!"

Thukuli just raised his hand, not moving his eyes off Kasai, and a swath of stone ivy shot for Doux.

He tried to back off, but the ivy encased his legs; only his iron skin kept him from getting hurt. Kasai could see he was barely holding his ability together though.

Thukuli glanced at Doux for a second and muttered, "Well, that's interesting," but kept his gaze on Kasai. "What do you think you're doing?"

Kasai stood, most of his weight on one leg. "You didn't say you were going to launch an assault on the entire base!"

Thukuli shrugged, flicking some ash off his shirt. "Plans changed. You would know if you hadn't been living with your brother for the past three weeks."

Everyone froze.

Doux met Kasai's gaze, held fast by the vines encasing his body from the neck down. His eyes blazed; not mad at Kasai, but pissed he couldn't defend him better. That the base had fallen under his watch. Kasai knew his brother was proud of his position.

Oxe was watching Kasai, his gaze hesitant and...afraid?

Why would Oxe be afraid of him?

"Oh yes, I know about that." Thukuli's voice stayed calm. A mountain in a storm. Unmovable. Steady.

Furious.

A building heat surrounded Kasai, only to condense into small, encompassing flames. White and yellow flickers showed up among the usual red and orange.

Thukuli sneered, cocking his head. "I wouldn't try anything, Kasai."

Shots of blue flickered through.

"You see, if you attack me now, I'll tell your brother your secret. About home?" Thukuli's eyes hardened.

Doux's gaze turned dark, his eyes on Kasai.

Kasai froze. No...did he know? *How?* The flames retreated.

Thukuli nodded. "That's what I thought."

Oxe had taken a few steps closer, only able to stand the heat because of his familiarity with it. Kasai met his frightened gaze and glared, trying to tell Oxe to stop.

Oxe froze for a heartbeat, then dashed for Velu.

Thukuli watched him help Velu to his feet and gave a small frown, then turned his gaze to Kasai. "Head for the ship. Now."

Chapter 31

Oxe

THIS WASN'T LIKE KASAI. His flames, usually darker shades of red, were softer but more controlled. These flames, bright oranges with some white and shot through with blue, these *couldn't* be Kasai's.

He was too careful, too controlled. Never wild.

But the charred bodies said otherwise.

Oxe didn't think Kasai even knew what he had done. He watched Ironwood stalk up to Kasai and grip his jaw, jerking his head up.

He leaned down and whispered something to Kasai and Oxe was startled...no, *frightened*, by the wave of fear that came rushing through the fire.

Overwhelming the smell of ash. Of burned flesh.

Of death.

Kasai was terrified; Oxe watched his body shudder, quickly turning to trembling. He fell to his knees. His face was both blank and terrified, his eyes wide.

What could Ironwood have said to have such an effect on Kasai?

Kasai jerked himself up and limped towards the dock.

Ironwood clenched his fist and Oxe watched Doux collapse. He was still breathing, Oxe could tell even from here, but he was completely immobilized. Ironwood followed Kasai slowly, his fist at his side.

He paused by Oxe and Velu. "Get to the ship. You'll know the one."

Oxe wanted to growl, but fear kept him silent. He focused on Velu instead, guiding him around rubble and debris as they walked. The heavy bag at his side felt awkward, but he wouldn't leave the face-crys behind. Na'vira had risked the danger and ran it to him at the edge of the forest; he knew it was important to keep it hidden.

"What did he tell Kasai?" Velu asked quietly once Ironwood was out of earshot; Oxe could see him saying something to Kasai, who looked furious.

"I don't know." Oxe glanced at Velu.

His hand was pressed against his shirt, partially wrapped with the bottom edge, but Oxe saw the heavily blistered skin, could smell the boiled blood smell that sometimes came with burns.

Velu saw his look. "He didn't mean to. I could tell."

Oxe nodded. The ground turned to wood beneath them.

"He's lost control of his powers, hasn't he?" Velu asked.

Oxe glanced at Kasai, who was heading up the gangplank. "I think so. But...something else has changed."

Velu shot him a look.

"I think... He got his body port removed, and he's acting different. He's not...stable with himself." Oxe struggled with the words.

Velu was quiet as Feluna approached. The ship's doctor had been mostly silent since Kasai had found Oxe, and she was hesitant to approach him. None of them knew why. "Come on. We have other injured, but that's the worst."

Oxe let them go ahead, meeting Dina at the foot of the gangplank.

She looked furious. "Did you see what happened?"

Oxe nodded. "Yes. Kasai lost control of his powers and burnt Velu."

She shook her head. "Not that! We have new crewmates..." She jerked her head at a group of gaunt looking people nearby. About ten people, at least that he could see, all older than most of the crew.

Oxe caught one of their gazes and a wave of malice flooded out. "Big names from the prison?" His resist wrinkling his nose.

Dina nodded. "Yes. Some of them have been here for over a decade."

Oxe shook his head. "We should get aboard." He hated saying that, but he wouldn't leave Kasai on that ship alone.

Ironwood was at the end of the dock, his hand still fisted. Oxe could see he was making sure everyone was aboard before he released his hold on the base.

He joined the original crew on deck and got a good look at their new ship.

Gleaming and already sea-ready, the carigate was a formidable-looking ship. Oxe could see the three masts were tall, with the front one being squared-rigged. A storm jib stretched from the bowsprit to the mizzenmast, and three sails were rolled up along it going up, but were off center from it.

The foremast, at the back, had two booms instead of one; both had triangular en-sails, which meant there was an engine. The mainmast had two large square sails, but the topsail had five sides and could move freely.

Oxe had a brief wonder if this was a brand-new ship, but was distracted by Ironwood leaping aboard. He held a box under one arm, and a sword in the other. "Cast off! Let's leave this island behind!"

There was a cheer, mainly from the freed prisoners, but most of the pyrates ran around to take care of the sails.

Ironwood stalked over to Oxe. "Tamotsu, take this to my cabin then help set up the lower decks."

Oxe nodded and set off. The box wasn't that heavy, but there was an earthy smell coming from it. He was stopped by Delta once, who told him where the captain's cabin was, and Oxe quickly went inside. It was at the end of a short hallway. Two other rooms sat across from each other; the surgery and a storeroom? He couldn't tell, but it didn't matter and he hurried into the captain's cabin.

The room was large, with only a bed, desk, and an empty chest in it. Oxe set the box down next to the bed and left. He could already feel Ironwoods presence in here and he didn't like it.

On the second deck, he was surprised at the row of cannons. Eight on both sides, with cannonballs stacked in various spots. The deck appeared to run most of the length of the ship, with a powder room sectioned off at the back of the ship.

The third deck was busy, full of pyrates beginning to set up hammocks and move around the various crates and boxes. Some of them were familiar, members of Bek's crew, but others were new, dressed in the drab prison garb of the base.

"Tamotsu, right?" One of these women came over to him, her greasy hair hanging over her shoulder. "One of Ironwood's crew?"

Oxe nodded.

"Not a talker? No matter. Where should we bunk?" She hooked her thumb over her shoulder to the group of now-ex prisoners behind her.

Oxe shrugged. "Find a spot for your hammock, even if there's not enough of them to go around yet. I was sent to help get the bunks set up."

She nodded and spoke to the others, who promptly broke apart and began choosing spots for themselves.

Oxe grabbed one hammock for himself, then hung it near the stairs, wanting to be able to leave without waking people. He needed to talk to Kasai, and bring him the face-crys, as soon as it was safe.

"So what's this?" The woman was back. She reached out for Oxe's bag, but jerked back when he glared at her. "Hey, easy, I was just curious!"

Oxe shook his head. "Just some stuff I bought with my wages is all." He needed to hide the bag.

She gave a bitter snort. "Wages? Did you really buy into that labor work crap?"

He gave a shrug. "Meant we got you out, right?" Oxe didn't like this woman, but he would act like he was a true pyrate if it meant she would leave him alone. "Who are you anyway?"

She snorted again, then started laughing. "Seriously? You don't recognize me?" Her laugh sent chills up his spine, set his hackles bristling. "I'm Nona, once known as Distortion?"

"I'm not familiar with too many pyrates that are around right now, let alone any from a while ago," Oxe told her.

Her grin fell. "Had your head in the sand?" She shook her head. "No matter. I'm sure we'll get along fine."

Oxe watched her leave, then laid down. He might have been sent here to help set things up, but he was tired and sore. Today had been...exhausting.

He hadn't known about the explosives and his nose was burning, and almost numb, from all the scents. And then meeting Na'vira and making it back to Kasai had been difficult. He had fought off a few Seaborne, but he only knocked them out.

At least he hoped they were just knocked out.

He watched the others through slitted eyes and kept the bag on his stomach, one arm over it protectively.

"GET OFF!" OXE GROWLED and deflected the sword with his claws. The merchant gasped as his sword was knocked away with a spray of sparks.

Three months, at least two ships a week, and he still had yet to get close to Kasai. He glanced over at his mate; Kasai was standing back from the fight, a frown etched on his face. Oxe rarely saw him anymore.

Kasai had shut himself in the engine room most of the time and didn't let anyone join him. Not even Oxe.

Oxe knew they couldn't be together, not without raising suspicion, but it still stung.

When Kasai did leave the engine room, it was to eat twice a day, use the head, or because Ironwood called him to his cabin. Oxe always felt uneasy after the event, unlike Kasai, who always seemed furious when he reappeared.

The ones from Bek's crew, who were now Ironwood's because Bek had been killed during the assault, had grown wary of Kasai.

He rarely spoke, according to what Oxe heard, and snapped at people when they tried to talk to him. Velu had tried to talk to him not long after they left Locke Island, but when Kasai had seen his arm...

Ironwood wasn't happy when they had to replace the sails only two days after leaving. That was when Kasai had shut himself away.

Dina and Nona came over, the former holding an en-pist and the latter wielding some kind of club. Nona swung it at the merchant, who raised his sword again, and there was a tremendous *bang!* as he was sent flying.

Oxe glanced at her. "Thanks." As much as he hated doing this, attacking people and being forced to hurt them, he was finding it annoying now. The merchants, as that was usually who they attacked and robbed, didn't seem to understand when a pyrate was trying to kill them or when someone was just trying to get them to back down.

Not that Oxe blamed them. As far as anyone knew, he was one of the pyrates.

Nona shrugged. "No problem. You looked bored of him." She waved her hand towards Oxe and he felt the pressure from the blow clear, leaving him a little lightheaded.

He shook his head. "Did you see Kasai joined today?" He jerked his head towards Kasai. While only North, Velu and Feluna knew about their connection, he showed some interest in Kasai around Dina and Nona. Not a lot, but enough that they knew he wanted to talk to him.

Dina glanced towards Kasai and her lip twitched downward. "Thukuli forced him. At least, that's what Delta said."

Nona nodded grimly. "She was correct. The captain's not been happy with Kasai since Locke, and has been trying to get him to leave the engine room more."

Oxe wasn't surprised she knew that. She was the second mate of the crew now, thanks to being a pyrate for over twenty years before being caught. "Any idea why Kasai looks so angry when the captain talks to him?" The question was rhetorical, but he wasn't surprised when Nona answered. He turned as another merchant crewmate ran at them, blocking his slash and shoving him away.

"He's been trying to get Kasai to use his powers," she told him.

It took Oxe a minute to realize what she said. Once he did, he jerked around to look at you. "What do you mean?"

Nona shrugged. "Not sure why, but Kasai hasn't used his powers as often for weeks. When he does use them, he's forced, but it's clear he's uneasy."

Oxe frowned, but couldn't say anymore as Ironwood called everyone back over to their ship. The moment everyone was over, some of the crew stopped and watched the merchant ship; Oxe could see it was sinking and wondered who had done that. He met North's gaze as the older man limped below.

He made a mental note to check on him later.

"Delta, how much did we get?" Ironwood looked excited, which made Oxe nervous.

Delta had been one of the last ones across, overseeing the ones who were gathering whatever they stole. She didn't answer for several moments, then finally looked up after making some marks on a piece of paper in front of her. "Le, both spiced and not, about five casks. That was the bulk of what they were carrying."

Five casks weren't a lot, not for a crew this size, but it was a decent amount for the merchant ship. Oxe had a much better understanding of how they thought about cargo after these last few months and had to admit, he was impressed. It might be stolen, but Ironwood was surprisingly fair when it came to the goods. At least with his crew.

The gunners mate, a former prisoner who Oxe avoided, stepped forward. "Are we keeping any ourselves?"

Ironwood frowned. "Not this time. The le will be sold." There were groans as he looked at Delta. "Anything else?"

She nodded. "Spices, about four large crates worth, and maybe over twenty kinds. A large crate of wyne, and some fruit. The cooks already taken the fruit, but I don't think anyone has a problem with that."

Oxe thought Ironwood did, from the cool look on his face, but the captain said nothing.

"Oh, and Kasai raided the captain's cabin and found several hundred kinas, a few books, and a now broken face-crys," she finished.

Oxe glanced at Kasai. He was leaning heavily on his new cane, one that must've been carved from a single tree, his hand tightening around the colf-head handle. His hair was down, like it had been for a few weeks, and he looked more tired than usual.

Ironwood glared at Kasai. "How did it break?"

Kasai shrugged. "The captain fired and missed me." His voice was ragged, rougher than Oxe had ever heard it. He hadn't been sleeping again, but he really hadn't been speaking much by the sounds of it.

Ironwood looked at him for a heartbeat, then turned away. "Alright, we're heading to port. We have too much cargo now, and I'm sure everyone would like a break."

There was some agreement from the crew, especially the ex-prisoners, but everyone went quiet when he raised his hand.

"After that, we're going hunting in the Western Region for a while." His words were met with silence.

Delta looked up. "Er, captain, are you sure?"

Kasai went pale.

Ironwood nodded. "Yes. We've been in the Northern Waters for a while, and went into the Eastern Area a few times, but everyone's gotten used to us." Oxe felt a twinge at that. "But the Western Region would be unaware of us."

"And we'd be targets for Razora." Someone called out.

A heavy silence descended upon the ship.

Oxe didn't miss the fear that flitted across Kasai's face.

Ironwood sighed, his gaze flicking over his crew. It landed on Velu. "Razora is a formidable foe, that is true."

The crew scrambled to get out of his way as he walked towards Velu.

"But she has one ship there, one crew." Ironwood stood in front of him.

Velu looked nervous, but his voice was steady. "Yes, but she doesn't tolerate other pyrates in her territory. If we go too far south-"

Ironwood hadn't moved, but a strand of ivy came shooting out of the bag at his waist and wrapped itself around Velu's neck. Oxe could see it was still in contact with Ironwood, which meant he had greater control over it.

"If we go too far south, then we'll deal with her," Ironwood said evenly.

Kasai turned away, but no one noticed but Oxe.

Oxe looked back in time to see Ironwood walking back towards the center of the ship. Velu was gone. There was a distant splash, and Oxe saw a few drops of blood on the rail.

Ironwood stopped when he was in the middle of the crew. "We are currently in the Northeastern part of the seas, below the ice line. We'll stop at a few ports along the way, spread out our goods. If we happen to chance upon another ship, we'll take it. But it will take at least seven months to reach the Western Region."

The crew listened in silence. The original crew knew his temper, but the newer ones hadn't seen him like this. Not this bad. Oxe had a couple times, but this was the worst.

"Does anyone have a problem with going to a new territory for a while?" Ironwood looked around, his face calm.

No one spoke.

"Good. Get to work on the sails or find something to do." Ironwood stalked off, pausing to say something to Kasai, then disappearing to his cabin.

Oxe met Kasai's gaze but he didn't recognize the fear, or guilt, that bled through before Kasai turned away.

Nona walked over. "Tamotsu, go help the cook with anything for now. Then I want you to check with Kasai about the engine."

She must've seen the look on his face.

Oxe nodded and headed for the mess area.

Chapter 32

Kasai

"WHAT?" KASAI MET THUKULI in the captains cabin a few minutes after he had dismissed the crew.

"Easy, I just wanted to ask about the face-crys." Thukuli held a hand up. "That's all, I swear."

Kasai grit his teeth. "I don't know how it got smashed."

Thukuli looked up from the garden bed he had set up under the windows. "It was melted, not smashed."

Damn.

It had been an accident, that much was true, but he had flared out heat. Every time he found one, he thought about taking it and every time he lost control. He didn't know why.

He also didn't realize someone had seen it this time.

"You need to get your powers under control." Thukuli's gaze turned dark. "I'm serious. Want to avoid the crew? Fine. Don't want to, or I guess can't, fight? Whatever, as long as you watch the engine and obey my orders. But your powers-" He stopped with a gasp.

Kasai clutched the handle of his cane hard, trying to pull back the heat before it caused a fire. The surrounding air rippled.

Thukuli waited until it stopped, then glared at Kasai. "That's what I'm talking about!" His shout made Kasai's ears ring in the enclosed space.

Kasai shrugged, ignoring the daggers in Thukuli's gaze.

"Get to the engine. Stop messing up." Thukuli ordered.

Kasai bit the inside of his cheek to keep from lashing out. As if he meant to do that with powers.

He left the cabin and made his way downstairs.

As if he were in control of them.

The gun deck had a few people walking around, all of them ignoring Kasai. The crew deck was nearly empty; the door to the mess was open and voices could be heard inside.

As if his own abilities didn't scare him anymore.

The cargo deck was packed with various crates, barrels, boxes, bags, everything they had gathered over the last three months. They could go longer between ports now, but the crew was stretched thin. They would need more crewmembers.

Even after freeing a dozen and a half people from Locke, this ship was massive and meant for a crew of at least 80, not almost 60.

Kasai stopped to grab something from a nearby crate. Thukuli was unaware of it, and he only got it out when he knew he'd be alone. No one else knew about it yet and he wanted to keep it that way.

The engine room was quiet, the wood a little damp from being under the waterline. It made the room cool, a good thing anymore. Kasai sat down on his bed; he had a proper bed for once, not a cot or a hammock. He leaned his cane against the wall and set the hurdur on his pillow.

He had found it on the second ship they attacked, and it was brand new. The designs were made by Marric; Kasai recognized the swirls and curves along the sides. The new strings, from the same ship, needed a quick retuning because of dampness.

Kasai reached under his bed, to the little niche he had carved out with a long knife, and pulled out a packet of papers, a pen-quill, and a notebook. He hadn't started doing this until he found the hurdur, but it felt good to be hearing music again.

Unlike the previous crew, this crew didn't sing often. He remembered North and Arat singing, badly, and even Brinar had joined in occasionally, and during storms the crew would sing a kind of song called a shanty to help make the work easier.

He had joined in a few times until his voice was damaged. Him and – he stopped the thought before it formed and set down the papers as flames licked along his hands.

Kasai bit back a growl and tried to focus on the flames flickering along his arms. While his newest arm, provided by Cifius, was of much better quality and could take a lot more damage, he didn't want to risk it melting. The flames slowly receded.

He breathed a sigh of relief as they disappeared. The flames were unpredictable still and much harder to control, and he was sick of telling Thukuli that.

Since leaving Locke Island, Thukuli had been pressing Kasai to use his powers more and more. But three weeks ago he threatened Kasai if he didn't start using them.

Kasai growled as the conversation flashed through his head.

"You have powers. You can't just not use them!" Thukuli growled through his teeth. He stood in front of Kasai, a strand of stone ivy twined around his arm.

Kasai blinked before answering. "It's not like I'm doing this because I want to." His voice was dull. He was tired. Tired of...everything. "My flames aren't working like they used to. These aren't like normal."

Thukuli snorted. "So? Learn to use them."

Kasai suppressed a sigh and bit back his response.

"Going to play silent? Fine." Thukuli went over to his desk and pulled out an en-crys. "Maybe you need

some...incentive." He set it into the hookup and it glowed softly.

Kasai tried to ignore the knot forming in his stomach. Wasn't the threat of death enough?

"You asked me a few weeks ago how I knew about Kira's death," Thukuli tapped the lit up en-crys. "This is how."

"Yea, it was him. He doesn't realize he did it though. At least, I'm pretty sure he doesn't. Why do you ask?" Kasai's head shot up at Naomi's voice. "Seriously, though our brother was a lot closer to our mom, Kasai is probably still torn up about her dying." There was a pause. "I know you won't let me talk to him, but tell him that I know he caused the fire. But I'm not mad or anything. It was an accident."

Kasai felt sick. He hadn't dreamed it then. HE caused the flames that destroyed the house, HE killed their mother, and Naomi was alive...

And in contact with Thukuli.

The message continued, her voice growing hard. "Look Thukuli, I know you're a powerful pyrate and everything, but remember your deal with Razora-"

Thukuli cut off the connection with a snap.

Kasai fell back in the chair, his eyes burning. "So I didn't just dream it...you weren't kidding..."

Thukuli gave Kasai a long look. "I've talked to your sister quite a bit in the last year. I like her. She's like you, but not as restrained with her powers."

Powers? She was a genetic too?

"But if you learn how to use your powers, start using them, I'll tell you where she is." Thukuli dangled the words in front of Kasai's nose. "I can even take you to her."

It was several minutes before Kasai could respond. When he did, his voice was choked. "Why hasn't she tried to find me?" He hadn't even known she was alive. Though he kept worrying about her, he had finally decided that if she was alive, she was safe and happy. If he found her, he found her. If not, he just hoped she was happy.

But actually hearing her was not something he had expected, not like this.

Thukuli gave him a sympathetic look. "I don't have an answer for that." He did, but he wasn't telling. Kasai could see it in his eyes. "But I also heard you talking in your sleep once about that, so I contacted her and asked."

Kasai felt a pang. He had slept so badly during his recovery, and since then; nightmares, restlessness, constantly torn between waking up frequently or being stuck in the nightmare that the flames the night his mother died were his. But he didn't realize it wasn't a dream, but a memory.

But he couldn't ignore how creepy it was that Thukuli had been there while he slept.

He relented. "Fine. I'll try to use them again." He closed his eyes briefly. "But let me talk to my sister."

Thukuli snorted. "Not a chance." He didn't back down from the flames that crawled along the floor. "But if you burn my ship down, you'll never figure out where she is."

Kasai called the flames back; they jumped to his hand and formed his pronged staff. "Fine."

Thukuli grinned as Kasai stood up. "Follow my orders from here until Valai, and I'll arrange a meeting with her."

Kasai didn't respond, ignoring the cruel edge to Thukuli's grin, and stalked out.

Kasai fell back against the wall with a groan. He had been doing his best with his powers, at the very least controlling them, but he couldn't continue to ignore the guilt he felt. So many ships attacked, so many lives lost. Most of them at his hands.

There was a knock and the door opened.

Nona came in, Oxe at her heels. "Kasai, Feluna reassigned Tamotsu to watch you. I guess he was doing that before this ship, but then something happened and he wasn't on that duty for a while."

Oxe looked uncomfortable and gave Kasai an uneasy blink.

Kasai frowned a bit. "I mean, sure, but he won't be able to bunk with me like before."

Nona snorted, crossing her arms. "He stayed in the room with you?"

Oxe nodded. "I had a cot before, on the previous ship. Feluna was concerned about Kasai's headaches."

Not that they had bothered him in a while now, but that had been the deal before.

Nona shrugged. "Doesn't matter to me, but I thought she wouldn't be so obvious about setting you two up together."

"Obvious?" Kasai was confused.

Nona grinned, and Kasai could tell she was trying not to laugh. "You're partners. That's been obvious to me from the start."

Oxe stared at her, and Kasai closed his eyes. He had been careful to keep his distance from Oxe, partially out of fear of discovery, but also because he knew Oxe would ask and Kasai wasn't sure if he could tell Oxe about his secret...

Nona chuckled. "Don't worry, I won't tell Thukuli. He's a good captain, but he's also a ruthless psychopath."

"Yea, that's for sure," Kasai muttered. He noticed Oxe give him a strange look and sighed. "Alright. But sometimes I might send him back up so Thukuli doesn't get suspicious."

Nona nodded. "If you really do need help, I could ask North to come check on you. He told me you were old crewmates." When Kasai gave her a worried look, she raised her hand. "That's all he said to me, and it was because I asked him. I heard him talking to Velu a few days after we left Locke and I was curious."

Kasai leaned back. "So why send Tamotsu down now?" He was nervous and glad. He could finally talk to Oxe, but he also knew that a very uncomfortable conversation would follow the moment they were alone.

Nona glanced at Oxe. "I know he's been waiting to talk to you, and after earlier...I thought this would be a good moment. I know about the face-crys."

Kasai saw Oxe's alarm, but kept his gaze on Nona. "Were you the one who told him?" Flames sprouted along the floor.

"I have to, whether or not I like it," she responded dryly. "Now I need to get back topside before Delta comes looking." She turned and left quickly, shutting the door behind her.

Kasai didn't meet Oxe's gaze. Oxe set his bulky bag on the bed and sat against the wall. He could tell Oxe wasn't avoiding him, but giving him space.

Kasai sort of wished he wouldn't right now.

Chapter 33

Oxe

KASAI GLANCED AT THE bag but didn't move.

Oxe wished he could sit with him, but he wasn't sure if he should. He didn't want someone walking in and seeing them, but he also wasn't sure if *Kasai* wanted him there.

"I'm sorry for before," Kasai said quietly.

Oxe watched him, not daring to move.

"I should've stopped him. But I didn't know he could do that." Kasai glanced at him.

Oxe didn't miss the fear, or hurt, in Kasai's gaze.

"I..." Kasai stared at his hands.

"What did he say to you?" Oxe whispered.

Kasai flinched. Fear flooded out from him, moving with the flames that flickered around the room slowly.

Oxe didn't think Kasai had ever been this afraid before. He sat closer, within arms reached, and watched his mate sadly. "Kasai?"

Kasai looked at him. "He knows Naomi."

"Your sister?" Oxe blinked in surprise.

"Yea. She went missing when we escaped Cloud Village and..." Kasai took a deep breath, "I think she's with Razora."

Oxe's hackles raised. "Why do you think that?" He could tell there was more, but didn't press.

Kasai laid down so his head was near Oxe. "He's been talking to her for a year. He had a message from her on a crys."

Oxe leaned his head against Kasai's. "But why do you think she's with Razora though?"

"She mentioned a deal with her," Kasai told him darkly.

Oxe kissed Kasai's forehead, then sat up. "Maybe there's a good reason." Kasai glared at him but said nothing. "I'm serious. Maybe she turned pyrate like you and ended up with Razora."

Kasai curled up, his eyes closed. "Maybe you're right. But *Razora*?" He groaned and rolled onto his back.

Oxe flinched as flames raced around the floor. "Kasai? Why are your flames different?"

Kasai sat up. "I think because I can't take my medicine anymore." He called the flames to his hand, and Oxe noticed the flickers of white. "This doesn't feel right."

Oxe frowned and tried not to flinch from the heat. "It's hotter than before."

Kasai flicked his hand and the flames vanished. "I thought they might be."

"Kasai, why have you been...visiting the captain lately?" Oxe couldn't hold the question back any longer.

Kasai grimaced. "He's been pressing me to use my powers. Finally...he threatened me."

Finally? Oxe knew, or guessed, that Ironwood had threatened Kasai before. But had he threatened something worse?

"If I follow his orders, I do whatever he says, he'll arrange a meeting with Naomi," Kasai said bluntly.

Oxe felt a stab of irritation. While not unexpected of someone like Ironwood, it was still a low blow. Using something, or in this case someone, as leverage against Kasai. "Kasai...do you think you could find her without Ironwood?"

Kasai sighed. "I don't know. She knows where I am apparently, but she hasn't reached out. I don't know why."

Oxe sat on the bed next to him. "Maybe she's unable to, the same way you can't get away from Ironwood right now."

Kasai hung his head. "I really don't want to think about that."

Oxe felt a rush of sympathy, but grabbed his bag. "Here. Take this."

Kasai took the bag, but grimaced as he felt the weight. "You grabbed this from Na'vira, didn't you?" He clearly knew what it was. His tone was bitter, and annoyed.

Oxe resisted grinning. "She insisted I give this to you." His grin faded as he continued, "She said you need to call-"

He flinched as fire shot out, almost blistering the air. There was a sizzling sound.

"*If you say Brinar I swear...!*" Kasai snarled at him. He snapped his jaws shut, looking away.

The fire, a pale orange shot through with blues and white, whirled around as if there were a strong wind inside the room. The walls steamed from the heat, and smoke came from the bed.

Oxe flinched against the wall, cringing back from a tongue of white-fire. "I'm sorry!"

Kasai sighed and stood up and leaned against the opposite wall. The flames shrank and turned darker, though they didn't disappear. "Just...why does everyone insist I talk to him..."

Oxe watched him before he spoke. Kasai was angry, and upset, but Oxe couldn't tell why. "Because he can help you better than you think."

Kasai snorted.

"And because you two never talked after..." Oxe's voice trailed off.

"After I nearly killed us both?" Kasai said bitterly. He sank against the wall, knees to his chest.

Oxe nodded once.

"I hate how I lost my temper that day..." Kasai laid his head against his knees. "But then...he refused to talk to me for *weeks* and it still hurts..."

Oxe waited, listening. He knew that sometimes Kasai needed to talk things out. It seemed to help him far better than someone asking the occasional question.

"I'm afraid he hates me," Kasai whispered.

The flames flickered darkly along the floor, then went out.

Oxe didn't move, though he wanted to. "Kasai, he doesn't hate you." That was true.

He'd spent months with Brinar after Kasai's disappearance. They had talked many times, mostly about Oxe's home, their customs, talks about what may have happened to Kasai. But Oxe had asked Brinar about after the arena exploded when they returned the clipper ship.

"Brinar was upset after you were both hurt, but because they wouldn't let him treat you," Oxe told him.

Kasai looked up, his eyes wide. "Wouldn't *let* him?"

Oxe nodded. "Because he was too injured mostly, but because they needed him to research the book he had."

Kasai sighed. "The one about the brain, right?"

"Yes." Oxe shifted to the edge of the bed. "No one could understand it as well as him. He even read while they healed him." Oxe had been impressed with the healers of Witch Island.

Within an hour of being knocked unconscious, Brinar was awake and mostly well. Well enough to read at least. Kasai had already been in surgery by that point, and the damage discovered, but he had already been taken to the recovery room by the time Brinar reached the information they needed.

And the entire time, they had worked on him as well. But he never stopped. Not until they told him that Kasai was waking up. It was only after that did he agree to rest before they left.

But he told Oxe, on the night Kasai had snuck into their communications room, that he felt terrible for not being able to help more.

"Kasai, he wished he had done more. And after you fought Blacksmoke..." Oxe hesitated.

"I trust you, Oxe, that he didn't abandon me," Kasai said tiredly.

Oxe grimaced. "I am glad you do, but he..." He hesitated again, unsure of what to say. "He wanted to bring you back to Witch Island. They were going to let us live outside, on the mountain. Kasai, he wasn't going to give up on helping you."

He almost got up when he saw tears on Kasai's face, but Kasai looked away. "That's why he was going to join Thukuli's crew, wasn't it? He just wanted to help..."

Oxe nodded, his throat tight.

"I'm glad he didn't then," Kasai growled. "He wouldn't have made it very far in the crew before Thukuli would've killed him, or we would've lost him when the Seaborne destroyed our ship."

Oxe couldn't disagree with that. Brinar might be a strong fighter, despite his almost pacifism, but against Ironwood...

Kasai stood and the flames appeared again, licking around the engine. He flicked his finger and they raced to his hand. "But I can't."

Oxe bit back a sigh. "Why not?"

Kasai glared at him, the flames going out. "Because Thukuli would find out somehow. And I can't risk that right now." He sat down next to Oxe, leaning against him. "Even if I can contact him, what can any of us do? It's not just me now. You and North are on the crew, and Linota's being held in the cargo hold."

Oxe still didn't understand why. A month ago, one of the ex-prisoners had accused Linota of biting him and Ironwood chained her against the bow, just above the bilges. The man had bite marks along his arms that matched her jaws, but Oyx wondered if he had provoked Linota. He wouldn't be surprised if she *had* been provoked.

He had seen Kasai bring her food, and had checked on her once himself, but he couldn't guess why Ironwood was really keeping her like that.

Oxe wrapped an arm around Kasai. "But if you can...try, alright?"

Kasai nodded but stayed quiet.

Oyx resisted the urge to pull Kasai closer as he would've done before. He rubbed Kasai's arm gently but jerked away, shooting to his feet as the door opened.

Nona came in. "Easy, it's just me. We spotted another ship. Captain wants everyone on deck. There's a pressure buildup going on, a huge storm is coming. He wants to get this ship before it hits."

Oxe frowned. Storms in the Northern Waters could come on quickly. "Are you sure we'll be able to?"

Kasai shot him a look, but Oxe could tell he was thinking the same thing.

Nona shrugged. "Probably. My own abilities can stave off the worst of it, but we need to go *now*."

Oxe waited for Kasai to grab his cane, tucked in the space between his bed and the wall, then followed them out.

IRONWOOD APPROACHED Oxe. "Nice work, Tamotsu." Oxe tried not to flinch. "I'm serious. You've really gotten good at this."

Oxe tried to contain the grimace he could feel threatening to show itself.

Ironwood gave him an odd look, but thankfully walked off.

The woman at Oxe's feet stared up at him, her arms around the child curled against her. "Please...don't hurt us."

Oxe turned away, but didn't leave. This was a new low for the crew.

This wasn't a merchant ship they had spotted; it was a travel ship. For families.

Oxe had tried to keep from attacking, but Delta spotted him. He knew the cut along his jaw would scar; it was too deep. He watched the crew round up the remaining travelers, herding them to where Oxe and a few others were keeping them contained.

North gave Oxe a sympathetic look as he brought someone over.

"Tamotsu, come help us." Ironwood waited at the entrance to the ship's upper cabins with Nona and Kasai.

Oxe met them but avoided Kasai's gaze. Linota, crouched at his feet, whimpered. He was glad Kasai had freed her, but the large cut across his nose was painful to look at. Ironwood sliced Kasai as soon as he saw Linota, but then again when Kasai openly defended releasing her.

It had taken every fiber of his being, and Nona and North keeping iron grips on his arms, not to spring at Ironwood.

Ironwood busted down the door and stepped into the narrow hallway. Oxe pricked his ears as he heard a whimper, not from Linota, but said nothing as they reached the captain's cabin. Linota backed away and fled down the hall; Oxe glanced after her, confused, but stayed with the others.

Ironwood jerked his head at Kasai, who toppled the door in a burst of heat and a knock from his staff, and Oxe stayed in the doorway while the other three entered the wide space.

Ironwood reached forward. "What's this?" He grabbed something from the young boy sitting in the middle of the room.

Oxe saw a heavily decorated bag and felt a stab of empathy for the boy.

Kasai sighed and grabbed it from Ironwood. Oxe couldn't resist a quiet gasp.

Nona gave Oxe a shocked look, the fear in her gaze startling. He returned the shocked look. This was more than defying Ironwood.

This was basically mutiny.

Ironwood stared at Kasai, his eyes narrowed. "What are you doing?" His voice was dangerously quiet.

Kasai tossed the bag to the boy, who caught it and scrambled backwards. "We have enough. That bag? I've seen them before. It's part of a culture from the Western Region."

Oxe glanced at the boy and noticed intricate, though nearly skin toned, tattooed spirals along his arms. The bag probably had the same pattern. His own people must be like Oxe's then.

Kasai must've met people like them before, maybe when Oxe was recovering. He knew his mate was sensitive to other cultures.

"So? Why does that matter? We came to find things to take and sell. That's one of them." Ironwood shrugged, but Oxe felt a tremor of fear as a vine snaked from the pouch at his waist.

If Kasai saw it, he gave no indication.

Kasai finally said, "It's one thing to take something from the cargo hold, or another room, or even from someone's bag. But I won't take this from someone's hands."

Ironwood struck out, startling Oxe, and then picked the bloody bag from the boy's hands. "Now we can take it from a corpse."

Oxe couldn't react, his body frozen. A sideways glance at Nona told him she felt just as sick as he did.

The room began smoking, white flames licking along the walls and windows. Where the flames touched the windows, Oxe saw them *melt*. Kasai walked past him, his eyes fixed ahead.

Oxe flinched back from the heat, then again as Ironwood shoved past him.

Nona grabbed Oxe's arm and hissed, "Get out there before he does something stupid!"

He wasn't sure who she meant, but it didn't matter. The tension alone was making his hackles rise, but the look in Ironwood's eyes terrified him.

If he didn't act, there would be a fight.

Between Ironwood and Kasai.

With a whine, Oxe shot down the hallway and barely slowed himself coming through the doorway to the deck.

North steadied him as he came out, nearly knocking the older man down. "What just happened? There was a blast of white fire and suddenly Kasai's out here covered in flames," he whispered. The fear in his voice set Oxe's nerves on edge.

Linota approached them, whining.

"Kasai just went against Ironwood's orders." Oxe told him. Nona came out and stood next to them.

"Thukuli's going to kill him." She told them.

Oxe and North stared at her. Linota let out a loud snarl.

She nodded. "I overheard him with Delta yesterday. He told her that if Kasai went against him again, he would make an example of him."

Oxe clenched his fangs, his muzzle bursting forward almost painfully. "He'll have to go through me first."

Nona shot him a dark look. "He expects you to." Oxe couldn't hide his shock as Ironwood approached Kasai. Nona turned towards them, speaking to Oxe and North from the corner of her mouth, "North, I'll need your help if this goes...bad."

North nodded and Oxe didn't like the look they gave him, but he looked at Kasai.

Above them, the skies were growing darker. It wasn't raining...yet, but Oxe could taste it on the wind. The waves were kicking up bigger than before, sending both ships rocking.

Linota whined and pressed herself against Oxe's legs.

"You really won't help anymore, will you?" Ironwood's voice dripped with contempt, his face set in a sneer. He spoke above the rising wind easily.

The crew went silent, gathered in a loose semicircle around the two men. Oxe noticed Delta grinning and forced his attention away from her.

"I never said I wouldn't help," Kasai sighed. "But taking a cultural item straight from a kid's hand is too far for me."

Oxe noticed some of the crew looking uneasy at that. He knew that very few of them would attack a kid, even among the more bloodthirsty members of Bek's crew. Stealing? Yes, all of them agreed with that. But if a kid put up a fight for something, most of them backed down and just took something else.

But only Thukuli would kill a kid to take what he wanted.

He blinked as the rain fell. Slowly at first, then faster as Kasai and Ironwood faced each other. Wisps of steam were rising from Kasai, blood running thinly down his nose.

Oxe took a step forward but felt North grab his arm. He didn't look back, but didn't move forward. Linota gave a quiet yip.

"But you're supposed to follow orders." Ironwood snapped. "I warned you what would happen if you didn't listen."

Oxe was surprised to see Kasai call flames to his hand, forming a spear. He hadn't seen Kasai use a spear since the training with Marric.

A few crew members hissed.

"Is he really going to attack Ironwood?"

"I figured he would've done this ages ago..."

"I thought Kasai was smarter than this..."

"If Thukuli doesn't kill him, I'll do it myself." That came from Delta, standing not too far from Oxe. Her eyes glittered, and she looked straight at him.

Oxe tried to ignore her, but couldn't resist the whimper that rose in his throat.

"Do you really think you can beat me Kasai?" Ironwood scoffed.

Kasai narrowed his eyes. "No, but I'll defend myself if I need to."

Oxe wondered if Kasai knew what was about to happen. He seemed too sure right now, glaring down Ironwood with a hard look on his face.

A crack of thunder sent most of the crew cringing; it was the beginnings of a hurricane. Oxe's nose was burning from the rising smell of salt and the acrid touch of lightning.

A few of the travelers bolted for the doorway leading below deck. No one stopped them.

A large wave sent the ships shuddering, and the crew bolted for Ironwood's ship. Oxe nearly followed, but his instinct to protect Kasai won out. North and Nona stayed with him, but Oxe's eyes widened as Linota bolted for Kasai.

Nona hissed. "She's just going to get herself killed!"

"Not if the hurricane gets us first." North's voice was unusually dark and Oxe glanced at him. North was staring at the clouds whirling above them, and Oxe whimpered. He had seen these kinds of clouds before.

This was the same type of hurricane that he had faced with Kasai on their way to Witch Island. His ears had rang with every crack of thunder, his vision gone for a second with every flash of lightning.

North nudged him. "Let's get to our ship." Oxe glared, but North met his stare harshly. "I'm serious. Kasai will be fine, alright? As long as he's on this ship, they can get him away if Ironwood decides to leave him here."

Nona grimaced but said nothing as they backed away, then leaped onto Ironwoods ship. Oxe was the last one over and he stayed at the rail, watching Kasai.

Ironwood was circling Kasai; neither man seemed to notice the wind whipping around them. Ironwood struck out, "You know you can't come back now." The vine flashed strangely in the storm's light.

Linota was trying to keep herself between Kasai and Ironwood, but Kasai kept nudging her away.

Kasai deflected the blow easily. "Who said I wanted to?"

Linota growled and feinted for Ironwood. He kicked her; she yelped and pawed her nose.

Oxe wanted to hiss. His claws dug into the rail, creating deep furrows. If Kasai stayed there, Oxe would leap over before the ships were too far apart.

Ironwood struck out with his sword this time. "So, you really want to leave?"

A gash in Kasai's arm leaked; Oxe felt sick at the sight and smell of oil. "Yes. I've paid you back for this. I don't owe you anything more."

Linota growled and bared her fangs at Ironwood.

A bright flash of lightning made everything blindingly white, and there was a yell which was quickly drowned out by a tremendous *crack!* The ships rocked horribly, and Oxe dug his claws into the railing to avoid being thrown over.

North pulled him back. "Oxe!"

Only when his vision cleared did he see what happened. He stared at the now-empty space before them.

The other ship was gone, pieces floating in the growing white-capped black waves.

Ironwood clung to the rail of their ship with a strand of ivy, but pulled himself up as Oxe watched.

The crew that weren't dealing with the sails or double checking ropes had mostly disappeared below decks. Nona, North, Oxe, and Delta were the few left above deck unnecessary for sailing in the storm.

Delta helped Ironwood over the railing. He said something to her that Oxe didn't catch, then turned towards him. "So...you are Oxe."

Oxe barely heard North's uttered curse, not backing down from the anger in Ironwood's eyes. He said nothing, but he knew he was caught.

Ironwood stalked up to him unsteadily. Oxe caught sight of a large wound through the fabric of his shirt; where his arm met his shoulder was a strangely familiar black and red mark, the scent smokey even in the driving rain.

He had been struck by lightning.

"I will deal with *you* later," he snarled in Oxe's face, then stalked off towards the surgery.

Delta sneered and shoved past him.

"Oxe..." North's voice broke him out of his rising terror.

Oxe looked over the railing, hoping to see Kasai clinging to the ropes, but all he saw were thrashing waves, bits of plank and rigging, and some barrels that were already being thrown away by the storm.

Kasai and Linota were gone.

Oxe felt the breath leave his body and everything went black.

Chapter 34

Kasai

THERE WAS A TREMENDOUS crash and Kasai felt his hair stand on end as lightning streaked between them. Linota howled and he instinctively clung to her fur, his fist clenched so tight his knuckles hurt.

He felt the ship rock, then burst as it broke apart. The familiar static of lightning in the air gave him a strange, and unexpected, sense of comfort despite his terror.

"Linota!" He clung tighter, pulling her to him as they were knocked into the water.

He didn't know, or care, what happened to Ironwood, but he would not lose Linota. If he could just get to the ship...

They met the water with a *slap!* that was lost in the sound of cracking wood, thunder, and screams from the people in the travel ship. He held his breath as they disappeared under the water, but then kicked upwards as best as he could. It was hard, but his head broke the surface just as his lungs were about to burst.

Linota, still held in one arm, whined and gagged, but she paddled in his arms, trying to help. Despite her extra weight, he was glad she was here with him. And having her help was probably the only reason he could even swim with her.

Kasai could hardly see anything between the dark skies and his right eye; he couldn't see out of his left eye at all right now, but he didn't want to think about that. A dark shape nearly slammed into him, but he struck out and dug his fingers into the wet wood. Linota yipped and dug her claws into the wood and pulled herself out of the water.

It was a piece of the hull, Kasai noticed as he pulled himself out of the water. He shuddered as he thought about the travelers; none of them would've survived. How could they?

How would he? Or Linota?

The rain drove into his face and plastered Linota's fur to her body. The cut on his face stung, but he had experienced worse injuries. The waves picked up, and he looked around as best as he could.

In the distance, already too great to swim even without the storm, he could see Ironwood's ship. A wave rose and the ship disappeared. Linota whimpered, and he gripped her tightly.

The only thing they could do was pray they didn't get tossed back into the water.

The storm carried on for at least a few hours, and Kasai clung to the planks and Linota's fur until he couldn't feel his fingers.

It didn't help that oil kept leaking from his arm either. It didn't hurt, but if it ran out, he'd lose the ability to use his arm.

Finally, the sky cleared, and he and Linota relaxed a bit. Linota sagged against him, panting from fear. Kasai held onto her tightly and watched the waves finally calm as the night sky showed through the clouds. The moon was full and if he wasn't so thirsty and tired, he could almost appreciate the beautiful glimmer on the water. The storm had only been about around four hours long, and he was glad it wasn't longer.

Linota whimpered and nudged him.

He swallowed heavily. "I don't know if we'll make it out of this Linota. Do you think you could try shifting into something that swims or flies and try to find help?" A slim chance, for both her shifting and finding help, but there wasn't anything else he could suggest or even think of.

Linota flattened her ears. Kasai could tell she couldn't. She was stuck in this form, whether they liked it or not.

He scratched her ear. "It's alright. I just wish you had stayed with Oxe." Kasai couldn't forget the look of fury and horror on Oxe's face as Ironwood and Kasai faced off.

Linota grumbled and laid her head on Kasai's arm.

He sighed. "Try to get some sleep, alright? We'll just..." The words died in his throat. Just what? Wait to die? For help that probably wouldn't come?

He felt like there was something he could do, but he wasn't sure what.

Kasai moved to sit more comfortably, though there wasn't much room, and watched the sky for a while.

As the clouds cleared though, he got the feeling that something was...familiar.

North had taught him the stars, and while Kasai wasn't as good as the navigator, he had learned enough to get by. He could tell the directions, and read the constellations well enough. The only time North had ever been too injured to navigate, after a bullet had pierced his leg and gotten infected, Kasai had been the navigator for a few days alongside...

He jerked away from his thoughts and looked at the stars again. Tracing their shapes, he felt a jolt. He recognized where he was. Ignoring the fact that there was still a slim chance of any kind of rescue, he held onto Linota and tried to hold on to that slim hope...and idea.

"IS HE AWAKE?"

"I don't know yet, dear. Give him some room."

"Daddy, the animal is awake!"

Kasai bolted up, sending a group of people falling back. "Linota!"

There was a weak whine and she came limping over the...deck?

"Excuse me, are you alright?" Kasai turned to see a man speaking to him. From the rich clothing he wore, and the other people behind him, Kasai guessed they were merchants.

Linota sank against Kasai's empty right side, nudging him.

Kasai reached over and pet her while he spoke. "Where am I?" He had an idea, but wasn't sure.

"Aboard the *Midnight Glimmer,* my dear man. We saw you adrift and when we checked, you were both still alive, so we brought you up," the man told him. "My name is Captain Yan, this is my wife and son, Ione and Ril."

Kasai glanced at the woman and the younger boy; the boy couldn't have been older than six. "A merchant ship?"

Yan nodded and helped Kasai up. "Yes, out of Sussard Port."

Sussard Port, a little south of Brimna Atoll. Kasai had been there briefly when Thukuli sold some goods just before they first met North's crew. A quaint town, mostly known for clothing and jewelry.

"Heading to Valai, I'm guessing?" Kasai asked.

Yan nodded. "Yes. We have goods to deliver and a contract. I know there's been pyrates in these waters, but the pay was too good and my family wanted to see Valai for themselves."

Ione stepped forward; a lovely-looking woman, her hair was black flecked with silver and she couldn't have been much older than Kasai. "Dear, why don't we let him eat and rest before we talk?" She gave Kasai a small smile.

Kasai grimaced as his stomach growled. "Please. We've been adrift for three days."

Yan's mouth dropped open. "Three days?! By the stars, it seems that we have picked you up just in time! Ione, go let Trill know. Ril, head to the cabin, alright?"

Ril watched Linota nervously, but didn't move. "She won't eat me, will she?"

Linota flattened her ears and pressed against Kasai's legs. He reached down and brushed his fingers along her ear. "No, I promise she won't," he smiled.

Ril didn't look too convinced, but raced off.

Yan walked with Kasai, on the other side of Linota. "What's your name, sir?"

Kasai hesitated, but he knew that even if he wanted to take a ship, he could never do it alone. And he no longer had any desire to do that, especially since these people just saved his life. "Um...Kasai."

The ship went deadly quiet and Yan took a step back. A few people in the rigging jumped down and brandished swords at Kasai.

Kasai held his hand up quickly. "Wait! I promise, I won't hurt anyone! I got swept overboard and lost in the hurricane!"

Linota whimpered and shrank behind him.

Yan watched him, scared but cautious. "Why should we not just throw you back overboard, Inferno?" His voice shook, but Kasai had to admire the firm undertone.

But he didn't have a good answer for that.

"Maybe we should take you to the Seaborne," one mate called out. Kasai glanced towards the voice and saw a man on the quarterdeck. Considering his demeanor and position next to the wheel, Kasai would guess he was maybe the first or second mate, or the navigator.

"Then do." Kasai told him. "I don't care."

The ship was silent.

Ione came out just then. "...why?" She must've been listening.

Kasai glanced at Linota, who pressed her muzzle against his leg. "Because I'm done being a pyrate."

Yan stepped forward, his eyes narrowed. "But you've destroyed many ships, attacked and even killed merchants like us. Why should we believe you?"

Kasai wanted to shrug, but he was feeling very drained now. "I don't have an answer for you. But just before I was knocked into the water, Ironwood Thukuli was about to kill me."

Kasai saw the merchant's crew exchange bewildered looks. Yan motioned to someone behind Kasai and stepped forward. "Ironwood was going to kill you? Why?"

Kasai felt someone grip his arm, hard, but ignored it and didn't resist. "Because I wouldn't take something from a traveler's ship we had just attacked."

The man from the quarterdeck appeared from behind him; he was the one gripping Kasai. "A pyrate who wouldn't steal?"

Kasai could tell they didn't believe him, but pressed forward. "I don't want to steal anymore. I'm sick of hurting people."

Yan was quiet for a few moments. "Well, forgive us for being hesitant with having you aboard now." Kasai shrugged slightly, but met his gaze. Yan took a deep breath before continuing, "I will speak to the crew about this, but I am willing to be civil as long as you are. If you do not attack us, we can drop you off at the next port we stop at."

Kasai felt a weak relief at that. It wasn't much, but better than being tossed overboard.

Ione walked up to her husband and whispered with him briefly, then walked over to Kasai. She nodded at the mate holding him, who released his grip, and spoke to Kasai. "I'll take you to our mess for something to eat while the crew discusses what's to be done."

Kasai nodded, then looked at Yan. "I promise I won't attack anyone while I'm here."

Yan didn't look too sure of that, but said nothing as Kasai and Linota followed Ione through a doorway nearby.

"YOU REALLY HAVEN'T eaten for days, have you?" Ione sat across from him as Kasai finished a third bowl of food.

Kasai shook his head. "No. And I'm sorry for my manners, but this is really good." He felt a tad embarrassed by his lack of them, but he couldn't help it right now.

She smiled. "It's alright, I can understand. I've gone without food before, though not nearly as long."

Linota yipped and put her paws on the bench.

"She doesn't look like any colf I've seen before." Ione said unexpectantly.

Kasai glanced at Linota. "Well...she's a shifter. She can look like any animal, but she's stuck like this."

Ione gave Linota a sympathetic look. "Well, I hope you're at least happy like that. But can I ask you something, Kasai?"

Kasai raised an eyebrow. "Of course."

"Will you really not attack us? I hate to think that you would attack someone who just saved your life." Her words were light, but Kasai saw the worry in her face.

"I swear, I will not harm anyone here. I have no desire to, for one, but like you just said, you just saved me, so I need to repay that." Kasai didn't blame her for asking. "Even if I did, what could I do on my own? I can't sail a ship like this." He raised his left arm but jerked his head towards his right shoulder.

"Do you need that looked at?" Ione asked.

Kasai grimaced. "No, but thank you. It's an old wound. I lost my arm years ago, and the most recent mechanical one was damaged and fell off yesterday."

He had to admire the fact that she didn't look sick at that like most others did.

She leaned back but jerked up as Yan and the other man came in. A younger woman was with them.

"Kasai, I have spoken with Alcaris and Viza, and the rest of the crew, and we are all in agreement that you can stay on the ship until the next port," Yan told him. "But if you cause any harm to anyone on the ship, Alcaris here will shoot you."

Alcaris, the man who had held his arm, glared at him. "We'll have you stay in the small brig we have, but we won't chain you...yet."

Viza nodded in agreement, but didn't speak.

Kasai didn't expect this, but wasn't surprised. "If I may ask something..."

Yan looked suspicious at this.

"I noticed the stars last night. We're a week's journey from a certain port you could take me to." Kasai's stomach lurched as he spoke, but what choice did he have?

"Which port?" Yan asked slowly.

Kasai met his gaze evenly. "Witch Island."

Chapter 35

Oxe

"WHAT ARE YOU DOING here?" Ironwood sat across from Oxe. Delta and Nona sat on either side of the captain. North, at Ironwood's request, sat with Oxe. They were in the space before the engine room, a table temporarily set up for them.

Oxe stared at the chains around his wrist. He didn't flinch at the sprig of ivy that crawled up his leg and wrapped around his neck.

"You may as well answer him, Oxe," North hissed through his teeth. He was in just as much trouble as Oxe right now, but because Oxe had lied and tricked his way onto the crew, only he was in chains. North hung his head, his eyes closed.

Oxe looked up. "I came to find Kasai." The ivy tightened, but Oxe didn't react.

Ironwood glared at him. "Why?"

"He disappeared after his fight against Blacksmoke. We didn't know where he was," Oxe told him truthfully. "Then I saw him in Sedgeliss and asked around to figure out where your crew would have gone."

Ironwood relaxed his hand and the ivy loosened a bit. "But he couldn't leave then. So you lied to get close to him, and free him from the crew."

Oxe blinked but said nothing.

"But why not give up on him? Why keep going when he made it clear he had moved on?" Ironwood smirked.

Oxe knew he must be referring to the months before Kasai knew who Tamotsu really was. "Because I had to."

Ironwood frowned but looked at Delta. "What do you think we should do?"

Delta shrugged. "I have an idea you might enjoy, but it will mean meeting Razora."

North and Oxe froze. *Meet* Razora? Oxe cut a glance at North, who looked sick.

Nona shook her head. "Not a good idea, captain. She's insane. She was already insane when I got locked away, and keep in mind that was when she was barely an adult."

"So? What's your idea, Delta?" Ironwood sneered at Nona and turned to his first mate.

Delta eyed Oxe thoughtfully, then looked at Ironwood. "He won't remember me, but years ago I was with a crew that was hunting for exotic animals."

A chill ran down Oxe's spine. *No...*

"We found an island with these strange creatures called wolves. It was my job to spot likely specimens for capture, and determine their worth." She smirked at this. "I didn't realize we had caught a man at first."

Ironwood gave Oxe an appraising look then guessed, "So he got away, you somehow found out his true nature, and now you want your money back."

Oxe could see North trembling and he could maybe understand why. North had approached Oxe about her not long after they left Brimna Atoll; she had been a member of Sonus' crew when they left Veridey's. He thought she had been loyal, at least enough to never be a problem. But now it was clear she only joined to follow Oxe.

Delta shook her head with a laugh, distracting him. "When I found out he was a man, I didn't really care about money at that point. Oh, it's nice, but do you know about Razora's...collection?"

Ironwood suddenly glared at her. "I might be ruthless, Delta, but that's going too far. I don't know how badly I want to subject him to her experiments, no matter what he's done."

Experiments? Oxe exchanged an uneasy look with North.

"But she'll exchange goods for goods. We lost Kasai, probably the most powerful member of the crew next to you, and I know someone on her flagship that we might trade him for." Delta cocked her head.

The pressure around Oxe's body felt off then, and he looked to see Nona's face twisted into a snarl.

"You would barter with a human?" Her voice was quiet, but Oxe was sure that no one could miss the rage simmering in it.

Ironwood flicked his wrist and another strand of ivy shot out, the sharpened end against her neck. "Yes. Normally I wouldn't, but I've already struck a deal with her. Now that Kasai's gone, I need another bargaining chip. He's not as good, but maybe I can rework the deal."

North was struggling to hold himself back. Oxe nudged him and shook his head when North glared at him. North nodded and looked away. Oxe knew he had been in charge of tracking Razora for years, making sure she never encountered Sonus, but he clearly didn't know she was trafficking in humans.

Nona glared. "Then what will we do in the meantime?" Oxe had to give her credit for not flinching.

Ironwood didn't answer immediately. He stood and walked to a chest that he had brought down before talking to Oxe. He pulled something out and came back, throwing it at Nona.

She caught the bundle of clothing, which clanked, and looked at him.

"We keep him from leaving. And *you* will be in charge of him," Ironwood told her darkly.

OXE WHINED AS NONA approached. Fully as a wolf, it was much easier for him to bear this treatment than if he were human.

Nona sat down two bowls; water and a small chunk of meat. "I'm sorry, Oxe..."

Oxe laid his head on his paws and watched her.

She sat down heavily on a crate nearby. "We'll be in Valai in about two months from now, but Ironwood has no plans to stop anywhere. I don't think we'll be able to get you out."

Oxe wagged his tail once. Surprisingly, when she spread the word through the crew about what Ironwood was planning, the crew had been divided. Many of them were against selling a human, but some didn't care if it meant being safe from Razora somehow.

Ironwood had been furious, but there were too many people against him to lash out at Nona then.

Oxe cocked his head as North appeared.

The older man met his gaze. "Oxe, I managed to get ahold of Doux and Na'vira using the face-crys."

Oxe stood and wagged his tail. The chains around his ankles clanked loudly, but he ignored them. In the month since the storm, they had never once been removed.

"They haven't been able to get ahold of Brinar, but they don't think Kasai's dead," North said.

Nona shot to her feet. "But how?" She had been told of Oxe's true connection to Kasai, and Kasai's connection to the Seaborne. She hadn't been as shocked as they expected, but was glad they included her now. It helped that they had another person to talk with since Feluna had refused to help.

They weren't sure why still, but she wouldn't help, then disappeared at the port they stopped at just after the storm.

Ironwood was angry, but more because there was no ship's doctor now.

Oxe whined, his tail between his legs. He wanted to believe Kasai was alive, but how?

"I told them where we were just before the storm, and Doux told me we were on the edge of a well-used shipping lane." North didn't look too excited, but Oxe understood why. Just because they were near the merchant routes didn't mean Kasai had been picked up. Even if he had, what were the odds he wouldn't be killed on sight? "He's gotten ahold of a few merchants, but aside from one that stopped at Witch Island, none of them were near that area."

"Witch Island? They allowed a merchant to stop there?" Nona asked him.

North nodded. "It's not often, but sometimes during hurricanes they'll offer protection to travelers. We've stopped there once during a hurricane ourselves."

Oxe whined.

"No, they didn't pick up anyone, Oxe." North gave him a sympathetic look, then turned to Nona. "But the main reason I came down here is the captain wants a word with you."

Nona nodded and left immediately. North waited until she was gone, then knelt in front of Oxe. "They had a message for Doux and Na'vira, who passed it to me. Kasai's alive, he's with Brinar."

Oxe wanted to howl, but wagged his tail furiously instead.

"Yea, I didn't think he'd die so easily either," North told him, grinning.

Oxe cocked his head at North. While he could've turned human and talked to him, the manacles around his ankles cut into his skin and he didn't want to deal with that now.

North glanced behind him before speaking. "I'll contact Brinar as soon as I can. But for now, we'll just have to stay put." He grimaced as Oxe yipped. "I'm not happy about that either, but we don't have much of a choice. And we have bigger things to worry about."

Oxe couldn't argue with that.

North stood and glanced around. "I know you've had a hard time being down here, but we might have a chance to get away in Valai. But Oxe?"

Oxe gazed at him warily now, not liking the tone in North's voice or the worry on his face.

"If we can't get away and we meet Razora..." North paused for a moment. "If we can't get away, we won't be able to."

Oxe whimpered as North left. He didn't know what North meant, but he knew it wasn't good.

Part II

Flame

Chapter 36

Kasai

"YOU HAVE NO IDEA HOW glad I am to be able to stop here." Yan looked up in wonder at the twin peaks high above them.

Kasai wished he could share in some of the enthusiasm, but he just felt nervous. He had lied to Yan about being from here, but he didn't know where else he could go. He just hoped that the island was okay with trading just once with the merchants for bringing Kasai here. He wasn't sure if he could even get inside, but it was either this or they turn him into the Seaborne.

Linota flicked her tail warily, but Kasai could tell she was excited to be out and about, without someone threatening to chain her.

Kasai waited as they pulled up to the dock before saying anything. Only when a few dockworkers began tying the ship up did he turn to Yan. "I hope they'll be open to trading with you for bringing me here. I know they're not always very open to strangers usually." He caught sight of someone on the dock and felt a tad more confident about his idea now. "Let me go down first. I'll talk with them and they'll let you know if they can trade or not."

Yan nodded excitedly, and Ione touched Kasai's arm briefly. He followed her to the side. "Is something wrong?"

She shook her head. "Not with me, but are you alright? You look scared."

Kasai wasn't surprised she could tell. "I'll be fine. It's just...the last time I was here wasn't exactly a pleasant moment."

She nodded. "You're not from here, are you?" Kasai shook his head. "I guessed as much. But you know someone here, someone powerful enough to give us a trading pass. At least today."

Kasai nodded, feeling a lump in his throat. "Yes. He was... I sailed with someone that is very much respected here."

"Does he know you're coming?" she asked softly.

Kasai shook his head, his eyes stinging now. "No. And I'm not sure if I'll even be accepted onto the island. But I recognized one man on the dock. If I can talk to him first, it'll be easier for...everyone."

She hugged him suddenly, surprising him. "I'm sure it will be fine, Kasai."

If he wasn't so nervous about meeting Brinar, he would've cried. He had gotten unusually close to Ione over the past week and he would miss her. When she let go, she placed a hand on his cheek, then left to stop Ril from going down the gangplank. He blinked back some tears. She reminded him of Kira. But he shook himself and waited at the top of the gangplank.

Linota waited at his side, her nostrils flaring as she took in the unfamiliar smells.

The dock workers motioned for him to come down, but they froze as he approached. Kasai felt the weight of disbelief and apprehension in the stares directed at him, but he disregarded them as a man of about his height came forward. Linota whined nervously and nudged Kasai; she must smell his fear.

"Kasai, what are you doing here?" Edward had a sword held loosely in one hand, his eyes hard.

Kasai noticed his gaze flicking from him to the merchants on deck and back. "I need to see Brinar. These merchants picked me up from some driftwood about a week from here, and I asked if they could drop me off at this port. I told them if they did, I would ask if you would trade with them, at least this once."

Edward didn't speak for several heartbeats, then sheathed his sword. "Come with me then. Will your pet behave?"

Linota flattened her ears.

"She's not a pet. Long story. But yes, she won't be an issue." Kasai bit back a sigh and resisted glaring. He couldn't do anything wrong, not when too much was at stake.

Edward nodded and set off, pausing only to speak quietly with someone, before leading Kasai and Linota into the tunnel. Only when they reached the soft, blue lights did Edward make him stop. "Okay, you understand that *no one* knew you were coming, right?" His voice sounded loud, nearly a shout, and almost angry.

Kasai nodded, not trusting his voice right now. Linota gazed at Kasai, but flicked her ears at Edward.

"And the last time you were here, you nearly killed yourself, Brinar, and destroyed our arena?" Edward asked. His words were like a physical blow, but Kasai just hung his head.

"The arena's destroyed?" Kasai hadn't heard about that. Linota gave him a worried whine and he grazed his fingers along her head.

Edward nodded, his eye twitching. "Yes. And a lot of people got hurt." He suddenly relaxed. "But I'm glad you're okay."

Kasai attributed the previous harshness to the surprise of his arrival.

"Seriously, me and Amalia thought you were dead, Kasai. Brinar and Oxe were the only ones who wouldn't give up on you." Edward closed his eyes briefly. "But...Brinar should be at home. It's still pretty early here."

"Home? Somehow I expected Brinar to be with other doctors or in a study somewhere." Kasai kept pace with Edward as they walked. Linota stayed at his heels, but occasionally brushed against his leg.

Edward snorted. "Yea, but not since River...well, you'll find out about that soon enough."

River? Edward said it like a name, but Kasai couldn't guess who he meant. "What happened after I went missing? I know they had to bring the clipper back. And I've met with North and Oxe, who explained what happened after the fight."

Edward nodded. "I knew you had met with them." He cut a sideways glance as they entered the underground town. "Brinar's been keeping me informed about any of that. But we brought the clipper back, Amalia gave birth to twins not long after and scared the hell out of everyone, and North and Fayde split the remaining crew up."

"Amalia had twins?" Twins weren't very common as far as Kasai knew. He glanced around, but few people were paying attention to them. There weren't many people out yet, and the few they saw on the same street barely gave them a look.

The buildings here hadn't changed. Most of the windows he could see were dark, though a light shone down on each door. A potted plant was spotted here and there; Kasai briefly wondered how they grew, but pushed the thoughts away. It didn't matter.

Linota gazed around with interest, her tail flicked excitedly and her ears swiveling around.

Edward laughed. "Oh yea, a boy and a girl. And Bronwen is a terror! They're three years old now and like night and day."

Kasai smiled at the image and shook his head. "I bet they have their hands full with the kids then."

"You'll meet them in a few minutes." Edward stopped outside one of the carved stone buildings. Linota cocked her head, sniffing around the edge of the door.

Kasai couldn't see anything to make it stand out except for the strange glass door, which looked so foggy you couldn't see through it, until he noticed the plaque by it.

Dr Brinar Rutar and Dr Amalia Negasi

Edward must've noticed his confusion. "Oh yea, people from the other islands don't have surnames, do they? Last names?" He pressed a button and Kasai heard a faint melodic chime from inside the house.

Kasai shook his head. He could feel his heart thudding but tried to keep his voice steady. "I hope they're okay with me being here." Linota licked his hand and curled her tail around his legs. He scratched her head, trying to block out his fear but failing.

Edward gave him a long look. "It'll be a shock, that's for sure. But I'm a little more worried about Mihel."

Kasai had a feeling he knew the name and was on the verge of asking when the door opened.

"Edward? What are you doing here so early?" Amalia hadn't stepped where she could see Kasai yet, but he could see her well enough. Having kids had made her body less slender, and she looked more tired than he would've thought, but she did say it was early. Maybe she had just woken up.

She was wearing a kind of robe that Kasai hadn't seen in a while; it reminded him of Marric's outfit when they first met. She had a mug of something steaming in her hand and slippers on. Her hair was loose and a little messy.

Edward shot Kasai a glance and coughed. "Um, well, you have a visitor. Well, visitors."

She gave him a confused look, then opened the door better and took a step to where she could see Kasai. Her eyes widened, and she nearly dropped the mug, but Edward shot forward and caught her. She handed him the mug absently and stared at Kasai. "What...how...*when*?"

If it had been better circumstances, Kasai may have laughed. He couldn't ever have imagined her being flustered before, but he couldn't even bring himself to be amused. He just felt too awkward.

Linota nudged his hand again, but he didn't react.

Edward handed her the mug back after a moment. "He just arrived...on a merchant ship. They picked him up in the Northern Waters on some driftwood. He can fill you in, but I need to go figure out what to tell Mihel."

Before anyone could say anything, he ran off.

Amalia watched him for a moment, then turned to Kasai. "Well, come in for now. Brinar's still asleep, and so are the kids. Watch your feet." She stepped back inside and Kasai followed, shutting the door behind him as Linota slipping through.

He stood in the entrance of a nicely decorated living room, the beige walls covered in artwork, photoglasses, and some drawings of various birds that he was pretty sure Brinar had done himself.

Amalia walked into a little kitchen area and leaned against the counter there. "So...a merchant crew?" Her eyes were fixed on him, her expression unreadable.

Kasai shrugged. "I got...blown overboard in a hurricane and they found me and Linota on some driftwood."

Amalia glanced down at Linota and pursed her lips. "Will she be okay here, Kasai? We don't keep animals in the town."

Linota crouched down, her tail wrapped around her haunches.

"Yes. I don't know if we'd be able to stay here long. But when I saw where the merchants were and the direction they were heading...it seemed safer to stop here than somewhere where the Seaborne could get me," Kasai shrugged.

"But why come here?" Amalia asked quietly.

Kasai glanced at her but fixed his gaze on Linota. He had seen no judgement, no anger in her eyes, but he couldn't ignore his nervousness. "Where else could I go?"

Amalia sighed deeply and Kasai heard her set the cup down. "I guess you've got a point. Um...why don't you sit on the couch for now? Take your boots off first though."

Kasai looked up to see her pointing at a low, plush looking couch. He quickly slipped the simple yet fine boots the merchants had given him and set them with a few pairs of plain looking shoes next to the door.

Linota looked at Amalia, who was studying her, then laid down on the floor at Kasai's feet.

"I heard you had lost your arm." Amalia sat down across from him in an overstuffed chair, the mug in her hands. The smell coming from it was bitter and harsh, but also strangely invigorating.

Kasai shrugged. "Feluna had no choice but to amputate it."

"Feluna?" Amalia looked at him in surprise. "What was she doing in Sedgeliss?"

Kasai cocked his head. "Do you know her?"

Amalia nodded and set the cup down on the low table between them. "Yes. She was a resident here for years, but then she disappeared about five years ago."

Flames sprouted up, and Kasai had to bite his tongue.

Amalia's eyes widened. "Kasai...?"

He raised his hand, his eyes closed, and called the flames. Once they were gone, he looked at her. "Feluna said she met Brinar in Cernu years ago, during the epidemic."

Amalia didn't speak for several heartbeats. Kasai internally winced at the alarm on her face, but waited until she was composed enough to talk. "Well, that is true...but Brinar brought her back here when her parents died and raised her alongside some of the other kids here. She learned how to heal from him. She wanted to be a doctor, but Mihel wouldn't let her since she wasn't born here."

Kasai sighed. "Well, at least she didn't lie then."

Amalia watched him with wide eyes. "Kasai, how long have your powers reacted like that?"

Linota flicked her tail, looking up at him.

"Since my body port was removed," he said bluntly. "I haven't been able to control it as well."

She nodded and opened her mouth, but jerked her head towards the hallway Kasai had seen. "I'll be right back. I need to check on the kids."

He thought he had heard someone crying, but leaned back as she left. Linota nuzzled his hand. "What?"

She jerked her head towards the hallway and gave a quiet yip.

Kasai glanced towards it but shook his head. "No, I think she really is just checking on her kids. I don't think she's getting Brinar."

Linota flattened her ears for a second, then trotted off before Kasai could stop her.

He silently cursed, but could do nothing as she disappeared into the hallway. He closed his eyes and leaned back while he waited.

It wasn't that long of a wait.

"Where's Linota?" Amalia sounded wary.

Kasai cracked his eye open. "I think I know...but I'm not exactly thrilled about it."

Amalia sat back down in the chair. "You don't think she got..." She shot up but sat down slowly, staring at the hallway.

"Amalia, who's the animal?" Brinar's voice, sleep heavy and slightly annoyed sounding, drifted from the hallway.

Kasai froze, unable to hide the alarm on his face. Amalia gave him a strange look, but quickly stood and stopped Brinar before he appeared. "Brinar...we have a couple...guests..."

Linota yapped and trotted over to Kasai. Her tongue lolled between her teeth, and Kasai could only describe her face as *smug*.

"Who?" Brinar appeared and then turned towards Kasai. "Ah..."

UNCOMFORTABLE, KASAI couldn't look Brinar in the eye. They sat across from each other at the kitchen table, a plate of food in front of Brinar. Amalia had offered Kasai something, but he declined.

"I figured Ironwood was crazy, but I'm shocked that *you* faced him down," Brinar growled. He had changed from the stripped pajamas he wore before into a plain beige shirt and pants.

Kasai shrugged. "Not like I had much of a choice."

Amalia snorted lightly into her cup of coffee. "You did, but you had horrible timing." She glanced over at Bronwen, who was sitting at the low table and drawing. River, the boy, was still asleep in the kids' room.

"But why come here? I still don't understand *that*." Brinar's gaze turned critical.

Kasai hesitated. He wasn't sure what he could say exactly, but he tried. "I couldn't think of anywhere else to go." True, but he knew there was more than that.

"But..." Brinar closed his eyes briefly, then glared at Kasai. "After your reaction in Brimna Atoll, I would've thought here was the last place you would want to be."

Kasai could feel the accusation, the judgement, in his tone. And the hurt.

"Brinar, enough. I think he feels bad enough without being reminded of that," Amalia chided gently from behind Kasai.

Kasai felt her hand land on his shoulder. "I am sorry about that..." he whispered.

Brinar waited a few heartbeats, then leaned back in his chair. "I believe you, and you may have done me a favor."

Kasai still didn't look up. Instead, he placed his hand on Linota's head and scratched her ears.

"Brinar, why don't I take the kids to the center while you two...talk." Amalia set down her cup. "It's time for River to get up, anyway."

Brinar stared at Kasai for a moment, then looked at her. "Alright. Take the tab. I'll call you later."

She picked Bronwen up, then disappeared into the hallway.

Kasai kept his gaze down while she appeared a few minutes later, both kids in her arms.

Don't hurt daddy please.

Kasai jerked his head up and met River's green and brown eyes just as they disappeared through the door.

Brinar snorted. "Guessing you just heard from River?"

"Is he a genetic?" Kasai couldn't hold back his confusion.

Brinar nodded, a little sadly...or maybe nervously. "First in three hundred years here. Telepathy."

Kasai met his gaze finally. It still unnerved him somewhat to see the doctor look barely older than North, but he was already getting used to it.

"Why were you so mad at me in Brimna Atoll?" Brinar asked.

Kasai looked down at the table for a moment before answering. "I was afraid you were mad at me. For before."

"You mean for the arena?" Brinar asked. Kasai gave a barely perceptible nod. "I was never mad Kasai." His voice softened a tad.

Kasai looked at him.

"I'm serious. Yes, I was upset, but never mad." Brinar took a drink from his mug before he continued. "I just wanted you to talk to us."

Kasai bit back the retort that threatened to burst out, because he knew it was no excuse.

"I still do. I've heard from Oxe and North about how you've...changed." He seemed...not hesitant, but uncertain.

Kasai glanced at Linota, who nudged him and jerked her head at Brinar. "I just...everyone kept so much from me, I couldn't just believe I could trust you." He forced himself to meet Brinar's gaze.

Brinar nodded slowly. "That's understandable, but now's different. Just by looking at you..."

Kasai mentally groaned and prepared himself for another doctor's assessment.

"You've been through more mentally than physically lately, haven't you?" Brinar's words surprised him.

Kasai nodded. "Because of Ironwood." And Naomi, and the knowledge that his nightmares about him causing Kira's death were really memories, and Oxe hiding himself for months, and inadvertently causing North to join Ironwoods crew and Arat's death.

"It's more than that," Brinar said, but didn't press. "But unfortunately, I won't be able to help you yet."

"Yet?" Kasai was torn between being glad Brinar wanted to help and suspicious, but he tried to hold on to the former thought.

Brinar nodded and scowled. "Before you can stay any longer, we have to let Mihel know."

"Who is he? Edward mentioned him before, and I think you did when I first came here," Kasai asked. He had an idea considering the look on Brinar's face, but didn't want to say anything in case he was wrong.

"He leads the island. Anyone comes here, anyone wants to partner up, have kids, perform any kind of research, get any kind of work done, they have to go through him first." Brinar's voice was bitter as he explained, his brow lowered. "If he doesn't approve it, nothing can happen."

Kasai waited a moment before asking, "And if he says I can't stay?"

Brinar met Kasai's gaze darkly. "Then you'll be forced to stay outside at the docks until you find a way to leave."

Chapter 37

Oxe

IRONWOOD JERKED THE chain and Oxe stumbled forward, barely catching his paws in time. The dock was mostly empty, but the air was almost over-saturated with fear. "Either walk on your own as a wolf, or as a man, I don't care. But you *will* follow."

Nona walked at Oxe's side, North just behind her.

There was a group of people at the other end of the dock, but Oxe could tell these were not merchants or townspeople.

A tall woman strode forward, with a younger woman behind her. The older woman had thick black hair that was tangled and wild looking, sunburnt skin along her arms, and wore a strange assortment of necklaces and rings. Her ears were pierced at least six times on each side, and she wore a set of bangles on each arm.

Oxe had never seen a woman quite like this, but a strange, unusually acrid wave of fear caught his attention and he glanced at North. It overpowered everything else.

The older man was visibly holding himself back from running. He caught Oxe's gaze and shook his head slightly.

Oxe yelped as Ironwood jerked him to attention.

The captain glared at him, then turned to the woman. "Razora, I'm glad you agreed to meet." She was several feet away from them, but clearly had no issue hearing them.

Her gaze fell on Oxe, but then she glared at Ironwood. "I see a filthy mutt, but no Kasai." Her voice cut through the air like a jagged knife. "You promised me my nephew."

Ironwood grimaced. "Unfortunately, Kasai was lost in a hurricane."

Razora scoffed. "Then we have no deal."

Oxe watched the other woman flinch as though struck. Grey eyes, dark blonde hair. Despite those differences, she reminded him of...

"Naomi, round up the men. We're leaving." Razora barked at her.

So that was Kasai's younger sister. Oxe exchanged a worried glance with North.

Naomi walked forward a couple of paces. "Wait, Auntie, Ironwood has an idea for something else if he still showed up like this." She walked up to Ironwood and stood in front of Oxe, gazing down at him. "If Kasai's dead, why show up towing...this?"

Ironwood grinned. "This-" he jerked the chain, causing Oxe to stumble forward, "-is a shifter. And Kasai's partner."

Naomi snapped her eyes to Oxe, then looked back at Ironwood. "So?"

"Delta, my first mate, had the idea that we could trade him for someone to join our crew," Ironwood explained. "Someone that can match Kasai's power and help us control the Eastern Seas."

Razora looked at Oxe, but shook her head. "We have no need for another full shifter. We have too many as it is."

Another? Too many? Oxe's head spun. Brinar had always made it sound they were rare. Was he wrong?

"Wait, Auntie, I have another idea." Naomi walked over to Razora and whispered something to her.

Oxe waited, his tail between his legs.

Razora shot Naomi a glare, but stepped up to Ironwood. Oxe could smell her over the salt from the ocean now and the fear from

North; she smelled like a storm. Ozone, wild winds, dark clouds. Oxe had to resist cringing away.

"My niece just gave me an interesting idea, but I would need a fair trade. Not the shifter, but something, or *someone*, else," she stated.

Ironwood cocked his head. "Of course. If it is something I have, or a specific crew member, such as one of the former prisoners, I only ask that you leave me Delta."

Razora grinned, but Oxe shuddered at the cruelty in it. She turned to North. "I'll trade for him."

Ironwood barely glanced at North, a slight frown on his face. "Why North?" Not shocked, only curious. Naomi looked a tad bored, writing something down on a piece of a paper Oxe hadn't seen her pull out.

Razora walked up to North and grabbed him by the jaw. "Because this man is the reason I couldn't find Sonus for all those years. I'm due for some payback for that being ruined."

North didn't respond, only stared ahead.

Oxe bared his fangs, but was shocked when Naomi approached him.

"Naomi, leave him. We're not taking him," Razora growled, releasing her grip. Oxe saw the look on North's face and tried to ignore the dread in his eyes. But North shook his head and Oxe knew he could do nothing to protect him.

"I just want to give him this," Naomi shot back, holding up a folded piece of paper.

Ironwood tried to snatch it but had to brace himself at the sudden gust of wind that threatened to knock him over. Oxe crouched to the ground, his ears flat and tail tucked tighter.

Naomi stood over Ironwood and glared. "This is for Kasai's partner *only*." Her face twisted into a snarl. "Not. For. You." The wind stopped as suddenly as it began.

Nona stepped forward. "Excuse me, but what is it you want to give him?" She didn't seem as strongly affected by the wind, but Oxe figured she changed the surrounding pressure.

Naomi glanced at her, but didn't turn away from Ironwood. "A note for him, that's all. But only he's allowed to read it." Still looking at Ironwood, she knelt in front of Oxe and held out the folded piece of paper. He gently took it in his teeth, flicking an ear at her.

Oxe glimpsed movement and saw Razora approaching with a girl. The girl's wrists were lightly bound and her hands were covered in strange gloves.

"And why should I let you do that?" Ironwood glared at Naomi, but Oxe could smell the nervousness emanating from him.

Naomi curled her lip and the wind started up again, but stronger. Ironwood, as well as several of his crew that were standing at a distance behind them, were knocked down from the powerful gust.

Fear trickled over Oxe as he lay with his belly on the ground. Naomi was a genetic, and a powerful one. Kasai had never mentioned this; maybe he hadn't known?

Before he could be blown over, the gale stopped, and Naomi took a step back. "Akir will be my contact." She must've noticed the girl with Razora and either knew or guessed what she was planning.

Oxe glanced at the girl again; unremarkable mostly. A dark tan, shockingly white hair bound in a messy bun, and wearing shabby clothes, she didn't make much of an impression.

Except for the dead look in her eyes.

Oxe twitched his tail, but focused on Razora as she spoke to Ironwood. "This is Akir, one of my...projects. She's incredibly powerful, and a genetic. I've never seen abilities like hers before, but I'm willing to trade her for North."

Ironwood glanced at the girl and scoffed. "She doesn't look like much, but I know you have an eye for power." He glanced at Oxe, then looked at Akir. "Can you speak?"

Akir shrugged, but flinched when Razora shoved her forward. Akir stumbled and fell in front of Oxe; his nose burned from an intense coldness that radiated from her.

"She doesn't speak much, if ever, but if you can get her to listen, you'll be pleased with the trade," Razora told him. She walked back over to North and tied his wrist together behind his back. "The trades done, I'm heading back. Get gone if you don't want to get caught in our winds."

Oxe watched as she forced North forward and took a step, but stopped at a thin shard of something glittering in front of him. He barely got a glance of something clear before it melted into a puddle.

"Don't."

Oxe willed himself to not react to the barely breathed word.

Akir picked herself up slowly as Nona approached, who helped her up. Akir stood between him and Nona, her gaze on the ground.

Ironwood approached them, coiling the chain tighter. "Come on, let's hurry." Oxe was quick to follow, not wanting to be jerked but also because he wanted to get away from Razora as much as possible.

Nona walked at Akir's side, her hand on the girl's shoulder.

Ironwood glanced over. "Akir, since you'll be a part of my crew, but from Razora's, you'll need somewhere different to stay that's not with the rest of the crew."

Nona frowned but said nothing.

Akir's gaze flicked to Ironwood, but she stayed silent.

Ironwood's lip twitched and he nearly snarled, "I don't do well with the silent treatment. Learn that now. Nona, take her down to the engine room once aboard. She can stay there until she gets used to the crew. We'll give her a few days to rest, then she'll start helping with the rest of the duties."

Nona nodded, but said nothing as they reached the ship. Delta was waiting for them at the foot of the gangplank; the rest of the crew had disappeared, already aboard and getting ready to leave.

Delta glanced at Oxe and frowned. "So she wouldn't take the trade?"

Ironwood shook his head. "Not exactly. Instead of trading Oxe, we ended up trading North for Akir."

Delta could hide her disappointment well, but Oxe nearly flinched from the wave of anger that rolled off her. She whirled around and walked deliberately up the gangplank.

Ironwood led Oxe up, then took him down to the engine room. Akir and Nona followed at their heels.

The moment Akir entered the engine room, there was a soft crackling sound, and the air chilled to where Oxe felt as if he could almost see his breath. She kept staring at the floor, but Oxe saw her glance at the bed, then at Ironwood, and wanted to growl at her flinch. He dropped the scrap of paper in the corner when Ironwood wasn't looking, then kicked a fallen blanket over it.

Ironwood turned on her. "Nona, go help the crew leave. We're going back to Brimna Atoll. Delta's in charge until I'm up there." Nona nodded and left, while Ironwood stood in front of Akir. "You're an ice genetic, aren't you?"

Akir gave a single nod and Oxe thought he saw a flash of fear in her eyes.

"This is where you'll stay until the crew is used to you. In a day or two, you'll start helping. Scrub the deck, coil ropes, help with the guns, be a messenger for the coxswain, anything that's asked of you." Ironwood's tone grew dark. "And whatever orders I give when we take a ship, you listen. Understand?"

Akir nodded once again, but flinched back as Ironwood stepped forward threateningly.

Oxe couldn't help it; he stood between her and Ironwood, baring his fangs and snarling at him. His tail stood straight out behind him, his ears shoved forward.

Ironwood flicked his wrist, but Oxe caught the strand of ivy in his teeth before it could wrap itself around his muzzle. Ironwood took a step back; there was a hint of nervousness in his scent. "Geez, I won't get any closer. But Akir, you need to explain what your powers are."

Akir placed a hand on Oxe's back; he felt her curl her fingers into his fur as she spoke in a thin, brittle voice. "I'm made of ice, and I can freeze water and air. Razora made me trap ships in ice so she could take them."

Ironwood nodded, his eyes gleaming. "That's a useful ability indeed. Then that's what I'll have you do whenever we decide to take a ship. Stay here for now."

Akir glanced at Oxe. "What about him?"

Ironwood paused, fixing his gaze on Oxe for a few tense moments. "Ever had a pet?"

Oxe flattened his ears, but Akir gripped him tighter. "No. But he's my responsibility?"

"Yes. Though, I'll be back in a few minutes with the key so he can roam in here. But if he leaves this room, he's required to be chained until I say otherwise," Ironwood grunted. "Now stay here for a moment." He pushed past Oxe, handing Akir the chains as he left.

She looked at Oxe and whispered, "I'm sorry. I heard them say you were human, but I promise I won't treat you bad like he does."

Oxe nudged her to let her know he was grateful, but they turned as Ironwood came back. Oxe whined as he spotted the thin, chainless manacles in Ironwood's hand and tried to stay still as Ironwood approached.

Chapter 38

Kasai

THE SPACE OUTSIDE MIHEL'S office was tidy, larger than Kasai would've expected, but it felt strangely...hostile. A few other people sat on benches nearby, whispering between themselves. Brinar fidgeted next to Kasai. Linota watched them, but shifted her gaze to the doors, Kasai, Brinar, and back in an erratic motion.

The door opened. "Brinar." The person beckoned to him and Kasai, then disappeared behind the now cracked door.

Brinar stood. "I would suggest you say nothing unless he asks you something directly."

Linota flicked Brinar with her tail and stood beside Kasai. Brinar gave her a strained smile but said nothing.

Kasai nodded and mentally braced himself. If there was someone who could make Brinar this nervous, he would probably be worse to Kasai. He stayed close to Brinar's heels, his borrowed cloak held tight in his left hand. Brinar told him to wear it for now, as his missing arm would attract more attention than the scar on his face.

Linota trailed Kasai closely, making him fear she might trip him. Once inside, the person closed it and disappeared elsewhere.

The inside of the office was a startling contrast to the rest of the town. Dark walls of wood and stone, at least one long couch and four short ones, and numerous stuffed chairs were scattered between the uncountable amount of plants that filled the space.

"Noticing my plants?" Kasai jerked his head around at the voice, but it didn't come from Brinar. A man approached them, carrying a pot. Except for the white-blonde hair that was cut short, and the few inches of difference in height, he looked exactly like Brinar. "You must be Kasai." Even sounded like him.

Kasai nodded.

"Oh, don't be so quiet. You're welcome here." Kasai cut a quick glance at Brinar when the man, who must be Mihel, turned away and saw a surprisingly annoyed look on his face. Mihel turned to them. "Well? Is my favorite sister going to introduce us?"

Sister?! Kasai couldn't help the shocked look on his face. Linota cocked her head but crouched down at Brinar's quick glare.

"Enough Mihel," Brinar grunted. "You know why we're here. Let's just get this done so I can get back home." He shot such a heated look at Kasai that the younger man flinched.

Mihel shrugged and set the pot down on a small, rounded table. "Alright, fine by me. No need to be snippy." He beckoned them over to a cluster of chairs nearby and Brinar and Kasai sat next to each other while Mihel sat across from them. "Now, I know you came here under...unusual circumstances, but I've already told Sirak to trade with them this time. They rescued a person in need who has a connection to this island."

Linota laid at Kasai's feet, her gaze on Mihel.

Brinar twitched. "But he's not a resident here. I'm a little surprised you agreed."

Mihel waved a hand at him. "Only because of his connection to you. If it were anyone else, I would've only allowed a refilling of their food and water, then had him leave with them." He leaned back in his seat, crossing an ankle over his knee, and spoke to Kasai. "But now we have a new problem. You came here unannounced, and without permission. Not only that, but you destroyed the arena the last time you were here, nearly killed my sister-" he ignored

Brinar's glare at that, "-injured well over one hundred people-" Kasai flinched, "-and put some of my top specialists in danger."

Kasai closed his eyes briefly.

"But, as I understand it, you have been seeking sanctuary from the Seaborne, among others. Well, you and your...friend," Mihel finished, glancing at Linota.

Kasai shot Brinar a confused look, who shrugged. "He means you want somewhere you can be safe without fear of being jailed or worse," he explained.

Kasai nodded. "Yes. It doesn't have to be here, but I couldn't think of where else to go."

"Why not to your brother? Brinar's explained that he's a Seaborne captain, but that he wouldn't be willing to turn you in," Mihel asked.

Kasai didn't respond immediately. Linota whined softly and nudged Kasai's hand.

Brinar glanced at him, then looked at Mihel. "Kasai told me that Ironwood Thukuli was about to kill him when he got knocked into the water. He survived, along with Linota here, for three days before the *Midnight Glimmer* picked them up. I think, given the circumstances, there *was* nowhere else for them to go."

Mihel appraised Kasai briefly, then nodded. "Yes, it would've been much more difficult to go elsewhere then." He stood and moved over to the plant he had set down. "Well, for the time being, I'm willing to grant you entrance to the island...on a few conditions."

Kasai had expected this and waited.

Mihel didn't look at either of them as he began tending to the plant. "Number one, you must stay with Brinar or Amalia at all times, and Linota is under the same rule." No surprise there. "Number two, Brinar's household is responsible for both you and Linota." Again, not a surprise, though Brinar didn't seem to mind too much. "Number three, and Brinar and Amalia can help you with this, you will be expected to have something to do each day. We don't allow laziness here, unless there is a good reason for it. And number four, and most importantly," he set down his tool and met Kasai's gaze, "if you step out of line even once, powers or not, you and Brinar will both be exiled."

Linota growled, but Kasai placed his hand on her head. He glanced at Brinar, who looked angry. Kasai was amazed he didn't explode, or at least attack Mihel.

Mihel didn't look at Brinar as he spoke next. "I'm serious. He's *your* responsibility, Brinar, and anything that he does will reflect on you. Now, I believe you two will need to talk about Kasai's stay here, so stop by the Store to let them know about the change in your household."

Clearly dismissed, Kasai followed Brinar out. Linota kept up with their quick pace, her fur bristling. Once they were outside, Brinar barely glanced at Kasai and jerked his head for him to follow.

Afraid of the anger on Brinar's face being turned on him, Kasai kept quiet and followed.

"I'M GUESSING IT DIDN'T go well?" Kasai glanced up from his book to see Amalia coming through the door, Bronwen asleep in her arms and River peering at him from behind her legs.

"Mihel insulted me, again, and threatened me and Kasai." Brinar shot at her from the kitchen. They had been back for several hours now, but Brinar had been so agitated that Kasai thought it might be safer to read something from the shelf near the couch. A storybook from the old world, but he could hardly focus on it.

Brinar finally decided to cook something for dinner before Amalia and the kids came home.

Amalia glanced at Brinar, then looked at River. "Why don't you go play for a while?"

River shook his head and walked over to sit by Kasai. He grabbed one of the picture books on the low table and flipped through it.

Amalia watched him for a moment, then looked at Brinar. "I'm going to put Bronwen down, but then I'd like to hear what happened." She disappeared down the hallway.

Kasai looked down at River. The toddler seemed engrossed in his book, but looked up at Kasai. The second he did, Kasai heard River's voice in his head again.

Uncle Mihel's mean.

Kasai nodded, but looked back at his book, unsure of how to respond.

"Yes, River, he was being mean again," Brinar called over.

River pouted and looked at Kasai. *Did he call Daddy a girl again?* Kasai grimaced. "Yes."

Brinar glanced over but said nothing as Amalia appeared.

"Bronwen might be asleep for a while; we'll save her a plate. River, Kasai, why don't you come eat?" Amalia sat down at the kitchen table after grabbing a stack of plates for Brinar.

River ran over after placing his book down, but Kasai followed more slowly. Linota stayed by the couch.

"Kasai, you're not averse to fish still, are you?" Brinar asked suddenly, his back to them.

Kasai suppressed a shudder. "Sort of."

Amalia grinned. "Brinar told me how you refused to eat fish even well after you left the Expanse."

Kasai snorted. "Can you blame me?" He sat down next to River, who kicked his feet excitedly. "But after I got thrown overboard, I'm not as picky now." He had eaten fish a few times with Yan's crew, at Ione's supervision and suggestion. She had understood his reluctance, thankfully, but he didn't want to go hungry again. And he didn't want to be rude. There or here.

"I'm just glad you and Linota survived that." She took a plate from Brinar and set it on the floor. "Linota, you can have this."

Linota huffed and came running over.

Brinar sat a plate down in front of River and another in front of Kasai before sitting down with a plate for him and Amalia. "You seem to have more in common with your father than you think."

Kasai shut his eyes, but at River's cry, he snapped them open and called the flames from the floor. "Sorry..."

Brinar eyed him warily. "Amalia wasn't kidding. You don't have a lot of control anymore."

Kasai sighed. "No."

"We can work on that tomorrow," Brinar sighed.

They ate in silence, but Kasai didn't have of an appetite after that. He noticed Brinar kept glancing at him, but Kasai tried to ignore him.

After River was finished, and nearly falling asleep in his seat, Amalia picked him up. "I can take care of dishes tonight, Bri, but I want to talk to you two before I do." She disappeared down the hallway, leaving Brinar glaring at Kasai.

"Doux told me you had become unstable," Brinar told him. "But I'm surprised at how the flames reacted to you."

Kasai shrugged. "Ever since my port was removed, they've been like that."

"Kasai, did you understand what Mihel meant when he said whatever you do will reflect on me?" Brinar asked.

Kasai paused for a moment, but could only guess, "That if I do that and someone gets hurt, he'll blame you."

Brinar gave a curt nod. "Mihel, and quite frankly myself, do not like people being idle. So tomorrow I'm taking you to the combat training center to help you learn how to control your changed abilities."

Kasai nodded, and Linota nudged his arm.

"I'm also going to see if we can't replace your arm." This was unexpected. Brinar looked at Linota, then back at Kasai. "I'm a little surprised Cifius' arm is missing, so you'll have to get a different kind."

Kasai felt a twinge in his shoulder. "Thukuli opened an oil vein, and it slipped off the day before Yan's crew found us."

"I'm going to warn you now, the arm we provide won't be like anything you've had before." Brinar leaned back in his chair slightly. "This one will be a part of your body, though it will be mechanical."

"What do you mean?" Kasai couldn't imagine what he meant.

Brinar pulled out a strange, flat object. It reminded Kasai of a face-crys, except this was just black and slimmer, and there was no hookup. Brinar tapped the surface and an image appeared! It reminded Kasai of the screen that Amalia had used in the arena, but much smaller. Brinar tapped a few more spots, then another image popped up.

It showed a grey bar inside the outline of an arm, with round joints at the shoulder, elbow, wrist, and small ones within the hand.

"This is what I want to give you. This won't be able to come out easily, if at all, and it's covered in a special sleeve that will look and feel like a real arm, minus the blood or any oil," Brinar explained.

Kasai frowned, skeptical. "The arms I had before all had a neural-connector. How will this one move?"

Brinar shrugged and tapped the screen; it went dark. "Same way, except it will be connected to your nerves directly instead of a chip. If you get cut, you will feel it like you do on your other arm. It's also filled with self-repairing nanos that are also self-replicating, but they will only replicate themselves if their numbers are below a certain threshold."

Kasai nodded, confused but not willing to show it, as Amalia came back in.

She glanced at the screen. "Showing Kasai the arm design?" Brinar nodded and slid the tablet to the side. "Now, what did Mihel do this time?"

"Called me his sister again," Brinar scowled.

Amalia made a face and came over to hug him. "You'd think after two hundred years he would stop."

"Did you really think he would? If he had been in charge then, he wouldn't have allowed my transition. No one's been allowed since he took over," Brinar retorted, then glanced at Kasai. "Oh right, you didn't know about our aging system."

Kasai immediately wiped the shock from his faced, not wanting to seem rude. "Are you really that old?" Kasai couldn't believe it. The oldest person he had heard of was 90, but 200?!

Amalia watched Kasai for a moment before explaining, "We have a special medicine that we start taking when we're eighteen. It slows down how the body decays over time, but it's mandatory after we've taken it for thirty years."

Kasai tried to think if he had ever seen Brinar taking medicine before, but couldn't.

Brinar must've guessed what he was thinking. "I had to take a modified version while I was...away. It didn't work that well, but it kept me from dying at least."

"But if you were born female, how did you two have kids?" If he hadn't heard them in the night, then been told about Amalia's pregnancy, he would've assumed they adopted.

Brinar exchanged a glance with Amalia, who shrugged, then looked at Kasai. "I had an operation that allowed some changes to happen. Unfortunately, I can't explain it to someone who's not from here more than that."

Kasai wasn't surprised, so he asked no more. "Where should I stay while I'm here?"

Amalia smiled. "Here. But you'll have to use the couch, unless we can get a cot for the spare room we had set up a year ago."

He felt a little relieved at that, and didn't mind the idea of the couch. At least he wasn't being kicked out. "Thanks," Kasai told her as Brinar's tab lit up.

Briner tapped it. "Well, I know the first place we'll stop tomorrow now. They approved your arm."

"So tomorrow I get it?" While excited, Kasai felt a trickle of dread, which got worse as Brinar answered.

"Yes, which means a hospital visit." Brinar shook his head, clearly trying not to grin at Kasai's expression.

Kasai groaned and closed his eyes.

Chapter 39

Oxe

"AKIR, I THINK IT'S time they waited for us," Ironwood called down to her from the quarterdeck.

Akir nodded and raised one hand. The crew flinched, except for Oxe, as the air chilled immensely and the water cracked and solidified before their eyes. The merchant ship jolted to a stop as the ice caught their hull. There was a short but thick skin of ice between the ships, sturdy enough for the crew to cross.

Ironwood's ship pulled up smoothly alongside the merchants, and he jumped down to the railing. "Alright crew, take what you want!"

Oxe pressed himself against Akir's legs as the crew roared out and leaped over the railing to attack the merchants. She reached down and grabbed his shoulder fur, gripping tightly.

Only three days out from port, and it was the second ship. The first one, yesterday, was almost too easy, giving up the second their ship was trapped in ice. This one however, got brave and shot at them before fleeing.

Oxe flexed his paws as he and Akir stood and watched the crew, wishing that he could move better in the heavy manacles. They kept him from shifting, or risk breaking both wrists and ankles, and were heavy enough he knew if he fell overboard, he would drown.

"Akir, why don't you take part this time?" Ironwood walked up to them, his sword dripping blood.

361

She glanced at him, but didn't respond. Oxe kept an eye on Ironwood from the corner of his eye, but the captain just hissed through his teeth and walked off.

Oxe nudged her and she nodded, heading for their cabin. Delta glared at them as they passed her, but he bared his fangs at her and she said nothing.

Akir led him down the stairs, the chain around his neck held loosely in her hands and swinging between them, and sank onto the bed after she shut the door.

Oxe whined and sank to the floor next to the bed. He flicked an ear at her and she shook her head.

"Do you think I could escape with you?" She stared at the ceiling. "He's hardly better than Razora. I don't think she would find me if I escaped this time, not with this being a different ship."

Oxe sat up and cocked his head.

She looked at him. "I'm serious. If I could figure a way for us to escape, would you take me with you?"

Oxe nodded and placed one paw on the bed. She nodded and he jumped up to curl around her. He could tell she needed some kind of comfort, and he could maybe guess why.

She laid her head on his shoulder. "Can you speak like this?" The question was unexpected.

He shook his head, lowering his ears briefly.

She sighed. "Sorry. Some of the other shifters could, but I wasn't sure if you could or not."

Other shifters? And they could speak human while as an animal? Were they full shifters, or just partial? He wanted to ask, but couldn't.

"Nona called you Oxe. Is that your name?" Oxe nodded and she gave a small smile. "My name's not really Akir, it's Xicía. Do you think you could shift human so we could talk?"

Oxe whined and lifted a manacle. He would if he could, but these were tight enough that even as a wolf, they hurt. If he turned human, it would be far worse.

She frowned and laid a hand on it. "Would Ironwood get mad if I froze these off?"

Oxe flicked her with his tail and he shook his head.

"Maybe some other time then." She understood thankfully and removed her hand.

Oxe laid his head on his paws, watching her. He was surprised that she could understand him so easily. Even Kasai had trouble guessing his thoughts when Oxe was a wolf.

She laid against his side, not speaking, and he got the feeling that she had never had any sort of friend. She had an air about her that made him wonder what she had been through and where she had come from. Considering her clothes, he thought she must've been some sort of slave. The thought made him grit his teeth, but he stayed quiet.

She shifted a bit and he glanced at her again; she had fallen asleep.

Oxe nudged her lightly, but she didn't move. With a small grumble, and more because of the manacles, he laid his head on his paws and closed his eyes.

"TRY AGAIN." DELTA STRUCK out and Oxe leaped back, his lips curled, and he growled at her.

Xicía hesitated, but when Ironwood stuck her with a thorn, she rushed forward and Oxe followed as she ran at Delta. Xicía was a surprisingly good fighter, but Ironwood insisted she practice against the crew, and many other members practice as well.

Delta barely avoided the ice-sword as Xicía struck, but smacked her with the flat of her blade as Xicía stumbled forward. Oxe took the moment and leaped at Delta.

He clamped his jaws down hard, but she shook him off, sending him rolling across the deck. Xicía stood next to him, an ice sword reforming in her hand quickly.

"Better, but next time don't let your mutt attack for you." Delta snorted, glaring at Oxe. Blood trickled down her arm from his fang marks.

He couldn't deny how satisfying that felt.

"I'm not a fighter," Xicía told her. "I do better when someone helps." Her voice was hollow, and Oxe could tell she was getting tired already.

Delta shrugged and swung out; Oxe barely dodged as the sword clipped his ear tip. "You need to be able to fight on your own."

Xicía shot a look at Oxe, who flicked his tail down. She nodded and her sword lengthened just as she swung at Delta.

Oxe felt a sting as he watched her; it was just like fighting with Kasai again, but as if he used ice instead of fire. Her style differed from his, but some weapons she had already formed were similar. Sword, scimitar, and a broadsword.

Delta dodged and Oxe leaped again. But this time, he went for her ankle and was rewarded with the taste of blood.

"Agh, you bastard!" Delta kicked out.

Oxe yelped and landed against the wall below the quarterdeck.

Ironwood, leaning against the railing, laughed. "Nice kick, Delta."

Oxe laid still as Delta approached him. "Captain, I think I have an idea for him."

"If Razora didn't want him, what else can we do with him?" Ironwood sounded bored.

Oxe kept his gaze on Delta, though Xicía ran over and helped him up. Her cold aura helped with some of the aching, though he didn't like the disdain Delta shot at her.

"What about the pens in Brimna Atoll?" She didn't look away from Oxe as she spoke.

Ironwood gave a strange sounding snort, then burst into laughter. "That's not a bad idea! Bring him here."

Oxe reluctantly limped up to Ironwood, Xicía behind him, after Delta prodded him. He refused to lower himself before Ironwood, but flattened his ears.

"The animal pens of Brimna Atoll are going to be your home once we get there," Ironwood told him.

Oxe's hackles rose and he shoved his ears forward, snarling, but Xicía laid a hand on him before he could lunge at Ironwood. She gripped his fur as she spoke. "You're going to make him fight?"

Ironwood glared down at her. "For his freedom. If he wins enough fights, then I'll set him free."

Xicía blinked at Oxe, then look at Ironwood. "And if he doesn't?"

Ironwood shrugged. "Then he'll die."

Oxe suppressed a growl and watched Ironwood walk off. Xicía nudged him slightly and he followed her down the stairs to their bunk. Ironwood was clearly done with them both, and the crew was already moving around to adjust the sails.

Oxe limped to his corner but before he could lay down, Xicía burst out, "I want to take him out!"

Oxe whined and flattened his ears. He shot his gaze towards the door, then tucked his tail briefly.

"I know..." Xicía sighed and laid back on the bed, staring at the ceiling. "But I'm against slavery of any kind..." Her voice was low, but it couldn't hide the pain.

Oxe watched her for a moment, then laid his head on his paws. He wanted to ask her why, but he felt she would tell him anyway.

And he was right. She sat up and looked at her lap. "I can't stand Thukuli...but he's better than Razora."

Better than Razora? Oxe found the difficult to believe.

"Razora took me from my parents when I was three," Xicía said quietly. "She heard I had powers, so she stole me from my home."

Oxe twitched an ear in the silence that followed.

Xicía closed her eyes; the soft crackling of freezing water sounded in his ears. "She keeps people on those...islands. Everyone is a genetic, and there were over five hundred when I left a few months ago."

Five *hundred?* Oxe couldn't hide his surprise. He had met a few outside of the tribe; Kasai, Sonus, North, Doux, they were the first ones to come to mind. Brinar had talked about how genetics were rare, but Oxe didn't think he knew about the ones on these islands.

If he knew, why would he have said they were rare?

Xicía sniffed. "I'm one of the few who got to leave the first island, and even the second."

Two islands? Oxe's head spun with this.

"There was even a wolf there, but he couldn't speak like us." Those words caught him off guard. Xicía turned when Oxe huffed; his ears were pressed forward, his lips curled back in both fear and anger. "No, I don't know where he came from. But when he shifted, he looked like you, but with dark brown fur."

Oxe didn't know of anyone with dark brown fur, aside from his grandfather's younger form, but that didn't mean much. He settled back down, his eyes on Xicía.

Xicía was quiet for a few moments, then sat up. "Oxe...do you think your friends could help rescue them?" She pulled out a scrap of paper.

Oxe growled; he had forgotten about the letter Naomi had given him. Since dropping it into the corner, and being unable to read it, he had just pushed it from his mind.

Xicía cringed away. "I'm sorry...I took it after you fell asleep the first night. I didn't want it destroyed or taken."

Oxe stopped growling, but flattened his ears in disapproval.

Xicía unfolded the letter with shaking hands. "I did read this, but that was before I realized what this was."

Oxe huffed, impatient. He stood up and walked over, but didn't jump up behind her like he normally would have done. He nudged her hand.

"Sure, I can read this for you. It was for you and Kasai, anyway." Xicía paused for a moment, then read aloud.

Kasai and Mate,

I'm alive, I'm safe. Razora's been training me, teaching me to use my own storm abilities. She told me about Sonus and I'm glad you found him. Thukuli never let me talk to you, and I don't think he told you I was alive.

If you can, here is my code – I'm sure Brinar will be okay with you calling me from Witch Island. Glad you found someone. Didn't expect a Nuveri warrior though.

__-.—=_.

- N.

Oxe sat back, his ears pinned to his head. Naomi knew he was a Nuveri warrior? She knew *Brinar*? *She knew Kasai was alive?!* There were too many questions. He felt himself sway and stumbled before Xicía caught him.

"Oxe?" She sat on the floor against him, bracing herself against his flank.

Oxe whined and paced the room. Xicía watched him, never taking her eyes off his face. Finally, he turned and barked at her, huffing once and flattening his ears.

Her eyes went wide with understanding. "Brinar...he's not someone you can easily find, is he?" Oxe shook his head fiercely. "She might have ears on Witch Island then. But that means..."

Oxe flattened his ears and tucked his tail. Witch Island was a fortress, a natural mountain reinforced with defensive weapons that hadn't been used in over three hundred years. Oxe had asked Brinar about the island once, but all the older man would say was, "Only the most confident of fools would try to penetrate the island again. Our defense system, built into the mountain itself, will brook no assault of any kind."

But if Naomi knew Brinar, that meant there was someone inside the mountain who was in contact with Razora.

Chapter 40

Kasai

"YOU HAVE TO REMEMBER that the staff isn't a gun, or even a sword. Brinar, over there, is one of the few on the island who has mastered the weapon." Edward spoke to the small group in front of him, but almost as one, their eyes turned to Brinar on the other side of the room.

Kasai suppressed a grin at Brinar's obvious discomfort. The doctor had made Kasai come here to observe Edward's weapons class, but Kasai didn't think Brinar had expected any attention.

He turned to Brinar. "Did you want me to practice with a staff today?" It had been almost a full month since he had his new arm, but he had yet to use his powers. Brinar usually had him practicing with various weapons, including the scythe that Edward had used on Kasai years ago.

Brinar snorted and turned away from the class. "No. We're going somewhere different. But I wanted you to hear some of his tips today. I just didn't think Edward would have them pay any attention to us."

Kasai followed him through a few more training rooms, mostly resembling the first one, but sometimes with different dummies or a different floor design. Finally, Brinar stopped in a room that was made of stone. Kasai felt his breath catch and glanced at Brinar.

He groaned as Brinar said the damning words, "Today you're working on your fire." Brinar was obviously trying not to grin, but kept himself in check. "I've noticed that, except for a few times at home, you haven't used it."

Kasai sighed. He had lost his temper once with Brinar, and then again with Amalia; both times his flames had popped up around the living room, scaring Bronwen and making River cling to him. Another time, he had been woken from a nightmare by Brinar, who had found the couch in flames.

He was suddenly very glad Brinar had insisted Linota stay at the house today.

Brinar narrowed his eyes. "If you want to safely get Oxe away from Ironwood, you'll need to understand how they've changed."

Kasai nodded in reluctant agreement. "I know I can't face him without my fire, but I still can't figure out how to use it."

"What usually triggers your flames?" Brinar's voice wasn't judgmental this time, thankfully, but curious and professional.

Kasai paused, staring at a ripple along the wall. "I'm not sure. I know it's my emotions, but I don't know which one specifically."

"Fear." The certainty in Brinar's voice was more surprising than the emotion. "I think they show up when you're afraid."

Kasai thought for a moment, then nodded. "Yeah, you might be right. But I'm afraid of a lot of things."

Brinar gave a strange snort. "You're afraid of hearing more about-"

His words were cut off by a flash of orange-blue fire. Kasai quickly called the flames back and they raced to his hand in an instant.

Brinar's lip twitched, but Kasai was glad he kept the outburst quiet. "Sonus. Ever since I first started getting reports about you from North, which came as a complete surprise by the way, he told me you get upset whenever he's mentioned."

Kasai's hand twitched; the flames grew into a pronged staff. "It's not like I mean to."

Brinar's gaze flicked to the staff briefly. "But that doesn't change the fact that you do."

"And you expect me to stop it like that?" Kasai snapped the fingers of his right hand, feeling a tad proud that the arm was finally responding properly, and the staff glimmered slightly.

There was a tense pause, then Brinar took a step back. "No. But I would've thought you got over the hurt feelings enough to listen about him by now."

Kasai closed his eyes and the staff disappeared with a *pop*. "Sorry. I *am* still hurt," he started. He still found talking to Brinar difficult, but he knew the doctor was right. "But I still have a hard time..." The words died in his throat.

"You still have a hard time dealing with what happened," Brinar finished for him. Kasai opened his eyes to see sympathy cross Brinar's gaze before disappearing. "That's more than understandable, given the...events of Veridey's Island. But not once did you ever ask North about him, or Cifius. And I know you met with him."

Kasai nodded and sat against the wall, his head between his knees. "I just can't forgive myself for what happened."

There was a soft tapping sound, then a sigh. "It wasn't your fault. I know you don't want to believe me, but none of us knew he would go back." The tapping stopped and Kasai looked up in time to see Brinar sit in front of him. "If he were still here, he would've gotten hell from everyone after that." He gave a wry snort. "Hell, I probably would've killed him myself."

Kasai leaned against the wall as flames licked along the stone floor.

Brinar eyed them thoughtfully. "You were upset when you found out I had never told you I met Sonus here. I don't blame you, but I never thought that would've been important enough to tell you about."

Kasai watched him warily; the flames grew more erratic, blues shooting through the orange.

"I found him in the same manner Captain Yan found you and Linota." Brinar gave him a sympathetic look. "His ship had been destroyed, and there were no other survivors around. We didn't know until many years later that Cifius and most of his crew had survived by clinging to hull for two days before being found by someone else."

Sonus had been with Cifius? Kasai hadn't expected that. The flames grew low and dark.

Brinar watched the flames idly, but Kasai could see he was gauging his words carefully as he spoke. "Starving, dehydrated, barely able to cling to that plank, it was a miracle we found him when we did. My crew was already heading home, so we took him with us. We weren't far, maybe a week away."

Kasai snorted softly. Maybe the same area where he and Linota had been.

Brinar cut him a glance, then watched the flames disappear. "I brought him here, and he told me he had to get back home. When he was well enough, I offered to escort him back to Veridey's."

"Why? Why not have him go back some other way?" Kasai couldn't resist asking.

Brinar laughed. "You've known me long enough, Kasai, that you should be able to guess. Your father was a genetic of rare ability, and he knew someone else with a more powerful one. I couldn't resist meeting them."

Kasai cracked a grin at that. It made sense, as Brinar got excited when Kasai first discovered his abilities. Kasai also knew that the Telekinetic Elemental chapter had heavily featured his own abilities in Brinar's latest book.

Brinar shook his head. "I didn't expect running into two genetic when we returned."

"My mother's sister, right?" Kasai briefly remembered overhearing North talking to Oxe, or really Tamotsu, once, but they had clammed up quickly when they saw him.

Brinar nodded, surprised. "Do you know who she is?"

Kasai shook his head.

"Razora." The name cracked out like a whip and flames shot up, higher than Kasai when he stood. Brinar didn't flinch, but he glanced at Kasai before watching the flames. "What do you know of her?"

Kasai took a deep breath before answering. "That she has my sister."

"Naomi?" Brinar's voice took on a dark edge. Kasai nodded and Brinar growled. "That is very bad. Razora is a storm genetic, and I've heard reports of another with her. It might be your sister."

Kasai closed his eyes as the flames turned dark blue, then shot through with white.

"Kasai," Brinar snapped out. "Enough."

Kasai opened his eyes in time to see the flames spreading up the walls and tried to call them back. They fluttered, but Kasai shot up when they flashed around erratically.

Without thinking, he stood in front of Brinar as the flames raced towards the stunned researcher and caught them. He heard rapid footsteps, but before they could reach the stone room, the flames had condensed into a wide sword, held tightly in Kasai's left hand. His fingers were white from his tight grip around the white-blue handle. The blades tip sank into the ground, the stone steaming.

"What happened?" Edward shot through the doorway just as Brinar got to his feet. "Kasai? Brinar?"

Brinar calmly dusted off his pants; bits of ash fell. "It's nothing Edward. Just helping Kasai master his ability is all."

Edward glanced at Brinar, but then fixed his gaze on Kasai's weapon. "That's new."

Kasai nodded, unable to speak from the effort of containing the flames that were struggling to break free. The sword stayed still in his hands, but Kasai knew no one could miss the unmistakable hurricane-looking swirls trapped within the blade.

KASAI FELL TO ONE KNEE as Brinar stepped back, panting heavily.

Brinar cocked his head slightly. "This takes more stamina than you're used to." Not a question, merely a statement in regards to the broad blade that had flashed into nothing the second Kasai let go.

Kasai waited a moment, then got to his feet when his breathing was better. "It's not that."

Brinar narrowed his eyes but stayed quiet.

"They don't listen to me," Kasai spat out. He was angry, but at himself. Three weeks of this and he still couldn't control them.

Amalia's voice startled him. "Sounds like their user." He turned to see her standing in the doorway, River at her side. Before anyone could react, River ran and leaped at Kasai. Linota yapped, appearing behind Amalia, but didn't come forward.

Kasai barely caught him in time. "Geez, a little more warning next time."

Sorry. The word flashed in his head at River's grin.

Holding back a sigh, Kasai looked at Amalia. He still didn't understand River's attachment to him, but now wasn't the time to think about it. He shifted the toddler to his back and asked, "Is it seven already?" At seven, the training center closed for the night and no one was allowed inside after that time. It also meant time for Kasai to babysit the twins, much to Bronwen's annoyance. She didn't like him, but he didn't blame her.

Brinar had told him about her first interaction with genetics; an unstable Linota and an angry Oxe. Kasai would've been surprised if she had been okay after being scared by them.

Amalia nodded. "Yes. And I wanted to ask when you two were going after Oxe."

Brinar's eye twitched, and Kasai resisted flinching. "We don't know where he's at, and we can't go blindly out there to look for him."

Kasai also knew Brinar wasn't happy with his progress, or lack of. He was determined for Kasai to be much more prepared for a fight this time. But Kasai couldn't keep up his flame sword for more than ten minutes without feeling like he was about to lose control of the flames.

Amalia gave them a sympathetic look as she turned to lead them out. Kasai reached down and scratched Linota's ear as he followed the couple out. He could hear them talking quietly, but paid them no mind. "What were you doing today, River?"

Mommy ran another test. River pouted, his arms around Kasai's neck.

Kasai squeezed his hand in empathy. "I hope it wasn't long this time." The doctors were baffled by River's ability, and occasionally they ran mild tests on his brain to try to figure out why he was a genetic when no one else in his family was.

River shook his head. *No. Boring. Tell me a story.*

Kasai sighed as they left the building. "I've told you all my stories." Maybe not *all*, but the ones that Amalia and Brinar would approve of, at least.

River was quiet for a minute, his eyes on Linota. *What's the strangest island you've been to?*

Kasai shook his head. "There aren't many strange places I've been to. Maybe Brimna Atoll, one of the world's only tundra atolls, but..." He paused, thinking. "There was the island with the tucowary."

River grinned. *Tell me more!*

Kasai opened his mouth to answer but slammed into Brinar, who had jerked to a stop. Kasai took a step back. "Sorry, Brinar."

He felt a surge of anxiety as he observed Brinar and Amalia's faces. A few people, from the training center or other nearby places, had stopped and were staring at Kasai. Some had their mouths dropped open, but every single one of them had an identical look of *fear*.

Brinar wheeled around, startling him. "What did you just say?"

Kasai gripped Linota's shoulder fur, his voice shaking slightly. "I got shipwrecked on an unmapped island with some of the crew. There were hot springs and a wild tucowary there."

Brinar stared at him, then snapped at Amalia, "Get Mihel. Head for the council room. Get someone to watch Bronwen." Without another word, he grabbed Kasai and pulled him back the way they came.

Linota whimpered as Kasai hurried to match Brinar's rapid pace. He wanted to ask what was wrong, but the fear radiating from Brinar was great enough Kasai could almost taste it. He was sure Linota was probably being overwhelmed by it.

They didn't slow down, not even when they reached the Leadership Building. But once inside, Brinar didn't head for the wide doors at the end of the hallway, where Mihel's greenhouse was, but instead took them to a long but low stone room just to the left of it.

Once inside, Brinar motioned for Kasai to sit and started pacing alongside the long table inside. Linota crawled under the table, laying her head on her paws. She was shaking, and Kasai didn't blame her. He had never seen Brinar this agitated before.

Or scared.

The door flew open with a bang and Mihel stormed in. He rounded on Kasai, his eyes blazing. "Is what Amalia just told me true? You've been to an island with a wild tucowary and hot springs?" Kasai nodded mutely and Mihel hissed, "Was anyone else with you?"

"The few surviving members of Thukuli's original crew." Kasai forced the words out. River, still clinging to his back, clutched him tighter and Kasai moved him to his lap, wrapping an arm around the shaking child. "Why?"

Mihel turned on Brinar. "You told me no one would find that island!"

Brinar snarled back, "I didn't anticipate North being on the crew!"

Kasai watched in a shocked silence.

"If Ironwood figures out what we-" Mihel glanced at Kasai and shut his jaws with a loud snap. He pinched the bridge of his nose for several minutes, his eyes closed and breathing harshly. When he had calmed down, he spoke slowly. "We *cannot* let him go back there."

Brinar glared at him for a moment, then turned to Kasai. "Who *exactly* was with you?"

Kasai closed his eyes while he thought, saying each name clearly. "Ironwood Thukuli. North. Oxe. Feluna. Jen. Daro. Linota." He opened his eyes and watched the two older men. "North could feel the island, and we were attacked by a Seaborne ship. We were just trying to escape them. I don't think any of us knew about the island until we landed there." He paused. "North said that there were very few islands with hot springs, but that didn't mean anything to the rest of us."

It may have to Thukuli, but not much. *Right?*

Amalia came in quietly and sat next to Kasai. "Mihel, Brinar, you need to explain why you're reacting this way before you scare them."

Brinar finally seemed to register River, still clutched in Kasai's arm, and sighed. "I'm sorry. It just caught us by surprise."

Mihel nodded and sat down, glaring at the table. "Brinar, you explain."

Brinar nodded once and looked at Kasai. "If you ever repeat this to anyone, I will turn you over to the Seaborne myself. And not even alive, if it comes to that."

The room grow cold and flames licked along the floor silently. Kasai waved his hand and they disappeared. At his feet, Linota whined.

"When you got here, we briefly explained our medicine. How it slows down the aging process," Brinar began. "We did not develop that technology here, or a fair amount of our medicine, actually."

Kasai watched, stunned. But slowly, as Brinar talked, little dots began connecting. He stayed silent though, not wanting to interrupt.

"Mine and Mihel's father found that island over 900 years ago." Brinar's voice was harsh. Kasai couldn't hide his shock. "Yes, over 900 years. Are you familiar with invitro?"

Kasai nodded numbly.

"We were frozen until a mother was found and deemed good enough to carry on his genes," Brinar said shortly. "Anyway, He found the island had unusual soil."

Linota yapped at this.

Kasai touched her head briefly. "Her and Oxe found a body there, decaying. But it held an assortment of items from 200 years ago. There's something there that kept people from aging?"

Brinar's eye twitched. "Yes. Our father found a way to use it in medicine, and from then on, we were known as the medical marvels of the world. But then we..." He looked away. His fist, on the back of a chair, was shaking.

Amalia touched Kasai's arm briefly. "We created the tucowary by accident. The world's animals? The mutations? Those all stem from that island. Some escaped the island, though we aren't sure exactly when or how. But if someone smart enough finds out the truth behind Witch Village..."

"It could be devastating." Mihel's voice was flat. He shot a glare at Kasai. "We've had scientist go missing from time to time, always disappearing when they stop at islands below the equator."

Kasai nodded, immediately understanding. "You're afraid if Thukuli finds out something, he could copy your island's work, or find a different way of using it."

"He could potentially mutate humans and create genetics. He could bypass the generations needed to produce them." Brinar's words were a shot in the air.

Mihel's head shot up. "Would that be possible?"

Brinar gritted his teeth and hissed the words out. "Yes. It would be devastating for whoever gets abilities that way, but it's a possibility we have to consider at this point. Ironwood's a lot smarter than I gave him credit for, and he has connections with Razora."

Mihel shot to his feet. "Brinar, take Kasai and track Ironwood down. He needs to be taken out before he tells her of that island." With that, he left as quickly as he came.

Amalia watched the door shut, waiting until it was closed before she spoke. "Do you think Ironwood's smart enough to realize what can be done with the island?"

Brinar sat down heavily, staring at the table. "Not by himself. But if he's in contact with Razora..."

Amalia nodded, though Kasai didn't understand fully. Amalia gently took River from Kasai's arms. "Kasai, you and Brinar need to discuss what you're going to do now. I'll take River home. Edward picked up Bronwen for us, and he'll want to get home to Emily."

Brinar nodded, but Kasai could see he wasn't paying attention. When the door shut, Brinar looked at Kasai. "We need to get to Cifius. He has enough contacts to find out where Ironwood is, and Oxe. And Kasai?"

Kasai raised an eyebrow.

"I need to ask you...if it came to it, could you kill Ironwood?" Brinar's voice was ice.

Kasai glanced at Linota, who whimpered. He closed his eyes, drumming his fingers on the table for a moment. "I'm not sure. If you had asked me before Locke Island...maybe. Now? I'm not so sure."

"Even if he threatens to tell Doux it was your flames who killed Kira?" The words shocked Kasai. Brinar met his gaze evenly. "Yes, I'm aware of that. I've known for years it was you."

Kasai blinked back the tears that threatened to show. "How?"

"You talk in your sleep," Brinar explained. "Most of the crew knew after you got your first scar."

Kasai groaned and closed his eyes.

"I'm serious, Kasai." Brinar's voice turned harsh. Kasai looked at him. "You're going to need to kill Ironwood. That island? *No one* can know about it. Knowing Mihel, he'll find a way to round up the others you mentioned and get rid of them. *Permanently.*"

Flames flared up around them.

Brinar held a hand up. "Not you and Oxe. Or North. Mihel's aware of my trust in you three. I can't say anything about Feluna, but then again, he probably won't worry about her."

Kasai sat back in the chair, the flames receding. "So, what are we going to do?"

Brinar sighed and stood up. "Come on, we have to call Cifius."

Kasai and Linota followed at his heels, but exchanged an uneasy look. If Cifius didn't know where Thukuli was, would they be able to take him down and find Oxe?

Especially before it was too late?

Chapter 41

Oxe

OXE GROANED AND SLIPPED into his human self slowly. Outside the bars, Xicía watched him silently. He could feel her eyes linger on the scars he had received over the last month. Claws, fangs, even a hoof, all had left some kind of mark that persisted even to his human body.

"Oxe?" Xicía's voice was quiet, scared. Fear saturated the air inside the small room.

He grunted and collapsed on his side. Curling up, he closed his eyes and tried to calm his thudding heart.

Xicía didn't speak for several moments, but her voice was barely a whisper as she said, "I'm going to get you some medicine."

Oxe's eyes flew open and he croaked, "Don't."

He heard her shift, then she was in his sight. "Please. That last fight was bad." Oxe snorted; *all* the fights were bad. "Please. I'll get you some extra food, too."

Oxe hesitated, then gave a quick nod. "Just be careful."

Xicía disappeared through the door, the flap hanging heavily across the door. Heavy enough, it didn't move hardly, and barely let any light in.

Oxe struggled to sit up, but finally sat against the corner where he was supported. The rings around his ankles and wrists, angry marks, stung, but at least the manacles were off. At least until the next fight.

He growled as he thought about the auruchs bull he had just felled. A huge brute, burn marks and scars dotting its body, it had nearly trampled him. And before that, the hork had run over his leg. And before the hork, the colf had taken off part of his ear. Oxe had lost count of his wounds, the scars he now bore. But each fight meant he got to live, and as long as he was alive, Kasai could find him.

He wished he could let someone know he was more than a wolf, but Ironwood had threatened to kill him right out if anyone found out. Especially Cifius.

Oxe huffed as he thought about the town's leader, who was here every week to deliver the food for the animals locked up in the tents. He never got close to the tent where Oxe was kept, but Oxe could smell him every time he came. It didn't help that Ironwood had somehow paid the caretakers off so that only Xicía could feed or treat him.

Oxe knew Ironwood was keeping the fact that he had a human in here a secret. If it was found out a shifter was taking part in the animal fights, something Oxe was sure that Cifius was unaware of, Ironwood would be killed for dealing in humans. While there weren't many laws on Brimna Atoll, that was an absolute. It was why Razora was not welcomed here.

Oxe growled in disgust, but kept as quiet as he could.

Xicía appeared, a bowl of meat and another of water in her hands. Oxe could see a bulge under her shift briefly, before the flap closed, where she must've stuck some medicine. She handed him the bowls, sliding them through the narrow slot at the bottom of the cage's door, and pulled out a tube of ointment. "It's all I could get. Kelli was watching."

Oxe pricked his ears; he winced as the remains of the left one twinged. "Kelli?"

Xicía nodded. "Yes. She's taking over for Cifius for a while. I guess he had to leave? He got an urgent message a few days ago, but I haven't heard anything else."

Oxe downed the water quickly, but was much slower with the food. "You can trust Kelli. She's related to Cifius."

Xicía nodded, but he could see something was bothering her.

After his meat was gone and the bowls pushed back through the slot, he reached through the bars and touched her shoulder. "What's wrong?"

Xicía glanced at him nervously, then stared at the floor. He knew she did this when she got scared. It was several moments before she whispered to him, "They set you up for another fight...but Oxe...I don't think you'll survive this one."

Oxe bristled, fur bushing out painfully over his body. "Why?"

She hesitated, and the fear scent got stronger. "It's...have you heard of a quilva?"

Oxe sat back, thinking. Eventually, he shook his head. "No. It's not from any of the islands I've been to."

Xicía's fear grew. "It's not much smaller than you as a wolf, with thick fur and an armored belly. Their vicious, Oxe. I've seen them before."

Oxe looked at her sharply. "Where are they from?"

"Jehengo Island." The name on Xicía's tongue was vaguely familiar, and it took Oxe a moment to recognize it.

"It's from the Southern Ice?" he asked. He never studied charts like Kasai, but he'd skimmed a few over the couple years while looking for his mate.

She nodded. "I don't know how they got one. They're nocturnal, and sort of loners. Only the infants stay with their mothers, and that's only for a few months. It's hard to catch them."

Oxe bit back a growl. "How do I fight it?"

Xicía almost answered, then the flap opened as Delta stepped in. "As well as you can. But don't worry, we'll dispose of what's left of you in a dignified manner." The sneer on her face wasn't nearly as bad as the scorn in her voice. "Tomorrow night, you'll face it."

"And if I win?" Oxe knew they wouldn't let him go, but he had to ask.

Delta laughed. "Well, then I get my money back." With a cruel laugh, she left. She paused only once, calling over her shoulder, "Xicía. You're coming with me."

Xicía gave Oxe a scared look, but she followed Delta out.

Oxe had no idea what she meant, but it didn't matter. He knew he only had a night to think, but he knew he wouldn't be able to guess from what little Xicía had managed to tell him.

With a sigh, he tipped his head back. If only he could let Kelli know he was here. And secretly, he hoped Kasai was on his way. He would guess that Oxe was with Ironwood still, but would he be able to find him here? He hoped so.

IRONWOOD GAVE THE CAGE a vicious kick. "Get up."

Oxe gritted his teeth, sliding into his wolf form, and stayed silent as Ironwood clamped the manacles around his ankles again. Once they clicked shut, Ironwood led him out. Outside his room, the inside of the tent was a cacophony. Screeches, hisses, roars; if it could be made by an animal, it could be heard here.

Oxe wasn't sure what they really did with all these animals, but he knew very few were used for fights. And each time, they were taken out during dark so they weren't seen by anyone who could stop this.

Delta greeted them once they were outside. "Come on. They have it ready."

Oxe shuddered, but the other two didn't comment. They briefly gazed at the glass crater, but no one said anything as they continued.

As far as Oxe knew, they had no idea who was behind that.

They reached the seashore side of the cliffs within an hour, where an enormous wall made of crudely fixed driftwood hid the cave used for the animal fights. Just before they reached it, Delta stopped them. "Captain, will you keep your end of the deal if he dies?"

Oxe pricked his ears.

Ironwood scoffed. "I have the money with me, don't worry." He patted a thick bag at his waist. Oxe heard the clink of kinas. "But if he somehow wins, you get half."

Delta bristled. "You said I would get three quarters if he won!"

Ironwood snarled at her. His hand twitched and a sprig of ivy shot up Delta's leg. "I told you half. You'll get the other half through your shares the next time we go out."

Delta backed down, but Oxe could smell the anger rippling from her.

Ironwood knocked on the wall, whispered something to the man behind it, then pulled Oxe inside.

The smell of blood, fear, and le touched his nose immediately. He didn't resist as Ironwood led him to the pen where he would stay until the fight, but snapped at the man who closed the door behind him. The man just chuckled before turning to Ironwood. "This thing got a good following, but the quilva has more money on it tonight."

Ironwood scoffed. "Just means more money for me if he wins."

Oxe shuddered and waited. There were screams from something already fighting, and losing, and a roar followed by a wet, ripping sound, then silence. A sudden snap sounded, and a grumbling roar exploded as the winning animal was driven back.

"Well done to the Cre'ch neixe for that powerful blow!" The announcer's voice rose above the clammer of people groaning in defeat or others laughing at their good fortune. "And now we have a special treat. Ironwood Thukuli's creature is back once again," chuckling followed this, "but they'll be facing off against a quilva."

A deadly hush fell through the cave.

"Yes, people, I said a quilva. Brought by a crew who recently traded with Razora herself, this creature is rarely seen outside of its natural habitat." The announcer sounded almost excited. "And now, let's start the show!"

The inner door slid open and Oxe snarled as someone smacked his flank with a club, forcing him into the arena. The door quickly shut behind him and he was left facing the strangest thing he'd ever seen.

A dull brown-ish grey, the quilva confused him. A short, thick tail, its back was covered with dense looking fur. A long snout dipped towards the ground in a thin trunk, while its much smaller bottom jaw revealed tiny sharp teeth. Its eyes were tiny black dots on a thick-skinned face, and its armored underbelly reminded Oxe of a beetles back.

Its hind legs were much thicker than he expected, ending in a thick foot with four short clawed toes. Its front legs however, were thin and seemed almost too long. Its front hands, for they resembled hands more than feet, were long fingered and each one was tipped with six-inch claws thicker than his own.

As it snuffled around in the dirt with its surprisingly supple trunk, Oxe blinked as he took in the long quills near the base of its tail. And were those shorter ones interspersed through the fur all along its back? Xicía had said it was vicious, but it looked no worse than a boar. Just pricklier.

There was a quiet hush as the people waited, unnerving Oxe. He could hear whispers, but nothing distinct enough that could let him know what he was facing. Getting to its underbelly would be an issue; the armor may be too tough for his claws or teeth. The fur was dense, and if there were quills, it would be painful.

The quilva stopped in its snuffling and whipped its head around to stare at Oxe. With a low snarl, it lowered itself until its belly scrapped the ground and fixed its beady eyes on him.

Oxe barked a warning at the quilva, but the strange creature growled and launched itself forward with surprising speed. It used its hind toes to dig into the ground, but Oxe yelped as its front claws pulled it forward even faster.

Racing around the ring, he wasn't sure how to attack it. The colf he could flip onto its side or back and claw the underbelly. The auruchs bull, he had clamped onto its throat as tightly as he could until the windpipe was crushed. This thing was barely shorter than a colf, but the neck was protected by thick looking skin.

Oxe sprang at the wall, then pushed himself off at the quilva.

There was a scream and Oxe backed away, pawing his nose and whining loudly. A cluster of short quills quivered in his muzzle, which was going slightly numb.

It was *venomous?!* Oxe furiously rubbed his head against the ground, trying to dislodge the quills. The quilva huffed and snarled, crouching with its belly to the ground. Oxe gave a slurred growl, stumbling.

A hush fell over the spectators, and Oxe heard some muttering from Ironwood and Delta.

The quilva screeched, startling him, and launched forward, claws outstretched.

Oxe reared up, leaping over the quilva's bristling back. A searing pain shot through his leg as he landed hard, a startled yelp escaping him as he saw the long quill embedded in his haunches. The quilva's tail lashed once and Oxe bit back a whine. *It could shoot quills with its tail? How can I fight this thing?!*

A deafening bang echoed through the air, sending Oxe sprawling to his side as a cold muzzle clamped painfully over his snout. A strangled, high-pitched whine tore from his throat. A sharp, agonizing pain lanced through his head, and blackness consumed him.

Chapter 42

Kasai

KASAI LEANED AGAINST the rail, his elbow on the wood while his other hand hung limply at his side. Linota whined softly, nudging his leg.

Idly scratching her ear, his gaze didn't leave the faint outline of Brimna Atoll; they were approaching the atoll quickly. It'd only be an hour or less before they arrived.

"Kasai," Brinar called out.

Kasai turned to see the doctor leaving the door below deck. Behind him, Edward's tenseness was obvious in the lines on his face, the stiffness of his shoulders. "Yeah?"

"We need to talk about what to do once we get there," Brinar said, leaning against the rail next to him. Smoothing back a few stray strands of hair, he fixed his gaze on the approaching atoll.

"Do we know if Thukuli's still there?" Kasai asked.

Edward shrugged, crossing his arms and shifting his weight. "No, but it sounded as if he was planning on staying awhile."

Kasai groaned, thinking back on the call they made to Cifius a few weeks ago.

Thukuli was back in Brimna Atoll, but there was no sign of Oxe. The crew had scattered over the atoll, settling in for the winter. Thukuli himself had disappeared after a few days, and no one had seen him since.

Supposedly.

But his ship was still there, and Delta frequented the local brothels and bars.

Kasai thought it was a bit strange, as Thukuli hated the cold, but he had stopped questioning the man months ago.

"We'll find him, Kasai," Brinar said, patting his shoulder briefly. Kasai shot him a worried look, but Brinar met it with a steady gaze. "From what Cifius learned, we know Oxe isn't dead. That means he's being kept somewhere. We just have to find him. Cifius said he'd start looking around, getting some answers, and try to meet us on the docks."

Kasai cocked a brow. "On the docks? Is that safe?"

Brinar shrugged. "With this ship, it would be suspicious if they *didn't* stop at the docks."

Kasai glanced up at Yan standing at the helm, then nodded in understanding. "A merchant landing elsewhere would bring up too much attention."

He was glad they could contact the merchant captain, and Yan was glad that in exchange for a ride to Brimna Atoll, he got trading rights with Witch Island.

Iono appeared then and walked over. "Kasai, why don't you leave at night? Brinar and Edward could leave earlier, but I doubt they would be recognized."

Brinar shook his head. "Edward won't be, but I would. I tried to get into Ironwood's crew, so even if he's not suspicious of me being there, I'll still be recognized." He exchanged a look with Edward, then looked at Kasai. "But she's got a good idea. You can leave tonight once night falls. And I know it might be uncomfortable, but wear a cloak. It'll keep people from wondering why you're not reacting to the cold as much."

Kasai stifled a groan and nodded. "Of course. But...where will we meet?" He wasn't terribly fond of wearing a cloak. They made him feel crowded at worst and uncomfortable at best, but he knew the importance of blending in.

"The Drowned Bird," Brinar said immediately. "Cifius is giving us rooms there while we stay and try to find Oxe."

Kasai relaxed against the rail. "Alright."

Iono tapped his arm, and when he looked at her, she motioned for him to follow. He walked just behind her, stopping when they reached the bow. She sat on a barrel, her gaze on his. "Kasai...are you going to be okay?"

It wasn't the first time she had asked, but Kasai was grateful for her. "Yes. Or at least, okay enough. I need to get Oxe back. I need to stop Thukuli."

She watched him quietly, then laid her hand on his arm. "But...you're willingly going to take a life." Her gaze softened. "How can you do that?"

Kasai gave her a sympathetic look. "Because if I don't, more lives will be lost." He understood why it bothered her, and part of him regretted confiding in her like he had, but he wanted someone other than Brinar and Edward to talk to. And it wasn't like he could talk to River; the kid wasn't old enough, even if he was unusually mature for his age, to understand this.

To be frank, he felt Iono treated him like a mother would. Like Kira had. And he missed that.

Iono dropped her hand and nodded, her brow furrowing. "I understand it will be bad if you don't, but can you not just capture him?"

Kasai shook his head. "He's too powerful. He needs to be taken down for good."

With a sigh, Iono pulled Kasai into a hug, startling him briefly before he returned it. "Kasai...when this is over, make sure you come talk to me if you need to, alright?"

Kasai nodded, his throat tight. "I will. I have a face-crys, and I'll make sure I have your call pattern. That way we can talk even if we can't meet." If he settled on Wolf Island after all this, and he intended to, he knew she wouldn't be able to visit and he had no intentions of leaving.

She smiled and walked off as Brinar approached him.

"Kasai, head below for now. Get some rest," he ordered. "We're going to need it."

Kasai nodded, not bothering to argue against the truth, and headed below.

"HE. DID. *What?!*" Brinar's voice shot through the bar like a bolt of lightning.

Kasai took a deep breath, forcing the flames sparking around the room to recede. Finally, he stood and paced to the window, then back. "Cifus, I don't give a shit about your rules. Thukuli isn't leaving here alive," he all but snarled.

Silence met his words.

Kasai looked behind him to see Cifus glaring at him. "I'm serious. He's trafficking in humans by bringing Oxe into this."

Lightning cracked out. Cifus' eyes flashing dangerously. "I agree, but we need to do this right. Kasai, if we just rush in and confront him, *he will kill everyone.*" The last words are punctuated by a crackle of electricity so powerful the lights flicker erratically. "I've talked to some of his crew. They told me about Locke Island. He does that here..." Cifius scoffs derisively. "The city isn't made of stone, Kasai."

Kasai grit his teeth, but said nothing, not trusting his voice.

"What do you suggest?" Kelli asked after a moment.

Silence, then the static in the air faded. "Kelli, go take over at the pens. Bring them food, water, go about business like normal. But try to figure out which animals fight, which ones are in the most danger.

Ask around about any special animals, but make it look like you're just doing a count." Cifus got up and paced, talking quickly. "Some of them are obviously in these fights, but it seems like they're animals that are naturally hostile or territorial."

Kasai waited patiently.

"Brinar, go find Renela. Tell her what's going on, make sure she's prepared for any injuries," he ordered. Brinar nodded and raced out immediately. Cifus turned to Edward. "Find Ironwood's crew, any of them aside from Delta. Talk to them. Get any information you can. If you can find Nona, she'll be invaluable. She hates him as much as I do." Edward gave a grim nod and left quickly.

Kelli appeared next to Kasai, touching his arm gently. "I think you should stay out of sight for now. If anyone sees you-"

"-it will mean trouble," he finished. "Don't worry, I won't be going out until I need to." Cifius may have struck him if he tried, and while that alone was enough of a deterrent, she was right. He couldn't risk running into anyone who could report he was alive and here.

He'd hardly reached the steps leading upstairs when Brinar burst back in, fury etched on his face.

"Ironwood's here," he growled.

Silence choked the air. Kasai's breath caught as Brinar's gaze locked with his.

"And he has Oxe in the caves on the north side of the beach," he finished.

Lightning lit the room as white flames burst out.

Chapter 43

Oxe

THE HEAT BLOOMING THROUGH the air woke him. Groggily, he lifted his head.

Xicía stroked her hand along his head soothingly. "A fire broke out a moment ago. I'm not sure where exactly."

Oxe groaned and struggled to sit up. His muzzle stung, his hip felt numb still, and a creeping pain radiated down his leg and along his flank. Whining, he flashes the whites of his eyes at Xicía.

She opened her mouth to speak, but the tent flap keeping him separated from the rest of the animal pens was flung open and Delta came stalking in.

"You're coming with me!" she snarled, reaching down and yanking Oxe to his feet harshly by the collar around his neck. His yelp was muffled by the muzzle still clamped over his jaws. Delta was tall enough his front paws cleared the ground by a few inches and he forced himself to limp alongside her rather than be dragged.

"Leave him alone!" Xicía shouted. Cold pierced through the air, only to be beaten back by the intense heat that met them outside his space.

Stifling before, it was unbearable now.

But Oxe *knew this heat!* He whined, his tail wagging, and tried to jerk from Delta's grasp. Kasai was here! No one else could wield this kind of heat, and most people couldn't withstand it for long.

Delta struck him across the heat with her free hand. "Shut up. You're not going back to that volatile matchstick." When Xicía came running at her, Delta snorted and knocked her into a metal cage with a powerful backhand.

The girl sank to the ground in a heap, a trickle of blood leaking from under her hair.

Oxe's eyes went wide as Delta continued dragging/walking him away.

Muttering under her breath, Delta ignored the flames, the animals howling in fear or pain, the yells of people trying to figure out how to fight the...

White flames? Fear trickled down his spine. He'd seen Kasai's flames changing, but they were blue. Shot through with white, but blue nonetheless. *Unless he's really pissed off.*

No, that made sense.

If he found out Oxe was here, it would be entirely like Kasai to let his temper get the better of him.

Oxe's thoughts were broken as Delta suddenly flung him down a steep slope. He rolled, his limbs flailing as he tumbled over and over down the rocky terrain, finally landing in a heap at the bottom.

Ironwood met them as Delta slid down the slope. "I don't care how the hell he survived, I'm ending both of them today!" He dragged Oxe back by his tail. "You're getting paid after this, and you'll get an extra half if you help me kill Kasai," he shot at Delta.

She grinned, her sharp teeth gleaming. "Keep it. I just want my payment for this thing." She kicked Oxe for emphasis.

He yelped.

Ironwood sneered. "Fine. But don't come begging afterwards for it."

Being dragged backwards, Oxe saw him first. Flames raced down the slope after them, like thin wires of heat and sparks. The little flames almost looked harmless.

Except for melting the rocks they touched.

Kasai's yell greeted Oxe's ears and he thrashed in Ironwood's grip just as his mate came racing forward from the bottom of the slope.

Ironwood let go with a snarl, bringing his blade up to meet Kasai's...arm?

When did he get a new arm? Oxe didn't give himself time to think, though. Leaping to his paws, he charged forward and rammed his head into Delta's side as she ran to Ironwood's defense.

She fell back with a gasp. Clearly, she hadn't expected this.

Panting heavily, unable to open his jaws completely, Oxe growled at her lowly. The heavy manacles around his ankles clanked as he moved. Digging his claws into the ground, Oxe leaped forward.

Delta barely rolled out of the way in time. "Stupid mutt!" Bringing her blade out, she slashed at him.

Oxe ducked, swinging his head against her leg. The heavy iron muzzle hit her knee with a satisfying *crack!*

She yelled and struck again.

A yelp, a spray of blood...

And Oxe sank his fangs into her arm.

Gasping, Delta used her other hand to grab her sword, slamming the hilt against his nose.

Howling in pain, Oxe let go and staggered back. But the pain was worth it, as it just proved even more the muzzle was gone.

White fire shot between them. "Get away from my mate, you bitch!" Kasai's voice was like heaven to Oxe's ears. He never thought he'd hear it again.

Standing against his legs, Oxe lowered his head and snarled at her.

Kasai laid a hand on his shoulders. "Oxe, get the girl and get out of here. I'll handle these two."

Growling, Oxe shook his head. He was going to stay. *He* wanted to take Delta down. Meeting Kasai's gaze, he let out a loud huff.

Sighing, Kasai nodded once. "Fine. But be careful." He sounded so much better than Oxe had ever heard him since finding him in Sedgeliss.

Ivy sprung up through the rocky ground. Oxe leaped back. Kasai burnt them instantly.

"Nice to see you survived the hurricane," Ironwood drawled, standing next to Delta. Blood streaked down his face. A fresh burn mark scored across his nose.

"No thanks to you," Kasai spat. "Either give up now or I'll burn you again."

Delta chuckled darkly. "Does he think we'll listen?" she asked Ironwood.

The captain grinned. "I think he's serious, dear." A thick strand of dark ivy twined up his leg. It twined around his sword, thorns studded all along the vine, until the metal was completely encased. "Care to show that mutt what you can do?"

Delta chuckled, the sound sending shivers down Oxe's spine, and suddenly darted forward in a burst of speed.

He barely had a chance to register her newfound speed when she slammed into him.

They tumble away from Kasai and Ironwood; from the corner of his eye, Oxe notices Kasai's strangely glowing blade clash with Ironwood's ivy sword.

Delta's teeth in his leg snap his attention to her. Howling, he raked his claws across her face.

She cackled and let go, leaping back in time. "Nice try, mutt!"

Oxe curled his lips back. Leaping for her, he sank his fangs into her hand. Blood touched his tongue.

She laughed and threw him back.

Landing heavily on his side, Oxe yelped. *Damn, she's fast!* Scrambling to his paws, he shot forward.

A flash of blue fire, a rumbling in the ground, and he dodged as burning ivy sprang forth. Ignoring it, he launched himself at Delta.

She ducked, slamming her fist into his throat.

With a chocked off yelp, Oxe stumbled to his belly.

Delta immediately hooked her fingers into his pelt. Heaving him back, she lifted him up and slammed him on the ground.

Pain detonated through Oxe's side as he crashed into the ground. Again.

His ribs screamed, but he barely had time to suck in a breath before Delta was on him.

Too fast—

A fist slammed into his muzzle, snapping his head back. The world blurred. His paws skidded against the dirt as he staggered upright.

She was already moving. A blur of motion, her boot striking out—

Oxe dodged. Barely. The ground where he had stood cracked from the force.

He circled her, panting. Every muscle ached, but he stayed on his feet. He had to.

Delta grinned, wild-eyed. Her body hummed with power, her stance loose but unnaturally quick, like she was seeing everything before it happened.

"You're tough," she said. "But I can do this all night."

Oxe didn't respond. Couldn't. He only bared his fangs.

She was too strong. Too fast. He had fought fast opponents before, but this—this was different. She wasn't just quick; she moved like she was ahead of time itself.

And worse? She wasn't tiring.

She must have a genetic ability. It was the only thing that made sense. How else could she be fighting like this?

Another strike. Oxe twisted away, but her elbow caught his shoulder, sending a jolt of pain down his spine.

I can't win by matching her speed.

But she was using too much force. Too much energy.

Oxe circled slower now, watching. Letting her come to him.

Delta lunged. Oxe sidestepped, barely avoiding the blow.

She snarled, whirling—faster this time.

Another dodge.

Then another.

She struck again— Oxe howled as his leg snapped. She grinned.

Oxe staggered back with a muted whimper. He lifted his leg off the ground. Blood soaked the fur where the bone tore through. But...

There. She's pushing harder.

It wasn't much. A slight hesitation. A tremor in her fingers before she reset her stance.

She wasn't untouchable.

Delta launched forward again. Oxe twisted away clumsily, and this time, she over-corrected.

She caught herself, but her breath came faster.

She attacked again. And again.

She still hit him—hard—but her movements weren't as clean.

He tumbled back, whining as his leg hit the ground. But he couldn't miss her reaction.

Her hands trembled for half a second before she clenched them into fists.

Oxe's heart pounded. *It's working.*

Delta didn't notice it yet. Or maybe she did, but she didn't care. She just forced herself forward, pushing her body harder.

Oxe had seen fighters like this before—ones who relied on power until their bodies betrayed them.

But none of them had ever been this strong.

Delta growled and threw everything into her next attack.

Too much.

Oxe dodged and rammed into her midsection. Pain shot up his leg, but he ignored it.

She stumbled.

He saw the flicker of shock in her eyes—not at the hit, but at herself.

She tried to swing, but her arm jerked mid-motion.

Oxe lunged. His fangs clamped down on her forearm, hard.

Delta screamed. The taste of blood filled his mouth.

She wrenched back, but her body was locking up. Her legs buckled, and when she tried to stand, nothing responded.

Whatever her ability, it had finally burned her out.

She gasped, hands twitching, trying to force her muscles to move. But she was spent.

Oxe stood over her, panting, blood dripping from his muzzle. His limbs trembled, but he stayed standing.

Delta's chest heaved. Her eyes darted to her arms, her hands. She couldn't move.

Oxe didn't need words. She knew she'd lost. With a snarl, he sank his fangs deep into her throat.

Chapter 44

Kasai

KASAI NOTICED DELTA'S burst of speed, but ignore her. Keeping his gaze fixed on Thukuli, he moved forward. "Give it up. You've gone too far."

Thukuli sneered. "Really? Says who?" Vines burst through the ground. "You?"

Blue flames seared the ivy instantly.

"Cifius?" Thorns poked through the earth.

A shot of white-flecked fire incinerated them.

"Brinar?" The earth rumbled.

Flames shot through the cracks as Kasai burnt the ivy as it appeared.

"You aren't going to win, Kasai," Thukuli taunted.

Kasai flicked his hand. Flames formed into the large sword he'd finally perfected. Well, sort of perfected. It was still a little wieldy, but he was strong enough to handle the claymore. White flames swirled among the orange beneath the surface.

Thukuli raised a brow. "That weapons new." He sneered. "Sure you can handle it?"

Kasai stepped forward. His blade clashed against Thukuli's. "Better than you ever could." The impact sent shockwaves through his arm, but he shoved Thukuli back.

The captain grunted, his feet sliding back a few inches. "Big mistake coming here," he growled.

Ivy shot through the ground. Kasai easily dispatched the strands with a burst of fire. His sword clashed with Thukuli's again in a burst of sparks.

Kasai took a step back. "Just give up, Thukuli." A yelp from Oxe caught his attention, but he didn't tear his gaze away from the man in front of him.

If he did that, it would be the last thing he ever did.

Thukuli's sword whipped through the air. Kasai barely twisted in time, feeling the sting of a thorn slicing across his cheek.

He hissed, stepping back.

Thukuli chuckled. "Getting distracted, Kasai?"

More vines burst from the ground, twisting toward his legs. Kasai slammed his blade down. Fire erupted in a wave, scorching the ivy before it could entangle him.

Thukuli didn't flinch. His blade lunged forward.

Kasai parried, but the captain twisted with the momentum, forcing Kasai's sword wide. A thorned vine snapped toward his throat.

Kasai ducked, rolled, flames trailing his movement. He landed in a crouch, heat surging up his arm. He wasn't going to win this by playing safe. *Where the hell did he learn to fight this good!?*

He knew Thukuli was a good fighter on land. Locke had proved he could control vines with far more finesse than Kasai had known or expected. But where had he learned this style of fighting?

It didn't matter. If Kasai didn't end this fight quickly, it could go badly.

A deep snarl caught his attention and he looked to see Oxe standing over Delta. Blood dripped from his fangs. His foreleg was lifted, blood pouring down his leg.

For a split second, Kasai's focus faltered.

Thukuli moved.

Ivy lashed out, wrapping around Kasai's wrist, wrenching his sword arm wide. Before he could counter, Thukuli drove his knee into Kasai's gut.

Pain exploded through his ribs. Air rushed from his lungs. His grip on his sword wavered. Flames sparked around them.

Thukuli sneered. "Too slow."

The thorned edge of his sword sliced down.

A harsh roar filled the air, and Kasai looked up in time to see Oxe slamming into Thukuli.

Thukuli snarled, knocking the wolf away. "Bastard!"

Oxe landed heavily but scrambled to his feet, blood dripping from his muzzle.

Kasai stepped up beside him, bracing a steadying hand against his mate's shoulder.

Thukuli sneered, spitting blood onto the ground. His grip on his sword was tight. "You should've stayed down, mutt."

Oxe tossed his head – a challenge. His chest heaved, his ears pinned flat, his injured leg trembling beneath him. But he held his ground.

Kasai tensed, preparing to move. Blue flames shot across the ground. *I can still fight. I can –*

Oxe lunged.

A blur of dark fur and raw power shot forward before Kasai could even react.

Thukuli barely had time to raise his sword before Oxe slammed into him. The impact sent them both crashing to the ground, vines snapping beneath their weight.

Thukuli twisted, trying to bring his sword up—too slow.

Oxe's fangs snapped down on his arm.

A sickening crunch.

Thukuli screamed. His sword clattered to the ground, fingers spasming open as his wrist shattered.

Kasai staggered forward, flames flickering weakly around his fingers, but there was no need. His sword disappeared in a burst of flames.

The wolf wrenched his head to the side, dragging Thukuli down. The captain hit the ground with a strangled gasp, his struggles weakening as Oxe's fangs tore deeper.

Kasai forced himself to stay still. His fire burned low, his body screaming for rest, but his gaze stayed locked on Oxe.

He didn't have to finish this.

Oxe would.

A final, brutal snap.

Then—silence.

Kasai exhaled sharply, his entire body sagging with exhaustion.

Oxe lifted his head, breath ragged, blood dripping from his muzzle. His brown eyes met Kasai's. For a moment, neither of them moved.

Then Oxe took a step forward—too unsteady. His injured leg buckled, and Kasai caught him, fingers curling into thick fur, holding him up.

"Easy," Kasai murmured, voice hoarse. He knew Oxe couldn't answer. Didn't need him to.

Oxe let out a heavy breath, his weight pressing into Kasai.

Kasai closed his eyes.

It was over.

Thukuli was dead.

He was free.

Epilogue

River

WATCHING AS THE KIDS raced among the huts, River couldn't help but stare. Short, round buildings dotted the forest, neatly hidden among the trees. The kids here had skin ranging from light tan to rich copper.

So different from the mountain, where pale was the darkest he usually saw!

A warm hand touched his shoulder, and his father's voice sounded close to his ear. "Why don't you go play?"

I want to stay with Kasai, River sent the thought without speaking.

Brinar smiled, his expression soft. "I know, but the grown-ups are talking to him right now. You'll have to wait a while."

River pouted, crossing his arms. *Then I'll find Linota.*

Brinar chuckled. "She's busy with the pack. Go on, River. Bronwen's already playing with the kids and I'm sure she'd love to have you with her."

River glanced toward his twin. Bronwen stood out. She was taller, her skin much paler, but she had just as much energy as the other five-year-olds. She laughed as she tumbled into a pile of leaves with the others.

It looked fun.

"Go on," Brinar urged, nudging him.

But River shook his head.

405

Brinar sighed, then turned and disappeared into the hut behind them. The voices inside briefly filtered out.

"...can be built on the northern shore..."

"...live there......on Alpha duties..."

Most of the conversation was in the common tongue, but now and then, that other language slipped in. The one Oxe sometimes spoke. Kasai was still learning it, but River knew some sounds were hard for him.

River already knew a little. Not because he studied—but because he could hear words inside people's heads as well as when they spoke them.

Curiosity tugged at him.

What were they talking about?

River crept closer, slipping under the hut's flap-door.

Inside, Kasai sat near Oxe, his mate's arm in a sling beside him. The other adults turned when River entered. Some looked amused, some annoyed. His father looked exasperated.

Kasai smiled. "River, you should be with the others."

I want to be with you, River told him.

Kasai glanced at Oxe, then sighed in defeat. He stood, pressing a quick kiss to Oxe's cheek before crossing the room. "How about me and you go see the northern shore while the others finish talking?"

River brightened.

Kasai held out his hand, and River grasped it immediately.

THE JUNGLE SMELLED different than the mountain. The air was heavier, thick with damp earth and flowers so bright they looked painted.

River gazed around curiously as they walked. He'd seen these plants before. His father had drawn them in his books, but seeing them in person was different.

"You're quiet today."

Kasai's voice broke into his thoughts.

River tilted his head up at him. *Are you really staying here?*

Kasai nodded ruefully. "Yeah. I know I said before I was going to come to Witch Island with Oxe, but..."

Did Doux say something?

Kasai let out a small laugh. "Yeah. But that's not the whole reason."

River frowned. He'd met Kasai's brother a few weeks ago—when the Seaborne captain arrived at Witch Island's dock. Doux had been nice, but River couldn't believe he and Kasai were related.

Kasai led him to a large rock jutting from the jungle's edge. Sitting down, he pulled River into his lap, arms wrapping around him.

"I can't tell you everything," he murmured. "You're too little."

River huffed. He wasn't that little.

Kasai didn't seem to notice. His gaze drifted to the sea beyond the trees. "When I was younger, I left home because I lost my mother."

River stilled.

"I looked for my father," Kasai continued. "I found him, but it cost me... a lot." His voice cracked, and he closed his eyes.

River gripped his arm.

Kasai's eyes opened again, softer this time. "After that, I got hurt really bad. That was all before you were born."

River's gaze flicked down. He hesitated, then reached out, touching Kasai's fake arm. The skin felt weird. Cold. Not like real skin at all.

Kasai nodded. "I lost my arm. A man helped me make a new one, but... he said I owed him. And he wasn't fair. He made it impossible to repay him. He made me do things."

River frowned. *He hurt people, right?*

Kasai's expression darkened. "Yeah. And made me hurt people too."

Silence.

River didn't know what to say.

Kasai sighed, rubbing a hand down his face. "That's why I'm here. Doux said this is the only place where I can live without someone trying to hurt me. I won't be able to leave once you and Brinar go back."

River blinked. *Is that why only me and Daddy were allowed here?*

"Yeah," Kasai confirmed. "Brinar helped these people a long time ago, so they let him visit—if he has a good reason. And we figured you and Bronwen might like to see other kids for a change, so we asked for permission."

River smiled.

He liked having other kids to play with. The children on Witch Island were all too big, and most of them didn't want to—or couldn't—play with him and Bronwen.

Do you think we could come back?

Kasai shook his head. "No, River. Brinar is only allowed because he's treating me and Oxe, and the healers need to know about our injuries. And you... you got special permission."

River frowned but didn't argue.

Instead, he curled against Kasai's chest, listening to the distant crash of waves.

Kasai squeezed him gently.

Neither of them spoke.

And for now, that was okay.

Pronunciation and References

ANIMALS

Hork *(hore-k)* - tall skinny creatures with long skinny legs, long necks, and short blunt snouts, their short thin coats range from white to black to blue grey to even red brown, they usually have short thick manes and thick flowing tails of a complimenting color

Quilva *(quill-vah)* – four-legged creature with a supple, short trunk, dense fur, armored underbelly, a short but thick tail, short quills interspersed through its back fur and longer ones at the base of its tail; usually shades of brown to grey

Tucowary *(two-co-wah-ree)* – enormous beast with a scaled hide, narrow jaws, four eyes (males are white-eyed, females have black), tiny triangular ears, thick paws with long nimble claws; native to the Western Waters

Ulcat *(ull-cat)* – small feline, two tails, small knub-horns, usually has short fur in various shades of grey or brown

Plants

Koris tree – a tall dark-barked tree with needle-leaves along the trunk and long branches with deciduous leaves on the end; loses the leaves in winter but keeps the needles year round

Rase *(raze)* – tall flower with sharp thorns along the stem, can be red, white, pink, or lilac colored

Other

Jra *(j-rah)* – a weak alcoholic drink, sometimes used as medicine
Le – an alcoholic drink

Also by Hollow

Pyrates
Burning Ember
Shifting Flame